The SPY'S WIFE

Fiona McIntosh is an internationally bestselling author of novels for adults and children. She co-founded an award-winning travel magazine with her husband, which they ran for fifteen years while raising their twin sons before she became a full-time author. Fiona roams the world researching and drawing inspiration for her novels, and runs a series of highly respected fiction masterclasses. She calls South Australia home.

PRAISE FOR FIONA McINTOSH'S BESTSELLERS

'A blockbuster of a book that you won't want to put down.'
BRYCE COURTENAY

'McIntosh's narrative races across oceans and dances through ballrooms.'
SUN HERALD

'This book is fast-paced, beautifully haunting and filled with the excruciating pain of war.'
WEST AUSTRALIAN

'A fine read . . . The moral ambiguity McIntosh builds into the novel gives it a depth that takes it beyond a sweeping wartime romantic thriller.'
SUNDAY HERALD SUN

'McIntosh weaves a diverse cast together, and you gain an appreciation for her depth of research.'
BOOKS+PUBLISHING

'A captivating saga of love, loss, and the triumph of the human spirit . . . Fiona McIntosh is an extraordinary storyteller.'
BOOK'D OUT

'A perfect blend of romance, action, mystery and intrigue by one of our best known and popular authors.'
NOOSA TODAY

'Sure to appeal to lovers of period romantic dramas like *Downton Abbey*.'
WOMAN'S DAY

'Written with zest and a talent for description that draws you into the world of the novel and its characters.'
THE AGE

'Everything I want in a curl-up-on-the-sofa read . . . an exquisite story that just bursts from the pages and leaps into your heart.'
WRITE NOTE REVIEWS

'Meticulously researched and beautifully written, *The Perfumer's Secret* solidifies McIntosh's place as one of Australia's most loved storytellers.'
BOOKTOPIA

'Spellbinding . . . [Stella is] reminiscent of our favourite literary heroines of the era, only feistier, sexier and more independent.'
BETTER READING

'Beautiful storytelling, emotional depth and complex characters captivated me from start to finish.'
WRITE NOTE REVIEWS

'A grand historical love story ideal for Francophiles and romantics.'
GOODREADS

'A lively tale with a rich assortment of ingredients . . . a well-crafted read.'
SYDNEY MORNING HERALD

OTHER BOOKS BY FIONA McINTOSH

AVAILABLE FROM PENGUIN RANDOM HOUSE

Fields of Gold
The Lavender Keeper
The French Promise
The Tailor's Girl
Nightingale
The Last Dance
The Perfumer's Secret
The Chocolate Tin
The Tea Gardens
The Pearl Thief
The Diamond Hunter
The Champagne War

In the DCI Jack Hawksworth series:
Bye Bye Baby
Beautiful Death
Mirror Man

FIONA McINTOSH

The SPY'S WIFE

PENGUIN BOOKS

PENGUIN BOOKS

UK | USA | Canada | Ireland | Australia
India | New Zealand | South Africa | China

Penguin Books is part of the Penguin Random House group of companies
whose addresses can be found at global.penguinrandomhouse.com.

First published by Michael Joseph, 2021
This edition published by Penguin Books, 2022

Cover design by Louisa Maggio © Penguin Random House Australia Pty Ltd
Cover images: woman and train by Rekha Arcangel;
cherry blossom by Makistock/Shutterstock
Inside cover images: castle and path by Christian Bäck/Mauritius Images
and Drunaa/Trevillion Images
Internal images: cherry blossoms by Plawarn/Shutterstock
Typeset in Sabon by Midland Typesetters, Australia

Printed and bound in Australia by Griffin Press, part of Ovato, an accredited
ISO AS/NZS 14001 Environmental Management Systems printer

A catalogue record for this
book is available from the
National Library of Australia

ISBN 978 1 76014 501 9

penguin.com.au

Prologue

Berlin

27 February, 1933

Max looked at his watch, and a sinking realisation that he was late plunged through him. His heavily pregnant wife was surely expressing her disappointment at this moment to her family. It was past nine and the time had got away from him. In his defence, slim as it was, he'd warned her that he had a meeting after work. Despite this, she'd insisted on calling together her parents and sisters for Jonas's birthday celebration.

'You don't have to be home for all of it. Just be back in time to see everyone,' Rachel had pleaded softly. 'Jonas will be asleep within an hour of them all arriving anyway.'

She rarely made demands on him. Theirs was a gentle, peaceful relationship. Two inherently quiet people had found each other; her laughter was a balm to his remoteness, and they always found plenty of amusement and love to share . . . especially for their son, turning three.

'So the celebration is really for *you*,' he'd teased.

'Of course. Any excuse to celebrate his life. Consider yourself lucky I'm not that religious or we'd be cutting his hair for the first time and having quite the ritual gathering.'

He pulled a face at the thought. 'I will be late, but I'll get home as fast as I can.'

'Thank you.' She kissed him and then stroked his face, lingering. 'I love you, Max.'

'Mmm. Well, if *that's* on tonight's menu, I'll definitely try to cut the meeting short.'

She laughed. 'Is that meeting really so important?'

He sighed. 'It is, I'm sorry. The expansion of our rail network waits for no one.' He planted a peck on her cheek. 'Be good for your mother, Jonas,' he said, crouching to kiss his son's head. Jonas managed a chubby wave and a beaming smile that showed off his glimmering infant teeth, now a complete set.

He remembered to get out of the office for some chocolate for his son, as well as a shiny silver Märklin model of the rail zeppelin. The original, built by the German Imperial Railway Company two years before, had been the first train to exceed 200 kilometres per hour.

Max also hoped the box of deep-fried cruller pastries would take the edge off his wife's frustration when he finally arrived home so much later than she'd hoped. He'd chosen her favourite, with the sweet lemon icing. He had anticipated flagging a taxi by now but the roads were thinly populated and it was such an icy night that he wasn't surprised to still be on foot, nose threatening to stream, his woollen scarf pulled up high around his mouth as he strode down Unter den Linden in the loping style of a tall man. It seemed only he and one other, presumably an impoverished student who had emerged from the State Library, were walking, so he doubted there would be any contest for a taxi should he spot one. Their footsteps helplessly synchronised, with Max a good twenty yards or so behind on the same side of the grand boulevard that connected the Stadtschloss royal palace to the Brandenburg Gate. Once a bridle path of the sixteenth century, it had been replaced by a broad avenue flanked by linden trees, most of which had now disappeared. Max loved this boulevard for its history and grandeur. He had been born in a tiny hamlet in Sussex – England was his spiritual home – but his father had pined for his homeland and brought his family to Bavaria when Max was six, to raise him as German. On a childhood visit to Berlin, Max had fallen for the avant-garde atmosphere of this most lively of cities.

He liked the melting pot of people, and though he knew his manner presented as conservative, his notions were all about liberalism. He considered himself part of that melting pot, being a mix of British and German, and his wife was a Hungarian Jew plus German and even a bit of French. What a pairing they were. Their son was unlikely to speak Hebrew, however, for his mother flouted many traditions in favour of modernity.

Jonas. That's what life was about now: making life the best it could be for their son and the child growing in Rachel's belly. What sort of a Germany, though, were his children to grow up in? There was so much poverty, and parts of Berlin could only be described as slums. The gamble on winning the war of 1914 and funding the four years of its misery on borrowings had failed. Reparations from the war had beggared the once proud nation as hyperinflation imposed its grip and the Reichsmark had less value than the paper it was printed on. Ten years earlier, Max had been appalled to learn that there were poor people in Munich throwing money into their hearths to burn, because it was cheaper than buying wood. The Wall Street Crash of 1929 had made it impossible for Germany to meet its debts as loans were no longer available.

But perhaps he could ensure Jonas's childhood would be happier than his. At nine, Max had watched his proud German father go off to die, among the two million other brave men who gave their lives. War was not something he'd wish on his son. Or being bounced around between family members as he had been, spending his middle teens in England again, before returning to Germany at seventeen. His mother died not long after, which allowed him to leave Bavaria for good and make Berlin his home.

And now it felt like a new Germany was rising from the ashes of the shamed Weimar Republic – but was it one to take pride in, or to fear? He didn't entirely share everyone's new optimism, although there had been no sign that the freedoms Berlin enjoyed would be curtailed by the small, pursed-lipped conservative leader who was known to be an antisemite and rabble-rouser.

Max did wonder about the Nazi Party, which was gaining in popularity. He was thinking about it now and how it was beginning to affect his colleagues' plans for the future. At work today the discussion had reached familiar territory: join the party or risk being on the outer, perhaps losing their jobs. No one really knew, Max realised, and so fear made most people compliant, but there was also Adolf Hitler's adroit way of touching a nerve among the masses. He was voicing what they wanted to hear; his speeches simmered with resentment at how the great German people were regarded in Europe, cunningly balanced with promises of how Germany would rise again.

Max appreciated Germany's precision in all things, especially in his meticulous line of work. He had so much opportunity sprawling ahead that he could look forward to a very handsome lifestyle for his family in years to come.

He was lost in these thoughts of the Republic while calculating that if he sped up, he could be home in under fifteen minutes. His home was in the privileged Mitte borough, the oldest section of the city in that eastern end, and any moment he should glimpse the glorious building of the Reichstag. *So . . . home in ten, maybe*, he thought, adjusting his estimate and widening in his mind the smile that Rachel would give him.

It was then that he heard what sounded like glass breaking.

It had caught the student's attention too. They both heard it again. *Definitely glass*, Max thought with a frown, watching the young man ahead of him break into a trot.

He did the same and his long legs soon brought him abreast of the youngster. They rounded the corner of Wilhelmstrasse together as more glass tinkled, this time seeming to blow outwards, and Max saw a strange orange glow above the grand building. His companion, unburdened by cakes or a precious toy train to keep safe, broke into a full run.

'It's on fire!' he yelled. 'The Reichstag is burning!'

Max halted, astonished, then heard another explosion and watched bright flames erupt and lick around the gilded glass cupola that sat over the Reichstag's plenary chamber. Black smoke had begun to billow through a hole in the glass roof, easing like a dark shadow above Berlin.

He heard the shot of a revolver and flinched. Now men were shouting. Max headed to where other curious pedestrians had gathered, including a police officer walking his beat. Apparently, through first-floor windows, they had seen someone acting suspiciously inside the building.

Max held back. There was nothing he could do. The screaming siren of a fire engine could now be heard, and he suspected pandemonium would soon break out.

He remained still, standing beneath a tree near the fountain in the formal gardens in front of the grand building, now properly aflame and lit from behind by the spreading fire that danced and licked around the edges of blown-out windows. Max watched the firefighters drawing water from the nearby River Spree as other spectators crouched at the sudden explosion as the cupola finally gave up all resistance.

Black cars began to arrive, spewing leaders. Max blinked in the shadows, noting Hermann Göring, interior minister, and not long afterwards a limousine brought the new chancellor, Adolf Hitler, together with his sidekick, Joseph Goebbels, whom Max had instinctively disliked on the day they were introduced. Goebbels had hardly noticed him, with barely more than a glance and a limp handshake . . . and Max was glad of that. He didn't want to be noticed by these shadowy men. Now he picked out the chief of the secret police and the aristocratic vice-chancellor, Franz von Papen, with ease.

Nevertheless, Max couldn't take his gaze from Chancellor Hitler, whose small, scrunched features reflected the glow of the flames; he managed to look demonic as he shook his fist and raged at his minions nearby. He was clearly enraged about the fire and the potential loss of the historic building. And yet something here felt contrived. Max couldn't pinpoint it but he trusted his gut; this situation felt bad in a dangerous way that he wanted no part of.

Max hunched deeper into his scarf, pulled his hat further down and eased away, moving through the cover of trees and buildings. He took the longer way home, less concerned about his wife's frustration and more worried about what the repercussions of this terrible night might mean for the people of Berlin.

At home, glued to the wireless and birthday celebrations forgotten, Max had watched the fire dissipate from his commanding vantage. As the flames eased, a vague and private sense of alarm intensified.

'So we're all safe,' Rachel said, her tension releasing as she lowered herself into his lap and curled up in his arms. 'Hold me close,' she whispered. 'And then I'll devour some cruller pastries.'

Max kissed the top of her head and they closed their eyes just before midnight in the armchair, in that embrace. Early-morning reports said that the fire had been started deliberately. The new chancellor blamed the arson attack on the Communist putsch.

Max had watched a new dawn break over Berlin and the smouldering ruin of the Reichstag. Somehow it felt symbolic. And the sense that it represented some sort of watershed was not easily shaken. He suspected this was because he, like every other politically aware German, had begun to pay even closer attention to wider reports later that morning – coming first out of Austria – that the fire was not the work of Communists or radicals but arsonists hired by the Hitler government.

Max turned this stunning notion over in his mind as more arrests were made and their details broadcast. He gathered it had been a busy night of rounding-up; not even clergymen or artists were spared. A whiff of left-wing economic thought, a mere sympathy expressed for the ideology, meant these people were judged as potentially hostile to the new Germany.

Less than a month later, Max was seated cross-legged on the floor of their elegant apartment, distractedly explaining the might of the flying Hamburger engine to Jonas, who was *choof-choof*ing a model train locomotive along some imaginary tracks, watched over by Rachel as she darned socks on the crest of her huge belly. Max knew in this moment he should feel as full as she looked, swollen with optimism and joy at his comfortable financial situation and his beautiful family. However, he had never felt more hollow. He did his best to shield Rachel from the rumblings of discontent that were beginning to sound through this most tolerant of cities.

With Adolf Hitler at the helm, Germany no longer felt responsible for Europe's pain. Its people were no more the miserable of Europe – Germany wanted its military returned, it demanded equality and all of its power back . . . and he suspected it would trample anything that got in its way.

As the notion clicked neatly into place like a jigsaw piece, Max reached the decision that had been nagging for weeks.

Time to leave.

As he felt his resolve harden, the telephone rang.

Max cut Rachel a grin and loped to the phone in the hallway.

'Max, it's Oskar.'

'She's darning socks. I'll fetch—'

'No, Max. Don't disturb her. I actually wanted to speak with you, er . . . discreetly.'

He frowned. 'All right. Is something wrong?'

'I'm not sure. It could be . . .' Oskar trailed off as if confused. This wasn't like him; Rachel's father was an ebullient professor of philosophy at Humboldt University, adored by his students for his wit as much as his brilliant lectures. He was never lost for words.

'Could be?' he echoed. 'What seems to be the problem?'

'There are rumours.'

He waited. 'About what, Oskar?'

'Government restrictions . . . which I can't quite believe, but it's not just me who is baffled. Others, more connected, are of the belief that it is true.'

'Oskar . . .' he began, sounding weary. 'You need to explain.'

'What I'm hearing is that our new government is planning to revoke the doctorates of all Jewish professors.'

Max gave a derisive snort. 'What nonsense. You know that's illegal.'

'I do, and still the rumours persist. One of my closest colleagues, who is connected into the highest levels of government, is telling me to protect myself and my family. He's suggesting we should leave Germany immediately, perhaps return to Hungary, as though it's still my home.' Max heard his elder groan. 'Max, we left there when I was half Jonas's age. Germany is my home. I fought for it. I bled—'

'Be calm,' he said, peeking at his wife and son, who were now reading a bedtime story. He couldn't have Rachel being frightened by this.

'Revoking our qualifications is the beginning. I'm hearing that the Nazi Party has decided that people of Jewish descent are first on their list to lose rights.'

'I can't give this credence, but I promise you I will look into it.'

Hitler had made no secret of his antisemitic tendencies, but Max believed that was surely just talk when Hitler was a young hoodlum trying to work up other rebels. He tried to reassure his father-in-law. 'Oskar, you're about to be a grandfather again in a fortnight. I don't want anything getting in the way of Rachel having a smooth, untroubled delivery.'

'I understand.'

'I promise to look into these rumours. I too have contacts that stretch into the higher echelons of our government.'

'Thank you, Max. I'm sorry for the late call.'

'Go to bed, Oskar. Tomorrow will be brighter – spring is around the corner.'

Fateful words. He wished he could take them back, go back in time and act on Oskar's warnings. It was the very spring he spoke about that brought death and the emergence of real trouble to come. Hitler celebrated his birthday month of April with new laws regarding the boycott of Jewish businesses, while stripping Jewish civil servants of their employment. Oskar had been right.

There was a new dawn indeed. But it was already too late for Max and Rachel.

1

North Yorkshire

Late spring, 1936

Evie Armstrong shielded her eyes from the sun as she looked up the hill, lifted her other hand to the person who had called her name, and waved. She recognised them as one of the villagers but wasn't in the mood for talking to others; she never was when she was here talking to Ron.

'Anyway, I'm leaving you with some of the cherry blossom,' she continued her cheerful conversation. 'It's been out for a couple of weeks and was so late this year I wondered if it would ever come.'

She didn't expect him to answer.

Mercifully, the icy chill of the North Yorkshire winter was past and spring had begun to sprinkle its heart-warming, life-giving magic across the moors, urging all the sleeping perennials to wake and start stretching in readiness for their summer flowers. Colour would soon erupt across the moors, which would be dominated by a pink blanket of heather, but even the blue harebells and the elusive ruby-coloured cloudberry would be spotted any moment.

Life. It was moving ahead without her. As much as she enjoyed these private times with Ron, she was not so lost in her memories that she could believe he felt the land warming around him.

The blossom had come and gone for six seasons since Evie had held him for the last time. As daunting as that recollection was, it was fading, and that in itself was troubling. What if she lost that too? She could remember Ron's voice, and the colour of his middle finger slightly stained with nicotine; she could even remember his cheerful whistle, but she'd begun to lose the sound of his voice. When had that memory started to fade? There had been a time when his absence was so keen that she could have sworn he was lying next to her, could still sense the length of his body against her in bed, long after he had died.

Ron was young and strong – too young to lose his life – but he had quite simply been where he shouldn't have been. He had made the fundamental error that every railway worker was warned to avoid. Ordinarily Ron would never have made such a mistake, but who could have foreseen a curious toddler wandering onto the railway tracks in little more than her nappy and a vest? No one. Least of all burly porter Ron Armstrong, which is likely why in his surprised horror he had reacted with none of the wisdom of the experienced railwayman he was.

According to what Evie could piece together, the child had escaped her mother's line of sight and the boundary of her home, appearing on the tracks as if magicked there by some wicked spell-caster. Carriages were being shunted off the hump track and were headed directly for the infant. Ron did not hesitate to consider the threat to himself: one second he was where he should be and the next he was in the path of danger, which didn't care that Ron was a good man, a dedicated railwayman, newly married and looking forward to starting his own family. Danger would have gleefully taken the infant as well, if not for Ron holding her up out of harm's way as he bore the full impact, the rolling wagons brutally sandwiching him at chest height as they rolled back down the man-made hump under their own weight and momentum.

'He never stood a chance,' her father had wept, looking on, wringing his flag in despair as a distant ambulance siren began to scream across the valley.

Curiously, Evie had not openly wept while she held Ron.

And Ron had used his last few heartbeats to apologise, of all things.

'I'm sorry, Evie. I wanted to give you that son we talked about.'

'Not for lack of trying, my love,' she said, knowing it was too late, amazed at her composure that told her to send him off with them both smiling.

He even chuckled, recalling the lovemaking of newlyweds. 'I worshipped every moment of loving you.'

'We're still here, Ron. Don't give up,' she tried, feeling useless, hating the hollow sound of her words.

'No, Evie. Let me say this.' He groaned but rallied with a great effort. 'Listen to me now. You're too young to spend years missing me. Promise me when you find someone worthy—'

'Stop it!' she begged. 'There's only you.'

He looked deep into her eyes and his breath turned shallow and ragged. 'Make sure you know happiness again sometime. Kiss me goodbye, my darling.'

Evie could see the light dimming in his acorn-coloured eyes and bent low to kiss him as tenderly as she could, ignoring the taste of copper pennies in his mouth. Ron smiled and sighed out his final rattling exhalation, as though his spirit were travelling on that breath as it left him.

Evie looked down now at Ron's grave and the crystalline white of the tiny snowdrops she'd placed there, knowing her father would already be looking for her at the station. Life needed to go on. It was such a cliché but how true it was; as much as she'd wanted the world to stop, it refused.

It was station work that kept her from despairing. Her father depended on her more and more now. She didn't mind; being needed, being busy and distracted had saved her from the corrosive force of her grief.

Evie shivered in the breeze that cut into the picturesque valley between Levisham and Lockton, whistling gently across the ancient yew and on through the ruins of the Norman-built St Mary's Church, in whose graveyard she stood.

Luminous drifts of daffodils danced in the sunshine, spreading their joy across Yorkshire's parkland. Tiny forget-me-nots guided her back up from Ron's grave to where life was full and busy. Wildflowers across the moors riotously competed for her attention and she was keen to get up onto those trails soon to pick all the new vibrant plants for her pressings, especially the shy bluebells. Even the birds were feeling the joy: suddenly so much song all around Levisham Station, and only the steam trains' arrivals and departures could drown them out.

Buds had burst into blossom in the orchards, and Evie was looking forward to a bountiful haul from the cherry trees that had been planted long before she was born – a gift from a traveller. She had no idea to this day from where that traveller had come – Japan, perhaps – but her father had duly planted the three tiny saplings along the station boundary. And they'd grown. Evie had personally grown another dozen trees from pits, and now those trees were their station's pride and joy, to herald spring and welcome or farewell travellers at Levisham. It meant a lot of work come harvest time: not just collecting the fruit but knowing what to do with it all. She had built a reasonable business out of selling many pounds in brown paper bags through the summer, not to mention dozens of jars of jam that sold well through the kiosk to the holidaymakers. Evie had taught herself how to preserve the cherries in liquor, plus her specialty was making her own glacé cherries.

She sold some for Christmas puddings but reserved most for her own cherry cake slabs, which she made daily and put beneath a gleaming bell jar. Placing the glass cloche over her special cherry cake that had cooled overnight was always the final task – like a ritual – and that meant she was ready for the day's business.

It was an optimistic weather forecast for today, so she presumed it would be a busy one. She checked her watch, gasped and broke into a run.

'Rosie?'

'Coming . . . coming,' her sister called, sounding offended by the edge in her sister's voice. 'You're not the foreman, you know,' she said, arriving back in the kitchen.

'What I do know is that you never get your chores done and you expect me to help you when you lag. Our father's nerves are stretched today.'

Her sister rolled her eyes. 'I will be *so* glad when this visit is over.'

'Won't we all? But in the meantime, can we please pitch in and help him? This time last year we were preparing for the King's Silver Jubilee, you may recall, but looking at how anxious Dad feels I think that was a breeze by comparison to the railway's short length prize. He wants this very badly for Levisham.'

She noticed her sister mocking her, rolling her eyes, but Evie was too well versed in Rosie's antics to react. 'Rosie, you have to help us. It's important. Now, I've got to go,' she said, glancing at the clock as it ticked over to eight-fifty.

'Why?'

'I'm checking in on Joe.'

'What's wrong with him?'

'Well, if you were less self-absorbed, you'd know he was sick yesterday and the day before. Dad and I have been handling his tasks.'

'You always get the good stuff.'

'That's because you never bothered to learn.'

'They'd sack Dad if they knew you were working in the signals box.'

'Which is why, Rosie, I've been dressed like a man for the past two days – had you even noticed?'

Her sister laughed. It wasn't unkind but there was still a gentle derisive quality underpinning it. 'Oh, I just thought you liked looking that way.'

Evie sighed. 'Please attend to the floors and then I'll need you to—'

'Floors again?'

'What now, Rosie?' She sighed. 'Do you need time to moon over Frank Evans a bit longer, or do you need to look at that new frock in the catalogue you've been badgering Dad for?'

'Don't scoff, Evie. I do think you're jealous because while you might be the smart one, I am the pretty one.'

Evie found a smile. 'Yes, well, that's why I change the railway points and you get to line up and be ready to greet our important guests, looking so eye-catching.'

'Do we even know when they'll come?'

'No,' Evie said with a slight groan. 'All we know is it's this week sometime, so we have to prepare each day as though it's the one.'

Evie stepped outside and skipped across the platform and onto the tracks. Realising she was late, she cursed in German under her breath as her Nanny Lotte had taught her. She had to be careful these days; what had been fun in her teens during the mid-twenties when the Great War had dimmed sufficiently was no longer as amusing.

She listened to the news on the wireless with her father daily and she also read the newspaper after he'd finished with it; Evie was more than aware of the threat beginning to emanate out of Germany once more. The situation that had seemed impossible just a few years ago was now plausible. A new leader with great ambition for Germany was on the rise.

She had noticed more conversations, more intense discussions up and down the platform about Germany and whether its re-armament was just the nation trying to rebuild itself, or something more sinister. The murmur was getting stronger that Germany's passionate, shouting chancellor was stirring the embers still glowing in the bellies of humiliated soldiers, who had returned feeling somehow robbed of their triumph over the world.

So, no one needed a Yorkshire lass talking in the German language. She understood most of Adolf Hitler's grandstanding orations, translating them as best she could for her father, who would shake his head with increasing dismay.

She looked now at his lovely face, presently creased with concentration and the stress of a busy morning as he discussed the day with Joe. The next train would be coming through on its way to Whitby. Then the goods train would approach from the other direction, bringing fish from Whitby and probably stone from the whinstone quarry at Goathland.

Evie climbed the stairs to the signals room and was immediately enveloped in the smell of Brasso. Rosie said that if Evie continued her ritual of inhaling the fumes of metal polish each time she stepped into the signal box, it would turn her soft in the head. It was true that the aroma of ammonia was strong, but once the fumes had dissipated and everything was polished and gleaming, the timber handles waxed and velvety, the whole masculine perfume became the smell of her father. It became a smell of home. She loved it in here, always had, with its tiny fireplace burning merrily through winter, ever cosy for the person who sat in the single comfy armchair. It was such a selfish little space for one, and on quiet days as a small child she used to sneak in here and sit on a tiny stool that Joe had set down next to him so they could look up and down the line together and talk about trains.

Evie knew from before her age was in double figures what every lever did, and sometimes Joe would let her haul those big handles with him, putting all their strength behind the levers that changed the points on the rails.

She climbed up into the signal box with a slice of yesterday's cake to go with Joe's morning tea.

'Hello, Joe. Are you feeling much better?'

These days there was no trace of the coal-black hair he'd once boasted. Now it had thinned and turned grey, while his beard was almost white rather than peppered as it had been when he'd first grown it. He'd make a good Father Christmas for the local children, if only he could remember how he used to laugh that big laugh of his. But the war had stolen his amusement and that of all his friends except her father, Alf, leaving him with cold, withering memories that came to haunt him from time to time. Her father said they made him tremble, take to his bed for a couple of days to lie and stare at the ceiling uttering no words until he emerged from the dark recollections. 'Just a sniffle. I'll be fine,' he said.

She didn't pursue it – was glad he was back among life and those who cared about him. 'I brought you this. Yesterday's but not stale, I promise.'

He beamed at the sight of the inch-high slab. 'I like day-old cake, love. Anyway, I think you just like being in the signal room. It's never failed to fascinate me how a pretty young woman like you takes such an interest in all this,' he said, pointing to the twenty-four levers, the dials, boxes with bells on them, gauges and switches.

'It's probably because I like language, Joe. To live on a noisy station is to witness people talking to one another but without being able to hear the sound . . . unless they shout, of course.'

Joe smiled and frowned.

'You know . . . you use flags and semaphore, you use the signals, you use lights, you use alarms and bells – not a single word spoken and yet up and down the line everyone knows what's happening at Levisham.'

He nodded. 'I'd never thought about it that way . . . I mean, that we have our own language.' He tapped his nose. 'But I've only recently learned that you and your sister can listen in on what people are saying.'

'And we don't have to hear a word.' She grinned. 'It began as a game when we were little, standing on opposite sides of the station and trying to talk above the screech of the steam and whistles. I've been unconsciously lip-reading strangers' conversations now for most of my life. I've become awfully good at it.' She put both hands to her cheeks as she blushed. 'That's embarrassing.'

Joe chuckled. 'I'll bet you've lip-read some stuff you wish you hadn't.'

She nodded knowingly. 'I've learned to look away, for instance when Mr and Mrs Dickson are having words on the other platform.'

'Who taught you that lip-reading business, then?'

'We taught ourselves. Sometimes I found myself on the opposite platform and needed to tell Rosie or Nanny Lotte something. We used to try shouting over the noise of the approaching train but that was no good, so we learned to mouth what we needed. It was Nanny Lotte who apparently had a deaf aunt and knew how important lip-reading was to her – she made us practise until we no longer had to exaggerate. Now we can just speak normally but silently, and we know what the other is saying.'

'And what everyone else is saying privately.' He chuckled.

'I promise, as an adult I try not to eavesdrop. Adults need their secrets, don't they?'

'Your father doesn't think Rosie is making much of a secret of her interest in that visitor from the south.'

She gave an exasperated sound. 'I've pleaded with her to stop flirting with that gentleman. Poor man. I can see how uncomfortable it makes him, and his awkwardness only emboldens her . . . it's like a challenge to Rosie. I can't blame her entirely. He's very handsome.'

'Oops,' Joe said, eyes widening, and she waggled a finger of warning. He didn't pursue it.

She gave him a smile. 'I'd better go – I promised to help Dad with the parcels, plus the next train is *his* train.'

She heard his soft laughter as she moved back onto the platform for northbound travel. She just knew in her heart that Rosie would have left the floor damp, probably to check her hair was perfect for the southerner.

She wished she had the luxury to do the same. Everyone thought she was some sort of ice queen, but if only they knew – her heart pounded too, at times; she just didn't like sharing the fact. She also didn't like that it tended to pound whenever she glimpsed the southerner.

Evie was sorting through all the post and parcels with her father, Alf Barraclough, before the train arrived, and they were sharing the midday news on the wireless. The clipped tone of the presenter had already announced the glum news that the British government would be tripling the size of its Royal Air Force in answer to the recent German rearmament. He continued, '. . . and today in Berlin, Germany has announced its new Defence Law, issued to ban all those of Jewish heritage from its armed forces.'

They looked at one another.

Alf's was a face that promoted cheerfulness. Whether he intended it or not, there was something helplessly genial in his expression, as though his eyes preferred the smile position, regardless of his mood. Unlike Joe, Alf had managed to return from the war entirely; he had left too many friends behind, but somehow he had escaped the ghosts. She'd talked to him about it on a few occasions and he'd said that he refused to let the enemy come home with him. She admired her father for that resilience, because she was sure he'd suffered as much as the next man; he simply refused to let it colour his life as a father and railwayman once again. She'd noticed his frame was slightly more stooped and he no longer looked as powerful as he used to. He was middle-aged now, with a slight paunch that his waistcoat buttons strained against. But he looked healthy, he knew how to tip back his head and laugh, and he had not forgotten how to love. She was grateful to have her beloved father in her life, safe and sound.

'Dad, there's a lot of confusion, isn't there, about Hitler's activities. Is there going to be war again?'

He patted her hand. 'I don't think so, my darling. I hope we learned our lessons from the Great War. Germany wouldn't be so thoughtless as to start another confrontation.'

'Then what's happening? Only a couple of months ago there was all that grumbling and protest here that Germany has introduced conscription.'

'Just a lot of chest beating, I'd say. Most of the balanced commentators are pointing out that Germany is trying to regain some stature in the world. Moving west into the Rhine area was simply that.' He didn't sound convinced.

'It feels so threatening,' she said.

'Well.' He sighed. 'I think this Hitler fellow is trying to breathe some passion and motivation into a country that has felt crushed – not to mention beggared – for years. They deserved to pay reparations for the war, but it was seventeen years ago; I don't blame a nation for trying to get back on its feet.'

'No, but this sounds ominous.'

'I don't want to think about war on a day like today. Let's just listen to some music instead, shall we?' He fiddled with the dial as odd sounds of other programs briefly filled their space and when he heard a familiar tune by Irving Berlin, he grinned. 'Jack Payne and his band . . . that will do us nicely.'

They were both humming as they handled letters and small parcels and didn't see the arrival of the local constabulary.

'Morning, Alf . . . lovely Evie,' the man said, wiping his damp boots on the doormat.

'Where did you spring from, Harry? I didn't see you there.' Alf picked up another bundle of letters.

Harry tapped his nose with a grin. 'They call us flat-footed, but I think us good ones are light of tread. Looks like you've got a light foot there, Alf.' He nodded at the stationmaster's leg tapping in time to the music.

'If Mrs Barraclough were alive today, I'd ask her to dance,' Alf replied, 'right here in the parcels office.'

Evie gave him an indulgent smile, feeling the old sorrow burn momentarily.

Harry removed his helmet and tucked it under an arm. 'Ah, well, why don't you come down to the local dance, then, Alf? There's any number of lovely ladies who wouldn't mind a journey around the floor in your arms.'

Alf waved this comment aside. 'How are things, Harry?'

'All quiet, as I like it, although I am here to brief you on something that London sent through.'

'Oh, yes. What's that, then?' Alf said, frowning and switching off the wireless.

'We're advising all the stations in the area to keep an eye out for strangers.'

Both Evie and her father gave a soft noise of derision.

'Strangers? We get dozens of those daily,' Alf replied.

The police sergeant nodded with a sigh. 'I know, I realise it is quite a curious instruction.'

Evie frowned. 'What sort of stranger?'

He shrugged. 'That's just it, even head office can't brief us any better.'

'What's this all about, then?' Alf asked, coming around from behind the counter. 'We need more information, Harry.'

The policeman sighed. 'I'll tell you what I know, but this has to be kept quiet.'

They both nodded.

'Seems we should expect some spies in our region.'

'Spies?' they chorused, but at his alarmed look they immediately hushed.

'Apparently,' he said, his tone admonishing them for their loud voices.

Evie whispered, 'From where, though?'

Harry tipped his head at the wireless, as though that should be all-enlightening. She waited. 'Germany,' he murmured. 'Adolf's lot.'

'You're joking,' her father said, his tone awed.

Harry closed his eyes and shook his head once. 'I wish I was.'

'But here?' she pressed. 'Sleepy Levisham?'

'Not here, specifically,' Harry continued, looking at their confused expressions. 'All stations in the north have been put on a sort of alert,' he admitted. 'All stations up and down the country have been cautioned, in fact, and now you have been too. What you're looking for, I can't tell you, but you know your passengers better than we do, so we're asking you to remain on alert and pass over any information you think is relevant – anything that strikes you as somewhat out of the ordinary, or that just doesn't sit right.' He began putting his helmet back on. 'Most of the people up and down here are locals or your regulars, so it likely won't affect you, I suspect.'

'Well, no, Harry, that's not quite right,' Alf noted. 'We're about to go into the high season for ramblers and tourists. We'll be awash with summer holidaymakers and sightseers.'

'All strangers,' Evie pressed.

'Just keep your eyes peeled, will you?' Harry said, sounding a fraction testier. It seemed he didn't set much store by the whole idea himself, and didn't enjoy talking about it. He departed and left them with their thoughts.

'German spies?' Alf said into the silence. 'Here? How ridiculous.' He looked at Evie. 'What are you frowning about, my love?'

'Well, the first stranger who comes to mind is Rosie's Londoner.'

Alf scoffed. 'That's because you're both obsessed with him. We have people on the trains daily that we haven't seen before.'

She shrugged. 'Just mentioning it in the spirit of duty – and, Dad, it's Rosie who is the one obsessed.'

'Anyway, that man is as English as cricket.'

'As strawberries and cream.' She chuckled.

'As warm beer,' Alf said, grinning. Then shook his head. 'That man's no spy. I heard him apologising to someone a week or so ago when they stood on his toe. You can't teach that . . . only an Englishman would be that daft or polite.'

Evie laughed. 'How about that old couple who like to go rambling around Goathland?'

'He's nearing seventy if he's a day,' he admonished, amused. 'Let's get a wriggle on, my girl. The train's due.'

2

The steam in the distance signalled that the train from York, which had travelled up from King's Cross in London, was on time. Vapours billowed up like snowy marshmallow above the tree line; soon she'd see the soot-stained cloud of steam at the helm and then the first whistle would announce its imminent arrival.

It was going to be a truly splendid spring day and she imagined the train would bring plenty of visitors, particularly trail walkers. She'd heard that the association now known as the Ramblers counted around six thousand members who walked Britain's pathways with the aim of increasing access, safeguarding paths, and promoting free and healthy activity for the public. She agreed with their mission to protect the right to walk Britain's amazing network of public paths as part of one's national heritage. Evie suspected that the southerner, whom Rosie was determined to get a name for today if he arrived, was one of those people who might argue that rambling benefited British society. Either way, so long as the eager visitors bought her tea, coffee and cakes, Evie would be happy to put more coin into her father's meagre coffers. She smiled at Alf as he emerged onto the platform, the buttons of his proudly worn uniform glinting in the sun, checking his fob watch and nodding. Once the train had left and all the passengers who'd alighted at Levisham had been catered for, she would help him in the parcels room.

The black engine lumbered towards them, pulling eight carriages painted burgundy. The driver's mate leaned out and leered at her, his face smudged with coal dust. She raised a hand in welcome, pretending she hadn't heard the wolf whistle. Rosie wasn't nearly so modest; at Evie's side in a blink, she was waving madly and calling out a welcome to the man who had risked a flirtatious moment with her big sister.

'Is the urn on?' Evie said, to focus Rosie.

'Yes,' her sister confirmed in a waspish tone.

'I need your help now, Rosie,' she warned, hating the matronly sound in her voice. 'We need to earn some money today and we want people to linger long enough for a quick pot of tea before they head off.'

'Evie, you say that to me almost every day as if I'm simple and didn't hear it yesterday . . . or the day before.'

'No, I remind you because you are so easily distracted.'

'Ooh, there's the handsome Londoner leaning out,' Rosie said, dismissing their conversation. 'Bags I serve him.'

'So long as he leaves some money behind, I don't care if Joe serves him,' she lied, sneaking a glance at the man.

'You're becoming so boring, do you know that?' Rosie accused her, coughing briefly as the steam enveloped them.

'It's called responsibility, Rosie – something you're yet to learn.' She sighed. 'I'll be behind the counter. Make sure you point people my way, including your southerner.'

Rosie gave a mock curtsy. 'I'll bring *him* in on my arm, if you like,' she teased.

Evie watched doors opening, a few already slamming shut. The train was off to Goathland and would only be at Levisham for another minute or so before her father blew his whistle and raised his green flag. She hurried to her makeshift kiosk to get behind the counter for those alighting; quite a few today. She'd set out small tables with chairs and she was serving directly out of their house onto the platform. The railway company didn't seem to mind her industry, but she wondered when the owner might finally get around to demanding a percentage of her modest takings to be paid back into company accounts.

Ah, well, something to worry about another day, she decided. Perhaps the weather would be fine enough next week that she could serve in the cottage gardens, always picturesque in spring. With the increased traffic, she might even sell a few of her 'frames', as she liked to think of her pressed wildflowers.

Customers began arriving and suddenly she was busy in a flurry of teapots and hissing steam from her urn, the train long gone. 'Where are you, Rosie?' she muttered beneath her breath.

'. . . and a slice of your cherry cake, dear, please,' said a woman, one of a middle-aged pair. 'My husband says yours is better than mine.'

Evie demurred. 'I'm sure he's just teasing,' she said, pushing the lever to fill a small metal pot with water over leaf tea. She placed it on a tray where cups and saucers were already waiting with a small jug of milk. 'Help yourself to sugar on the table. I'll just fetch your cake.'

'No, really, it's delicious,' someone waiting behind said. 'I hold off buying anything at Malton or even Pickering, which has a proper kiosk. Your cherry cake is the lure, Mrs Armstrong.' He was an older gentleman who had been alighting at Levisham for years. He touched his hat with respect.

'Thank you, Mr Brand. Er . . . a slice each?'

The woman nodded, casting a smile over her shoulder at Mr Brand.

'You won't regret it,' he assured her with a wink.

'That will be sixpence, please.'

The husband counted out the correct number of pennies and paid.

'Thank you. Enjoy the lovely day.'

Evie served two more customers, including Mr Brand, and as he paused to talk, she risked looking over his head with guarded fury that Rosie had not turned up as promised. She served another couple who appeared behind him.

'Thank you, madam. Are you rambling today?'

'Can't waste this weather, and I want to walk to Goathland before the pathways get too crowded.'

'It can be muddy up there. Be careful.'

The woman waved away her concern. 'We'll be back for an afternoon pot soon enough and some of that cake everyone's talking about.'

'I'll save you some.' Evie smiled and turned away to fetch a new pint of milk. When she returned to the table that acted as a counter, she was met by the smiling gaze of the southerner.

'Good morning,' he said.

'Good morning, sir.' She blinked: Rosie was nowhere near, and she was slightly disarmed by his grin. Normally he was reserved to the point of seeming distracted, but he was making full eye contact. 'Are you rambling today?' she asked, feeling ridiculous because of course he was, wearing that garb.

But he answered in a conversational tone. 'It's time to do the Hole of Horcum,' he replied.

'Oh, you'll love it. We call it the Yorkshire Grand Canyon,' she said.

'Yes, so I've been told,' he remarked, and it arrived – that curious silence that seemed to follow him around. Rosie had tried desperately to engage with him, and had said: *he's just one big awkward pause, but I'll keep working on him.*

Evie filled it instantly. 'What can I get you today?'

'I'll have a coffee, please, and a slice of your cherry cake.'

Evie cut him a sideways glance. 'Are you sure? I have some nice rock buns this morning.'

He frowned. 'I'd prefer the cherry cake. Your sister tells me you bake it daily.'

She busied herself with the coffee and shrugged at him. 'People seem to like it . . . but I didn't think you did.'

'Oh? Whatever makes you say that?'

'Well . . .' She gave a nervous chuckle. 'You always waste the fruit. It comes from our own trees at the end of the platform and I work very hard to turn them into glacé cherries.'

He looked momentarily disconcerted. 'I hardly noticed. Have I offended?'

'No,' she lied. 'I just thought I should offer something else.'

'Now I'm embarrassed, and so I shall buy two slices to make up for my carelessness.'

She laughed.

'No, I'm serious. One for now and one for later, on the moors.'

They could use the extra pennies, but she was feeling badly for shaming him. 'I don't mean to scrutinise . . . it's just that I couldn't help noticing. Most people think they're the best bit. I, er . . .' Good grief, she was blathering. 'Please, let me give you a slice with my compliments.'

'Absolutely not.' He grinned. 'I'm very happy to pay. I do like your endeavour here at this country station, Miss, er . . .'

'Mrs Armstrong – I'm Evie,' she said, slightly self-conscious herself beneath his hesitant look, which only now she could see spoke of pewter-coloured steam that billowed from the head of a train, stained by the coal that powered it. They were lovely stormy-coloured eyes with a melancholy quality she had noticed even from afar, and she found them deeply attractive.

His gaze landed lightly on her, but it quickly slipped away, like mercury. 'Sorry, you . . . you don't wear a ring. My mistake.'

'Gosh, how observant. Maybe you are the one.'

'Pardon?'

She gave a dismissive laugh, shaking her head. 'We've been asked to look out for strangers.'

'Oh? Aren't most people strangers on trains?'

Evie gave a small shrug. 'On this branch line we do see a lot of regulars.'

'I hope you count me among them,' he said, his voice soft, earnest even.

She met his frown with one of her own. 'Of course. We look forward to your regular visits.'

'Who asked you to do this?' he said, digging in his pocket for change.

'The local police.'

'How very vague.'

'Vague and silly, if you ask me. How could we recognise a spy?'

'Spy?' She nodded at his derisive tone with an equally disdainful look. 'Well, I have no idea what that's about, nor do I wish to, but in my experience, I think you'll find the villains always wear black,' he said, tapping his nose. 'Very easy to spot.'

Evie chuckled, glanced at her fingers. 'I'll bear that in mind. I should be wearing my ring – you're right. But my hands are either in suds or Brasso, or I'm digging around the moors for wildflowers, and it was always really rather a fragile ring; it gets battered.'

'Your husband doesn't mind you taking it off?' He grinned.

'He might, if he were alive. I'm a widow.'

He looked back at her with such a wounded expression, she couldn't tell if it was with empathy, or for his misstep. But it was writ deep enough in his features that she felt guilty for her candour, and all talk of spies was forgotten. 'I'm sorry. I find it's easier to be direct, especially on this subject.' She shrugged. 'People make judgements, get the wrong impression or just reach the wrong conclusion.'

His face was yet to resume its previous relaxed pose. 'No, I'm very sorry, stumbling around like a clod.'

'It really is all right. How could you possibly know?'

His smile eased its way forward again as he gave an apologetic shrug of his own. 'I'm Roger Hall,' he introduced, looking towards her bars of cherry cake beneath the glass dome.

She let herself enjoy his cultured English accent, which spoke of grammar school and warm scones with clotted cream, as she blew a wayward curl of hair away from her face. 'It's very nice to finally meet you properly, Mr Hall. My sister will be disappointed to have missed you. I can't imagine where she is, or you and I would not have had two seconds spare to converse.' She smiled as she sliced his cake. 'Would you like me to wrap those for you?'

'That would be excellent. I did see your sister . . . I'm getting used to her cheerful welcomes, but your father called her away. Something about parcels.'

She couldn't help a soft snort of laughter. 'Ah, I think my father is saving you the trouble of disentangling yourself from Rosie's warm greetings.'

He gave her a tight look. 'It's never my intention to offend—'

'You should not even think on it, Mr Hall. Rosie is far too gregarious at times. I'll have a word,' she promised. 'I hope it won't stop you visiting, though?'

'Not at all,' he said, holding eye contact with her. It was disconcerting to have this attention. 'Are you not allowed a permanent kiosk here?' he asked, suddenly looking away at the makeshift trestle tables and unmatched furniture.

'It's not that. The railway owners don't consider this branch line of Levisham large enough or busy enough to have one built, so I decided to fashion my own.'

'Well, I think you do a grand job. *Everything* about Levisham is beautiful.' His words sounded loaded, and when she noted how he was regarding her, she felt a warmth rising from her collar.

She curled the wax paper beneath the two slices of cake. 'Do you come up from York or London? Oh, I hope that doesn't sound too curious.' She was sounding like a loon.

He grinned. 'From King's Cross. I give myself a couple of days up here as often as I can.'

Rosie suddenly arrived in a cloud of perfume; from the first heady inhalation of the peach notes of Jean Patou's Joy, Evie recognised it as her own. She felt her throat constrict with frustration that Rosie had been indulging at her dressing table.

'Er . . . Dad asked me to see if you're available,' she said to Evie almost carelessly as she turned away. 'Oh, hello again,' she said in an exaggerated tone, as if only now noticing Roger Hall.

Evie watched him retreat. That open, slate-eyed gaze became hooded again and slightly worried. 'Er, yes, hello. Time for me to get on my way. Lovely to meet you,' he said to Evie and handed over some coins.

Evie felt the warmth of his skin inadvertently touching hers as he did so. He knew it too, and for a heartbeat they snapped a glance at each other before she quickly looked down at the silver sixpence in her palm. 'What about your change, Mr Hall? I owe you tuppence.'

'You did me a favour,' he said, holding up the wrapped cake. 'And thanks for the coffee – perhaps I'll see you on the return journey.'

'It gets in at eight minutes to four,' Rosie said.

He smiled. 'I'll be on it out of Goathland, which is a couple of hours on foot from your "grand canyon" and looking forward to another coffee if you're still open.'

He took them both in with a sweeping glance and strode out the door before either of the women could respond.

Rosie turned back to Evie accusingly. 'You've chased him off.'

'Rosie, if anyone is chasing off the customers, it's you. You terrify him.'

Her sister laughed. 'Rubbish. I think he's probably self-conscious because he likes me too much.'

Evie released a deep sigh of concern. 'Leave him alone or he won't come back.'

'Or leave him for you, do you mean?'

She shook her head as she might to a pouting child. 'What is wrong with you?'

'Well, when I walked in you looked like you were making a new friend.'

'I was simply being polite.'

'Then why are you blushing?'

'This isn't blushing,' she lied, more than aware that colour would be splotching her cheeks. 'This is called embarrassment at the way you moon over him. You smell like a perfume counter, and I haven't given you permission to wear my scent.'

'Well, someone needs to.'

'Oh, be quiet. You wear me down, Rosie. Please fetch all the trays in. Looks like most people have moved on. Let's get them washed and ready for the next train. What does Dad want?'

'What does Dad always want? Help!'

'Right, then. I'll be in the parcels room. Please get this place tidied. Looks like a nice day – we can set up in the cottage gardens for this afternoon.' She turned her back on Rosie's theatrical sigh and rolling of her eyes, wondering why Roger Hall never took tea like a true Englishman.

Stationmaster Barraclough introduced his daughters after the railway dignitaries had shaken hands with Joe. Evie had chosen a simple, plain-coloured frock of grass green with white and lemon accents. She felt it subtly complemented the station's lawn edged with pretty daffodils that she and her father had worked hard to cultivate in time for judging. Rosie, however, had gone all out. She was like a bright bauble on the platform in a drop-waisted raspberry gingham summery dress with two large shiny buttons below her waist and neat box pleats below that. She looked stunning but she knew it, Evie thought, smiling privately at her sister's perfect bob of finger-waved dark blonde hair and immaculately applied rouge and lipstick.

Evie hadn't bothered with either. She'd barely had time to glance in the mirror and push her own golden hair into some semblance of shape after making sure that all the tickets were sold, the parcels were distributed and the garden kiosk looked tidy and inviting. If the prize length – an annual award for the best mile of improved railway track by which they measured their individual efforts as well as the collective effort of their train station – might be decided this afternoon, she wanted to be sure it was awarded to Levisham. The prize length was revered by all railway workers up and down the country. Her family had given an enormous effort to this year's prize length just north of the platforms. Added to this, she was feeling uncharacteristically jumpy, looking out for the last afternoon train that would be carrying Roger Hall.

Evie and Rosie were standing on the northbound platform with the supervisor and a man who had been introduced but she hadn't paid much attention to due to being distracted by notions of romance enhanced by admiring the daffodils dancing in the mid-spring sunlight. Cherry blossom drifted across their vision, settling on their shoulders and catching in their hair when the soft breezes came. There was only beauty in these pale, floating petals. She leapt to the conclusion that the supervisor's companion was the prize-length judge, so Evie rallied herself to spend time explaining to him how they'd landscaped the area. Meanwhile, Rosie was charming the railway supervisor with an amusing tale about a lost parcel, while Alf and Joe prepared for the train that was arriving on the southbound platform, hopefully carrying her handsome southerner.

It chugged in with all of its usual noise and activity, her father blowing his whistle and the train answering with a piercing screech of its own. Steam wafted around them and they couldn't continue their conversation, so Evie politely stopped talking with a smile and turned with the others to watch the train's brief pause. She hoped, as it drew away, that Roger Hall would be left behind and she'd raise a hand in welcome with a bright smile. What Evie didn't expect was to see him deep in conversation with another gentleman in a carriage. He didn't stir from his seat as the train slowed, and when the billowing steam cleared, what he couldn't have known is that she was on the opposite platform looking at him. While the other man spoke, Evie watched Hall sneak a look out the window to where he presumably believed she or Rosie might be waiting for him. She noted him craning his neck for a better view before he turned back to his companion, leaning forward and pointing a finger as he spoke in what looked to her as rising anger.

She frowned, concentrated and helplessly lip-read.

Nothing was ever said about that. She watched Hall jab at the air. *I'm a rail engineer. We made a deal. I never agreed to this.*

Those are your orders, the other man replied.

From who?

From the highest . . . Evie couldn't be sure but guessed that the man had used the word 'level'.

Doors slammed as steam puffed from the chimney of the engine, drifting over them all in dramatic clouds. She heard her father's warning whistle and the train's answer. Evie waved at the vapours, and as they cleared she saw Hall sit back, looking angry.

I've done what I promised.

Well, they've asked for more, the man snarled at him, and then the train hauled them away. She glimpsed Roger Hall stand up and run a frustrated hand through his straw-coloured hair and mess up its neat lines. And then he was gone, off to Pickering . . . without stopping for coffee.

She blinked, her disappointment so overwhelming she didn't realise that her father was already back.

'Evie?' He shook her elbow.

The three men were staring and Rosie was looking at her as though she were naked and causing quite a stir. 'Oh, I am so sorry, I was away in my thoughts. Gentlemen, can I offer you some tea and cake in our station gardens? The cake features Levisham's own cherries.'

'Splendid idea, Mrs Armstrong. And we might as well stop you wondering. Er . . . Mr Plunkett?'

Ah, that's the fellow's name, Evie thought.

The short man spun lightly on his heel and addressed Alf. 'Stationmaster Barraclough, I'm very pleased to confirm that we will be awarding a prize length for your new landscaping and gardens around the platform, and also for the same care and attention at Goathland.'

Alf gave a small clap of bright pleasure, and while Evie couldn't help but hug him, it was Rosie who squealed with the joy they were both feeling. The guests could be forgiven for thinking that Rosie had had a hand in the hard toil that had delivered them the award.

She watched in astonishment as Rosie looped her hand around Mr Plunkett's elbow. 'Mr Plunkett, this is such wonderful news. Our family has worked with constant pride to keep a splendid station that the railway can be proud of. Do let me escort you to our tea garden. You'll be further impressed when you see what we've done there.'

Evie cut her father a look of exasperation as Rosie led the visitors away, but her sister's bold move was immediately forgiven as Evie was relieved of the need to entertain them. Now she could focus on her thoughts of Roger Hall and why he had avoided Levisham and her – but more to the point, why he might have had such an angry conversation with the man on the train.

3

Evie was balancing trays of used crockery and cutlery when she heard a familiar voice behind her.

'Good afternoon, Mrs Armstrong.' She turned and would have dropped it all if the man hadn't swiftly steadied her arm. Evie felt his hand covering hers beneath the tray. It was that familiar warmth she could swear she'd felt for the whole week of his absence. 'My apologies. Did I startle you?'

'No. I'm just clumsy.' She cleared her throat all too self-consciously. 'How are you, Mr Hall?'

'As we're no longer strangers, please call me Roger. I feel like I want to look around for my father when you address me so formally.'

She grinned to hide her irritation at being so delighted to see him. 'Then you must extend the same courtesy.'

'Evie,' he murmured.

'You remembered.' She nodded. 'Coffee?'

'Please.'

'Can I offer you some food?'

'Not today.' He tapped his belly. 'I had a big picnic lunch.'

The memory of his cross words on the train with the other gentleman hadn't dimmed. She was curious and now determined to find out why he'd effectively stood her up. 'Did you get up to the Hole of Horcum, by the way? We missed you last week on your return.'

'Yes, I did. I thought I might go back that way next week,' he said, not taking the bait.

'Do you work in the city?'

He nodded. 'I'm a civil engineer. Now, tell me, who is responsible for all the beautiful flower pressings I note around the station rooms?'

Evie felt the adroit shift but allowed herself to be distracted by the compliment. 'They're mine.'

'They are superb. I gather they're for sale?'

'They are.' She smiled.

'I've admired them for weeks now. My favourite is in the waiting room, to the right of the clock.'

She frowned. 'Show me.'

'Can you leave?'

'Yes, everyone's been served. You always somehow manage to be last. Feel free to bring your coffee.'

He followed her to the waiting room, which was empty while everyone was enjoying the sun on the platform or out in the gardens.

'This one.' He pointed, taking a sip of his coffee.

'Ah . . . yes, well, those are actually cherry blossom.'

He looked back at her with wonder. 'I didn't realise that.'

'My favourite too,' she admitted, surprised that of all the beautiful flowers she had pressed and framed, it was the cherry blossom he was drawn to. 'They come from the trees we've grown along the station siding.'

'I've noticed their beauty this spring, shedding their petals like soft snow crystals to catch in drifts by the platform.'

Evie grinned. 'Ready for me to collect. I plan to use them as confetti one day.'

'When you remarry?'

'I . . .' She hesitated. 'Actually, I was thinking for my sister's wedding, whenever that might occur. I shall just insist on a spring wedding date for her.'

'What about yourself?'

'Oh, no prospects,' she admitted, feeling her cheeks beginning to glow. 'I . . . wouldn't get much time to act upon it even if I had one.' It sounded pathetic – borderline desperate.

Evie was relieved when he gave her a nod that felt empathetic rather than sympathetic. He cleared his throat. 'And these are wonderful too.'

Glad to move on, she brightened her tone. 'These are fen violets, and that's called yellow-wort. Here is brooklime, and that furry white flower with the long green stems is called ground elder. And those, of course, I'm sure you'd recognise as—'

'Scottish bluebells,' he said. 'Red campion'—he pointed—'and thistle?'

'Musk thistle,' she confirmed, sounding impressed. 'You know your wildflowers?'

He swallowed another gentle gulp of the coffee and gave a sigh of pleasure. 'Not really. I'm learning gradually.' He reached into his pocket and withdrew a tiny book. 'I try and recognise them when I'm rambling. They're just beginning to emerge now.'

'Yes, I need to get out on the moors soon myself. Do you take long walks down south?'

'Sometimes. I prefer it here.' His look stole upon her; it felt more intense.

'Then come with me across the moors,' she said, hardly believing the words were hers; they were out before she could censor herself. How brazenly she was behaving.

His mouth was open in surprise, but as he leaned forward to answer, Rosie's voice cut through the bubble that had formed around them. 'Oh, there you are!'

Evie felt her arrival like a cold blast bursting into a warm world. She was shocked by it, unaware that she and Roger Hall had created such a shell around themselves. She watched his expression fall and close down in the same heartbeat.

They turned. 'Hello, Rosie,' Evie said, letting go of her frustration. 'All go well?'

'I got everything on the list, if that's what you mean. Afternoon, Mr Hall. I see my sister is claiming your time . . . again.'

Evie wanted to tell Rosie to hush but she smiled, embarrassed, instead. 'Mr Hall, um, Roger, is interested in buying one of my works.'

'Really? This old stuff?'

He nodded. 'It's charming. How much do I owe you for this one?'

Evie was surprised and delighted to think she would, in a small way, be sharing his daily life. 'Shall we call it ten shillings?'

'Gladly.' He took out his wallet and withdrew a crisp banknote. 'I still owe you for my coffee.'

'That's on the house. Let me fetch your change.'

'Not necessary. Please put it towards another frame of wildflowers. I'll choose one to pair it with next visit. I think I must also buy some cherry jam so I can taste the results of the blossom.'

Evie looked at the green £1 note he'd handed her with quiet astonishment; it was a lot of money.

'When are you next up . . . *Roger*?' Rosie asked, sounding slightly sarcastic as she looked between them.

'I really can't say – it just depends on when I can get away from the desk.'

'Oh well, you can be sure Evie will always be here. She never goes anywhere.' Rosie spun on her heel and departed.

They cut each other a hesitant glance and then grinned, just a fraction wickedly.

'I'm sorry. Rosie doesn't believe any man can resist her; that's the truth of it.'

'Few will.'

'You can, though?' *Stop it, Evie.* Too late; she was feeling ever so slightly out of control to have him alone and suddenly open and interested in her.

He nodded. 'That's because her sister outshines her in every noticeable way.'

Her mouth opened slightly; she wasn't expecting such directness.

'That was indiscreet of me. And yet I find it increasingly hard to visit Levisham and not look for you.'

It was the opening.

'You managed to come through last week and not stop, even though you said you would.' But now that she'd said it, how pathetically childish she sounded.

An awkward silence stretched between them. 'I'm sorry,' he said at last.

'Nothing to apologise for. I percolated some fresh coffee for you, that's all. It's nothing.'

'It is something. I let you down.'

Evie gave a slight shake of her head and a shrug, as if to say it wasn't a promise. 'I saw you on the southbound train, actually.' He looked momentarily caught out but he quickly gave a nod. 'You were with another gentleman, I believe, deep in conversation?' She framed it cunningly as a question; he needed to answer her.

'I ran into one of my colleagues who was travelling back to London and he decided to join me. I didn't want—'

She put a hand up. 'Actually, you don't have to explain yourself to me, Roger.' It was a test. If he did explain, she would stop acting suspicious.

He frowned. 'I feel I do. I didn't want to share my private time with a colleague talking about work but he insisted on joining me and discussing rail tracks.'

Evie desperately wanted to ask about the conversation and the deal they were breaking, but then she would have to explain how she knew they had been arguing and about what. She couldn't. 'To be honest, we were busy with some VIPs who were visiting the station to—'

He interjected. 'You're missing my point. He stole my time away from you.'

They regarded each other in silence. It was Evie who broke it. 'They say that if you wear a garland of bluebells, you will be compelled to tell the truth.'

She watched the shadowing of his features as his brow knitted into a frown. 'You don't believe me?'

Evie tried a smile. 'Just sharing some local folklore to get us past a tense moment.'

'Then let's go find some bluebells and make a garland,' he offered. 'Evie, will you walk with me onto the moors . . . just for a few minutes?'

Hall met her just outside Grove House, the big property that was nestled at the foot of the moors at the station's entrance. They followed the pathway that led up the rise and onto the moor. He seemed to understand that she didn't want her family to know about him just yet. They crossed the sheep grid halfway up the fence line. Trees in full leaf burst would soon form a familiar canopy, creating a natural frame over this part of the path and she cast a glance at the tree, which looked sturdy enough but she knew from the other side was hollow. It was where she and Rosie used to hide what they considered precious finds from their playtime on the moors. Everything from shiny pebbles to a brooch had once been stored in its depths and her father had not yet had the heart to chop it down for firewood. Evie smiled at the memory as she sensed some damp in the air and imagined there would be a shower in the next hour or so.

Out in the open with only the sounds of nature around them, they both seemed to relax. Nothing had been said since she'd told her father she was going for a stroll, and she was glad she hadn't had to confront Rosie. But now, up on the scrubby terrain, they were out of sight of the station

He smiled tentatively. 'You mentioned a tense moment – is that because I made you feel uncomfortable?'

'I don't know what you're doing to me, to be honest. Weakening me, I think,' she admitted. 'I find being attracted to you a little humiliating.'

He waited.

'I'm not a teenager who suffers crushes. I look for you, most Wednesdays. You don't always come and I'm disappointed when you don't; quietly elated when you do.' She gave a shrug. 'I gather most women find this period of attraction exciting. Me? I find it . . .' She couldn't grasp the right word and settled for 'distracting. And almost debilitating.' She saw a smile threaten to break through but he halted it, perhaps understanding she felt ashamed of her admission.

'What did your father advise his daughter?'

'Well, we did discuss it, but he laughed at the notion that you're a spy.'

'You think I am?' He sounded shocked.

She trusted his spontaneous incredulity but still persisted, almost teasing. 'Why not?'

'Spying for whom?'

'Germany.' Now he looked genuinely affronted. 'I'm sorry I said that,' she admitted quickly. 'It's not at all fair.'

'No, it's not. That's a horrible accusation, particularly when I'm a patriot.'

'Honestly, Roger, I was simply teasing and did not mean to offend. I feel embarrassed now. Everyone's a little jittery over whether there may be another war coming; the thought is so heinous it's making me behave badly and forget my manners.'

'Evie, I see nothing wrong in the warning from the authorities – or your diligence. I'm glad of it. Not exactly the front line, but why shouldn't people who work with the public contribute to keeping us all safe?'

She gave him a grateful smile for his generous attitude.

'What else did your father say about me?'

'Dad laughed.' Roger looked baffled. 'He was laughing at my admission of frailty, but he was full of affection when he said, "My darling child, I speak from experience when I say there is nothing stronger than love."' Evie sighed and clutched her cheeks. 'Gosh, this is awkward.'

Vertical creases in Roger's cheeks, like dimples but larger, deepened with his smile, which was characterised by puzzlement, his previous affront evaporated. 'But you've never shown any—'

'No,' she jumped in, understanding his confusion. 'I leave that behaviour to my sister, but I can't help myself. I like your remoteness. I want to mistrust you – that's the truth – and yet I trust my instincts and I sense you are a person who prefers no falsity.'

'You *want* to mistrust me. That's curious.'

'You're a perfect stranger, Mr Hall. I've even been warned about them.' She twitched a grin to make sure he could tell she was being playful. Then her expression became more contemplative. 'Your smile strikes me as honest, if a little sad. You make no secret of your desire to travel alone, happy in your own company. I'm afraid I recognise a kindred spirit, and I know I would hate to be misunderstood as someone up to no good simply because I like my own company and don't chatter to anyone and everyone.' Evie shook her head. She stepped around him. 'I'm sorry to make you feel in any way self-conscious—'

He caught her elbow as she made to walk on. 'I don't,' he said gently.

'You don't what?' She raised her gaze.

'Feel awkward, or obliged. I do feel entranced, though. By you, your honesty and openness, by your artistic talent . . . the way I watch you move around this station with such competence and confidence. It's obvious everyone admires you – likes you. And heaven knows we all come for the great baking.'

'Except—'

'The glacé cherries, yes . . .' he said, nodding and looking like his big secret was out.

They both laughed, and then the easy amusement shrivelled once more into unease.

'I'm twenty-eight. I don't want to be like Rosie, all but swooning over anyone who shows the slightest interest.'

'You are nothing like Rosie.'

Suddenly self-conscious, she was grateful to feel momentarily distracted by the joyous signs of spring, from buds and blossom to the new lambs frolicking around their patient mothers. The process of connecting back with the landscape meant she could hear bees busy scouting the new heather that would be in full roar in a few months; in the meantime, there was a swathe of bluebells – one of early summer's most joyous sights. The dancing bells carpeted a copse to her left, and she could pick out emperor moths at the top of the hill. They wouldn't be around for long. The birdsong, full of the brightness of being alive, filled her heart.

'There are some bluebells,' she said, breaking into a smile. 'Truth time.'

She didn't intend to make the garland as she talked . . . it was more of a jest and yet she put her basket down and her fingers immediately began weaving the flowers together. It was as though her hands knew that this was a difficult conversation for her and the distraction would help her to say all that she wanted to with her gaze pinned elsewhere and not on him. 'Losing my husband just months after we married felt catastrophic. I couldn't imagine ever having feelings for someone again. And now there's you. My heart isn't up to any more pain. I've admired you from a distance, and even though my heart sinks a little each time you depart, I know you'll probably be back, and it's in that looking forward that the excitement lives.' She stopped weaving, crooking her elbow, a hand against her hip. 'Look, I'm as susceptible as Rosie to a handsome man and a kind word but I have more to lose.'

When she gave him the garland he grinned and put it on his head to amuse her. 'I want you to trust me.'

'Just like that? A stranger from the south, walking into my life?'

He gave a helpless shrug that suggested vulnerability rather than indifference. 'We're all strangers until we make the effort to know someone. I want to know you, spend time with you.'

'I don't wish to be hurt, which is why admiring you from a distance is safer, easier.'

'Ask me anything you like and I'll answer. Know me better. We have another twenty minutes at least before I have to board the next train. Let me help you pick the bluebells.'

Her gaze narrowed as she smiled. 'All right. Remember you're wearing the garland – it demands honesty.' He nodded dutifully. 'Do you have a wife?'

'No.' His answer was quick, as though he was ready for it. 'And if I did, I assure you I wouldn't be here with you now.'

She tested it further. 'No other girlfriend?'

He shook his head. 'I'm not involved with any other woman and haven't been for a long time.' He was emphatic.

'Why now, then?'

He looked surprised by her question. 'Who understands attraction? I'm drawn to you. And for as long as you say you've been watching me, I've noticed you too . . . except your sister kept getting in the way.'

This made her grin, although she felt privately embarrassed that she had been testing his answers against the warning from Harry of the local constabulary. 'She'll be furious if she finds out I've had you all to myself on the moor.'

'Can we give her something to be jealous about?' He stepped closer, and despite her reluctance to be weakened by attraction, she felt her pulse accelerate. He offered his arm. 'Up over there are some beautiful flowers I'd like to show you,' he said. She picked up her basket and took his arm, and for the first time, perhaps ever, felt every other unconscious aspect of her body quicken alongside her pulse. This was a new and exciting experience. 'You seem to like the quiet life, you told me as much yourself. Are you happy here?'

'Yes, but that doesn't mean I am without curiosity. I don't seek adventure but I'm not afraid of it; I don't seek travel but I wouldn't turn it down if I had the opportunity. I still want a man to intrigue me. Ron and I shared a love of station life, and we planned to run our own station one day. Perhaps I could lead the charge to be Britain's first station mistress.'

'I can picture that, although not in this outfit. You look very pretty today.' He paused a few beats as they ascended a small incline. 'So . . . do I intrigue you?'

'Wholly,' she said with a smile. 'Everything about you is a secret.'

'Still secretive? Then continue with your questions.'

'Do you live in London?'

'I live in Lewes, further south. I travel to London most days and work most weekends. I like to come up here midweek and stay overnight if I can. I can't do it every week, as you would have probably noticed.'

She nodded. 'And you work for the railways?'

He cut her a sharp look. 'What makes you ask that?'

Evie gave an exaggerated shrug. 'You said you were an engineer, and I suppose because you linger on the platform . . . you seem to like trains. I've sometimes seen you staring at the tracks almost as though you're studying them.'

He stopped walking and regarded her with what looked like respect mixed with surprise. And then it melted into a smile. Something about the shift gave Evie the impression that he'd had to conjure up that smile. It wasn't false but she believed he'd had to find it in that moment, as though she'd made him feel defensive.

'Perhaps I shouldn't be so direct,' she admitted, trying to let him off the hook.

'Not at all. Yes, I do love trains. You've seen right through me, Evie.'

She smiled. 'Train lovers aren't hard to spot, especially if you're one yourself,' she admitted. Do you work for the railways?'

'I do. I'm with Southern Railway – you'd know it as one of the Big Four. Unlike up here, most of our revenue comes from passenger traffic, rather than freight.'

She gave a sigh. 'Yes, and such romantic trains; the *Brighton Belle*, the *Golden Arrow*, the *Night Ferry*.' Evie felt her probing was enough. His answers had come naturally and conversationally. His expression, tone and lack of hesitation meant his response was clearly unrehearsed: Roger was no spy, but a railway engineer and railway enthusiast. Evie became weary of her own suspicion; she wanted Harry and his warning out of her head so she could enjoy the rare and delicious experience of being noticed and potentially even wooed.

'Here they are,' Roger said, not realising he was calling her back from her private thoughts about him. He was pointing, while some sheep, who were startled by their arrival, galloped off.

'Oh, they're exquisite.' She smiled, glad to return to this moment with no hidden motive. 'Look, these are called common eyebright.'

He bent down to cup one of the pale, creamy-toothed blooms. 'They're beautiful close up,' he remarked. 'That bright yellow centre and those streaks of purple look like they've been painted by an artist with a steady hand.'

She chuckled. 'I think you're every bit a lover of nature as I am.'

He stood and stared deeply at her. 'Well, I love being with you,' he admitted, to steal her words. Evie was focused on the space closing between them, as Roger straightened from his crouch to bend towards her until he was so near she could see the tiny flecks of gold in the charcoal of his eyes. He removed the garland. 'May I?'

She knew what he was asking and nodded, not trusting her voice, wanting more than anything for him to kiss her. He leaned in and their lips touched. He was gentle, hesitant; she was the one who deepened the connection, dropping her basket, reaching her arms around his neck and pulling him closer, giving him permission to make their kiss passionate rather than polite.

He obliged and Evie felt momentarily lost. She didn't care about the flowers spilling from her basket, or those they were trampling underfoot. In those heartbeats she didn't care if anyone saw them; she no longer wondered about Rosie taking offence, or her father tutting at such an outward display of affection. She registered a thought of Ron but was sure he was nodding wherever he was, giving permission. She felt lost, escaping somewhere private, as she felt his arms move around her now. One hand dipped into the small of her back, another found the curve between her shoulder blades, and politeness no longer mattered as he pressed her closer. She could feel his ardour against her, hard and filled with desire, while a personal electricity was igniting within, its current racing around her so fast she could believe she was glowing like fairy lights. That comical image pushed through all the sensory distraction and Evie finally pulled away. 'We might be seen.'

'Does it matter?' Hall bent down – as much, she imagined, to disguise his desire as to gather up the fallen bluebells. She took the opportunity to smooth her dress, but she helplessly reached her fingertips to her mouth, already missing his lips, fascinated by the effect his kiss had had on her.

He began to talk, his voice thickened. 'Evie, can I see you again? Properly, I mean.'

'Properly?'

He straightened and she was glad she stood on slightly higher ground and could look him directly in the eye. 'I'd like to take you out somewhere, away from here, spend time with you . . .'

'Yes, I'd like that very much. When?'

He blinked with surprise. 'Your father . . .'

'Is not my keeper. I'm nearing thirty, Roger, and I think he, more than anyone I know, will be pleased that I'm captivated by someone. We were raised to be independent, make our own decisions, and know the consequences of those decisions. He would anticipate that I've considered all the potential . . . um . . . complications.'

He laughed. 'Lovely word.'

Time to be direct. 'That is your intention, of course, to spend the night with me?'

She enjoyed watching him struggle. 'I wouldn't call it my intention so much as a desire . . . that if shared, we might act upon it,' he finally admitted. 'I don't want you to feel taken for granted, as you said only moments ago that you barely know me.'

'That was before we kissed. Now I want the same as you, Roger. I'm too old to be coy. I'd rather tell you what I want.'

They stared at each other, and he ran a hand awkwardly through his hair. 'Well, we can certainly . . . um, together . . . sort that out.' Evie loved his choice of words, felt excited by them, and laughed with genuine pleasure. 'I can't come up for a while,' he added, 'but how about in a couple of weeks? I'll hire a car and we can spend a whole day and night somewhere far from here.'

'Yes.' She grinned. 'Let's do that. Treat me with care, Roger. It's been six long years.' She took the basket from him.

Hall shook his head. 'Evie . . . I'm crazy about you,' he blurted. She could tell he hadn't meant to let that out. He looked as surprised as she did by the outburst. 'That whole time I was with my colleague, I wanted to rage at him to stop talking, to get off my train, to let me see the woman I'd travelled north to visit.'

It looked like you were deeply angry, she thought but banished the notion – he'd explained his frustration.

'I don't wish to frighten you off, but you said you felt you'd found a kindred spirit in me. I hope you mean that?'

She nodded. 'Why should I be frightened off?'

He let out a sigh of exasperation. 'Because I think I'm in love with you. And I realise we know so little about each other, but it's the truth – I do love you, it's as simple as that. If I could see you every day for the rest of my life, I would never be bored, never tire of your smile, never dread your voice or company. In fact, if I didn't think it would send you screaming off to platform two and across the tracks, I'd get down on one knee and ask you to marry me this moment. I know it's ludicrous – I am not known for spontaneous or emotional behaviour – but I've been in love only once before and I know what it feels like.'

She felt desperate to ask who he'd loved before her, and tried not to sound jealous. 'Snap!' she said instead.

He touched her cheek.

'Why aren't you with her? Where is she?'

'In her grave.'

She gave a soft hiss of despair. 'You too? Why didn't you say something earlier?'

He pushed back a curl of her blonde hair. 'I'm glad I have now. When she died I never thought I could emerge from my sorrow . . . it seemed impossible, heinous even, to countenance what people were saying: that I would find love again.'

She nodded her agreement.

'I didn't look for it. And maybe that's the best way . . . to have no inkling when someone you can fall in love with may appear. Now I think of you all of the time, and I'm frankly ashamed to sound so lovelorn. But there it is. Now you know most of what there is to know about me.'

'Hey, you two!' It was Rosie's voice piercing their bubble again. Evie wanted to scream. 'Dad says Mr Hall will miss his train if you don't get a move on.'

Evie schooled her features to be even, her voice to be mild. 'We were just collecting some wildflowers,' she called back, holding up her basket.

'Is that right?' Rosie said, her sarcasm reaching out across the moorland.

4

Later, alone with her father, Evie opened up, hoping not only for his guidance but especially his approval.

'Are you quite sure about this, my girl?'

She smiled softly. 'As night follows day, Dad.'

He gave a sad sigh. 'Did you just quote Shakespeare?'

'It's easier than saying I want to spend a day and a night with this man more than anything in the world. I probably shouldn't have told you the truth, spared you the agony of knowing your daughter is going to drive off to some hotel and sign in as Mr and Mrs Smith or something.'

He looked away and shook his head.

'It's just that I don't like lying to you . . . to anyone.'

He looked understandably embarrassed.

'One of the best pieces of advice Nanny Lotte ever gave me was to know a man before I committed to him. Ron and I—'

'Stop! Your mother and I stepped out together for three years before we became engaged.'

'Well, lucky you. I don't have that luxury of time. I'm going to be sure of the man whose name I take, who has my love, who fathers my children and who shares my life. It will be for keeps with me, Dad, for better, for worse, for war that may be coming . . . and all that.'

Her last comment gave him pause. 'Do you think it's to be Roger Hall?'

'Well, that's what I'm going to find out,' she said gently. 'Is this love?' She shook her head, amazed even to be discussing it.

'Well . . . that's a question only you can answer. You seem very struck by him. I shall have to pay more attention to this Roger Hall. I have to admit his polish, plus those looks and ways, don't immediately suit the country boy he seems to want to be.'

'That's because he's from the city, although maybe he grew up on a farm – I have no idea yet. I can't help but notice he is hard to reach. He barely passes the time of day with others; keeps very much to himself. Spends an awful lot of time wandering around alone on our moors.'

Alf looked at her. 'I suspect that's what you like about him, though, eh?'

She smiled. 'You're right.'

He nodded, then paused somewhat dramatically, she thought, before he spoke again. 'Of course, a man like that . . . he has secrets.' Alf looked back at her apologetically for airing that thought. He lifted his hands in defence. 'Being that cagey means he may well be running from something . . . or someone.'

'I didn't say he was *cagey*. I said he keeps himself to himself. It's not the same thing.' Evie groaned. 'Dad, he's not the spy, if that's what you're thinking.'

'Good grief, that thought never crossed my mind,' Alf replied, looking genuinely taken aback. 'But I wonder if it should have?'

She gave a sound of exasperation. 'No, we're both agreed, he's the consummate Englishman with all the traits, as far as I'm concerned. And I've asked him some questions that he answered firmly, swiftly and with candour. He's a widower, by the way.'

Now her father looked further surprised but she held a warning finger up. 'It feels like we were meant to be, Dad. He understands everything I've gone through and all the challenges inherent in even being open to a new relationship.'

'Should we mention him to Harry? I mean, now that you feel quite serious about him?'

'Please don't,' Evie said, looking mortified by the suggestion. 'Who I fall in love with is hardly a matter for nosy Constable Field. It will be all over the village and beyond within hours if he gets wind of it. No, Dad, it's too new, too precious to be gossiped over. Remember, everyone really loved Ron. I should never have aired my thoughts.'

Alf gestured submission with a wave of his hands. He opened the door of the ticket booth and came around the counter to give her a hug. 'I'm glad you did, love.' He kissed her head. 'I agree. It's Barraclough business only. I've longed for someone to come into your life who is worthy of you. Bring him to see me on Wednesday – I'd like to talk to him.'

'Oh no, Dad. What are you going to say?'

'Nothing tricky. I just want to take my own measure of the man. See if he strikes me as evasive.'

She tried not to look overawed by the sleek Singer in cream and black that Roger had driven up in. Rosie, however, did all the open-mouthed gawping for her.

'Well, he certainly knows how to spoil a girl,' she said, pushing past Evie in a huff.

'Oh, come on, Rosie. Don't be like that.'

'Like what? Like a woman who has had the man she's sweet on stolen from her . . . by her sister, of all people?'

Evie shouldn't have been as surprised as she felt. 'Rosie,

you can grasp that he's not sweet on you, can't you? Attraction has to work both ways.'

'Well, that's obvious, Evie, thank you for that lesson in romance,' she sneered. It made her exquisitely pretty face turn ugly, which was such a pity, Evie reflected. 'But you see, you never gave me a chance with him to find out just how attracted to each other we might have been.'

'Stop it,' she cautioned. 'Roger and I . . .'

'What?' her sister snapped, clearly needing the argument to unfold, get more heated, to help assuage her fury.

She didn't mean to let a winsome smile play at her lips. 'We have a connection,' she said with a shrug.

'Oh, please stop,' Rosie fumed. 'Don't be so wet, Evie. You set your sights on him and you won. Congratulations!'

'That's such a wrong accusation. I had no intention of—'

'And yet here we are. You off on a romantic trip with one of the most handsome men who has ever stepped onto Levisham platform and me left behind to help Dad in the parcels office.' She looked fit to explode with despair. 'And I saw him first!'

Now Evie did laugh. 'It's time for you to grow up, Rosie. I'm really very tired of your childish tantrums. He doesn't feel anything for you other than embarrassment that you have so shamelessly pursued him. Accept it and move on. There'll be dozens of eager fellows falling over themselves for you – don't begrudge me this single romantic attention from the first man who has interested me since . . .' She couldn't say it, and Rosie clearly couldn't see how much the mere thought demanded of her sister.

Instead she came straight back at her like a whip crack. 'And I'm tired of your big-sister lectures. There's only a few years between us, Evie, but you act like you have some sort of supervisory role over me.'

'Someone has to look out for the child of the family,' Evie said, and felt immediately disappointed with herself. It was an unnecessary barb that she considered herself above. For years she had successfully deflected Rosie's petulance, expertly redirecting it without any of today's toxic words. Rosie was angry. Fair enough. But her anger was unfounded. And she refused to feel responsible for her sister's proprietorial attitude to Roger Hall, or for her subsequent offence that he preferred Evie.

'I could hate you for that!'

Don't say more, Evie pleaded with herself, but out it came, her recent emotional upheaval making her impetuous. 'One day, when you're a proper grown-up, Rosie, you'll have perspective. But right now you're acting like a peevish, spoilt adolescent rather than your twenty-three years – go away and sulk and let me enjoy my special time.'

Rosie flounced off, scowling at her father who was admiring the car. She all but sniffed her disdain at Roger, ignoring his salutation.

Sitting now in the plush seat, the polished leather warming beneath her, Evie looked at the map she had unfolded. 'Scarborough. I haven't been there since I was about seven.'

'I thought about Whitby because it's pretty, but Scarborough's bigger and we can move more freely without worrying.'

'Scarborough's perfect. It's 1936, Roger, and we're adults, not fumbling teenagers frightened of our parents. Speaking of which, what did Dad say?'

'It was touching, actually. He made it very clear that I was not to hurt you, not after all that you've been through. He made me promise that I was sincere in my intentions. I made it equally clear I would never injure you in any way or do anything to harm your heart. He seemed satisfied.' He clasped her hand. 'This feels good, doesn't it?'

'It feels exciting.'

Roger smiled at her. 'I'm going to spoil you rotten.'

'Good. Definitely my turn to be spoiled.' She grinned.

'Rosie?'

'Oh, quite vicious. Really most affronted that it's me here with you.'

'I can't help that it's only you I want here with me.'

Evie shook her head sadly. 'We haven't fought in years, not since we were children. And over a man. How mortifying.'

Roger squeezed her hand, ignoring her last comment. 'I'm guessing the lack of fighting is because you make room for Rosie and her ways,' he said. 'You demur. Except this time, you've eclipsed her – not intentionally, so I'm happy to take the blame that she's not the centre of attention.'

Evie nodded. 'Thank you. It doesn't make it easy on my heart, unfortunately – there's just the two of us.'

'I know, but who *I* love is not *your* fault.'

The remark made her give a slightly teary laugh. And after she'd dabbed at her eyes, a more amused one followed. 'You're right. Rosie does this to me constantly. She makes me feel guilty.'

'Not this time, Evie. I want you to be happy and have an entirely selfish and indulgent time.' His gaze was tender, sparkling with romantic intent.

It was infectious, warming her, pushing Rosie's tantrum aside. 'I agree. So what shall we do first?'

'Well, let's check in to our hotel and then I thought a walk through the gardens, down to the seafront and perhaps lunch at the Grand and then—'

'Let me guess . . . a visit to North Bay miniature railway?'

'Only if you want to?'

'It's very sweet. I rode on it as a child,' she said, looking out the window across the moors she loved. They'd soon be clothed in the purplish velvet of the heather cloak that lunged down to the incline, halting at the various deep dales that gave North Yorkshire its dramatic landscape.

'Well, we won't plan. Let's just allow ourselves to be led by instinct.'

She smiled. 'This is the North Riding Forest Park that we are skirting. It will be filled with bluebells and other spring wildflowers.'

'Do you wish to stop?'

'No, the flowers would wilt before I could preserve them properly, and I think there's a work camp going on anyway.'

'Work camp?'

'Yes – they call it *reconditioning*. Essentially and rather cruelly, they are toughening up men that many believe have turned soft – their words, not mine – through unemployment and the lazy 1920s.'

'Really?'

She nodded. 'If there's war, we need our men to be strong, so said the leaflet I read a couple of weeks ago.'

'I see. How many men?'

She shrugged. 'I don't know. They've been brought up from the south, some of them. Lincolnshire was the origin of the last batch, I believe. Anyway,' she said, forcing a brighter tone. 'Let's not talk about war. Tell me instead more about where you grew up.'

'A place called Ditchling.'

'In Sussex?'

'That's right.'

'There's something about your accent.'

He turned, and the smile that had come easily now looked frozen. 'What do you mean?'

'Oh, it's just that I have a good ear for language and there's something else in there. Your accent is obviously southern, but forgive me, I do hear an additional quality.'

'Oh yes?' He sounded guarded. 'What's that?'

She gave a small gust of embarrassment, wishing she hadn't mentioned it. 'Well, there's a European note in it somewhere.'

'Ah. That would be because my father was born and raised in Europe. It must have rubbed off. I think my mother sent me to a very good school to get that European note chiselled away.' He gave a soft note of query. 'Hmmm, it's getting hilly, isn't it?' She felt him steer her away from the topic but was still determined to follow her strong and reliable instincts. 'I hope this car can handle it.'

'I do too.' She grinned. 'Because it's a hilly drive all the way. This is Thornton Dale. We head east into the village but keep going into Allerston and onwards to Snainton. We take the fork at Ayton onto Racecourse Road, all the way to Riggs Head.'

'Don't you love English place names?'

'Yes,' she said in a sighing voice. 'It's easy to be patriotic, don't you think?'

He turned to look at her and there was something puzzled in his gaze, as though he was unsure whether her question was rhetorical. 'Er, is this the A170 we're on?'

She nodded. 'It is. We'll see the coast shortly.'

'Excellent. I want to say "Now I can relax" but I sense the road is going to twist and turn.'

'It's a dangerous road, actually. Few enjoy it because of its height and hairpin bends. But I love the view it will give us.'

He smiled. 'I have something for you. Open the glove box.'

'For me?' She popped the glove box open and inside spied a shallow cardboard container.

'It's very pretty – like you. It's wonderful to buy something purely for its beauty and have someone to give it to.'

She looked at him, feeling tongue-tied as she withdrew the box. It had been a long time since a gentleman had given her even a posy of flowers, but a gift? 'May I?'

'Please. I want you to open it.'

She saw the label on the box. 'Selfridges.' It came out not much louder than a whisper.

'Have you visited the department store?'

She shook her head. 'I haven't been to London.'

Roger cut her a shocked glance. 'We have to change that, Evie. I wish I could walk with you through the great department stores of London and Paris.' He could see her expression falling.

'You've been to Paris,' she breathed, sounding impressed.

'Yes. I speak fluent French.' He smiled again, looking self-conscious. 'It was drummed into us at school, along with German – that I'm also fluent in but try not to use just now, and, of course, Latin. My father was a great traveller and took us with him. I've travelled through France, Holland and parts of Spain in my time.'

'I know I said I didn't want to talk about the prospect of war, but seriously, how do you feel about what's happening given all the travel you've done?'

She watched him swallow. 'I feel wretched,' he replied. 'You'd think we'd have learned the first time around, wouldn't you? All those lives lost and here we are again, contemplating war. And if you and I are talking about it on our special time away together, you can be sure that governments are . . . and the military.'

'I hate it that we're all so blinded. If I can remember twenty years ago, surely the decision-makers in Whitehall can.'

'What's their choice, though, Evie, with such a powerful and persuasive new force guiding Germany?'

She shook her head because she had no answer. 'Hitler does seem to be very popular.'

'He is. And a keen observer can see what he's doing. He's come along and he's offering not just hope but a sense of dignity . . . a future.'

Evie frowned. 'You sound like you admire him.'

'No, it's not that. I can see his cunning. I certainly can marvel – with some dismay – at his clever moves in rallying people, making them feel pride in their country and themselves as Germans. But no, Evie, the man himself – I loathe him. I feel he's leading them down a pathway of regret. He is so small-minded and conservative, still dreaming of the days of Prussia's military bearing and might. He wants to burn down the Weimar Republic and all of its freedoms and liberal attitudes to life and people.' He sighed, sounding helpless. 'Democracy is stepping backwards in Germany under his watch. He is a dictator in the making and very soon, before the German people realise it, he will control every aspect of their lives. He'll instil fear, suspicion of each other; he'll ruin us as he follows his crazy and singular path of what I believe is hate masquerading as patriotism.' He blinked. 'Sorry.' He looked shocked by his own passion and admissions. As was his way, he shifted position with a disarming smile and a change in topic. 'I think we must agree not to talk about Germany or war again on these two days.'

'Agreed. It scares me.'

'Please open your gift.'

She did, lifting the lid of the box, but her thoughts wanted to explore what Roger had just shared. In her mind she had tripped at his words and even as she considered what might have snagged her, she saw the silk scarf. It had a warm butter-coloured background upon which was painted a trailing array of flowers picked out in grey-blue and rich cherry red. Cherries were hanging out of baskets at each corner. The restrained but beautiful depiction of flowers and cherries with pale green leaves was framed by silk the colour of hot English mustard. The label was Hermès. His taste was exquisite.

'As soon as I saw it – with all those cherries – I could only think of it gracing your neck.'

'Roger,' she breathed. 'It's magnificent.'

He looked relieved. 'No, you're magnificent. It needs to keep up with you.' He smiled. 'Put it on. It suits what you're wearing,' he said, nodding at her soft grey frock.

Evie pulled off the cheap scarf she'd tied that morning and took the large silken square from its tissue, holding her breath at the joy of lifting it from the box. It felt feather-light in her fingers. She bent forwards to place it around her neck and Roger pulled the visor down so she might view herself in the mirror. He couldn't have known what she'd wear today and yet it looked as though it had been bought to go with the outfit.

'My gosh, I love it. Thank you. I've never owned anything so . . .'

He waited.

'I want to say expensive, but that sounds crass. Truly, I can only guess at what you've paid . . . and from Selfridges.'

'I have no woman in my life to spoil. It's my pleasure.'

'I'll never take it off now.'

He pointed. The start of their journey had been open farmland before turning wooded, now they were surrounded by a patchwork of fields, separated by hedges rather than the dry-stone walls they'd been passing. 'There!'

She could see the sparkle of the sea in the distance and felt a shimmer of excitement within.

They left their bags at the guesthouse on the Esplanade to take advantage of the lovely day.

She felt a surge of something powerful. It was a rush of bright attraction and the thrill of knowing she'd be alone with him in private later, but there was more. It wasn't just physical – Evie was beginning to admit that her connection to him felt so strong: she didn't know how she could look forward to her days without him.

The feeling was sudden, irrational; she couldn't explain it to herself, so she had to accept it taking over her life. She remembered experiencing a fierce feeling like this when Ron first asked her to dance at the local village hall. He had been new to the town but wasn't shy with the girls.

'My late husband, Ron, died in a terrible accident at the station,' she confided to Roger now. 'He was saving the life of a little girl who had wandered onto the tracks during a shunting. There, now I've told you and we don't need to visit that subject again.'

He seemed to understand. 'My wife died soon after childbirth. Her blood pressure had soared during an obstructed birth. And I couldn't save my little girl on that miserable day. She simply didn't get enough oxygen during the obstruction, I was told. Let's not talk about it.'

She gave him a look of sympathy, squeezing his arm. 'Our shared losses bind us.'

He nodded as she stared out across the water.

'This sea breeze is so wonderful,' she said, giving a heavy sigh. 'I'd forgotten how good for the soul the taste of salt on one's lips is.' She licked her bottom lip and grinned.

Clearly, he found her action irresistible, and with a quick glance around he bent and stole a soft, fleeting kiss. She tasted the salt from his lips and knew that neither of them would ever wish to be apart. She could hear the advice – *it's too soon, you barely know one another, you've only just met* . . . All true. But Evie knew herself and believed that if she had one skill it was to be able to take a fast and accurate measure of a person's character.

'Come on, I want to walk you through the South Cliff Gardens – have you seen them?'

She shook her head.

'Well, you're in for a surprise.'

Evie took his elbow and walked alongside him, allowing his lovely voice to immerse her in the history of the gardens, some of which had originally belonged to the Prince of Wales. She let him talk, forbidding her mind to wander where it was demanding to go. *Later*, she told the nagging thought.

The sensation of being given a second chance with a man she found irresistible provoked a sort of mad giddiness of private joy, as though she had a pleasurable secret that only she knew. She blinked out of her romantic thoughts and focused on Roger's narrative.

'. . . originally as the gardens for the spa that people could enjoy. Look, there it is, all the way down near the Esplanade. Can you see it?'

'A dome?'

He grinned and nodded. 'Two hundred feet below, and what you can't fully see yet is a castellated building that the sea wall protects, where Victorians used to take their healthful leisure in the spa.'

She chuckled. 'And here?'

They'd arrived, navigating a slow descent through layered gardens into a rose garden.

'Something like fourteen hundred rose bushes were originally planted here in Lord Beeforth's Rosary.'

'Amazing,' she gushed. 'How do you know all this?'

'I like the engineering of it. Imagine: it was just acres of cliffs but over decades it's become these gloriously constructed layers of gardens down to the sea. It's extraordinary and wonderful.'

He took her hand and she felt his strength ease through her like a pulse, and Evie enjoyed the feeling of safety in his grip. They continued walking, wafts of perfume from the drifts of spring flowers welcoming them as they passed.

'I could spend a lifetime in here,' she admitted.

He bent to pick a tiny violet multiheaded flower and gave it to her. 'What a colour,' he murmured.

'This little beauty is called thrift,' she said, taking it from him. 'It likes to look out from ledges over the sea, which is why its Latin name is *Armeria maritima*.'

'Show-off. Keep going. I like listening to you.'

'These little pincushion-style flowers come in a variety of colours, although most commonly in hues of pink. Sometimes you'll encounter white but violet is the hardest to find.'

'Do you know what the colour violet signifies?' he said, guiding them alongside sentinels of tall trees through which glimpses of the sea sparkled.

She shook her head. 'I always think of violet as imperial.'

'Ah, well, purple maybe. Violet is from the light spectrum, of course, whereas purple is not. Violet is often connected with the spiritual – a transfer of the soul.'

'Roger, are you making this up?'

He laughed, pretending that he was deeply offended. 'Certainly not! I promise you, violet is symbolic of harmony of the mind and soul. It's . . . er, well, it's how I feel when I'm with you. You bring peace to me.'

They paused to regard each other. Evie felt the weight of the moment invisibly pressing on her shoulders.

'I have to admit the same,' she said, shaking her head.

'Good,' he replied and pulled her close, no longer caring who might see them and click their tongue.

They kissed, and for a few heartbeats Evie felt weightless, as though in a separate violet world of soul transference. They heard footsteps and pulled away, smiling.

'I hope you're going to ask that gorgeous woman to marry you, young man,' said an older woman, walking briskly down the slope with the aid of a walking stick. A small pug at her feet regarded them with a baleful stare; they could hear his heavy breathing.

'Actually, madam, that's exactly what I was going to do.'

Evie gasped.

'So you should,' the woman replied matter-of-factly. She pointed with her stick. 'And you'd better say yes, young lady.'

'Do you think so?' She grinned, feeling like she really had entered some new and incredible universe.

'Good luck, you two. The way the world is going, love is precious – don't squander it.' She strode off, using the stick but refusing to limp for it.

They turned to stare at each other with a sense of wonder as much as bewilderment.

'I think she was an apparition, entirely for our benefit,' he said. A pause arrived and they looked at each other. 'I meant it,' he said. 'Will you marry me, Evie?'

She swallowed, breathed out slowly. Thoughts of Nanny Lotte, her father, Rosie, even old Joe, crowded in. And then there was Ron. She could swear his hand was in the small of her back, shoving her forward. They all wanted happiness and family for her. War was coming, she was convinced. Meanwhile, men as fine as Roger didn't come along more than once in a lifetime. He was special; she knew it, and so did the seer and her pug – and she was certain of how she felt about him.

She looked up into his gaze and suffered no doubt, staring into the earnest depths. 'Yes, I will.' And then she let out a soft squeal of horrified delight.

He laughed, picked her up with ease and spun her around once before kissing her again, hard and fleeting. 'You mean it?'

She nodded. 'I never lie.'

He dug in his pocket and withdrew a small, battered ring box and she gasped that this wasn't the spontaneous decision she had thought it was.

'Well, I hope you're as serious as I am,' he said, voice slightly shaky. He popped the catch and Evie caught sight of the large, round diamond in a square setting, the corners filled with smaller diamonds. There was milgrain detail on the shoulders of the platinum ring, each one adorned with a round-cut diamond.

She let out a sigh, and her mouth remained open – speechless – when she looked back up at him. 'But your wife . . .?'

'She used her grandmother's ring. This is my mother's,' he said, filling the quiet. 'She lost her wedding ring in 1910. She'd begun to lose weight around then; the, er . . . the cancer had her in its grip. My father had another ring made for her. He took me up to London with him and we visited a top jeweller in Mayfair and designed a ring together. Being so young, I came up with the oddity of a square-shaped setting for a round diamond.' He chuckled. 'The jeweller thought it inspired, but more importantly, my mother loved it. So it feels right to ask you to wear this ring – I feel so very connected to it.' He shrugged. 'We'll have it properly sized for you. Will you try it?'

With a sense of trepidation, she watched him lift the ring that clearly meant so much to him from its velvet couch. The sun roamed around the facets of the central diamond, which threw off sparkling glints like the sea below them. 'Oh gosh, it's stunning, Roger.'

'May I?'

She nodded, eyes moistening.

He eased it onto her hand, and like the story of Cinderella and the glass slipper, it fitted as though it had been made for her finger. 'How's that?'

'It's perfect.' She stared at her finger, bedazzled by the exquisite ring that looked back at her and spoke of the future. 'I don't know what to say.'

'Only that you love it and that you love me.'

She couldn't help it. All the emotion fizzed and spilled, helplessly. 'I love it, I love you more and I love the thought of being married to you.'

He scooped her up into his arms and they kissed freely and at length. They heard footsteps and the snort of the pug going by again. Even the familiar voice didn't break their kiss. 'Be happy, you two. Remember, no problem's too great when there is love.'

5

Evie felt as though she floated down to the promenade. They waded in the shallows, Evie screeching as the dying waves frothed and foamed past her ankles and further up the beach, stranding her in the sinking sand. Roger rolled up his trousers and carried her out of the water, kissing her as he did so. She imagined herself in a film, the way they were behaving, so careless of onlookers.

'I didn't know I could be this reckless,' she admitted.

'I love seeing you this windswept, with such colour in your cheeks. I'm glad we didn't go to a restaurant.'

'Salty fish and chips with vinegar on the beach and straight out of newspaper is very hard to beat.'

'You're so easy to please, Evie. Now, did you know that a pier once stood here?'

Evie shook her head and smiled. 'Go on.'

'It was built by Eugenius Birch and when it opened in 1869, it was plagued by problems – from storms to too many owners back in the day.'

'What else can you tell me?'

'About fifty years ago, people had to bathe in machines – and be dressed from head to toe. The men's machines were there by the Grand Hotel, where we shall have afternoon tea.'

'And the women's?' she said, licking at a teardrop of ice cream running down her wafer cone.

He pointed. 'There, by the aquarium. Just sixpence per hour, including two clean towels and a bathing gown.'

Evie laughed. 'How very proper. How did they cope with all those rules?'

'Mixed bathing followed soon enough, and then public baths and the swimming pool after that. Come on, throw that ice cream away.' She looked offended. 'I want to take you to afternoon tea.'

'Roger, I look a sight.'

'You look a picture. I adore you, and the Grand's restaurant is there for excursionists, not toffs.'

'You know there's a skating rink attached too,' she said with a smirk.

'I'm dangerous on ice.' He winked as he hauled her up from the sand and they kissed.

'Shall we forego afternoon tea? It's a long way back.'

'I thought you might be peckish?'

'Oh, I am . . . just not for food.'

He looked at her stunned, his mouth ajar at her deliciously wicked innuendo.

'Let's just go back to the guesthouse,' she suggested.

Roger cleared his throat. 'This way.' He took her hand as they began the walk back up. They didn't say much, instead simply enjoying leaning into one another and the anticipation of what awaited them at the top of the cliffs. He led her past the parade of seaside stores and entertainment venues.

'I feel we're walking in the wrong direction,' she remarked.

'Well, the ascent is harder than the way down, so I thought we'd take it in a shallower zigzag. Besides, don't you want to pass

Gala Land and the fun palaces? They once had Unthan the Armless Wonder, who could play a violin and fire a gun with his feet.'

She had wanted to stay in her dreamy mood but his remark made her explode with laughter. 'You liar. You just made that up.'

'Absolutely not. How dare you!'

She cackled with amusement.

'A kicking mule came later, as did concert bands, minstrels and circus acts, puppet shows, a dancing skeleton if my memory serves me right, shooting galleries and of course—'

'The miniature railway,' she finished for him. 'Come on, I know an easier way to get to the top.'

He frowned.

'Ah, see, I may not have been taken to all the pleasure palaces that you know about, but I do know about the funicular.'

Roger looked delightedly stunned. 'How could I not know?'

'There are a few of them in and around Scarborough. Come on. I think the cars have been replaced since I last rode in them. But there's no station for the St Nicholas tramway – you just have to step on from the pavement, so be ready.'

They arrived back at the guesthouse. The place was busy with guests moving around for evening walks, evening drinks, dinner in the dining room.

The harried husband behind the counter handed them the key. 'Will you be eating with us tonight, sir?'

'Er, no, actually,' he said, glancing at Evie, who shook her head. 'We ate a huge lunch and we're exhausted from the drive here and the walk to and from the promenade. An early night, I think.'

The man smiled. 'It's all the fresh sea air. My wife had your suitcases put in your room. Enjoy your evening, Mr and Mrs Hall.'

Evie took Roger's hand as they ascended the stairs.

'Well, Mrs Hall,' he began and they both laughed, feeling like schoolchildren.

'I do like the sound of that – Evie and Roger Hall.'

As he fiddled with the key, he frowned at her. 'Evie . . .' He paused.

'Something wrong with the lock?'

'No, I . . . listen, there's something I need to tell you. It's imp—'

'Not now, Mr Hall. I have plans,' she said as the door opened and she pushed past him, dragging him into their room.

'Evie, please . . . let me say—'

'Hush, Roger. If you're going to ask if I'm sure, this is the last time I'll say it. I'm sure about you!'

He gave her a look of sorrow that she read to be hesitancy, but as she took the lead and began to undress, Roger – like most men, she guessed – was easily distracted by the sight of a woman slowly peeling off the layers of her clothes.

Evie couldn't believe she was behaving so provocatively, but it had been six years since she was touched by someone. Long enough. The sight of his trim, hard body being revealed as he undressed quickened her breath again. She watched him walk around the room, carelessly bare-chested but still in his trousers, turning on two small lamps, closing the curtains and giving her a chance to neatly lay her discarded clothes on the chair nearby before sliding beneath the coverlet and sheets. She still wore her silken scarf, though; it felt all the more sensuous on her flesh now that she was naked.

He turned and for her benefit, deliberately and with care, took off the rest of his clothes. 'May I join you?'

'Never ask again. The answer will always be yes,' she assured him.

As their skin warmed against each other and Evie sensed herself trembling with a need for him to cover her with his broad body, he whispered to her.

'Promise me you'll marry me, no matter what.'

Even though he looked so intense and grave in that moment, Evie believed he was playing and so she smiled. 'No matter what, I promise you I shall.'

Roger pulled the coverlet above their shoulders and in a single movement he was above her. Evie held his face, and the dim lamplight turned his hair the colour of the bronzing glow at twilight. The feathery touch of a lock of his hair falling forward onto her face, like the light scrape of her scarf against her neck, her nipples, ignited the feeling that had been threatening to explode all day.

He felt it too. Responded to her need. And there were no more words to be exchanged. Roger laughed and gently put a hand to his lips to hush her before slipping deeper beneath the coverlet to teach Evie that she didn't know everything yet about answering her desires.

It was a night of urgent lust that turned to gentle lovemaking by morning, in between which Evie slept curled in Roger's arms. She stared at him with some wonder as he slept silently, facing her. Evie wanted to touch the soft stubble along the line of his jaw, but she didn't want to wake him just yet. His hair was straight and bright, probably golden bright during July and August, and she could tell it tended to be floppy, which she rather liked in this unkempt moment. Normally it was immaculate, short at the sides, parted on one and slicked back with a little brilliantine, tapering to a broad vee at the back. She smiled, wanted to run her fingers through that sweep of thick, golden hair, imagining his ancient ancestors as Vikings.

She lifted a hand but stopped, arrested by the sight of the stunning engagement ring as it caught a shaft of morning sunlight, which fractured into dozens of tiny spotlights around the walls. Without warning and into her gentle thoughts and full heart finally galloped what she'd held at bay since yesterday's drive. Evie didn't want to, but she ran back over their conversation in the car when Roger had been talking about Adolf Hitler.

He'll instil fear, suspicion of each other, he'll ruin us as he follows his crazy and singular path of what I believe is hate masquerading as patriotism.

What had he meant by *us*? Did he mean the British? Yes, of course he had! Roger did not like to talk much about his past. He had a way of answering a question while adroitly steering her away from the heart of it.

He stirred as if disturbed by her negative thoughts. He opened his eyes, looked at her and smiled. The irises she knew were blue appeared so dark as to be colourless in the shadows.

'Good morning,' he murmured.

She returned his smile, melting away from gloomy notions. 'Hello.'

'Are you watching me?'

She nodded. 'Can't get bored of it.'

'I charge for that.'

'How much?'

'I level my fee in kind. I'm afraid I accept no other currency but your body.'

She gave a theatrical sigh. 'Right, well, I'd better pay up, then.' She grinned as she rolled to lie above him, smiling. 'Still in love?'

'Desperately,' he admitted. 'Hungry first for you and then for breakfast.'

Back in the car and headed for Levisham once again, Evie felt a push of sorrow that their trip had been so swift; she didn't feel ready to let this wonder pass.

'What happens now?' she said, after she had given him the directions to navigate out of town.

'You mean for us?'

She nodded.

He slipped up a gear to start one of the many ascents they'd have to make, and then took her hand. 'We need to speak with your father formally . . . or at least I do. It's only right.'

'Thank you. He's quite old-fashioned – he would appreciate that.'

'And then break the terrible news to your sister,' he teased.

Evie laughed delightedly. 'She'll have to survive. I'm not giving you up. Where shall we live?'

'There's no rush, is there?'

She gave him a glance, looking up from the map. 'How do you mean?'

'To get married,' he qualified. 'I mean, we can announce our engagement and then . . .'

'And then what?' She kept her voice even, not wishing to sound needy.

He shrugged. 'What I mean is, we don't have to marry immediately, do we? Let's enjoy our engagement; I've barely courted you.'

She deliberately smoothed away the frown. 'Of course. But does it mean waiting at a country railway station from one week to the next to see you? Not knowing when that might be?'

'Just at the start. I'll get organised, let them know at work and plan something more suitable.'

'Basing yourself in Yorkshire?'

'That would be my aim,' he answered, giving no other information.

The ring was a commitment but his words were vague. An alarm distantly sounded but it was soft enough not to panic her.

'Well, no one's throwing me out of the porter's cottage. I think we could live there, and if you found work in York, you could commute.'

He smiled back at her as if in agreement, but she sensed he was placating her.

'Maybe you'll want to live in Paris when you see it?' he offered. 'I thought we'd honeymoon there.' That lifted her spirits. She'd never imagined they might choose somewhere else to live . . . even for a while, living abroad would be adventurous and exciting. Perhaps Scotland or Wales . . . even Devon. Evie felt fresh exhilaration at this.

'I noted a lovely little teashop at Thornton-le-Dale. I thought we might stop there,' Roger said. 'What do you think?'

'Sounds lovely,' she answered. 'We can probably take our refreshments by the stream that runs along its streets.'

'It's such a pretty village, just like a chocolate box.'

They travelled in a pleasant quiet, holding hands in the car, stealing smiling glances, until they'd left Scarborough far behind and finally began their approach into Thornton-le-Dale.

'I could live here,' he admitted, 'in one of those cottages by the stream, curled up in each other's arms by night. We'd have a dog, of course, and take long walks.'

Evie grinned, relief washing away the hesitant worry of earlier. It didn't manage to carry off the nagging kernel of misgiving that had begun to feel like a hard pit in her stomach. She refused to confront it. 'The waterway is called Thornton Beck,' she said. 'Nearest station is Pickering.'

'Perfect,' he replied, and cut her a look of such affection that if he'd said, *Let's just set up home here today*, she was sure she'd say yes on the spot. Right now, she wished he would.

He didn't, though. He helped her out of the car, and they went the long way to the tearooms, taking the extra few minutes to stroll by the forge.

'This pub is the Fox and Rabbit. It has very good food.'

'Next time,' he said, smiling, and they made their way arm in arm down to the tearooms, which sat in the buildings that ringed the edge of the green, where children played and a small dog ran in ever decreasing circles.

Evie spied a telephone box.

'Do you mind if I take a minute to call home?'

'Not at all.'

'I thought I'd let them know we are on our way and perhaps . . .'

'Warn them?' He grinned.

'I don't want Dad having a heart attack from the shock of the marriage proposal,' she said, laughing. 'I'll just pave the way a little. Tell them we have some wonderful news to share.'

He kissed her cheek. 'Whatever you think best. Now, tea or coffee?'

'I'm a Yorkshire girl – has to be tea,' she said.

'A beautiful Yorkshire girl,' he said, adjusting her silk scarf.

She wanted to kiss him long and hard but instead she smiled and gave him a push. 'Oh, go on with you and your flattery, Roger Hall. I won't be long.' She began digging in her bag for her purse and some pennies.

Evie asked the operator to put her through and after what felt like an interminable wait, she heard her father answer.

'Levisham Station, Barraclough here.'

'Dad, it's me.'

'Evie, my girl! How wonderful to hear your voice. Everything all right?'

'Everything is just perfect.' Even she could hear the dreamy tone in her voice. 'I'm ringing to ask how Rosie is. I don't really want to walk back into another argument.'

'Your sister is sullen but resigned. I'm convinced it's not really you or Hall – more that she's not the one enjoying being romanced. You know how she is, she wants everything to be like a fairy-tale . . . or what she sees at the Saturday cinema. I'm sorry you argued, love.'

'I'm sorry too. I should have bitten my tongue and not fallen for it. I blame myself because I really do know better, especially where Roger is concerned, but she just caught me off guard, Dad, and was determined to ruin my happy time by making me feel guilty.'

'You have nothing to feel guilty about,' her father insisted.

'Thanks. Anyway, I wanted to check in on her before we arrived so that she won't be impolite to Roger. And also to warn you that it may get worse before it gets better.'

'What do you mean?'

'Are you sitting down, Dad?' There was a pause. 'Dad?'

'Do you have news?' It was obvious he'd guessed.

No point in playing coy. 'I do.'

'My gosh! Really?'

She smiled at the receiver, loving his excitement. 'I said yes but I'm trying to avoid another scene from Rosie. If you think she's going to get upset, it might be good to send her on a long errand . . . perhaps into York?'

'I'll take a measure, don't worry, and we'll have it sorted before you return. Congratulations, my darling.'

'We're on our way home now – we're just at Thornton-le-Dale, and Roger wants to do it the right way and speak to you, even though it's unnecessary. It's not as though I haven't been here before.'

'No, I applaud his courtesy.'

'I also rang to ask that you don't make a fuss or tell anyone. I think Roger would like to keep it sort of quiet for now, and you know how much I hate unnecessary attention.'

'I couldn't be happier for you, darling Evie.' She could hear his relief as much as his joy.

'Thank you, Dad,' she said and started to laugh and cry at once. 'I'm just frightened Rosie will get the pip, but you'll help me with her, won't you?'

'Leave it with me, Evie,' he soothed her. 'You can't plan love. This is your moment and you deserve your happiness. I'm very, very pleased for you. He's a good catch and I respect your decision.'

'I realise it's happened very fast, but I've admired him from afar for so long – for as long as some couples court – and to be honest, I love him so much, Dad, I reckon I could just burst. He's prepared to relocate to Yorkshire, so you're stuck with me.'

She heard her father give a soft whoop of delight. 'That is the best news of all, Evie.'

She dabbed at tears of relief and happiness. Sniffing, she laughed. 'Thank you. Now tell me, how is everything at Levisham?'

'Oh, fine, fine. Apart from Rosie being in one of her moods. I find it easier to just do everything myself than bother to ask. Oh, actually, there has been some excitement, I must admit, but it can wait.'

'What could possibly have happened since I hugged you goodbye yesterday?' She wasn't alarmed, more amused, anticipating her father saying something benign, like the points were sticky and a maintenance gang were on their way, but his next words shocked her.

'Well, you know all that stranger business that Harry was muttering about?'

'Mmm,' she answered, waiting for more and frowning, feeling a gentle frisson on the rim of her mind, as though this part of the conversation had been inevitable; something that was going to spoil her happiest day.

'Well, apparently it's been confirmed. There's a spy in our region – and not just our region but right here, around Levisham and Pickering. They think he's using our line to move around and nose about the north.'

'Oh, Dad, no,' she said, instantly frustrated that something potentially dramatic would eclipse her enjoyment of this moment, forcing her to get involved in something so negative and worrying.

'Yes. There have been some clues, including the discovery of some equipment.'

'What equipment?'

'Measuring tools – the sort engineers use. They were stashed in the hollow of that broken tree just up from the station, past Grove House.'

'The tree stump that Rosie and I used to hide our stuff in?'

'The very one. Some young lads were larking about on that bank, opposite the path, and came upon it. It was a satchel full of equipment, definitely meant to stay hidden, according to Harry. Not that the officials are saying much.'

'What do you mean by officials, Dad?'

'Oh, some of the bigwigs have been up from Whitehall.'

'From London? Yesterday? And I missed it?'

'I'm afraid so, Evie. Came unannounced in black cars. All very formal and abrupt. Men in suits and trilbies. Asking lots of questions that we couldn't answer because we don't know anything.' His voice turned amused. 'Of course, on the quiet, your sister is trying not to show that she's excited. It's a feast of new potential—'

Evie blinked in irritation. 'What *do* they know?' she interjected.

She could picture her father shrugging as he spoke. 'Whatever it is, they're not telling us.'

'Oh, how exasperating. How can we help if they won't enlighten us? They must have some clue if they're poking around Levisham. I mean, that equipment – even if it is what they fear, it could belong to someone who's snooping anywhere in Yorkshire.'

'I suppose the whole idea of a German spy among us isn't very amusing, but between us there is one small titbit that is likely to make you smile.'

'Me? Why?'

'It's connected with your most popular of tearoom offerings – your station cake.'

'Whatever are you talking about, Dad?' She laughed, suddenly nervous.

'Seems the fellow they're hunting likes your cake. That's how they know he's using our line. Harry recognised some of the crumbs.'

'Good grief. How ludicrous. Surely it could be any cake?'

'Well, Harry's convinced it's yours and told the bigwigs as much; this spy in our midst likes your cake but really doesn't care for the glacé cherries. They found a little pile of them cast aside in the grass overlooking the old Group 4 RAF airfield at Elvington.' He chuckled, waiting for her response, but received only silence. 'Evie . . . are you there? Evie?'

6

The distant alarm now sounded like a thousand great bells clanging in her mind. The little black seed of concern in her belly had bloomed, turning her vision narrow and accelerating her pulse. It took her several long moments to even register her father's voice in her klaxoning terror.

'Evie?'

'Yes, yes . . . Dad, sorry. I'm . . . I . . .'

'What is it?'

'I just thought I saw an old schoolfriend, but it wasn't,' she fibbed. 'Erm . . . look, I'd better go. I've left Roger long enough and we'll be home soon.'

'Right, then. I'm glad you rang. Gives us reason to celebrate. Come safely.'

'Bye, Dad,' she said, staring out across the stream that wound around the village, hardly aware of putting the receiver back into its cradle.

It had all looked so picture-perfect five minutes earlier . . . just like a chocolate box, as Roger had said. Loud around her was the hum of bees, busy in the riot of pink hawthorn overhanging the fence and the white blossom of the horse chestnut nearby. Swallows dipped and zigzagged overhead, while swifts, silhouetted against the pearlescent turquoise of the sky, flew straight and strong. There were the sounds of vehicles and people going about their day, and children fishing in the beck giggling over something. She could hear the metallic ring of a bicycle bell and she watched a woman raise a hand and wave to a grocer's boy, who blew her a kiss. Normally that would have made her smile, but her expression remained frozen with disbelief. From behind her came a soft hum of conversation from the tearooms and the regular clink and clank of crockery being washed or stacked. The minutiae of the village was suddenly crowding her mind with sound.

But louder still was the bedlam of her thoughts.

And the sound of that bedlam was her howl of betrayal.

She had to act.

Evie rang the operator again and was connected for a terse and teary conversation that lasted less than a minute.

'You're quite sure?'

'Yes,' she said, feeling ill. 'Don't tell anyone.'

It wasn't a long drive back to Levisham but Roger slowed down so they could enjoy the scenery, and because he said he wanted to prolong their time together. To Evie, however, each agonising revolution of the wheels felt like an eternity.

Evie needed time not only to sort through the scatter of her thoughts but to line them up as well – what she knew to be true on one side, and what she now suspected was a queue of lies on the others.

'You're very quiet?' Roger said, squeezing her hand.

'Am I?'

'I thought you might be feeling travel sickness, because you barely drank your tea.'

Evie stared out the window to catch glimpses down the valley of Newton Dale. Out it came. 'You must have nerves made of cast iron.'

'It's not the nervous system that causes travel queasiness. It's all connected with the ears and balan—'

'I mean for all the lying.'

He turned, staring at her quizzically. 'Pardon me?'

'Oh, just stop, Roger. Stop the car!'

He kept driving, appearing utterly confused. 'What?'

'Stop!' she yelled and now he responded, looking around wildly.

'This is dangerous here. Wait, just give me a moment to find a safe place. Are you going to be sick?'

'Yes.'

He swerved onto the verge, but the hedgerow was further back, and she was able to open the car door. It was just in time. Evie lost her breakfast – the one that she had eaten with only affection in her eyes, stealing loving, amused glances at her fiancé. Now she didn't think she could look at him directly, although she knew she must. The least she could do was give him warning, especially as she'd already taken precautions against him fleeing.

'Darling Evie. Oh, I'm so sorry.' He'd got out of the car to come around and crouch nearby, reaching for her, sounding so tender.

'Don't touch me, Roger.'

He pulled his hands back as if he'd just put his fingers into an open flame. He said no more but handed her his handkerchief. She reluctantly took it and dabbed at her mouth, feeling the rough bump of his embroidered initials. Touching her lips with his name made her think of how many times she'd kissed him in the last forty-eight hours. She heaved again; acid scorched her throat, and that which had prompted its sour pain burned in her mind.

'How could you,' she said, more a statement than a question.

Still he said nothing, but in raising her head and pushing back her hair to regard him briefly, she saw only confusion in his expression. He was waiting for her to explain her hostility. But she glared back, unaware she was capable of such naked aggression.

'Evie, I'm lost. Tell me what I've done and let me make amends.'

'I can forgive most people any transgression except one. I have no sympathy for anyone who blatantly lies to my face. And you are a deviant who has set out to deliberately violate my trust.'

His voice took a harder edge. 'What are you talking about?' He reached for her again.

'I said don't touch me,' she warned as she straightened up. 'You should know that there are people looking all over the Levisham region for you.'

'People?' He frowned, his handsome face creasing in lines of bewilderment. 'For me?'

'Police, to be exact, but also men from Whitehall.' She watched his golden complexion blanch. 'Less puzzling now?' He swallowed, and she could all but hear the gears of his mind shifting. 'Don't lie again. And don't think of leaving me here on this hilltop and fleeing. You won't get far. I've already left your identification papers with the teashop owner back in Thornton. By now she will have passed them on to her delivery boy, who is picking up parcels from our station and will leave them there.'

'You stole my papers?' He sounded hurt.

'You stole my heart,' she snapped, breathing hard.

'Evie—'

'Don't. Frankly, I want nothing to do with a German spy, but while most might think that's your lowest point, you and I will know that taking advantage of me yesterday . . . last night'—she shuddered—'speaking of love, and promising me a life, is truly the mark of an immoral and depraved evildoer.'

'I need to explain something to you.'

'Roger . . . is that even your name? I can't imagine it is . . . I can't—'

'It's not.'

She stopped talking and had to take a calming breath to stop the bile rising again.

'My name is Maximillian Ryker Hall.'

She gave a groan and began to shake her head. She didn't want to hear this.

'You must listen to me.'

'Why?'

'Because I love you. Because nothing I said or did with you was a lie.'

She gave a mocking laugh of despair. 'Just the spying bit, you mean? Oh, well, that's fine, then. I'm sure I could live with that,' she growled. Her words came out like a curse on him. Evie was shocked by her own shaking rage. She swallowed air, sucking in two deep breaths. No, she would not compromise herself any further. 'Let's go. Even if you are going to run, the least you can do is get me a little bit closer to home.'

'I don't want to run. I want to explain.'

'Take me home, please. I need time to think without you speaking your unfaithful words of affection.'

They travelled in a frigid silence so cold and brittle Evie was sure she could feel her teeth chattering.

Lockton's claim to fame was that it was mentioned in the Domesday Book. Evie was sure that Roger, or Maximillian, or whatever his name was, would already know this; she sensed he liked history as much as she did. As they passed through the village in horribly taut silence, it teased them with its spring hedgerows and a splendid cricket green looking ready for the summer games. A church service had just finished at St Giles and children were tumbling out of Sunday school for their carefree day of play, while their mothers thought about the roast lunch and their fathers hoped for a pint or two at the Durham Ox before they enjoyed that family meal. It all sounded so normal and English . . . meanwhile her mind was full of swastikas and the guttural German language turned ugly by the country's shouting leader, who the man next to her clearly followed.

She swallowed the temptation to retch and let her gaze rest on the mill at the bottom of the valley as they approached. St Mary's church would come up next, and then the Horseshoe pub, which enclosed the village shop and the post office at one end. They passed the pond and she pointed for him to turn left.

He obeyed her instructions.

'At the junction coming up you need to take a sharp left or you'll end up on the moors.' *Perhaps that's where he'd prefer to be*, she thought, looking for the sycamore tree she had always thought was like the train guard welcoming people to Levisham Station, just a minute or two away now. 'I'll get the gate,' she said, relieved to be able to leap out as the car slowed. When she got back in, she allowed herself a moment to be dazzled by the way the road dropped away to give spectacular views out across the valley and over Levisham Station. A dry sob caught in her throat.

'We should have been coming back to announce our engagement,' she said, helplessly allowing the emotion to spill over.

'Let me talk, Evie.' He stopped the car once they were through the gate and got out, sucking in air.

She followed him as he walked towards some untroubled Swaledale sheep, which parted in their own time. Their woolly coats were shaggy and ready to be shorn. A mother and baby passed by, the ewe's gaze fixed directly at Evie. It felt like an accusation, but Evie didn't know why. She was doing her patriotic duty, surely?

She heard a shrill whistle. That would be the midday train. The smell of warm grease and oil permeated the nearby countryside, along with the pleasant fragrance of burning coal and wood, as they made their gentle descent. These familiar layers wrapped around Evie to reassure her she was home . . . and safe.

'All right, Maximillian,' she said, his name sounding so foreign suddenly. 'Tell me.'

'It's Max, Evie. Roger was my English grandfather's name.'

She shrugged, feeling awkward about how ruthless she was being.

'I told you my wife died in childbirth – her name was Rachel. To be honest, I think she died of anxiety as much as complications with my daughter's birth,' he began in blunt fashion, making her draw a silent breath of shock. 'We were the happiest couple on this planet. That's how it felt. And until I met you, I didn't think finding that sort of joy again was possible.'

Evie said nothing but felt some relief that his sentiment matched hers. 'I'm sorry about your wife and baby.'

'As I am about Ron. But without their deaths we would never have met. Nothing about my time here, other than when I've been with you, has been comfortable or truthful. It was my intention to tell you everything while we were away – I tried to begin last night, before . . .' He shook his head. 'But it was so carefree and uplifting to be having fun, to be in love again, to not worry for just a few hours. I was selfish, yes, and wanted to enjoy our time.'

Evie bit her lip to stop herself saying anything. She could tell from his broken expression that he was recalling terrible memories. As betrayed as she felt, this was the man she loved and there was no pleasure in seeing him so cowed. 'It was a violent, bloody birth that came after a tense, frightening and protracted period. Our baby was delivered at home, weak and struggling. Being a wife and mother was all that Rachel ever wanted, and when that was threatened,

I think it frightened her so much that her anxiety prompted an early labour that turned into the obstructed one.' His voice had developed a tremor. 'Our daughter died the same day she was born – the same day as her mother – but Rachel did hold her and was able to kiss her before they both left us. She never had a chance to name our child but I think I'd have liked to call her Sarah.'

Evie had to look away as he frowned with deliberate concentration to stop himself breaking down.

'It was the worst day of my life. But my girls are in a better place, frankly, than being in Germany right now.'

'What does this have to do with you being a spy?' Evie was surprised by how easily she cut through the heart of this, their last few minutes together. She needed an explanation, some sort of architecture upon which she could make sense of what was happening to her.

'Rachel was Jewish. Our new government takes a deliberate antisemitic approach and in 1933 it was beginning to close in on Jewish freedoms. Now, the regulations around being Jewish are rampant and oppressive.'

She waited. They both knew he hadn't answered her question.

'I have a son.'

She gasped.

'He's six years old. He's half Jewish but has Nordic looks. He is blond and blue-eyed.'

'So . . . he's safe?'

'No. As far from safe as you can imagine for a child. No baby, no matter how Aryan they may look, is safe if born to a Jewish mother. At the moment he is vaguely protected by my blood and that of his grandfather, who can trace a fine Prussian line . . . but the way things are going, that advantage won't last.'

Evie felt ill that a child could be under such a threat. 'That's appalling.'

'It is. Rachel was far from religious. She intended to raise our family in an open manner that embraced her culture and my culture, and allowed both our religions to flourish around our children. She was modern and so liberal in her thinking. She was a proud German before she was Jewish.'

'Where is your boy now?' She bent down to grab the buds of some wildflowers growing nearby.

'Munich. I moved there after Rachel and the baby died. They're pretending he is being cared for by a friend – someone he knows, so he's not frightened. But this person is also a paid-up member of the party, of course, and a true believer.'

True believer? 'They'd surely not wish him harm?'

'There's fervour out there, and so much antisemitism. Jews are an easy target. These days you're either Aryan or you're not. And if you're not, you're . . . dispensable.'

'But you fit the perfect German. Doesn't that count?'

He shrugged, as if to say he couldn't help being what they admired. 'My son looks the part, as I told you, but they won't let me forget the Jewish blood that runs through his veins. And the so-called friend?' She nodded. 'She'd hand him over to be sent to a guarded Jewish quarter in a blink, because she's a fervent supporter of Hitler.'

'I know you're not. You said as much. Am I to trust that?'

'I loathe him and all of his henchmen and sheeplike followers.'

Evie sighed out the anxiety of all that she'd learned. She put one of the flower buds into her mouth and chewed as she thought. 'You're not lying about being English?'

He shook his head. 'I spent my early life in Ditchling, Sussex, as I told you, and then we moved to Germany, and while I had to live as a German because I was a child, England is home.' He touched his heart. 'I am English. I am patriotic to Britain.'

'You certainly sound it, and you act like an Englishman.'

'I don't act, Evie. I am one,' he pressed. 'I just happen to live and work in Germany because I was married to a German who had a large and loving family there. I was planning for us to leave Berlin when Hitler became chancellor, and we felt the first tendrils of antisemitism touch our family. I wanted to emigrate to Britain and had plans underway to make that happen, but then Rachel became poorly and . . .' He didn't finish. 'I vainly hoped her health might improve in time for us to leave but by the time I came to my senses my senior role in the railways had been noted . . . along with my dual citizenship.'

She raised her gaze to him. 'And?'

'They have my son. I'm helpless. Unless I agreed to spy on the British railway system for the Nazis, my son would have been sent away as a Jewish undesirable.'

'Sent away?' Evie frowned with consternation.

'Into the Jewish quarter, fast becoming a ghetto, and after that . . . I don't know. I would not be allowed to see him. There's talk of killing undesirables.'

She felt queasy again at his words. 'So what you're telling me is that you're being blackmailed by the German government, which is holding your child hostage?'

He nodded. 'Yes. Spy for them and have a chance to get him back or, refuse to spy and lose him. What choice do you imagine I had?'

'Why not say something? To me, at least?'

'I wanted to. I tried . . .' He didn't finish, his words trailing off as though he realised it was futile to explain. 'Anyway, they've got information that is negligible.'

'How so?'

'I've skewed everything I've sent back. Figures, statistics, measurements, calculations and my advice. None of it is correct but I've made it sound plausible, so until someone can come across here and check, they will be none the wiser.'

'You've lied to your blackmailers?'

'I told you, I'm patriotic. I will not betray my country, but I have to protect my son, so I'm giving them what they want to hear – they have no sense that it's false information . . . not yet, anyway.'

She recalled how he'd hesitated last night, tried to pause and tell her something, but she'd been in a recklessly romantic mood and she hadn't wanted anything to burst that bubble. She remembered shutting him down, dragging him into the room. 'I wish you'd said something, even this morning.'

'Breakfast was not the right time either – your eyes were shining with love and delight; I selfishly didn't want that to stop. I have not acted cynically, Evie, when it comes to you. I'm sorry to have let you down but a life is at stake. Besides, no one sees love coming, do they? It just happens. I had to put my child first but I would do anything to spare you being hurt.'

'Yet here I am, hurting.' He nodded and she saw the pain as much as contrition in those stormy eyes of his. 'All right,' she said, making a private decision. 'I'm prepared to trust you, Max.'

'You are?' He looked shocked, unsure. 'Why?'

'Because now that I'm in love, I don't know how to be out of love with you. I believe you. I think I would have known if you were pretending in your feelings towards me, and if you were a complete fraud, I swear I would have picked it.' She sighed, then breathed in audibly. 'Add to this that Ron and I wanted to start a family more than anything . . . He wanted a son – a whole football team of boys, if he had his way – so I feel it's my duty to safeguard a child. Your little boy asked for none of this. He's the innocent one we should all be protecting.'

'That's gracious of you, Evie.'

'I don't want to be gracious. I want to turn the clock back a few hours and still be in bed with a man who loved me without secrets.

I don't want to face my frailty where you're concerned. I should just let the authorities have you. But I can't!' Evie shook her head. 'I can't,' she repeated in a small voice.

He looked back at her with a wounded expression. 'So you haven't told anyone?'

'I told my father of my suspicions.'

'How did you work out it was me?'

'A few things that I tried to ignore, but the most damning was your inability to eat my glacé cherries.'

He looked back at her, confused. Evie explained and he hung his head with shame.

'I've asked my father not to breathe a word until we get ourselves home to discuss everything. He'll help us.' Evie sniffed back all the emotion that was threatening to overflow. 'We go back to Levisham and we make a plan for how we explain to the authorities what's going on.'

'They aren't going to believe—'

'They will,' she snapped. 'We are not at war with Germany. They have to hear and understand your side of this,' she added. 'I'll make them listen. And you will tell them how you've lied to Germany. Have you proof?'

'Of the lies I've sent back?' Max nodded. 'Yes.'

'There we are, then,' Evie said, as though it were as simple as day becoming night. 'We shall marry as we planned, and we have to get your son to England.'

He smiled at how decisive she sounded, but she read only his indulgence in it; she could tell he didn't believe her optimism. 'His name is Jonas,' he said.

'Jonas,' she repeated as if testing the name on her tongue. 'Good. So, come on,' she said briskly. 'We need to get ahead of the police and these officials from London.'

'Run, you mean?'

'If necessary . . . until they grant us the chance for you to be heard properly and without the lynch-mob mentality that seems to be appearing.' She turned on her heel and parted the calm sheep once again as she strode back to the car.

Max had no choice but to follow.

7

As the Singer turned onto the road that passed Grove House and led to the entrance of the station, neither of them saw the black car following them over the sheep grid. Evie, however, was fully aware of Harry and two policemen she didn't recognise, waiting for them, alongside her father.

'Max . . .' she began nervously, swivelling around in her seat and noticing the black car acting as a blockade. Men were getting out. They looked like wraiths with pale faces, and their dark formal suits melded into the surroundings so at first glance they had no immediate outline.

'It's all right, Evie. There never really was any other way.'

A slim man, older than his colleagues, stood next to her father and was polishing his spectacles as the car drew in.

At a nod from Harry, the police constables moved in swiftly and hustled Max from the car.

Evie leapt out of the passenger seat. 'Leave him alone! How dare you!' She ran at them, hating to see Max's hands raised in surrender. 'Wait! Stop!'

She watched as the man she was even more deeply in love

with now was being handcuffed.

Alf and her sister were instantly at her side, helping her away from the car.

'Evie?' her father tried in a tentative tone.

'Dad! What's happening? I thought . . . you told them?' She couldn't believe the betrayal. It felt worse in that moment than discovering Roger was actually Max and that he was a spy. Her gaze flicked angrily to her sister.

Rosie was mute. Terrified, even. The silence of the Barraclough family was overrun by male voices, giving orders to Max. She couldn't look his way until she'd worked out how on earth they'd managed to corner him before she'd had a chance to work out an escape plan.

Evie returned her attention to her father. 'I begged you not to—'

'It was me,' Rosie admitted, her gaze darting frantically from Evie, to her father, to the strangers and back again. 'I did it. Dad warned me to keep it to myself until you'd returned.'

A feeling of vertigo made Evie sway where she stood. If someone had told her that she was being held over the edge of a tall cliff by a thin strand that was about to break and tumble her against rocks and into the ocean crashing below, she'd have believed it. A gale seemed to be howling around her, drowning out sound, but she knew it was an internal shriek of anguish. It was her, screaming privately, her hands clenched claw-like as if she were about to pounce on Rosie and scratch at her.

Rosie's pleas reached her from far away. Repeated supplication. 'I'm so sorry, Evie. I was shocked at the news of you being engaged and I suppose I was angry or jealous – I just blurted to Harry what I'd heard.'

Evie turned and saw Max being searched. He looked back at her steadily. They ignored the people around them and whatever was being said. There was them . . . no one else. The thread that she'd pictured holding onto only moments ago on the imaginary clifftop was him. He was the line and he was holding it tight, drawing her towards him, not letting her fall. They were connected. She would not, no way on this planet, allow this man to be prosecuted. The thought snapped her back to the present.

Evie looked at Rosie as if she were simple. Her breath was shallow and she was aware of the rapid rise and fall of her chest, which was filling with resentment and despair. 'Rosie, they're going to arrest him for treason. Have you any idea what that means, you selfish little brat?'

Rosie began to babble her whining pleas again. It was the same claim repeated. She was jealous. She didn't mean to cause such trouble. She'd just mentioned it to Harry, not realising it would . . .

The slap was as much a surprise to Evie as it was to her sister. It silenced Rosie. Evie stared at her hand in slight confusion as though she didn't recognise it, and certainly did not feel responsible for its actions. Rosie, it seemed, was too shocked to react audibly. Evie blinked as she tracked her gaze from her hand to where Rosie clutched her cheek.

'Shut up, Rosie. Just shut up,' Evie heard herself saying.

Her father looked pale with a shocked expression, his skin clammy. Evie came to her senses: if she wasn't careful, she'd be crouched over her darling Dad as he had a heart attack or similar. And it wouldn't be over Max Hall – it would be over his two daughters fighting. 'Breathe, Dad,' she urged, as he tried to comprehend what he'd witnessed. 'Breathe and listen to the truth. You need to hear his side of it to know that he's still a patriot. Now they'll arrest him and—' She gulped.

Rosie had recovered, apparently accepting the physical rebuke as inevitable. 'Forgive me, Evie,' Rosie tried, beginning to cry.

'I can't. Your spitefulness is unforgivable,' Evie said, her own tears brimming now. 'I hate you for what you've done.'

'Girls.' Alf found his voice, desperately trying to repair the damage, but was cut short by the man who seemed to be taking charge.

He had continued polishing his spectacles while Max was being handcuffed and searched. Max was now flanked by men and a car door was opening. The man strolled up to the family. 'Good afternoon, sir, ladies. I'm Clive Elliott from . . . well, let's just say from Whitehall.' He did not make it more awkward by extending his hand to shake. 'My men and I will be accompanying Roger Hall to London.'

She watched Roger nod. Except it wasn't Roger.

'His name is Maximillian Hall,' Evie confirmed. 'He told me. Here are his papers.' She withdrew them from her bag.

Hall cut her a bruised look that said: *So I'm not the only one capable of lying?* She had to stay focused now; a maelstrom of emotion was threatening to sweep her away but she had to let it pass by her. Right now she had to forget her pain and her own sense of betrayal, and do everything she could to paint Max in the correct light so that the men from London would listen and not judge him without knowing his story.

'Sir, my name is—'

'Thank you, Mrs Armstrong. You've been most helpful,' Elliott said, dismissing her. He gestured for one of his sidekicks to take the documents from Evie. 'Come with us now, Hall, there's a good fellow,' he offered Max in a friendly tone.

'Gentlemen,' Hall said, stalling them, his handcuffs clinking loudly in the sudden silence. 'By all means keep me bound, but before I leave I would like a private conversation with Mrs Armstrong . . . perhaps in the waiting room? You can leave the door open and your constables can stand by.'

'I don't believe she has anything more to say to you,' Elliott replied.

'But I have things to say . . . and they're important. Please. Just five minutes.'

'Mr Elliott?' It was Evie stepping forward. 'Please don't ignore me, speak for me, or dismiss what I have to say.'

'I can assure you, Mrs—'

'And don't bring your fake politeness here either. I can see the glee glittering in your eyes that you think you have your man. But you are mistaken, and if you let him explain—'

'He'll enjoy every opportunity, Mrs Armstrong, to do just that in London in front of the right people. A courtroom really is the right place for Mr Hall to explain all his reasons for being an English citizen acting as a spy for Germany on British soil.'

'"Acting" is the critical word here,' she snipped. 'But I can see we'll need to consult someone higher up the ladder than you, Mr Elliott. So for now, yes, I'd like to speak alone to my fiancé. I'm sure you cannot begrudge me a few words.' She looked to her sister and her whimpering tears. 'Be quiet now, Rosie. This is not about you. Dad, are you all right?'

He nodded. His complexion had a slightly better colour but she wasn't convinced. 'Rosie,' she snapped, and her sister flinched. 'Go and make some sweet tea and get it into Dad. Take him to the other platform.'

Rosie obediently took her father's arm and he seemed content to be led.

Everyone held an uncomfortable breath.

'Mr Elliott?' she said, with firm demand in her tone. 'Deny me this and you will regret it.'

'Don't threaten me, Mrs Armstrong.'

'Why not? You've threatened all that I love. I'll do as I please. You're not my keeper, my supervisor or my prime minister, and I will take it all the way to him if you don't give me the simple wish of a few minutes with the man I intend to marry.' If Elliott could sense how she was trembling within, he'd probably keep smirking and give a flick to his men to continue bundling Roger . . . she needed to think of him as Max . . . into that car. But she was covering it well with her crossed arms and equally cross expression.

'Let's get this over with,' Elliott sighed, sounding bored, nodding towards the waiting room and withdrawing his pipe.

Embarrassed, Evie led the way, moving across the platform to the waiting room for southern travellers, of which thankfully there were none at this moment. She walked to its far end to stand in a shaft of sunlight streaming through the single back window, which she hoped might still the shivering that hadn't abated.

Evie turned at Max's footsteps as he entered. The space, hung with her wildflower frames and the familiar paraphernalia of the station – its notices, brochures, the smell of wax from the polish on the benches – all of it felt comforting until she noted the constables flanking the doorway. Outside she saw her distraught father shuffling from foot to foot; he'd ignored the tea and was instead murmuring to the two men in suits. Rosie was nowhere to be seen. Good. She had nothing more to say to her sister just now. White rage was obliterating her normally warm and endearing view of her sibling. Elliott stood away from everyone, loading his pipe with tobacco from a tin.

'I'm actually lost for words,' she admitted to Max, who stood close enough that she could smell the pretty citrus tang of the stitchwort he'd chewed on the moor still on his breath. 'And my mind is mush. I don't know what to do.'

'None of this is your fault. I made my own decisions, Evie, and I knew the risks. I had to take them for Jonas but I didn't have to involve you – that was me being selfish and just a bit helpless in your midst. I think if I leave here knowing you believe me, and trust my innocence, then I can face what's ahead.'

'I do believe you,' she reassured him. 'But what about Jonas?'

His expression darkened. 'I don't know how to help him from a British prison cell but I'll argue his case. Perhaps as he's got

English grandparents, the authorities here might be able to assist in getting him out.'

'Roger . . .'

'Max,' he corrected with a soft smile, lifting her hands and pressing his lips against them. 'I know all that you want to say. Just know I love you more,' he said.

'Mr Hall?' It was Elliott.

Evie glanced at Elliott with as much sourness as she could angle his way. He was now tapping out tobacco from the bowl of his pipe as if readying to leave. He never did successfully light it; she realised now it was just a way to kill a few minutes.

'No, wait,' Evie began.

Elliott shook his head. 'It's time.'

Maximillian Hall gave her a heartbreaking smile of encouragement. 'Goodbye, Evie. I hope when you get some distance from this terrible day, you'll keep close all that we shared and daydreamed.'

'Where are you taking him?'

'That's not for me—'

'Mr Elliott, if you don't tell me where you're taking Mr Hall, I will make the most terrible scenes for you, I promise. I think it's fair that our family know where my fiancé will be held while this business is sorted out.'

Elliott took a shallow breath to hide his sigh. 'Mr Hall will be held under guard in London. Nothing you should concern yourself with.'

'But what if I wish to—'

'What, Mrs Armstrong? See him? You likely won't again. But Britain thanks your family for doing its patriotic duty. Good day.' He lifted his hat politely and Max Hall cast her one final look.

'Mr Elliott?'

He turned. 'Mrs Armstrong?' His tone told her how tedious she was becoming.

'Do you have a calling card, please?'

Elliott stared at her as if he'd just noticed something unpleasant caught on the bottom of his shoe. 'Or you'll cause a scene?' he asked, his voice level but edged with poison.

'You have my measure, Mr Elliott.'

He blinked and managed to convey how vexing he found her pitiful threat, before he withdrew a small white card from his top pocket. 'I don't hand those out willy-nilly, Mrs Armstrong. I'll thank you to keep that private.'

'Of course. And I'll thank you to treat Mr Hall with care and respect until all the truth is uncovered. He's cooperating.'

'He's caught, Mrs Armstrong. Prisoners usually do cooperate when they know the game's up.'

'He's British – please don't forget that. Born and bred right here in England. He's no Communist or fascist sympathiser. Get to the truth, sir.'

He lifted his hat. 'We shall. Good day. Let's go, Hall.' He pointed towards the doorway of the waiting room.

She turned away from him and cast a look – half despair, half apology – to Max. And it felt like he was breaking open her heart, and sharing with the world what made it beat, with the smile of undisclosed affection he beamed at her.

'Never change, Evie,' he murmured as he passed her and was led towards the large black car.

It happened fast. One moment she felt her father's grip on her shoulder and within seconds the car had reversed, turned and was driving away, taking that broken heart of hers with it.

Evie moved through the next day as though snipped free from all that connected her to her normal life. She felt as though she were treading over treacle, its thick stickiness permitting only slow movement:

each action, whether it was selling a train ticket or serving in the tea gardens, felt like it was happening at half pace. She could swear that someone else was inhabiting her body, going through the motions as she watched. And yet a small voice, as if from a long distance, was calling to her to defy everyone and to take control.

She'd waved away her father's suggestion to take the day to herself to rest and she'd especially ignored Rosie's pleas to take on Evie's duties. Rosie's guilt sucked all the air from around them. Evie couldn't bear to be in the same enclosed space and found herself avoiding her sister, mostly because she didn't want to look upon her or hear any more apologies. No amount of regret or contrition would undo what she'd set in action and Evie was genuinely struggling with the notion that she might ever forgive her. She could feel her father's fear that their family unit was under threat and it was his angst that kept her civil, but that was the best she could achieve. The hot anger had cooled to a frosty silence.

Evie ground through the rest of the previous day after Max had been whisked away under guard, and when the final train had been given its green flag to proceed, she'd had the strange sensation of imagining herself returning to her body and having to face reality. Whichever guardian angel had given her the hours to function was now retreating and pushing her back into the world.

Her night had been sleepless and burdened by despair. She'd churned his words over in her mind. He was a spy . . . but didn't want to be. He was a patriot of England but lived in Germany and worked for Adolf Hitler. He'd asked her to marry him knowing there were so many secrets. Lies and truth blended to confuse her. But one thing was certain when she saw the first brightening of the dawn through the net curtains: her love for Max – as she was learning to refer to him – had only intensified. And that frightened her.

Another morning, midday and afternoon had passed as she moved through her duties like a wind-up toy. Her smiles at the customers were quick and forced, her bright tone dragged up from some primitive place of memory, her actions learned and robotic. Evie's mind was not here in Levisham. Her thoughts danced back and forth from lovemaking in Scarborough and the memory of his proposal, his kiss, his laugh, his plans, to the horror of yesterday's arrest. Each vignette was in sharp focus, from Elliott pretending to light his pipe to the lines of worry on Max's face as he earnestly explained the impossible choice he'd been forced to make.

Ever since she'd woken, something had been building. It wasn't her anger; that was somewhere else – that was visceral, deep in her body. This raced like a runner on a track around the rim of her mind. It was moving fast and she couldn't get purchase on it but it wouldn't let her go. Maybe it would tire before she did and allow her to snag it, pull it to the forefront of her mind and understand what it wanted, or perhaps what it was asking her to do. She found its company distracting; at least it was helping her to remain trapped with it, while her body moved through the motions of the day.

Between it and thoughts of Max, hours and hours passed, the silence awkward whenever customers were out of earshot.

'That's it,' Rosie sighed, and her voice dragged Evie back to the kitchen sink, where they were cleaning up after the last of the customers. She did not want to be here with Rosie but the more she pushed her away, the more her younger sister tried desperately to cling to her, or at least be near. She obviously held some vain hope that she might wear Evie's frigidity down until it no longer existed. She heard Rosie's words and her final thought as she left the memory of him was that he'd already been gone more than twenty-four hours. 'We're done,' Rosie continued.

'We are done, indeed,' Evie said. It sounded horribly final.

'You've got to stop this,' her sister said. Her hand was on her hip and she blocked Evie's pathway to the door. 'I've absorbed your rage, your insults, your physical anger, and even your silence.

But unless you want to see Dad in a coffin soon, I suggest you bloody well have it out with me here and now.'

'I've got nothing more to say to you.'

'Yes, you do,' Rosie said, shifting to block her passage as Evie tried to sidestep her.

Rosie began to wipe at tears she couldn't stem.

'Those won't work on me, Rosie.'

'They're not for you. They're for Dad, for me . . . even, I suppose, for Max.'

'Don't you dare feel sorry for him. You caused this.'

'No, Evie. I caused his arrest but I didn't make him a spy. I'm deeply sorry for my part in this. If I could turn back time I would, because I love you and Dad. There is no one else in my life and perhaps that's my problem. You've never had any trouble attracting men.'

'What?'

Rosie shrugged. 'It's true. You just aren't aware of yourself or how people are drawn to you. I don't have that quality, Evie. I'd give anything to have it, but I wasn't blessed with that magnetic something that has put two engagement rings on your finger and not so much as a long-lasting relationship for me.'

Evie said nothing but it was a startling new perspective.

'I'm jealous, I'm childish, I'm spoilt, I'm pretty useless at most things, but that's because you are everything I'm not. I walk in your shadow, Evie. And Roger, or Max – whatever his name is – was simply final, hurtful proof that I don't match up to you. It was a mental slap in the face that was still stinging when Dad mentioned your phone call.'

'Why are you telling me this? It won't bring him back, it won't change how I'm feeling, it won't stop him being accused of treason, Rosie.' Her voice broke and she had to put her hand to her mouth as she gulped; she did not want to cry in front of her sister.

'I'm so sorry, Evie. But can I ask you, what would you have done if you were me?'

The question caught her by surprise. Rosie was full of insight today, it seemed. 'I don't even know why I'm asking because I know full well what you would have done. You would have gone all the way to London yourself, if necessary, to tell the government that you knew who the spy was. He was romancing your sister. Take away the jealousy and spitefulness that I showed yesterday, Evie, and you're still left with the fact that I took the right action – for all the wrong reasons, admittedly. Nevertheless, it was my patriotic duty. And I don't know how you planned to convince our father because Dad has already admitted to me that he had every intention of forcing your hand. He would not have let Roger—'

'His name's Max.'

Her sister raised a hand; half surrender, half warning. 'I want to hear you say that you would not have acted any differently if the roles were reversed. Come on, look me in the eye and tell me you would have waited, would have kept the secret, would have tolerated the notion that a German spy was wooing your sister and potentially using her as cover while the police hunted for him.' They stared into each other's near-identical blue eyes, the familiar prominent limbal rings of navy encircling irises the colour of a summer sky. As afternoon slipped towards evening, the colour of their eyes turned cold.

'What do you want me to actually say, Rosie?'

'I want you to admit the truth.'

'Let you off the hook?'

She shook her head. 'Evie, this is hurting Dad. Really hurting him. I can't believe you would be that cruel to him. You've never been cruel – you've always been the kind, sensitive one. He's counting on that.'

'That I forgive you?'

'Of course!' Rosie snapped, as though her sister was acting foolish. 'There is nothing else to do. Hating me doesn't get Max back. Hating me simply bangs nails into Dad's coffin. And my point is, while I deserve your wrath for talking out of turn, I'll call you a liar and walk away from Levisham myself if you don't admit the truth.'

She was back on the precipice. Teetering. It felt momentarily tragic that for the first time her sister was behaving as her equal – and really quite impressive – she couldn't have liked her any less for being so clear-thinking in that moment. But she also couldn't escape the truth of Rosie's words. And that truth needed her to be the grown-up she claimed to be, who could admit as much.

'I would have done the same,' she said, her throat not closing and the world not collapsing on her.

To her credit, Rosie did not laugh or point, or clap her hands with glee or give any sort of sound of ugly satisfaction. She simply looked down, her shoulders slumping. 'Let me help you. I don't know how but let me help find ways to support you through this.'

All her animosity towards Rosie seemed to leave in a single sigh. Losing her family would be the knockout blow of a fight she was already losing. 'I'll just finish up here,' she said uselessly.

'You've cleaned that counter . . . twice.'

'Have I?' she said absently. 'Then I suppose it's time to think about getting some supper ready.'

'There's some stew left over, and we have fresh bread. We can make do, Evie. I think you're tired.'

'I'm not tired, Rosie. What I am is lost.'

'He spied for Germany . . . on Britain. Tell that to Joe and see if he has much sympathy. Our own father put his life on the line every day for nearly four years to protect countries that Germany was bullying. Why do you think any of us should feel sorry for him? It's you we feel for. Stop protecting him.'

'I just know the truth of Max. It was the ambush and the sneaky spilling of something I needed to sort out first in my mind that has sent me into this spiral.'

'Yes, and for that I am horribly ashamed of myself and I will do everything I can for the rest of my life to make amends. But it does not undo the fact that the man you thought you knew was tricking all of us.' Rosie suddenly grabbed her into a hug, sobbing. 'You've had so much grief in your life. And now this. Let me help.'

They were both weeping now and Evie, as she always had done with Rosie, found her composure and hugged her little sister back. The thing that had been orbiting the rim of her mind was slowing and in so doing was becoming visible, more tangible. 'I'm going to find a way to help Max.'

'How?'

She gave a watery smile. 'I don't know but I think he would do the same for me.'

'He's a traitor, Evie.'

She shook her head. 'It's about perspective. I can see how most people would only see it that way . . . but I know him—'

'You don't. You have barely had any time in each other's company,' her sister pleaded. 'He needs to face his fate.'

'I know what matters about him. I know his heart, Rosie, and there's nothing dark about it. I said yes to marriage and I intend—'

Rosie gasped. 'The ring.' She pointed. 'What will you do with it?'

Evie stared at the diamond ring she'd forgotten she'd removed hours earlier and put in a tiny china dish on the kitchen windowsill. There it was, catching the late afternoon sunlight and spraying sparkles of fractured light around the room. 'It's so beautiful,' Rosie admitted. 'I suppose you could sell it.' This sounded more like the Rosie she knew, and her sister even wore a slightly gleeful expression in an attempt to distract them from all the hurt.

Evie cut her sister a look of unbridled exasperation. 'This belonged to his mother. I'll need to somehow get it back to him.' She didn't see her father arrive quietly. 'The why of his actions. That's what there is to know. No one just makes up their own mind to spy on another country. And you forget, he's English.'

'Not with a name like Maximillian Ryker! I heard you tell Dad.'

'It suits him better than Roger, to be honest,' she murmured. 'I rather like the name Max . . . and Ryker is just the Germanic version of Richard and he was probably named that after his father's side. Please let's not forget that his mother is English.'

'Don't forget? Honestly, Evie, I love you and I am desperately sorry for hurting you and that your marriage to Mr Right has gone so wrong. But truly, I couldn't care less about him. He's probably getting paid plenty to use that clever English accent and look like one of us.'

'He *is* one of us,' she snapped, but quickly regained her composure, finally noticing her father in the doorway. 'But he's been compromised.'

Rosie looked chastened but still managed to pull a face that mocked her.

'Now, what's all this talk, Evie?' her father asked.

She moved her gaze from the sparkling ring. 'Max told me some things that have got me thinking.'

'Such as?' Rosie demanded.

'I told you, Dad, he's a widower.'

Rosie gasped.

'Well, his wife died in childbirth and so did his daughter. He has a young son who he is now entirely responsible for.'

They were both frowning.

'Jonas – that's his name – is half Jewish.'

She could see her father catching on fast.

'It doesn't matter that Max is British-born, or has a German father with a proud Prussian heritage. Jonas has a Jewish mother and that condemns him to who knows what.'

Her father was nodding; he understood, had listened alongside her to all the damning reports coming out of Germany.

'So?' Rosie said, presumably uninformed.

'So they – they being the Nazi government – have taken Jonas away from his father and they are using him as a bargaining chip to get Max to do their bidding. If he doesn't, Jonas will be sent to the fate of all Jews, and I really don't know what that means except many are fleeing, many are already dead and there is certainly a sense of dread among those who remain in Germany.'

'The German government is blackmailing Hall?' her father said incredulously.

'Exactly that. A six-year-old is expendable, apparently, so long as it gets them what they want. And right now they want information on British railways. But here's the truth. Max has been feeding them gibberish the whole time he's been supposedly spying.'

Her father's mouth was open and even Rosie's eyes glittered with intrigue. 'He's loyal to Britain so he's skewing the truth, pretending to give them valuable information, all of it close enough but actually rubbish, while he keeps Jonas safe and works out how to get him out of their clutches.'

They both looked astonished, perhaps even angered that she hadn't mentioned any of this to them before. 'And I'm sorry I didn't say any of this earlier but my mind has been scattered and I've needed to gather myself together, find a way through the shock.'

'And you trust this blackmail story?' Rosie asked before their father could say anything. 'We know he's lied, so he's going to say anything at all that might wriggle around the truth of what he was up to. One of the constables told me that they'll probably hang him.'

Evie retched. It came out of nowhere. She spun around and gagged over the sink. Nothing came out, fortunately, but a sense of hopeless wretchedness gripped her.

'Rosie!' her father snapped. 'Go on with you, saying rubbish like that.'

'It's not rubbish, Dad. We have to face this. What's more, one of those men in the suits agreed. It's treason and the price for that is life . . . and he qualified to me that this does not mean behind bars.'

Evie let out a groan that sounded like an animal in pain. She sensed her father ushering her sister away and then his arm was around her shuddering shoulders.

'Listen, my darling, none of this is your doing, and there is nothing more you can do for Roger.'

'His name is Max.'

Her father gave a grumpy and unintelligible mumble.

'I want to give his ring back.'

'Well, I don't know how. I suppose we could ask Harry—'

'No. I'm going to London.'

The unidentified intruder on her thoughts stopped dead. And she saw its final shape. It was the train to King's Cross. It was a building in Whitehall. It was a confrontation with Elliott or whoever would listen to her argue for Max Hall's life.

He swung her around. 'Evie, whatever for?'

Suddenly it all made sense and the path was clear. 'I need to see him. I wish to return his ring to him, not to someone else. And I have things to say to him and to Mr Elliott.'

'This is government business now, Evie darling. Even the Crown might be involved. I don't know how these things work but it's going to be a diplomatic incident. You really don't want to be involved.'

'I already am involved, Dad. I'm engaged to him.'

'Oh, for a few hours,' her father spluttered.

'No, Dad. In here.' She placed a hand over her heart. 'I fell in love with him. I agreed to marry him. I wanted to spend my life with him. And that was snatched away in the blink of an eye. Dad, he was coerced, and they used the most powerful form of persuasion – they threatened his child. Wouldn't you spy on England if they held a gun to *my* temple?' She pointed a make-believe gun at herself. 'Well, would you? Wouldn't you give everything, including your life, for Rosie and me?'

'Of course,' he replied gravely.

'Why is Max any different?'

'We don't know if it's the truth.'

'I'm leaving in the morning.' She twisted gently out of his embrace. 'Don't try and stop me. Help me instead.'

'But you don't know where to go.'

'I have a telephone number for Mr Elliott and I will not be ignored or fobbed off. I shall turn up on his doorstep unannounced if necessary. Just watch me.'

Rosie had been lurking by the doorway and had obviously overheard. 'Gosh, Evie, you sound so brave. I feel quite proud of you, actually.'

'I'm not brave. I'm angry. I'm going to make Whitehall listen to me.'

8

The ringing phone was answered. 'Clive Elliott.'

'Mr Elliott, this is Evelyn Armstrong.'

There was a pause as he made the connection. 'From Levisham? Er, yes, of course. Hello, Mrs Armstrong. Is everything all right?'

'Not really. I wish to see my fiancé, please.'

Another pause. She refused to fill it.

'Well, that is rather impossible, actually. Mr Hall is now a prisoner of His Majesty.'

'Even so, Mr Elliott, I have a right to visit the man I am engaged to marry. He's not a murderer—'

'We don't know what he is, Mrs Armstrong.'

'Mr Elliott, I am catching the eleven o'clock train to York and on to London. If you will not permit me to see Mr Hall, instead of coming to you, I shall go straight to Fleet Street and tell every reporter who wants to hear it my side of the story. I will be sure to let them know of your obstinacy and cruelty. I will tell them everything that Mr Hall has told me in private and that your people may be ignoring. I have a brilliant memory, Mr Elliott, for detail. Plus, I'm staring at your card and I will happily provide your telephone number to the press and indeed anyone else who would like it.'

'That is not becoming behaviour, Mrs Armstrong, and it is bordering on treason.'

'Oh, for heaven's sake, Mr Elliott. Do you plan to execute *me* now for making the perfectly reasonable request to see my fiancé before you hang him?'

'We're not hanging anyone, Mrs—'

'Good. Then please let me see him. I have something precious of his that I'd like to return. I would also like to talk to you.'

'Me?'

'Yes, sir.'

'What about?'

'What do you think I want to talk about, Mr Hall?' she demanded, her testiness racing the hundreds of miles to London where he sat and cleared his throat.

'I don't believe that you and I need to discuss him.'

'Then who is your superior, Mr Elliott? Don't test me because I will find out and I will barge into his gentlemen's club and embarrass both of you.'

'Good grief. You have more pluck than all the women I know rolled into one.'

'It's not pluck, Mr Elliott, it's mettle. I'm not asking for anything but some time with Mr Hall, and I'm more than comfortable for you to be in the room with us when I speak with him.'

'All right, Mrs Armstrong. The circumstances are unique, so I'll make an exception.'

'Thank you. May I have an address, please?'

'Give me the details of your train. I will have you met and brought here.'

'Even better.' She gave him the details with a triumphant smile.

An hour later, the pungent smell of the elderflowers that

grew wild around the station was pushed away by the hot scent of industrial lubricant and steam as the train arrived with its accompanying bluster.

'There's still time to change your mind,' her father tried, helping her on board.

'I'll only be gone overnight. I have the address of a guesthouse for women near King's Cross, and Mr Elliott has arranged for me to be met at the station.'

'Be careful, Evie. Telephone us from London.'

She nodded and blew him a kiss. 'Now, wave your flag, Dad, or you'll be late for perhaps only the second time in your life.'

He smiled. They both remembered that he was late waving out the train on the day she was born, and one of the first sounds Evie had heard outside of her mother was the screech of her father's whistle as he held his newborn child less than an hour after her birth. He stepped back, blew his whistle and raised his green flag.

The train jerked; steam billowed all around – she lost her father for a moment in the vapours – and then the train sighed and began its slow haul out of Levisham towards London via York, and she wasn't sure what would happen after that.

She was met on the platform by a man in a suit, overcoat and trilby. He was a younger version of the man who had come to pick up Max – that was how she thought of him now. He was now no longer Roger in her mind but firmly Max Hall. She twisted the ring on her finger. It seemed the safest way to transport it to London.

'Mrs Armstrong?' He smiled.

'Yes.'

He lifted his hat. 'I'm Edward – Ed – Cartwright. Mr Elliott sent me to pick you up.'

'That's very kind, thank you.'

'May I?' He gestured towards the tapestry bag, just large enough to carry her modest overnight needs.

'Thank you,' she said as he bent to pick it up.

She touched her small straw boater that sat neatly against her hair. It had been her father's birthday gift, which she'd loved on sight during a trip into York. The thinnest of black netting was expertly positioned by its maker to come just below her eyes and accentuate them. The thick satin ribbon was glossy black to match the light wool overcoat. It wasn't cold in London for a Yorkshire girl, she thought, but still, she was glad of the extra layer.

'How was your journey?' he asked.

'It was pleasant, thank you, although my mind's been in a bit of a whirl,' she admitted. 'I can't remember actually making any of the stops or changing trains.'

'Well, I'm not privy to the details of your visit, Mrs Armstrong – only that it's uncommon, to say the least, to take an outsider into SIS, so I suspect we can forgive your whirling thoughts.' He smiled kindly and she liked him for the generosity that was so lacking in his superiors.

'SIS?'

'Er, Secret Intelligence Service.' He looked instantly embarrassed, as though he'd said too much.

'The man I was to marry is apparently a German spy,' she said, to put him at his ease, knowing she too had revealed too much, but she didn't care about Clive Elliott's secrecy.

'Oh, that's unfortunate. I'm so sorry. Here,' he said, 'if you'll wait a moment, I'll fetch us a taxi.'

She gave a small smile. Once her eyes would have been wide with wonder and excitement. London. At last! But now here she was, and it held no interest for her. She had developed permanent nausea, it felt like, and her belly was roiling. Nerves she'd never known existed were on edge, and when something metal clanged loudly in the distance, she was startled. How ridiculous. Her whole life had been spent in and around a train station, with metal whining and sighing and jangling unexpectedly, yet she had never felt more uncomfortable or fretful as she did right now. She didn't even want to look up and take in the city. She knew the famous *Flying Scotsman* departed King's Cross for Edinburgh – Evie had seen it once and dreamed of travelling on it – but she had no interest now to turn and gaze at it, idle at the platform. She could smell fish cooking at the Restaurant & Grill Room of the busy railway station, and beneath that the meaty aroma of some sort of stew. She risked a quick look up when she heard laughter and realised the *Pullman Express* was in, and people were boarding. She yearned to travel on the gorgeous *Southern Belle* Pullman train from Brighton, and the even grander, still more exotic *Orient Express*. If she'd raised her head she might have noticed the pigeons bobbing at one another and looking down from the iron rafters, or admired the arched glazing that let in muted light across the tops of the trains. She'd have taken in the busy flows of people moving to and from the platforms. There were voices and the familiar shrieks of whistles, doors clanging shut and men yelling as they wheeled barrows of goods to the parcels office, while porters with suitcases dodged and weaved towards waiting cars and taxis. Even the brief glimpse she stole was such an overload of colour and activity that she refocused her attention onto the posters around the station, promoting everything from a new lipstick to London's latest cocktail lounge.

'Ready, Mrs Armstrong?' Ed was back. 'Follow me.'

The door swung closed on the Austin Taxicab as he clambered in after her.

'I've never been in one of these,' she admitted. 'Never been to London.'

'This is one of the new ones, called Low Loading,' Ed said with a grin. 'My uncle is a taxi driver and he still has one of the upright grands, sometimes known as a High Lot,' he said. She thought he sounded nervous but then so was she, so she appreciated his effort to make polite conversation.

'Nearly four hundred pounds to buy this beauty,' the driver said, joining in as he flicked a cigarette end onto the busy street. 'Where to, sir?'

'Fifty-four Broadway, please.'

'Right you are. Always wondered about that building.'

'Just offices.' Ed shrugged. 'International trading.'

He cut a glance her way and gave a small shrug. Evie turned to watch London going by in a grimy cacophony of vehicles, horses, double-decker buses and people. So many people!

'That's the British Museum,' Ed said softly; he leaned over to point, and she could smell the sweetish fragrance of Brylcreem that kept his neat hair strictly in place. 'As we go around the corner here on Bloomsbury Street, we shall start weaving our way towards Leicester Square.'

She craned her neck to watch the iconic museum building as they passed by, wondering if she might ever return under happier circumstances, to walk through it and see all the famous exhibits. It took them nearly forty minutes, and after lots of honking of horns and some time spent waiting around Trafalgar Square which she didn't mind, feeling her first twitch of excitement to glimpse one of London's famous monuments, they finally drew up outside a tall terracotta-coloured building.

'Here we are, sir, madam. Number fifty-four.'

Ed opened the door for Evie before he settled the bill with the taxi driver. He picked up her bag again and invited her to follow him into the building. 'This way, Mrs Armstrong.'

She stood back as Ed talked with an officious woman at a counter. She watched him withdraw a piece of paper, which the woman scanned, and then fussed with a file on her desk before looking over her half-glasses at him. She pointed and Ed turned back to Evie with a smile.

'Do you mind steps?'

'Not at all,' she said, intrigued, and followed him up four flights in all. She was glad that her trails over the moors had prepared her for this ascent.

'You're not even out of breath, Mrs Armstrong,' he remarked, impressed. 'I do this all day, so I'm used to it. You must be very fit.'

She shrugged a small smile at the compliment, unsure of how to answer him, before following him down a corridor past lots of closed doors and finally halted in front of one at the end. He tapped gently before opening it and they were greeted by another gate-keeper, Evie noted. Another woman, less hostile-looking.

'Mrs Armstrong?'

Evie nodded.

'We've been expecting you. Thank you, Ed. I'll show Mrs Armstrong through.'

Evie smiled at her escort. 'I'm very grateful for your help,' she said.

He grinned. 'I'll leave your luggage here,' Ed offered.

'I'll look after it,' the woman said. 'I'm Andrea Clarke, Mr Elliott's secretary.' Ed left as Andrea tapped on the inner door.

'Come in.' Evie recognised the voice.

The door was opened, and Andrea ushered her in. 'Mrs Armstrong has arrived.'

Elliott stood and walked around his desk. 'Thank you, Miss Clarke.' She closed the door softly behind her. No beverages were offered, Evie noted, not that she felt she could keep anything down. And finally she stood in the sanctum of someone she'd come to believe was her enemy.

'Mr Elliott,' she said, refusing to cower, keeping her tone neutral.

'Good trip?'

'Tense,' she admitted. 'May I see him, please?'

'He's on his way up.'

'From where?'

'From below,' was all he said. 'Please, do take a seat.'

She did so and he returned to his chair behind the desk. Only now she gazed out through small panes of glass onto the neighbourhood around St James's Park.

Evie was aware of Elliott making a steeple of his hands, but she only turned when he spoke. 'As I said, Mrs Armstrong, this is most unusual, so I will have to ask you to remain discreet about this visit.'

'Providing I have the access I want to my fiancé.'

'I'm curious as to what you might be hoping to achieve . . . I hope you understand this is a delicate situation.'

'I want to learn the truth, Mr Elliott. I hope you wish the same?'

'I do. But you need to understand that a cornered animal will try anything and everything to escape.'

'I was there, Mr Elliott, and all I saw was that Mr Hall came willingly. Made no fuss. Offered no resistance. He had ample opportunity to make a run for it, but he drove me home and was compliant with all your orders. I think we need to hear what he has to say.'

'That's exactly what we're doing, Mrs Armstrong. Listening.'

'And what have you learned?'

'He says he's being blackmailed.'

'And you don't believe him?'

He shrugged. 'I return to my original point.'

'Well, how about looking into his claims?'

Before Elliott could answer, there was a knock and suddenly Max Hall was standing in the doorway. He didn't look cowed, even with his arm held behind his back by a surly looking man. He was straight in his bearing to his full six feet and more; no one could have pushed past him, either, as he carried himself with his wide shoulders back . . . defiant. He clearly wasn't expecting her, though, and he smoothed his tousled hair back in an effort to neaten the blond thatch, which needed a wash and a comb. His eyes brightened and then widened at the sight of her and she felt her heart beating faster as she laid her gaze on him. She had wondered during her journey south whether all those feelings of affection may have quietly dissipated, knowing he had lied to her. Instead, they felt just as strong – perhaps even more intense. Through it all – the lies, the pain he'd caused her and her family, the future he'd taken from her after stealing her love – she realised that, for all this, her romantic feelings towards him were strengthened. And she could see nothing had changed for him either, which reassured her. This overwhelming, powerful feeling of need, desire, the determination to be at his side felt instinctive, and no matter what they were all seeing in Max, she was sure she sensed the truth of him.

'Hello, Max,' she said softly, pleased that all tears were banished. They would not betray her in front of Whitehall's men.

He smiled. 'Evie. You look . . . beautiful.'

'Thank you.' She glanced Elliott's way.

'Right—' He cleared his throat. 'Let's allow Mrs Armstrong to have a few minutes with Mr Hall, shall we, Johnson?' Elliott dredged up a twitch of a polite smile. 'Ten minutes, Mrs Armstrong, and then I believe I have discharged all necessary courtesies to you and your family.'

She loathed Elliott at least one hundred times more than she had yesterday.

'Thank you, Mr Elliott. Do we remain here or . . . go below?' she said, not disguising her sarcasm at his earlier use of the word.

'Here is fine, and I've cleared my desk accordingly,' he noted, throwing a warning look Max's way, as though he anticipated that the German spy might try a last-ditch effort to glean information.

She was delighted at finding a genuinely wry smile for Elliott. 'I promise I won't let him open any drawers,' she said in a droll tone.

Elliott left without another word, taking the silent Johnson with him. She wondered if they were both listening on the other side of the door as they closed it. And then she was alone again with Max, whose gaze searched her face, and she read pain in his eyes.

'How are you being treated?' she began, glad to find something to get them started.

'Fine.'

'Apparently they've got you below, whatever that means.'

'Behind bars,' he qualified.

She hadn't grasped that. 'A cell?'

He shrugged. 'How's everything at Levisham?'

'Exactly as you'd imagine. Nothing much changes there. Plenty of disappointment, of course.' She couldn't help the truth, and even that she was understating.

He nodded. 'I don't know how many different ways to say I'm sorry.'

'Don't try,' she replied. A silence gave a long yawn between them.

'Why are you here?' He frowned.

'Oh,' she said, stung into action. 'Er, to give you this.' She twisted the ring off her finger and held it out towards him. 'I felt I should . . . you know, return it.' He didn't reach for it. 'Do take it,' she tried.

'I don't want it back.'

'Well, I really shouldn't keep it.' She knew she didn't sound convinced. 'It's your mother's, let's not forget,' she said, trying very hard to not let any bitterness enter her tone.

'I really don't need it. I'm not asking you to wear it but I'd rather you had it – sell it, if you wish.'

'Max, you—'

'Evie, I'm to be executed.'

9

The blunt words hit her as effectively as if Clive Elliott had walked back in and swung a mallet at her. Everything stilled. The doves cooing at the window, the noise of traffic filtering up from the street, the muted sounds within the building from floors above and below . . . even the hammering on the anvil of her heart stopped. There was a thick, dread silence, which caused Evie to swallow. Even her vision seemed to narrow, just as it felt when a train entered a tunnel and the daylight blinked to darkness.

'Surely—' she began.

He shook his head. 'I'm afraid British secret intelligence would like to chalk up a win. I'm a good scapegoat. There will be a trial, of course, but I doubt I'm going to beat the accusation of high treason . . . or so Elliott assures me. Look, Evie,' he began in a placating tone. 'It's true I was spying, so I can hardly deny the accusation, but they won't pay any attention to my motivations, or the fact that I didn't send back a single truth. It's been lies both ways. I would never betray my birthplace for the dangerous bigot who is leading Germany.'

Evie couldn't think straight. The words *I'm to be executed* kept echoing in her mind as though bouncing around the walls of a closed space.

'There must be something we can do?'

'*We*? No, Evie. Go home. Thank you for bringing the ring. It meant I got to see you again and that's what I'll hang on to after you've gone.'

The word 'hang' was all she heard for the next few heartbeats.

'I feel honoured, given how badly I've hurt you, that you came.'

Her resolve to not let a good man die for no reason intensified. 'Max, no! We can't let this happen.'

'Evie. It would help if I knew you might forgive me for lying to you.'

She glanced up into his face to see a broken man; all of his pride and courage from moments earlier had been stripped away. He would have stayed strong through his arrest and interrogation but having her present had smashed through his defences. Now he appeared exposed . . . vulnerable.

'I can't explain how I feel. I'm hurt, yes, but I'm angry too, Max. I know too many who lost their lives during the Great War and so many who have come home and aren't the same; they might as well have died over there. You can't imagine what it feels like to know I fell in love with someone who is betraying those people and my life, my country, everything I love.' She said this deliberately to make him tell her again – she had to hear it again; be sure of him again while she was focused and rational, no longer in shock.

'I promise you on everything I love – on Jonas's life – that I have not given the Nazi government anything of use. I've deliberately sabotaged every word of my relays, so all information is corrupted in some way. No matter what happens, just know that in your heart.'

It was all she needed to hear. 'Tell them this! Tell them you've actually been working in Britain's favour by feeding the Germans your lies.'

'Elliott is not listening. He wants to see me hang.' Now the word felt like a bruise being deliberately pressed.

Her lips pursed as she frowned. 'Right,' she said, sounding determined.

'Where are you going?' he asked, astonished.

'To fight, like you should.'

'How?' He looked lost.

'Our ten minutes is up. If we're going to save you from a trial and . . .' She couldn't say it; dared not contemplate his execution again. 'I'm going to find someone who will listen.'

'I won't be here when you get back.'

She swung around, eyes glittering with an idea that was coalescing in her mind. She needed a few minutes alone to think it through. 'Tell Mr Elliott that I haven't finished with him and that if he doesn't receive me on my return shortly, I shall go straight to Fleet Street. Promise him that I shall ensure no newspaper editor will be able to resist the weeping bride-to-be when I tell them my story and how badly Britain's Secret Intelligence Service is behaving. I'll give them everything, including his name, his secretary's and exactly which floor they sit on in this building! They won't be secret any longer.' Evie didn't wait for him to reply, casting a 'trust me' smile at his flabbergasted expression, and closed the door behind her.

'Mrs Armstrong?' Elliott's assistant enquired. 'Is everything all right?'

'Yes, er . . . it's Andrea, isn't it?'

The woman beamed at her good recall, and Evie imagined that Andrea had probably got used to being invisible around Elliott.

'I wonder, do you have a manila envelope I might use, please?'

'Of course.' She opened a drawer and pulled out a single envelope. 'Might this do?'

'Perfect. Thank you. Um, Andrea, I am planning to continue my conversation with Mr Elliott. Would you excuse me so that I can use the ladies' room, please?'

'It's down the hall to the right. I'm sorry we didn't offer you the facilities on arrival, Mrs Armstrong. Most remiss of us.'

'I'm fine. Back shortly. Thank you for the envelope.' She stepped out into the hall and could see Elliott on approach, although he didn't see her as he was deep in conversation with an offsider. She fled towards the bathroom, hurrying around the corner to the right. But there she stopped, digging in her handbag for a pen. She scribbled her name on the front of the envelope so it looked official, and then doing her best to appear casual should anyone suddenly arrive into view, she peeped around the corner.

It felt somehow impossible to be contemplating such a thing but she was in motion, beyond any reasoning but her own. Elliott was nowhere. Time to backtrack. She followed her nose back to the sweeping staircase and continued the ascent up a couple of flights, presuming that the higher the level, the higher the office of the people moving around on it.

She reached a landing and deliberately pasted a frown on her face, as though she was meant to be here but working out in which direction to move, although if she was honest, it didn't take much effort. This level was much quieter. A couple of people speaking in hushed tones fell silent as they moved past her, picking up their conversation only when they were out of earshot.

Yes, she thought, *I'm getting close to where I need to be.*

Logic told her the senior staff would be at the end of th
building, where the corner offices gave the best views over I
They would also be to the front of the building, sh
took her bearings before setting off, hoping she a

in her stride while still giving the look of the new girl, bewildered by the building's warren of offices.

A man of around her age turned the corner. He was wearing spectacles and holding a clutch of files. She frowned deeper to herself, pausing to take stock.

'Are you all right?' He paused as they drew level. 'You look lost.'

It had worked. 'Do I? That bad? I've been sent from another office and this is my first time at Broadway, so I haven't a clue where I am.'

'Oh gosh, let me help. I'm Michael.'

'Evie.' She smiled and allowed a momentary awkward pause.

'Who are you looking for?'

'That's the thing, I don't really know. Mr Elliott told me to find his boss and give this to him.' She waved the envelope without really showing him anything more than vague writing scrawled on its front.

'Clive Elliott?'

'Yes. Andrea's very busy with that Max Hall they've brought down from Yorkshire. And I offered to run the errand but realise I've got no clue. I'm sorry,' she said, deliberately rushing her words, so he couldn't respond. 'I probably shouldn't have said what I have. I know how tight-lipped we have to be here.'

'That's all right. You've obviously got clearance, and we know about the German spy.'

All of a sudden that title for Max offended her; it was accurate, but she wanted someone to listen, let him fully explain. She did not allow her consternation to show. 'Phew,' she said, beaming her most disarming smile. He fell for it. She saw his eyes widen with pleasure. 'Any idea where I should drop this?'

He nodded. 'Down this corridor to the end. That furthest door. Mary Sharpe is the assistant to Elliott's boss, Mr Hugh Leadbetter, and she can certainly take that for you.'

'Hugh Leadbetter,' she repeated. 'You've been very kind, Michael, thank you.'

Michael grinned. 'My pleasure. Are you down for long?'

'A few days.'

'Well, perhaps we'll see each other in the canteen?'

'I certainly hope so,' she said, affecting the sort of coquettish body language she'd watched her sister display for most of their adult lives . . . and felt amazed to watch it work, like magic on poor Michael. Toast, as Rosie would say.

He pointed again. 'Have a great day, Evie.'

She walked on, reminding herself to remember the influence she could exert through her appearance and bearing. If you acted like you belonged, then others wouldn't notice you; she could hide in plain sight.

At the office door she took a steadying breath and knocked. There was no answer. She tried again with no result. Steeling herself, she risked opening the door to find the office empty. It was similar to Elliott's anteroom, where Andrea worked, except it was larger, more impressive. It seemed Mary Sharpe was running an errand. Excellent! From the other side of the door she heard a man's voice. It had to be Leadbetter, her target.

No point in wavering now, she told herself. *Come on, Evie – a man's life is in the balance here . . . the man you love*. Without further hesitation she crossed the carpet and rapped on the door. Not waiting for permission, she turned the handle and opened it.

'Mr Leadbetter?'

A silver-haired man with a neatly trimmed beard and a lit cigarette in his hand looked at her, astonished.

'Bloody hell! I'm giving dictation, if you don't mind.'

'So I can see,' she said, turning a smile on the woman, who had to be Mary Sharpe, glancing back with a perplexed expression from behind her boss's shoulder. It didn't seem like dictation, given Mary was on the same side of the desk, but it didn't look like they were up to anything they shouldn't be; probably sharing some familiar conversation. But in the next heartbeat she decided she might as well use their guilty expressions and discomfort. 'I'm sorry to intrude on a private moment . . .' She waited and allowed them both to air sounds of offence. Leadbetter began to bluster but she stopped him.

'Mr Leadbetter, my name is Evelyn Armstrong and I've come down from Yorkshire today.'

He blinked, trying to work out how that affected him. 'To see me? We weren't expecting . . .' Leadbetter looked to his secretary as she returned to her side of the desk. She too was frowning and shaking her head. 'I have no appointment for you, Mrs Armstrong,' Leadbetter said.

'Spies and their wives don't make them, I'm sure,' she said cryptically. Evie was feeling her way through here, privately shocked that she'd got so close to the man who might be able to exert some pressure. She watched Leadbetter repeat her words silently, as though trying to make sense of them. 'Let me get to the point, Mr Leadbetter.'

'Do, please,' he said, sounding baffled. 'Er, thank you, Miss Sharpe.'

Mary nodded to them both and left, stoking Evie's sense of victory. Now she had him. *Channel Rosie?* she wondered. No. Leadbetter wouldn't respond to flirting. He would respond to directness. *Be confident and convincing*, she told herself.

'How can I help you, Mrs . . .?' He'd already forgotten.

'Armstrong.'

'Mrs Armstrong,' he said, relieved.

'Mr Leadbetter, I am . . . was . . . engaged to be married.'

'I see,' he said, trying to sound intrigued but looking no wiser; he was more confused than ever, in fact, especially as she used the honorific of a married woman.

'I am a widow,' she explained. He nodded his understanding, not that it made the reason for her presence any clearer. She hurried on. 'I am an excellent judge of character, sir, and the man I agreed to marry struck me as honest, upright – patriotic.'

He frowned, perhaps beginning to catch on.

'Max Hall has been arrested as a German spy and you are holding him somewhere in this building as a prisoner.'

'I'm going to stop you there, Mrs Armstrong, and—'

'No, sir, you will not fob me off as your subordinate Mr Elliott has done. I refuse to be silent and I will tell you what I have told him.' She explained her threat to tell her story at Fleet Street.

'Ah, now we come to it,' he said, his tone turning neutral. 'You would jeopardise this special unit of government?'

'I would prefer not to. I would prefer that you just listened to me and my idea.'

He opened his palms. 'Go ahead.'

Evie laid out a lot of what she'd learned from Max.

'Let me get this right. He is a spy but has been lying to them?'

'Exactly, sir. He is a patriot, but he is being blackmailed in the worst way. Do you have children, Mr Leadbetter?'

He looked baffled by her switch in topic. 'I have three. I even have a grandchild, if you're so interested.'

'And you love them?'

'Of course! What kind of question is that?'

Evie nodded. 'And would you do anything to save their lives? Give your own, perhaps? Compromise yourself if you had to?'

His gaze narrowed; he knew he was being cornered. He didn't reply but waited.

She obliged. 'Adolf Hitler's henchmen have not just threatened the wellbeing of Max's son, but they have removed him to the care of a Nazi supporter. Now, it's not a long stretch to understand the threat here. Jonas Hall, Mr Leadbetter, has two grandparents on his father's side, one of whom is English, the other German. But on his mother's side, they are Jewish.'

She watched his understanding dawn.

'They are using the jeopardy of that lad like a stick to coerce Max into doing exactly what they need.' She took a breath but didn't let him speak, rushing on. 'He has the ability to move freely around Britain as an Englishman; he has the knowledge of the railways they want, plus he's an engineer so he's handy in other respects . . . and his most vulnerable point is that he is the widower of a Jewish woman. I doubt anyone in Germany who is Jewish is feeling safe right now, and Max is understandably fearful for his son, who is in the care of Nazi followers. But still he defies them, Mr Leadbetter. In spite of the peril to his child, he has risked everything to lie to those bullies. And he is more than prepared to show you everything he has communicated, to prove to you that every word of it is false. As he says, all the intelligence is credible but ever so slightly wrong. If you talk to him, you'll understand he's no Nazi supporter. If anything, he's a British patriot.'

'Why should you care, Mrs Armstrong? Surely he has wounded your pride, if nothing else?'

'Quite simply because I love him in the same way that you no doubt love your wife and would let no harm come to her. I don't let many people into my inner circle but I did let Max Hall into my life and I will not allow him to lose his right to be heard.'

He opened his palms, as if to ask why she was pursuing this so fervently. 'You can understand my confusion, Mrs Armstrong. A man we all believe has set out to deliberately—'

'I don't believe I am part of that equation. Max Hall did not know I existed before he returned to England on this mission. He is – dare I say – as much a victim of our romance as I am.'

'But he has been caught spying!'

She wanted to throw her hands up with frustration, but she

remained calm. 'But sending back deliberately incorrect information, to keep that enemy in the dark, surely shows his true colours? He is loyal to Britain. I am as patriotic as you are, but I'm not blinkered, and I think if you're as clever as your rank tells me you are, Mr Leadbetter, then you'll overrule Mr Elliott's decision to have Max Hall executed and instead put this English patriot to work for you.'

He stared back at her with astonishment. 'Work for the Secret Service?'

She nodded.

'Mrs Armstrong, I—'

'Hear me out,' she pleaded. 'I know it's a wild idea, but no one in Germany knows that Max has been caught. The truth is, I think he wanted to be caught, as I know he tried so many times to tell me.' That was a slight stretch of the truth, but she needed to latch on to anything that could give her argument purchase in Leadbetter's mind. 'Why don't you use Max to continue to feed false information to the Nazis? I know he would welcome the opportunity.'

'To save his skin?'

'If you met him, I think you'd discover that all he's trying to do is keep his son safe, and he would gladly give his life to do so. I do believe saving his own skin is his last priority right now.'

'We call this a *double agent*, Mrs Armstrong.'

'Well, if you have a term for it, then it's hardly such a wild idea. Why not take advantage of a potential double agent sitting downstairs and twiddling his thumbs right now?' She didn't mean to make light of Max's situation, but it seemed to work.

He gave a sly twitch of a grin. 'The practice of spying is as old as prostitution, Mrs Armstrong. I can take you back centuries and describe incredible creativity in how secrets were passed on.'

'Make Max your double agent, Mr Leadbetter – surely that's more useful than killing a patriot for telling lies to the enemy.'

'If that's true.' He held up a hand to stop her rebuttal. 'It has credence, I'll give you that.' He sat back and steepled his hands. *Ah, so that's where Elliott learned it*, she thought, *copying his boss*. 'The rub is, Mrs Armstrong, the Germans are hardly stupid. In fact, they are extremely wary – as cautious as we are. And I imagine they would be very suspicious of your fiancé if he suddenly started sending back lots of information.'

'Then drip-feed it.' She frowned as if it was obvious.

'The game of spying is not nearly as simple as you consider it to be. And deploying a double agent is like a chess game. Both handlers are involved.' He shrugged. 'Besides, Mr Hall is of no use to me sending information to Germany about British railways.'

Evie felt a tremble of fear begin. She thought she'd won him over but perhaps he had just politely heard her out, and was going to drop the executioner's axe anyway.

'Why?' she asked, trying to keep the begging tone out of her voice.

'Because he is of more use to us *in* Germany than here in Britain sending back false information. What we would appreciate is a spy on the ground over there, reporting back what we need.'

'Then send him back,' she countered, as if it all made such simple mathematical sense. If she had to lose him, she'd rather it was this way than to the hangman's noose. 'He wants to be with his son; make use of him.'

'He's of no use to us.'

'Why?' She was beginning to sound frustrated.

'Quite simply because we would never fully trust him,' he replied evenly, flicking at something on his suit collar.

She dropped her head, hating that she felt defeated. The thought of Max being executed was appalling; she was losing her argument and potentially his life with it.

'You're very plucky, Mrs Armstrong. And resourceful. I have

no idea how you even managed to find me, let alone break into this room. I admire you.'

Something about his expression caught her attention. There was the vaguest sense of amusement . . . no, it was more like intrigue, as though he was weighing up the value of Max. *Think, Evie, think!* It was the voice in the distance again, forcing her to use her wits as she'd done minutes earlier in breaking into Leadbetter's office. She had nothing left to give him . . . except herself.

The thought hit like someone had thrown a rock at her. She gasped to herself, the idea colliding with fear, with surprise, with determination. Could she? Would she?

'Mrs Arm—'

'Do you trust me, Mr Leadbetter?'

'Trust you?' He grinned. 'I think you're rather splendid and resourceful. You've shown cunning and real front. Yes, I trust you.'

'Then hire me.'

'Ha!' he exploded, genuinely amused. 'As what?'

'Your spy in Germany.' There. She'd said it.

'I beg your pardon?'

'Make me your spy in Germany,' she repeated. 'Use me instead.' She tried to shrug nonchalantly, although she wasn't convinced she'd pulled it off. 'I go as Max's new wife. Tell me what I have to do and I'll do my best as a loyal member of the British public to help your cause.'

10

Leadbetter blinked with consternation that seemed to be flavoured with intrigue. She could almost hear the idea being repeated in his thoughts, the cogs of his mind turning it over, considering it.

'When did you plan to marry?'

She could hardly dare believe he hadn't laughed in her face. 'Immediately. He was arrested the day after we became engaged. We were returning to Levisham to tell my family and make arrangements. I did not want a big wedding. I simply wanted to marry this man and I would have done so the next day if he wasn't trapped in London.'

Leadbetter actually smiled. 'Levisham. Pretty little railway station,' he remarked. 'Such a lovely part of our country.'

'My father's the stationmaster there,' she said, frowning, wondering if this was a new pathway into his good books for her and Max. 'I was born and raised there.'

'Good grief, you lucky child. I think I'd have quite liked to be a stationmaster.'

She found a smile for him. 'You and every other little boy growing up, I think, including Max Hall.'

He nodded. 'And your family?'

'My father and sister. My mother died when I was young, just after she'd had Rosie.'

'He raised you alone?'

'He had help.' She shrugged. 'A woman we thought of as our grandmother was actually a German refugee from before the Great War. She lived with us until she died and—'

'Mrs Armstrong,' he interjected, leaning forward. 'Might I ask if you speak German?'

She nodded. 'Yes, I'm fluent, as is my sister. I think I can probably curse in German, too. It's why I think I could do what I'm suggesting, as—'

'Good grief. Wait here, would you? Don't go wandering.' He stood up from his desk, the cigarette long ago burned out in the ashtray unsmoked, and he muttered something to Mary, who was standing in the doorway. 'Quickly, please,' she heard him instruct her as he closed the door. He returned his attention to Evie. 'I've asked Clive Elliott to join us.'

Hope swelled within her.

When Elliott arrived some fifteen minutes later, it was with Max in tow. He was led in, handcuffed. Max cut her a quizzical look and she gave a shrug with a soft smile.

'Are you all right?' she asked.

'Of course he's all right, Mrs Armstrong,' Elliott said, sounding condescending. 'We're not barbarians.'

'Forgive me,' she replied, just as fast. 'An hour ago I could have sworn you were talking about hanging him.' She turned her smile into something sickly sweet for Elliott. 'My mistake.'

'Children!' Leadbetter said, with an admonishing sigh. 'Take a seat, everyone.'

His office was large and airy. Sounds from the street drifted up the side of the building to tap at the window. Her good hearing picked up a burst of laughter from a woman making a high-pitched sound of amusement, but that was the only punctuation in the murmur and grind of the traffic below, and a low rumble that seemed to shake the building ever so slightly now and then. She presumed it was the Underground, rattling beneath them in the tunnels below the city.

'Let's try and play nicely, shall we?' Leadbetter said.

There was a clearing of Elliott's throat and a tight smile of guilt from Evie. She nodded to confirm she would do as he asked.

Leadbetter began. 'Mr Hall, your former fiancée has threatened us today with the exposure of her story . . . or rather, yours . . . to the ever-hungry press. If we take pride in one aspect of our work, it's our discretion. That said, perhaps Mrs Armstrong should have been a barrister, because she builds a good case for lenience to be shown in your case.' Everyone waited while Leadbetter deliberately paused for a couple of beats. 'Except as persuasive as Mrs Armstrong is, I'm afraid we cannot escape the fact that you have been rightly and appropriately arrested for spying on Britain, sending back information – truthful or not – to a country that we were locked in a massive, debilitating and ferocious war with. We lost more than a million of our brave people. And the walking wounded who did survive may never recover from their injuries, or indeed what they experienced, what they were required to do on behalf of King and country. That you have been sending secrets to a sworn enemy is treason, sir.' He paused again, taking time to blink, to sigh, to sit back and steeple his hands again. No one chose to interrupt, although Evie thought if he gave her an opportunity, she would. For now, she remained patient.

Leadbetter cleared his throat. 'Mrs Armstrong is rather impressive, Mr Hall, and it was she who posed the idea to use you as a double agent.'

Max's forehead creased, intrigued, but smoothed out soon enough as Leadbetter explained why sending Max back to Germany as a spy for Britain simply couldn't work.

'We would never trust you,' he reiterated, 'as I've explained to Mrs Armstrong. How could we know you wouldn't just be telling us the tall tales that you claim you are sending to Germany now?'

Max nodded. 'You couldn't know,' he agreed. 'It would have to be based on trust.'

Leadbetter acknowledged his honesty with a silent nod.

But Elliott pressed the point. 'Which we don't have,' he said, all too obviously, in his peevish way.

Evie cut him a look of spite, which bounced off him like a rubber ball; he was used to people disliking his manner, clearly.

'But we do have *you*, Mrs Armstrong,' Leadbetter continued, turning now to look at Evie.

'Wait . . .' Max said, frowning.

Leadbetter held up a finger. 'This is all her idea, Max. And I rather support it. Imagine what she could see for us. She could be our eyes . . . not only scrutinising you, Mr Hall – your behaviour, your information, your network of contacts – but far more importantly, Mrs Armstrong as Mrs Hall would be our spy, in the guise of the good wife of the German engineer.' Leadbetter thought about this for a heartbeat and his face creased with genuine pleasure. 'The spy's wife.' He even chuckled. 'Oh, I do like that, Clive. She could move around so innocently, so protected, so embedded in the Nazi Party's network that her information might be the price I'd be prepared to pay in exchange for your life, Mr Hall,' he said slyly, now turning his attention back to Max.

'So I leave for Germany . . . as Max's wife?' Evie repeated, suddenly terrified but determined not to show it.

Leadbetter nodded. 'That's the deal, Mrs Armstrong. You marry the man you intended to, and you travel to Germany as my brilliant spy.'

'Absolutely not!' Max responded.

'It would save your life,' he said. 'And if I'm not mistaken, that's what Mrs Armstrong's petition is all about?' He blinked, waited, and when no one denied it, he continued, turning to Evie. 'This can work, especially as you speak the language fluently. You learned it from a German, so presumably your accent will pass the scrutiny of those who may wish to appraise the adoring new wife of Max Hall.'

Max shook his head. 'Impossible! How do you expect us to pull that off?'

'Well, that's actually your problem, Max, not mine. You brought this upon yourself. As for Mrs Armstrong, you are in her debt for saving your life and giving you a fighting chance of returning to your son. You'd be wise to find ways to "pull it off".'

'I won't take her into that danger.'

'It's not your decision,' Evie objected. 'Max, this is for us . . . for Jonas.'

Leadbetter made a *tsk*-ing sound. 'Listen, Hall . . . this is your only option to remain alive, so I wouldn't be objecting if I were you.'

Max gave a sound of despair. 'I don't care about me. I do care about my son – and about Evie.' Max turned to look out of the window with frustration.

Leadbetter pressed his point. 'If they don't know your cover is blown, then there is no danger for her. She is simply the woman you met and fell in love with. She speaks German, she is a stationmaster's daughter . . . I couldn't have written the script any better myself. Look at her: beautiful, innocent, ready to be a wife and start a new life in her husband's country. What they can't know, must never know, is just how intelligent she is, how patriotic she is, and the fact that she's mine.' As he said the final word, he pointed his index finger onto the leather of his desk. 'She is *my* spy in Germany and you are nothing but her cover. So don't blow it, Max, or you'll be in a different prison, in a different country, facing a different execution, and this time you'll have your wife facing the same. I might add,' he continued conversationally, 'they executed two noblewomen in February using the blade. It's how they do it over there. Some executioners, like Carl Gröpler of Saxony, favour a short-handled axe and brute strength.' He looked from Max's horror to Evie's blanched complexion. It was clear that he was deliberately terrifying them. 'So medieval, really.'

'You bastard,' Max uttered.

Leadbetter snapped his attention back to Max, and Evie watched his navy eyes glitter with menace. 'Perhaps that is so, Mr Hall, but I'm not the one whose loyalty to his country is in question. Nor have I caused a beautiful English rose to fall under his spell and become enmeshed in his guile.'

Evie couldn't be bothered to tell Leadbetter that she needed neither his gallantry nor to be spoken of in such romantic terms.

'What I am suggesting is purely for the security of my country, and frankly I think it's a very good deal, given you were set for execution.'

'And there I was thinking there might be a trial in there somewhere, Mr Leadbetter,' Evie said, angered by his threats. She gave him a steely look of her own. 'I'm sorry but I have to agree with Mr Hall. You're all utter bastards.' She'd never used the word before. If her father could hear her language in this moment, his neat, straight hair would curl. She saved her private blushes by moving into German and cursing Leadbetter and the mother who birthed him. Max slid her an amused look.

To his credit, Leadbetter smiled. 'You see, I knew I'd made a good decision, Clive. Do you hear her? She's practically German – and with Hall as her surname, we'll embed her swiftly and easily.'

'I haven't agreed to—' Max began.

Just to spite them all, Evie reacted. 'When do we leave?' she asked, speaking over Max and winning a sly grin from Leadbetter. Perhaps he knew she'd not be able to resist this opportunity to save

Max's life . . . or perhaps he knew something about her that she didn't. She would study that later.

Leadbetter gave her a lazy glance. 'Oh, I think you should get yourselves over there for the German summer, don't you, Mrs Armstrong?'

'How do we do this?' She'd cut Max out of the discussion but could feel his shocked gaze against the side of her face.

'Evie . . .?'

'Be quiet, Max. I am getting you back safely to Germany and to Jonas. I think I'm the only one in this room who will ever be able to lie straight in bed again,' she said, looking at him briefly before turning back to Leadbetter. 'So, how do we start?'

'First things first. You need to become Mrs Hall.'

'I'd better plan my wedding, then,' she countered.

'Bravo, Mrs Armstrong. But you have no need to formalise it. I wouldn't ask you to legally marry a known traitor. No, we will have all the necessary paperwork drafted and craft the backstory for you. I'll explain that later. What I will need you to push through, no matter how hard it is, is a fake wedding breakfast so we can have photographs that attest to your happy union. Have it at Levisham. I'd like to return to that quaint Yorkshire station.'

'I wasn't planning to have you on the guest list, Mr Leadbetter.'

'No? Pity. I'm afraid you'll have quite a few strange names on your faked guest list. I suggest you keep it tight – the fewer of your real friends and family who know, the better. For caution's sake, only a handful will know the truth. To all intents, the pair of you will be married. Do you understand?'

He paused dramatically, waiting for them both to nod. Evie did so without hesitation but Max turned to her again, exasperated. 'I do not agree to this.'

'Actually, we're not asking your permission, Mr Hall,' Leadbetter confirmed. 'Unless you wish to swing on the end of a rope for treason, I suggest you take this once-in-a-lifetime opportunity to save your neck, save your child, and save your fiancée's broken heart. You're a lucky man to have such a loyal and brave woman by your side.'

'What about afterwards?' Max demanded.

'After what?'

'After you've got what you want from Evie.'

Leadbetter shrugged deeply. 'Mrs Armstrong will determine that. When we all feel we've got something out of this deal, we shall bring her home on the pretext of a holiday. By this time, presumably, you will have made arrangements for the safety of your son – and after that, Max, I couldn't give a flying fig what happens to you. You can rot in hell for all I care.'

Evie felt her throat close at the hate in his tone. She was the only obstacle standing between Max and the executioner's rope – frankly, she didn't think Leadbetter would be entertaining the idea of the double agent without her threat of exposing the matter to Fleet Street.

'Shall we set a wedding date?' he offered sweetly. 'Clive? Thoughts?'

'As soon as possible. Er . . .' He took out a tiny pocket diary and put on his spectacles to scrutinise the dates. 'How does Saturday the eleventh of July sound?' He removed his glasses and looked up expectantly.

'I think that has an auspicious ring to it,' Leadbetter said. 'Eleven in a football team, eleven men in an ancient Roman police force, and eleven happens to be my lucky number. Add to that, summer will be in full glory, so hopefully some good weather for our happy couple. A significant day indeed.' He grinned, amusing himself. No one else smiled. 'We'll drive Mr Hall up the night before. I want to make sure it's all done right, Evie – may I call you Evie?'

She shrugged as if she didn't care one way or the other.

'We shall get on with organising your passport, the travel arrangements for your honeymoon, and a photographer for the wedding. The British taxpayer will fund your wedding breakfast, so please send me your accounts. We want to make sure your album is full of wonderful photographs of your happy day. You will honeymoon in Paris for two days, and then your new husband'—he turned his attention back to Max—'will take you triumphantly home to Germany as his new bride, and perhaps not-so-triumphantly explain to his handlers that he's been compromised, his cover blown. They'll buy it – we'll make sure the discovery of his equipment is known – together with some chatter about spies in the north, so it holds water back in Berlin. Leave that all to us – we're the experts.'

'Do you mean Max has to remain here until the, er . . . wedding?'

'I'm afraid so. I can't let him out of my sight, nor will I, until I see you both off on the boat-train to Paris, where you will be observed by our people. Max?' He won his attention again. 'May I suggest that you go along with all of this – to do anything but play your role is to put Evie's life in jeopardy, and I can tell you don't wish that. But just so you know: if you do anything that compromises her cover or her security, I will personally see to it that you are killed. You've dodged one execution; you shall not dodge another if you earn it. That's my promise to you, Max,' he said, with a generous smile. 'You'll leave your child an orphan. I care only about Evie – not you, or your son.' He let that sit between them for a second, catching Evie unaware. She held her breath with surprise that he harboured this sentiment.

Max looked back at him with an iron expression; she'd never seen him more unreachable. Leadbetter had achieved nothing with the threat, but at least he was being honest, she supposed. None of them was being left in any confusion.

Leadbetter's smile died. 'So protect her with your life, Mr Hall, because it's only her life that protects the son you love.'

Later, when Max had been returned to his cell, Hugh Leadbetter took Evie to a meeting room. Over a cheese and chutney sandwich and a pot of tea, sitting across a large polished table, he spoke to her about spying as though discussing the weather for next week.

'You love this man, clearly,' Leadbetter began.

'I do. I also trust him as much as you don't.'

'Right. If your gut trusts him, then don't be afraid to use him.'

She looked at him in surprise.

'Max has contacts. Sift through them, find someone who might be useful. I'm relying on you to use your resourcefulness to know if someone might be helpful.'

'I can't just blatantly ask his friends or colleagues what they know.'

'Go out to social events with him and listen. Listen carefully. Play no cards of your own; keep them close to your chest, Evie. Have you ever played poker?'

She shook her head. 'Rummy,' she offered.

He grinned. 'Well, in poker, half the battle is not hinting in any way at what you're holding or what your strategy is going to be. Some people deliberately lose for a while to make themselves appear sloppy, unskilled, only to take the big pot at the end.'

She smiled.

'You understand what I'm saying, don't you, Evie?'

Evie nodded. 'You want me to play the innocent and charming wife with nothing much going on up here,' she said, tapping her temple.

'Exactly!' he said, sounding impressed. 'As vacant as you please. The more unworldly you sound, the less they'll notice you.

Don't be caught watching. Learn to listen without paying attention. Mirrors are brilliant – so are windows, teaspoons, anything reflective. Your naivety will be disarming and ultimately boring. That's what you want. You can move around his circle like a wife who waits for her husband's smile to light upon her.'

She gave a groaning sound.

'It will be your protection. Evie, you are to take no risks. None whatsoever. Let me confess something to you.'

'I'm listening.'

'As much as I don't want to be, and as much as the evidence speaks otherwise, I think I'm in your camp.'

She caught on. 'You trust Max.'

'"Trust" is a big word. No, I don't trust him, but I think he's telling us the truth of his situation. I do trust you, however. And I need you to keep your wits about you at all times. So lean on Max, but make your own decisions. Don't let him make them for you. In public, feel free to let him make all decisions – even be seen to order from a dinner menu for you – but behind closed doors, you make your own mind up about everything you learn, or hear, or see, or go after. He is not your keeper. I am. I am the person who will be looking after your best interests from afar. Are we agreed?'

She nodded.

'If you hear anything that makes your ears prick up, any genuine evidence of preparations for war, you are to let me know.'

'Can you explain that? I mean, we all know Hitler has violated the Treaty of Versailles several times over.'

'Indeed. But there's been no outward threat. At this stage it feels like he's sick of Germany being Europe's peasant and is determined to restore its dignity. Well, the British government is holding its breath and viewing it that way for now. So you may overhear conversations that make you believe actual preparations are being made for war—'

'Like a new railway?'

He shrugged. 'No, I was thinking more about war machinery. Being part of the engineering division, Max might be privy to information and certainly could be in contact with the various departments that might be involved in the production of that machinery.'

She frowned.

'Planes, tanks, weapons.'

'Oh, I see. And how do I let you know?'

'This is a very pretty scarf you're wearing.'

She blinked with surprise. 'Er, thank you. A gift from Max.'

'He has style. You are to hang this scarf in the window of your home in Germany – I hear you'll be living in Munich?'

She shrugged. 'I wouldn't know Munich from Berlin.'

'Hang this in your window, and one of my agents on the ground in Munich will meet you at this address.' He reached for the pad nearby and carefully wrote out an address in neat block letters.

'Carlton Teeraum,' she read aloud.

'Carlton Tearoom, yes. Quite famous, actually.'

'Why's that?'

'I hear Adolf Hitler likes to frequent this place whenever he's in Munich.'

She cut him such a shocked glance he laughed. 'Finished here?' he said, indicating the debris of their lunch.

'Thank you.'

'Come with me.' He gestured to the end of the table, where she noticed some items had been placed. Evie watched him open the door and usher in a nervous man of indeterminate age. 'Evie Armstrong, this is Allan Fisher. He's one of our clever people.'

She didn't know what that meant but cast him a welcoming smile, which Fisher struggled to return. His eyes darted busily behind his thick lenses.

'Good afternoon,' he said, pushing his heavy glasses back up to the bridge of his nose. 'Er, I've been asked to show you some tools.'

'Oh?' she said, sounding intrigued.

'That's a subminiature camera. A Minox. It's already loaded with film that can take around fifty frames, I believe.'

'Why do I need this?' she said, turning to Leadbetter.

'I don't know that you do. I am, as the Americans say, covering all bases.' He smiled disarmingly and she helplessly felt reassured. 'The inventor – a man called, rather charmingly, Walter Zapp – is a Latvian living in Estonia. Have you heard of these places?'

She nodded.

'Anyway, he rather cleverly designed the first of these. He couldn't find funding to go into proper production so he contacted the English representative of an electrotechnical manufacturing business in Riga. I heard about it through this representative and asked him to send me a couple. This is one of the most recent prototypes. So right now, Evie, you'll be one of the few with her hands on one of these. Allan will show you how it works.'

The apparatus was half the size of a mouth organ, and she learned the tiny film it held was no bigger than her fingernail.

Fisher picked it up. 'You simply pull it open'—he mimicked doing so—'and push it closed.'

'That's it?'

'Well, you do have to click here to take the photo.' He pointed to the button. 'Each time you close it'—again he mimicked the action—'it advances the film in readiness for the next photograph.'

'I can't imagine I'll ever need it, but thank you. And what's this?'

'A powder compact, but it also slides out a magnifying glass, like this.'

'That's cunning,' she said. 'Why would I need that?'

Leadbetter shrugged. 'It's one of the things our female agents have said could be useful. We're showing you a small range of things that may help. You may never need them.'

'The lipstick . . . I can't imagine myself wearing scarlet,' she said.

'You might pretend to use it,' Leadbetter offered. 'Show her, Allan.'

Allan flipped the top to reveal a tiny mirror. 'You might pause to fix your lipstick and check if you're being followed.'

'Good grief, I hope not,' she admitted. She watched him screw off the bottom.

'You can hide something in here. It would have to be very small, of course.'

'Like what?'

'That's up to you,' Leadbetter said cryptically. 'We're simply equipping you.'

She reached for the Agatha Christie book with the distinctive green cover of the new Penguin Books series. 'And this?'

'Flick through it,' Fisher instructed her.

She did so and discovered some of its pages had been cut out to form a little well. She caught on. 'To hide a message?'

'Bravo, Evie,' Leadbetter praised her. 'An innocent vessel for carrying information or for a dead-letter drop.'

She repeated his last three words.

'I'll let Allan explain.'

Fisher outlined how she would leave the book at a given spot in public and whomever she was passing the information on to would pick up the book.

'It adds a layer of protection because the two parties need not meet face to face.'

'I see.'

'Your contact at the tearoom will explain more.'

'This penny?' She picked it up.

'Is a handy cutting tool,' Fisher said, pulling back the concealed edge to release a tiny razor-like blade.

'Why?'

Fisher laughed. 'Why not? We don't know what our people need, so my team simply dreams up and crafts tools they might make use of.'

'My head is spinning. I don't think I need any more contraptions to worry about. I'd rather just use my eyes and ears.'

'Just one more little trick. May we borrow your scarf, please, Evie?' Leadbetter asked.

She touched Max's silken gift at her neck. 'Why?'

'I promise we won't damage it. Allan would like to keep it and I shall personally bring it back to you.'

With great reluctance, Evie pulled the scarf from her neck, its warming presence disappearing to leave a sudden chill; it felt like a loss. She helplessly touched her engagement ring, firmly back on her hand, and now her only physical connection to Max.

'See you in Yorkshire, Evie,' Leadbetter said, guiding her towards the door. 'Now, let me see you to your car and the driver who will take you back to King's Cross. And as much as you don't wish to see me among your wedding guests, I'm afraid I shall have to be one of the invisible attendees – not in the photographs, I mean. We have plenty still to prepare for your departure.'

11

Paris

July 1936

The hotel porter closed the door gently, his tip already pocketed, and left Evie and Max to the fragile relationship that was still holding together through their shared ambition to get Jonas out of Germany and the memory of an all-consuming love that was now being tested.

The notion that every girl dreamed of her wedding day was irrelevant to Evie; hers had been pretty, albeit rushed and entirely fake. Their secret 'wedding' was mocked up outside a local church far from Levisham, where the smiling priest in the background was a member of Britain's secret service and all the family line-up, save her father and Rosie, were stand-ins. Someone, probably Elliott, who was such a stickler for the rules, had even had the foresight to bring along a five-year-old flower girl and pageboy. She wondered which parents of twins he'd cajoled for the purpose and presumed that the mother had been hovering somewhere nearby.

Leadbetter, who had defied her and come along anyway, had sidled up during the staging for the photographs.

'It would have been more convincing at Levisham,' he murmured with a shrug.

'I told you, I wouldn't let this charade anywhere near my home. Besides, no one in Germany will be any the wiser that while we wanted a church wedding, we wanted a quick celebration in a local pub and had trains and ferries to catch.'

'Yes, your "husband",' he said, loading the word with sarcasm, 'can make up whatever story suits his panic to get out of England. Maybe all of this is for naught, but I like the layer of protection it gives you, Evie.' It was the first time he'd addressed her so gently and she heard a note of affection in it. He nodded. 'I know you believe all sorts of things about me but when you lay your head on that pillow of an evening, please know in your heart that I am not the enemy. I will be watching and waiting for your every word.'

'And Max?'

He shook his head. 'His wellbeing is not my concern. It's your neck that I'll be saving. And I promise I will keep my word about his son. But I need something for my trouble – and for essentially letting Max go – so let's see what you can find out, Evie. Why did they send him to spy on our railways? They can't be planning an invasion, surely? They're only just coming out of absolute poverty. It would be unconscionable for their government to take another generation into war.'

'And still he was sent.'

'I want you to take this.' He gave her a small oblong package, wrapped as a gift. She frowned as she opened it. 'I wish it were an innocent wedding gift . . . silver sugar tongs, perhaps, or a pickle fork.' He smiled. 'I'm afraid it's a pack of playing cards.'

She looked at him, baffled.

'The Queen of Hearts is your card. Peel back the picture and that's a private number we've set up. It will be answered as a female cousin of Max's. I believe her name is Greta and she lives in Ditchling – don't worry about all this; Max has filled us in.'

'Good grief.'

He grinned. 'All you have to do is say that it's you. When she asks how you've settled in to Munich, you are to answer: "I'm learning how to use the trams."'

'That's a code, I'm presuming.'

'Indeed. No matter what else you say, if you mention the trams, it will tell us that you are in trouble and need to get out. We shall take over from there.'

Evie sighed. 'I hope I never make that call.'

Leadbetter, who had not featured in any of the staged photographs, assured them the shots were 'really rather good'.

Her dress had been borrowed from a London store and a seamstress had fitted it to her. She had wanted to use her mother's veil but decided a few days out that she didn't want to tarnish her mother's memory with a lie.

'You use it, Rosie, when the right man comes along.'

'Oh, Evie, this was meant for you.'

She had shrugged. 'My wedding is not real. Yours will be.'

'You don't have to do this, Evie,' her father had railed yet again. He'd said it so many times, it no longer held any impact for her.

'I do, Dad. Apart from loving him, which I know troubles you, I'm doing this for my country but also for an innocent, whose life would be on my conscience if I didn't try.'

'The marriage certificate looks real enough,' Rosie said.

'It's a very good forgery, as are the records in the church books, and even the wedding breakfast was planned down to giving us a receipt for the cost. Leadbetter has left no cracks in our story. But I'm still Mrs Evelyn Armstrong, no matter what the forged documents attest.'

Her father shook his head. 'Germany with that sod,' he growled.

'Dad, please. He's the man you were prepared to let me marry, and you were so happy for me.'

'That's before I knew the truth.'

'Remember, the truth lies too. Trust his truth, as I do.' Curiously too, among the fear was a building excitement that she'd admitted to no one. Somewhere deep, beyond duty, beyond concern for the innocent, beyond her patriotism and her defiance of Leadbetter and his coercive minions, was a secret desire for adventure.

The realisation had come as a shock.

So now here they sat in their Paris hotel room, which felt a lifetime away from their bedroom of love in the small guesthouse in Scarborough. This room was palatial by comparison, the hotel itself deliberately ostentatious for impressing travellers from as far back as the mid-1800s on their grand tours of Europe.

'Leadbetter has spared no expense,' she remarked.

'I don't know how to do this.'

'Yes, you do. Pretend. Find that charm and wit, that easy way you had. It worked on me.'

His gaze darkened. 'I never pretended with you.'

'But you did lie.'

'I withheld the truth.'

She laughed. 'Brilliant. Look how slippery you can be. Use that quality. We need to look like a pair of newlyweds and very much in love. It's no longer just your life that depends on it . . . it's mine as well.' She waited. 'We are in love, aren't we, Max?'

He crossed the room. 'Of course. Why do you even have to ask?'

'Because look at you – you seem too frightened to touch me. We're free, Max. And to all intents, we're married.'

'I never wanted you to be caught up in this dangerous web.'

'Tough. I didn't want your life or your son's on my conscience, which is why I'm here, trying to save both.' She grabbed him by the elbows. 'I'm frightened, Max. We have to be seamless in how we present to the people waiting for us in Germany. I need you to play your role to keep me safe.'

'I don't have to play at loving you, Evie.'

'Then prove it,' she challenged him.

Max pulled her close. 'If not for Jonas, Evie, I would have run away with you, disappeared into Yorkshire, never to return to my life.'

'Well, let's go and get Jonas and keep Yorkshire bright in our minds as the beacon that brings us home to safety. But right now we're on our honeymoon, so let's go out, shall we? I've always wanted to see Paris – and presumably you know it quite well. Arm in arm down the grand boulevards?' She beamed him an encouraging smile.

He agreed. 'We mustn't ignore what Leadbetter said about us being watched. I doubt it's just by London's team; I suspect Germany's people will be watching too.'

'What have you told them?'

'The man you saw me with that day on the train?'

She nodded.

'He's what they call a handler. I told him my equipment had been discovered and they were suspicious there was a spy in the region. I let him think I believed myself compromised.'

'And me?'

'Oh, he thought you were a wonderful layer of protection. He didn't agree with my decision to ask you to marry me, of course. In fact, he was shocked. I let him believe my incarceration time was in Scarborough. He will have reported back to Germany about you.'

'And you don't know how your return will be greeted?'

Max shrugged. 'As far as they're concerned, I sent through valuable information. I'm compromised, no further use as a spy, but plenty of use in me as an engineer, given what they're up to.'

She looked relieved. 'So we can count on you being safe . . . for a while at least?'

He nodded. 'Come on,' he said. 'I think we should arrive in the lobby via the grand staircase, making a show of being newlyweds.'

Here goes my new life, Evie thought. She knew she was supposed to be pretending, but apart from the hard nut of fear trapped in her chest, she had never felt more alive. It was the danger as much as the tingling anticipation of knowing she'd pulled off an extraordinary trick to give her Max back.

They arrived in the lobby via the marble staircase and Max felt impressed – seduced, even – by Evie's sudden cascade of laughter and how she held him close as they stepped down arm in arm. She was looking at no one but him, her eyes filled with sparkles and amusement.

'Max!' she said, squeezing his arm with delight, 'you're truly wicked.'

He grinned. He had to hand it to her. 'You're amazing,' he murmured.

'Thank you,' she said, lifting a shoulder to shrug, the smile not leaving her expression. 'Come on, darling, show me Paris.'

Max had to match her courage and daring. He felt the warmth of her against him and smiled at the doorman, who gave a gracious nod and wished them a happy day.

'*Bonne journée, Monsieur et Madame Hall*.' He slipped into excellent English. 'May I fetch you a taxi? I'm sorry, it is how the English say, "spitting" today.'

Max glanced at Evie, who gave a helpless grin. 'I'm a Yorkshire girl. Rain doesn't scare me.'

'Mrs Hall prefers to walk in your beautiful city.'

The doorman looked impressed and cut her a wink. 'Wait, please,' he said, hurrying back into the lobby before returning with an umbrella. 'Please.'

'Oh, thank you.'

'My pleasure, Madame Hall. Rain means luck for the newlyweds,' he remarked.

'Are you sure you don't mind?' Max asked Evie. 'You're going to get wet.'

'Makes it harder for those who follow us. Now, kiss me beneath our umbrella.'

They both glanced at the doorman, who smiled as if celebrating the fun of their being young lovers.

'Where would you like to go?' Max asked, putting his arm around Evie as she snuggled up closer beneath the umbrella. They carefully descended the hotel stairs onto the busy street of the ninth arrondissement, hearing gentle rain hitting the fabric of the black dome above them. He gestured. 'That way, to the Palais Garnier,' he said, pointing left, 'which will give you plenty of cultural and architectural interest. Home of the Paris Opera, where you can see a grand performance such as a ballet. Also full of shopping.' He pointed a thumb over his shoulder. 'Behind us, towards Montmartre . . . or that way,' he said, angling an arm to his right, 'we can stroll all the way down to rue de Rivoli, where we'll hit Place de la Concorde and the junction of the Champs-Élysées.'

She shook her head with delight, and there was no pretence in the wonder he saw in her expression. 'Let's walk to that famous busy square today.'

He nodded. 'That's a long way in the rain.'

'Don't have the stamina? I thought you were a rambler,' she teased.

They began wending their way past the wide Haussmann boulevards built in the previous century, which gave this neighbourhood, the busy ninth full of shops and cafes, its distinctive style.

'Do you want to look in the Galeries Lafayette?' he asked.

She shook her head. 'I'm enjoying being outside and smelling Paris.'

'Smelling it?'

'Doesn't it strike you as so strange and different to England?'

'I hadn't thought on it.'

'That's because you travel, but I know I'm a foreigner here just from the smell of the coffee and tobacco on the air.'

'You are a beautiful foreigner.'

'Thank you, but the women here seem so elegant and composed. Notice how that woman holds herself as she stares into the shop window. I think I need to practise that pose, leaning off onto one hip – all poised angles from chin to toe.'

He laughed, genuinely amused. 'I think that's built into Parisian women.'

'Damn them,' she said, to amuse him.

They paused to glance around when a young woman let out a soft shriek at stepping into a puddle and the man she was with scooped her into his arms and walked effortlessly across the rue des Mathurins, dodging the traffic and blaring horns, and the angry cyclists who rang their bells with frustration. But the girl was oblivious. She tipped back her beret-clad head at a coquettish angle and kissed him long and affectionately.

He felt Evie hug him closer, obviously moved by the lovely vignette that had unfolded before them. To him it said everything about Paris; the city was as adorable beneath an umbrella, through the smudged, watery lens of a spring shower, as she was in the shiny sunlight.

Max cleared his throat. 'Let's take rue Tronchet – that will lead us down past La Madeleine, which is splendid.'

The shower intensified to become a harder pelt of firm droplets.

'We're not going to make it, are we?' she said, sounding amused rather than disappointed.

He pointed to a nearby cafe and took her elbow, urging her towards the last remaining table beneath the awning. He gave a look of apology to another couple, who arrived seconds too late. At least they laughed. 'Is this all right?'

'I'm in Paris! Everything is new and exciting; a sidewalk cafe – a dream.'

The waiter arrived. 'Monsieur, madame?'

Max slipped into French. 'Two coffees with milk, please. And an absinthe.'

'Just one?' the man asked in a droll voice, in English.

'*Oui, monsieur, merci*,' Max said, not to be cowed.

'Do you believe we're being watched now?' she murmured into his ear as though whispering something naughtily affectionate.

He smiled as he knew he was expected to. 'I suspect so.'

She shifted her chair, scraping it on the pavement to be closer to him and took his hand, leaning in, again speaking only just loud enough for him to hear. 'Perhaps we should be careful what we say in the guestroom. It's probably safer here outdoors to say all that we need to.'

'For instance?'

The coffees arrived along with the absinthe and Max observed Evie's intrigue as the waiter – who barely looked at them – turned up a palm in a silent question.

'Go ahead,' Max said in French.

He enjoyed noting how her interest intensified at the process. The waiter poured the liquor from a tiny carafe over a decorative silver slotted spoon that sat atop a curiously shaped bulbous glass. As the seemingly bored waiter poured, Max explained in English.

'This is called a reservoir glass and it contains water to dilute the sugar and alcohol.' He pointed to the sugar lump atop the spoon, which liquified as the liquor was drizzled over it and into the waiting water.

'*Merci, monsieur*,' Max said to the waiter, who briskly nodded, already casting his glance towards another couple leaving their table. The bill was expertly placed beneath the ashtray and he was gone.

'Such a colour,' she marvelled.

'Taste it,' he urged. 'It's full of botanicals . . . can you guess?'

Evie risked a sip and looked back at him, delighted. 'Bitter and aniseed?' He grinned that she was right. 'I want to say the licorice plant . . . or even fennel.'

'It's wormwood.'

'Ah,' she breathed, intrigued. 'I've read about wormwood. Latin name *Artemisia absinthium*.'

'You're showing off now.'

Her laughter arrived as genuine. 'I am.' He watched her take a sip of her coffee and he enjoyed her sigh of pleasure. 'Ooh but that's delicious and strong. Max, what am I walking into? You say we will be based in Munich. How does that differ from Berlin?'

He gave a snort. 'In just about every way. Berlin is the original Prussian capital and has become loud, vibrant, diverse – intoxicating, really. It used to be the most exciting city to live in before . . .' He looked around. 'Well . . . before.'

She nodded her understanding.

'Munich is the capital of Bavaria and surrounded by beauty – the landscape is more exhilarating than the city itself, which is traditional, almost cosy, you could say. They've walked very different histories and it would be fair to say they're competitive, especially now that the leader of Germany works from Berlin but likes to think of Munich as his home . . . and his playground.' He sighed. 'A woman called Giselle calls it home too. Not the city so much but a lakeside chateau in a place called Starnberg.'

'Why is she important?'

'She was charged with looking after Jonas.'

'Ah, I see. But I presume Jonas will be living with us now?'

He looked down as he answered. 'I hope so.'

'You have to insist he is returned. We shall be a family until we can get him out to safety.' Her words cut deep.

'Listen, I've been given no information on your role. Is it wise not to include me in your plans? I know you've made them with Leadbetter.'

She smiled brightly for any observers, as though he'd said something complimentary. 'No one trusts you. I've been asked not to tell you anything.'

She looked shocked as he nodded. 'Then don't. If following Leadbetter's orders gets you out of Germany faster with Jonas, I will do whatever you need.' He lifted her hand and kissed it.

'All of us are leaving Germany, Max,' she insisted, staring at him hard. 'Being a mother to Jonas comes with the territory of being your wife. We're in this together and I will tell you whatever I can.'

'You should,' he said. 'Otherwise how can I help?'

He took a couple of sips from the absinthe but left his coffee untouched. 'Come on, the rain's let up a bit.' He left some francs including a tip and offered help for her to ease out of the tight space.

The waiter descended, his black-and-white clothing suggesting a greedy magpie as he pounced on the money and pocketed it, taking the slip as he left. '*Bonne journée, monsieur et madame*,' he said over his shoulder. It came out rote.

They turned in the direction of the hotel.

'The Olympics are soon, aren't they?' she asked conversationally, linking arms with him.

'Indeed. Berlin will be bursting with excitement. This is Germany's opportunity to show off to the world its emergence from the doldrums.' He leaned in. 'It's also his plan to excel in every sport and show that the Aryan race is the superior one.

He's deeply intrigued by images of Greek gods and goddesses – fancies Germany can imitate. It's going to be the first Games broadcast via television. But Evie, I want you to be gone before the Olympics.'

'Then we must work fast. To hell with Leadbetter's caution. You're going to have to help me, Max, and I'm going to trust that you will never betray me again.'

12

Munich

July 1936

Munich smelled as different to Paris as Paris did to London but its air, scented by the oil and metal of trams that rumbled and screeched down the centre of the wide streets, was reminiscent of her home on the Yorkshire railway. That's where the familiarity ended for Evie though, who understood from the moment they alighted the train carriage that she was a foreigner in a strange city, and she needed to embed herself fast.

Everyone was dressed brightly for the German summer; there were few cars and a lot of folk on bicycles. Smart women walked holding the hands of girls in bright dresses and boys in lederhosen. The city gave the impression of affluence and a certain confidence, she thought, wondering where that emanated from. And then she remembered Max's comments that Hitler visited the city regularly through desire rather than necessity; that he really enjoyed being in Munich – like a spiritual home. Perhaps it was from this that its people derived a sort of collective self-assurance. She hadn't known what to expect with her limited travel experience but to her these people looked no different to the people of Britain – a lot blonder, maybe.

Evie had lived here now for just a few days and her immediate feeling was that Munich was a cultured city with a vibrancy to its arts and museums that was counterbalanced perhaps by its preoccupation with beer, which the region prided itself on producing. She'd learned that Munich possessed the largest factory, the oldest factory and the famous Oktoberfest to celebrate the beer industry, and she couldn't overlook the fact that it was a beer hall in Munich where Adolf Hitler chose to make his coup d'état almost fifteen years earlier as a young leader of the radicals that spawned the Nazi Party in government today. He'd failed, of course, in the well-known Beer Hall Putsch, but if she judged him by his meteoric rise, he'd obviously learned some lessons from being charged with treason and subsequently imprisoned. It had won him the national attention he'd craved and she now understood it had created the platform he used to build the nationalism that Germany these days embraced so fiercely.

She could not ignore the feverish support for the new regime that governed this country, still harbouring a deep grudge over its treatment after the Great War. As they sat in the apartment she was now to call home, Max explained in quiet tones just how far from their broad-minded and liberal attitudes the German people had been forced to leap.

'Are we safe to talk freely?' she checked.

Max nodded. 'I've been over every inch of this apartment, including the floor and the ceiling, and there is no listening device that I can find. You know that man who visited on our first day?'

She nodded.

'He's a reliable friend and an expert in this sort of clever technology and he assures me we are not being overheard . . . not yet, anyway.'

'Does that mean they don't suspect anything's amiss?'

He frowned. 'I suppose it does. I'm being debriefed tomorrow and then I'll have a better grasp of how I am regarded. You, of course, still carry enormous novelty.'

'And suspicion?'

He shrugged. 'I think we'd be wise to presume as much, even if they aren't suspicious.'

'Who debriefs you?'

'A great many levels below Hitler and his top henchmen, I'm relieved to say.'

'And yet you tell me we've been invited to this important cocktail party next weekend after that festival – what did you call it?'

'The Night of the Amazons.' He grinned, before he shook his head. 'How do I explain this? My work has been relevant for German railways but frankly I think the interest in me is more my pedigree.' He shrugged, embarrassed. 'My father came from a line of admired and very senior Prussian soldiers; my grandfather was a favourite of Alfred von Schlieffen, who was the chief of the army's general staff. And that respect percolates through: my father was one of the early members of the Imperial German Army.'

'Tell me about your parents.'

'My father met and married my mother in England, had me, brought us to Germany and then he went to war.'

'And then what happened?'

Max shrugged. 'He died. We returned to Britain, and then we spent some time back in Bavaria because I suppose I was searching for some sort of belonging to my father. Mum died, and I spent my late teens with my father's folk and then left for Berlin. The family name carries weight in the capital. That's what I mean about pedigree. I think I was employed more for the name than my engineering skills.'

She sighed. 'It's extraordinary that we haven't had the opportunity to discuss any of this. Is your family wealthy?'

'I suppose you would say so, but the wealth these days is on my mother's side, to be honest, and they're all in England. It's more because of my family background that I'm invited to these parties that I'd rather not attend. Now that I've returned with a German-speaking bride from England, everyone's interested – especially, I imagine, if I'm being watched or judged.'

'Suspicious of me because I'm English?'

'More intrigued to see who I have ended up with, after swearing I would never marry again . . . and perhaps collectively relieved.'

'Why do you say that?' She frowned. 'I need to understand everything, Max, so don't hold back.'

'Because me being married to a Jewess presented a host of problems that my supporters didn't want to face; Rachel's death solved a problem for them. Now I've brought into their midst a bright, blonde, beautiful wife who they can appreciate and admire.'

She pulled a face of disgust.

'I know, Evie, but we have to rely on those qualities of yours now and use them to their best effect.'

'And . . . is *he* at these events?'

'No!' He gusted a laugh, amused at such a thought. 'He avoids that sort of social interaction, as far as I can tell. Don't get me wrong – he can be incredibly charming, but even from my distant vantage I've noticed that he seeks out the spotlight only when it suits his needs. He does not seem to enjoy the petty endeavour of small talk with small-time officials. I might add I have not met him enough to be a superior judge of anything but his psychopathic attitude to certain people. He loves animals but he hates with true passion Jews, Roma and invalids.'

She looked appalled.

'If only when he was here, falling in love with Munich, that he'd shown some artistic talent, we may never have known him as anything but a gentle painter. Instead, he failed as an artist and entered the world of politics instead,' he explained. 'Anyone he chooses to dislike is now under grave threat. As of last year, a Jew like Rachel would not be permitted to marry me, an Aryan – or consider herself a citizen of Germany, even though her father fought bravely for our nation in the war. I'm just glad we are living in a small but fashionable clique in Munich, well away from the heartland of the Nazis in Berlin.' He turned sheepish. 'There is some bad news, though, regarding this apartment.'

'It leaks in winter?' she tried and won a gentle smile from him.

'Our Führer has his palatial nine-roomed apartment in the same neighbourhood. Not the same street, of course.'

She frowned. 'In Munich?'

'Munich is a Nazi stronghold because of its early importance to Hitler. It gave him his start, and the groundswell of support for him and his ideas happened here.'

Evie nodded and turned to look out the window. The compact penthouse apartment she now called home was set back from Prinzregentenstrasse – a long street that began at the Prinz-Carl-Palais and formed a boulevard of the former German royals. Their building was fashioned from a warm grey stone the colour of Horlicks, as she'd described it to her sister in a quick postcard home. She hadn't yet stepped out onto its balcony, but she planned to put a small table and chairs outside where she could enjoy a morning cuppa . . . or coffee, as it would have to be now that she was in Germany. The architectural style of most of the buildings in the neighbourhood was a richly structured and decorated baroque Art Nouveau. Their flat enjoyed two pretty oriel windows facing onto a wide, handsome street with tall trees in full leaf. There was no doubting its privileged setting.

'I think you'll like Munich. The rest of Bavaria is helplessly beautiful, from its medieval squares to its forests and mountains. King Ludwig II was known for his grandiose and almost fairytale architecture – it's hard not to enjoy.'

She smiled and nodded.

'So how are we going to approach this whole new life of ours?' He waited for her guidance.

She had given this question plenty of reflection. 'Our friend in London agrees with me that we press hard on the truth. To lie is to leave ourselves open – it's best we are economical with any untruth. So . . . we met exactly how we did. Our relationship blossomed with your various trips to the north. For my part, I'll say I know you as a rambler and a railway enthusiast. And although I didn't have a chance to get to know you very well, our romantic attraction was immediate and powerful. We fell in love almost instantly – and I can then start to embellish my life as a person who wanted adventure and travel. You offered me a way out of the quiet country life I was leading.'

'And how do you feel about living in Germany? It will be the first question on everyone's lips.'

'I'm excited and I shall ensure that this feeling shows.'

'I'm concerned I'll let you down . . . put you in danger.'

'You won't, Max. You'll be brilliant. Just be Roger again.' She turned back to the street. Distantly the sound of a tram moving down Prinzregentenstrasse reached them. 'One more thing – I want you to treat me like the good little wife at home.' She stood.

'How do you mean?' He stood and joined her close to the window, so that she was forced to look at his perplexed expression. She could feel the warmth of his body, wanted to touch the tiny wisp of blond hair that had escaped its neatly groomed companions and was swaying and catching the sunlight. It dared her to replace it, to stroke it back into place. She wanted to but they needed to focus on their homework, get their facades tailored – so she resisted the inclination and met his puzzled gaze.

'We need to convince all people we meet that my head is filled with nothing more challenging than being your adoring new wife. I want to cook for you, look good for you, be with you as much as I can. I want to give you children, I want to nest in our new apartment, I want to fall in love with Munich and Germany as I've fallen in love with you.'

'You want to appear empty-headed?'

She laughed without mirth. 'Not entirely. Just preoccupied with the novelty of being married and in love, with no room for much else just now. I don't want anyone to sense any ambition in me – then they'll stop noticing me.'

'Hardly. One look—'

'Let me put it like this. Anyone who might harbour suspicions will have them quickly allayed once they meet me and watch you with me. They'll base their judgement on our behaviour so we must nourish the notion that I am no threat. People will begin to speak openly in front of me; they'll stop thinking of my presence as anything more than innocent.'

He nodded. 'I understand. However, I'm not sure I'll be privy to the sort of conversations you and London anticipate. I could well be persona non grata.'

'You've told me your family name opens doors. Let me worry about their reticence around you – just get me into the right rooms with people of status. I'll worry about what information can be gathered to keep Whitehall informed.'

He looked lost. 'How long do we keep up this pretence?'

'As briefly as possible. Just go to your work daily as the engineer you are and behave normally. You are no longer a spy, remember. You're returning to your life and hopefully they'll allow you to do so without further pressure. Stop concerning yourself with my role – just enable me wherever you can. Whitehall will just have to be happy with whatever I can gather.' He nodded unhappily. She smiled. 'So, I shall meet Jonas tomorrow?'

'Yes,' he confirmed, his mood visibly lightening with the pleasure of the thought. 'I hope you both get on.' He ran a hand through his hair and the rogue wisp disappeared.

'We will. I promise. His new room is a bit bare.'

'They took a lot of things with him.'

'Shall we go and find some things to help him feel more at home?'

'If you think so.'

'It's been months since you left him. Too long without a parent. Come on. We have to make him remember what his home life used to be and reignite his affection for you.'

He touched her arm. 'I need to tell you something.'

She paused at the hitch in his voice, frowning in fear despite her curiosity.

'The woman who took him away, and who is responsible for his care . . .'

Evie nodded. 'Giselle, who lives in the chateau overlooking a lake at Starnberg.'

'Gosh, your memory is stellar.'

She shrugged. 'What about her?'

'She's . . . well, she's always had a thing for me.'

'A thing,' she repeated, slightly mocking.

Max shook his head. 'I haven't encouraged it, not even when I was a bachelor. But she's always been there in my circle of friends.'

'Unrequited affection?' she cut at him, despite understanding why most women would find him irresistible. His hesitation was a heartbeat too long. 'The truth, Max. Forewarning is my only weapon.'

'Look,' he said, sounding exasperated. 'I can't fathom a woman's sensibilities. Giselle and I didn't exactly grow up together but we've known each other since childhood. Our families knew each other well; we went to the same parties. She comes from a wealthy, well-connected family, and we've moved in similar circles since we were teenagers.'

'And?'

'And . . .' He looked frazzled. 'I might have kissed her in my teens – New Year parties, that sort of thing.'

'Have you slept with her?'

'Yes. A hundred years ago, when I was a pimply adolescent.'

'But she's in love with you?'

He moved further into their apartment and leaned against the fireplace. 'Her shadow has trailed me for years. I've learned to ignore it.'

'I asked if she's in love with you.'

'I don't know,' he said, sounding helpless.

'Yes, you do.'

'I've never understood Giselle,' he said, cutting the air with his hand in an emphatic gesture of frustration. 'She hasn't outgrown her fondness for me, no matter how I've discouraged her. I feel nothing for her, I promise . . . except perhaps pity. She's not my type.'

'What's your type?'

'Not her! I thought marrying Rachel might have ended Giselle's interest, but I think it got worse. So I've done my best to generally avoid her, but our paths have continued to cross nonetheless.'

'And now she has Jonas. Was this part of her plan to win you?'

'I can't say. She certainly put her hand up.'

'Sounds intense.'

'I can handle it but I'm just warning you that she's prickly and now she has my son, and I'm never fully sure of her intentions. I don't know whether she wishes me harm or . . .'

'All right, I'm warned. I'll be careful.'

Marienplatz had been the city's main square since the twelfth century, and Evie couldn't help but smile as she walked arm in arm with her pretend husband into Munich's heart. The New Town Hall that Max pointed out looked splendidly medieval but he assured her it had been built less than three decades before, in a Gothic style.

He pulled her towards a tower. 'Oh, we'll just catch it.' He grinned.

'What?'

He looked at his watch, then directed her gaze to the tower. 'It's a carillon. And it will chime in a few moments.'

She waited and noticed several people had gathered to do the same, chins tilted, smiles breaking across their faces in anticipation. Their attention was riveted on the city's clock. Hers was on the long red flag that hung from the top of the structure in a menacing blood colour, with a black swastika that stood out from its white disc.

Chimes suddenly sounded and people around her gave happy gasps as the colourful figures on the top level of the carillon began to move in a circular motion while the figures of the Duke and his bride looked on. Knights on horses then appeared in all their finery – one kitted out in silver armour, the other in gold. It lasted about seven minutes, before the brightly dressed coopers on the lower level, carrying bells, began to spin in their merry dance, drawing applause this time. Evie had to smile at the show.

'Has Jonas seen this?'

'Yes, of course, but never tires of it.'

'All right. Where else can we take him?'

'The English Garden is splendid in summer with its beer garden and Chinese tower.'

'There, that sounds perfect. We'll go this weekend. What does Jonas like?'

He gave a soft smile. 'Railways.'

'Oh no, a chip off the old block?'

'Afraid so.'

'What's new in railway toys?'

'There's a brand new Märklin locomotive, painted in black, red and gold.'

'Very Nazi,' she whispered.

'Very British, actually,' he corrected her.

'Let's find it. It can be a special gift from me.'

'Really?'

'Yes. I have to earn his trust, and when it comes to children, there's no better way than sweets and toys if it has to be done fast.'

He grinned. 'Are you an expert?'

'I don't know how many children I've entertained on our platform over the years: lost children, weeping children, overly busy children, children whose mothers have lost their patience and just need a moment's break. I've seen it all. Chocolate usually works wonders, as does a chance to get inside with the engine driver for a few moments.'

'Jonas loves chocolate.'

'Let's stock up.'

They spent a happy hour moving about the old market square, threading through the streets that led off and back into it so that Evie could get her bearings until, finally, exhausted, she sighed. They had collected a few bags of shopping, including the new boxed locomotive.

'Have we earned a rest?'

'I think we've earned a drink and a sit-down at one of the city's most fashionable spots. If you can stand one more very brief walk, I'll take you to the oldest cafe in Munich, which happens to be Italian.'

'Lead on – I'm already tasting good coffee . . .'

'Or a beer and an elaborate ice cream,' he promised.

It was less than five minutes' walk to Café Luigi Tambosi. The beer garden – or *biergarten*, as she now knew them to be called – was filled with happy drinkers. At his suggestion to forgo coffee, she looked doubtful.

'Come on – in Munich we drink beer whenever possible.'

'I don't drink it.'

'Then learn. Especially if you want to integrate.'

They were seated and within moments Evie was sipping a golden effervescing beverage that tasted nothing like the flat draught ale her father favoured. She made a slurping sound and the froth remained on her lips to be licked away. 'Refreshing,' she admitted.

'You were born for this,' he said, sounding like he was finally enjoying himself. 'You like the aniseed of absinthe and the bitterness of our beer. You'll do well in Europe.'

She tilted her face to the sun. 'It's lovely out here. What's this?' She pointed to the gardens.

'The grounds of the Residenz Palace. Are you going to have an ice cream?'

'Next time, with Jonas.'

He nodded. 'Tambosi is a place to be seen and to observe others. Inside it really is a traditional coffee house that smacks of a different age. They say Mozart drank here.'

She opened her mouth in surprise and then had to disguise a small burp behind her hand. She laughed helplessly, looking around guiltily, but no one except Max had heard. He shared her amusement.

'You'll have to learn to hold your liquor, my dear.'

His fake condescension made her grin wider. 'You see, Max. We can do this.'

13

She hadn't expected to feel as nervous as she did in this moment. Max was pacing near the window, looking out for his son's arrival. Evie had sent Max out earlier for pastries – regretting now that she hadn't baked a cake – and the smell of fresh coffee scented the air as it simmered. But now that everything was in place, she felt the first tendrils of genuine fear twisting in her belly like the steam curling up from the coffee percolator. This meeting was her first real test and she needed to pass it flawlessly.

Max looked into the small kitchen. 'They're here.'

She swallowed as she gazed at him.

'Are you all right?'

She nodded.

He didn't think so and she didn't resist him holding her briefly in a hug. 'You are amazing. You're going to charm them.'

She looked up at him from within the circle of his arms. 'Thanks.'

Max kissed the top of her head. 'And Jonas is going to love you on sight.'

She eased away, let out her breath and nodded. 'I'm ready.'

Evie smoothed the long skirt that fitted her body immaculately; it was pale olive with a small row of visible buttons leading down her left hip, and a pocket at her right. She wore a light knitted sweater with short sleeves in cream, and she'd tied her favourite scarf featuring cherries in a loose and jaunty fashion at her throat. It was the ideal casual but smart ensemble for a day that had emerged cooler than the previous few, even threatening a shower. She completed her outfit with flat brogues, so that she wouldn't appear too tall for young Jonas.

There was a knock at their apartment's door.

'I'm going to come out from the kitchen,' she said to Max softly. 'You answer and have a moment with Jonas.' She nodded. 'Trust me.'

'I do.' He smiled, then whispered, 'Let's perform and get him back!'

Evie returned to the kitchen and listened. She heard the door being opened.

'Jonas!' Max exclaimed with excitement. A child's laugh, and then she peeped around the doorway of the kitchen to see a small boy flinging himself into his father's arms. Max's voice was muffled because it was buried in his son's neck. 'Oh, I've missed you.'

She saw movement behind Jonas and stepped back, not wishing to be seen yet. She listened.

'Daddy, we just saw the clock again in the square. It's a glocken . . . a glockenspiel chime, Aunty Giselle told me.'

Aunty Giselle. Evie didn't mean to dislike her already but the thought was out now and dancing around the kitchen. How dare the German woman steal Evie's plans.

'Good morning,' Max said, sounding as though he was straightening to greet the adults.

'Darling Max . . . handsome as ever,' she heard a smoky voice say, followed by the sound of two kisses.

'Giselle. You look very . . . summery. Come here, Jonas.' It sounded like he'd picked up his son. 'Ooh, it's good to hold you again.'

She heard the woman bluster in. 'Well, it's July, darling. Once I pass mid-May, there's no going back for me in terms of my wardrobe.' There was a slight pause. 'Max, may I introduce Eric Becker; he's from the Hitlerjugend.'

'Heil Hitler,' a man said, and it came as a shock to Evie to hear it so loud and so real.

Evie heard Max's tone change. 'Herr Becker. Sorry, I have my hands full,' he replied, presumably to excuse himself for not returning the salute. 'My son is about a decade too young for the Hitler Youth, surely?'

'Never too young to learn how to ensure the future of Nazi Germany, Herr Hall.' He gave a gentle chuckle. 'But I am here simply for support, not conscription of Jonas into the movement . . . not for a few years, anyway.'

Evie sensed an awkward moment arising. She emerged all smiles from her kitchen.

'Hello, hello!' she greeted in German, pretending to wipe her hands on a small towel as if she'd been busy in the kitchen. She threw the towel back onto the counter. Then she gasped, just short of making it theatrical. 'You must be Jonas,' she said, ensuring her eyes sparkled and her smile was wide. The blond-haired boy in Max's arms nodded shyly. His father put him on the ground. 'But you're so tall. You can't possibly be only five.'

He grinned. 'That's because I'm six now,' he said with a delightful lisp through missing teeth, and held up six fingers to prove it, nodding vigorously.

'Well, well. And you look just like your father.' She crouched at eye level with him. He shared the same reticent expression as Max, as well as those stormy blue eyes that were more like a winter's day than summer. 'My name is Evie. And I am so thrilled to meet you, Jonas. I've heard so much about you.'

Jonas cast a shy glance towards Giselle. 'Are you my new mother?' he wondered, looking back at Evie.

The question was so direct she didn't dare answer it in a similar fashion. 'Well, I think we can have lots of fun together and we can work that out gradually.'

Before Jonas could say more, a long hand with tapering fingers and nails polished in shiny scarlet appeared before her face. 'I'm Giselle Kleist – I'm delighted to meet the woman who has won the heart of Maximillian Hall.'

Evie stood to face the woman whose words were friendly but whose eyes, the colour of the water that surged at the shoreline of Scarborough beach on an ill-tempered day, spoke of no friendship.

'Welcome, Giselle,' she said, smiling broadly, not missing a beat, despite where her thoughts were roaming. 'Splendid to meet you.' She also reached out her hand to the thin, hook-nosed man hovering in the doorway.

'Eric Becker.'

'Evelyn Hall.' She smiled and felt his limp handshake. 'Come on in, everyone. Oh, Jonas?' The little boy turned. 'There's something for you on the sofa.'

He ran ahead and she and Max laughed delightedly, although their companions didn't share the amusement. Evie didn't miss the look that passed between them.

'Please go through. I'll bring some coffee.'

She watched the tall, slim-hipped woman peel off her light coat, helped by Max; she slid a hooded-eyed smile over her shoulder at his touch, and allowed herself to be guided into their main sitting and living room.

'I'd forgotten how charming this apartment is, Max, despite

how small it is. Must be the windows allowing in all the light,' she heard Giselle comment.

Evie detested her already, sensing only guile in the woman, but busied herself checking all was ready on the tray. The coffee was hissing to full percolation and she was turning to switch off the gas when she felt a tug at her skirt and looked down to see Jonas. Once again, she crouched.

'Is this for me?' he said, holding the boxed locomotive and sounding nonetheless impressed for his serious tone.

She nodded, smiling. 'Do you know, Jonas, my father is a stationmaster, in charge of all the trains into and out of the railway station? I grew up living on that station watching all the trains coming and going through our little part of the railway track.'

His expression filled with wonder. 'You're so lucky. I wish I could do that.'

'Well, you can! Let's go and visit, shall we? Your papa and I can take you to England and you can see the station and wave in the trains, perhaps even blow the whistle, or help change the points like I used to.'

He gave a gasp of fresh wonder – clearly understanding all the workings of a station, which she'd guessed he would. He had been well educated by his father in this.

'Would you like that?'

He nodded with genuine pleasure. 'Thank you for my gift. Papa said it's from you.'

'It is. We can play with it together later if you'd like – you can tell me all about it.'

'Jonas?' It was Giselle, suddenly appearing at the doorway. 'Don't disturb your father's wife, darling.'

Evie hadn't shifted from her crouched position. 'Jonas, you can call me Evie,' she continued in flawless German. 'And you can disturb me as much as you like. I'm looking forward to us being together all the time now.'

'Off you go, Jonas darling,' Giselle said, giving him a push. Once he'd left, Giselle's near-colourless stare fixed on Evie and the smile didn't touch it. 'We're here to make an assessment on that, Evelyn. We mustn't presume or confuse the child.'

Evie deliberately frowned. 'Presume what? That Jonas is returning to live with his father? Forgive me, I don't understand.'

'No, my dear, perhaps you don't. It's not really something we can discuss either. It's to do with the sensitive nature of Max's work.'

'On the railways?'

'Er . . . yes.'

'Sensitive?'

Giselle demurred, as if she didn't want to discuss this matter. Instead, she reached towards the scarf that Evie was wearing. 'This is very beautiful. Hermès?'

'It is. Max gave it to me.' She didn't like Giselle touching it.

'May I?'

She really didn't want to but she unfurled the scarf and was surprised that Giselle took it and tied it around her own neck. It was an appalling overstep but Evie sensed it was a show of power. 'He has excellent taste.' She removed it and handed it back. 'Shall we go through?'

Evie tried not to bristle that her guest had not only deflected her but was now playing condescending host. She picked up the tray, unhappily following Giselle. 'Well, you may have to explain, Fräulein Kleist, because Jonas's father has now returned and we are looking forward to being a family.' She made sure there was only sweetness in her tone. 'I have certainly anticipated being a good influence on Jonas since I agreed to marry Max. Jonas was always his priority and I've known that since the day I met him.'

'That's very admirable,' Becker said, nodding at Max.

His encouragement won a tight non-smile from Giselle. 'I'm intrigued. How *did* you two meet?'

The men were already seated. Evie explained as she poured the coffee.

As Giselle accepted her cup and saucer, she smiled and there wasn't a wrinkle of sincerity in it. 'How charming. I've known Max almost all of my life, and I think most women chased him around for most of theirs until, ragged'—she chortled—'they gave up on hoping for a proposal of marriage from him.'

Including you . . . Evie wanted to say. Instead she smiled, turning towards her husband with a look of indulgent affection.

'I don't know about that. Perhaps I got lucky.' She shrugged. This time Evie made sure she was wide-eyed and especially innocent in her tone.

'Second time around, I gather,' Giselle said condescendingly.

'Two widowed people found one another,' Evie said, sounding like a summer breeze with only a sighing pleasure in her voice.

'Enough, Giselle. Have you forgotten Jonas is here?' Max murmured wearily. It was said in a way that only people who know each other extremely well can risk.

'My apologies, Evelyn.' Again, no depth to the sentiment or the tone.

'And in fact, Frau Hall,' Becker chimed in, 'you certainly appear as though you will integrate well into German society.'

She wanted to ask Becker if he was referring to her fair hair and strong constitution but didn't, of course. 'Oh, I do hope so. Max has spoken so highly of it and from what I've seen of Munich, I like it so much, and this apartment is lovely.' She reckoned Leadbetter would be proud of her gushy, innocent manner.

'I suppose coming from a grimy railway-station life, this must be rather splendid,' Giselle remarked. 'I mean, with all the coal and steam and brass polish,' she added, noting a look of admonishment from Max.

'Oh yes, it is,' Evie agreed wholeheartedly, covering her lie so well she could hardly believe it herself. She blinked at Max, who smiled, squeezed her hand and didn't let go. She could tell how impressed he was but Giselle, she grasped, was falling for the naivety and was giving off waves of scorn, as though Evie was far too simple to even pick it up. Well, she would keep absorbing it; that was the game she was now in.

'Frau Hall, I must say, for an Englishwoman your German is really rather good.'

'Thank you, Herr Becker. That is a high compliment indeed.'

'How did you become so accomplished in our language, may I ask?'

'My grandfather was held captive in Bavaria, actually, during the Great War. During his time in captivity, he fell in love and married a beautiful local,' she lied. 'And brought her to Yorkshire. Nanny Lotte started teaching me and my sister German from the day she arrived.'

'Really?' Giselle chimed in. 'I would have thought that almost dangerous after the war.'

Evie pretended a blank look momentarily before brightening. 'Oh, I see. Well, yes. It's why Nanny said we had to keep it secret. So we only ever spoke German when we were alone with her.'

'Splendid!' Becker said, sounding genuinely chuffed.

She turned, needing to extricate herself from this conversation. 'Jonas, would you like to see your room again and make sure it's all how you want it?'

He turned from the corner where he was kneeling, rolling his locomotive on the floorboards while making soft train sounds, and nodded.

'Come on, then,' she said, up on her feet and extending a hand. She was aware of Becker also giving a nod – but to Giselle. Evie pretended not to notice it. 'There may be some more surprises in there, but *shhh*,' she said, putting a finger to her lips, 'don't tell anyone.'

'I like the colour of your lipstick, Evie,' Jonas remarked as they left the room. Evie imagined Giselle was scowling at that comment.

By the time they returned to the small living room, decisions had been made. They began with Jonas and a rather emphatic announcement.

'I want to stay with Dad and Evie,' he said, as if he sensed there had been some doubt.

'I'm afraid not, little Jonas,' Giselle began, but Max interjected.

'Why?'

'You know why, Max. Let's not cause a scene.'

'I need an explanation. I'm home now. Jonas was living with you simply while I was abroad doing some business. Now we can be properly together and we have Evie in our lives too; we should be a family.' He turned to their guests. 'Aren't I right, Herr Becker?'

'Yes, I think we can—'

Giselle shot her companion a look of pure loathing. 'Jonas, gather up your things, please.' She didn't say it terribly kindly but Evie gave the child an encouraging smile.

'Let me help you, Jonas,' she said, purely to distract him, not for Giselle, but for Max's sake.

'Thank you, dear,' Giselle condescended. Evie turned away as if no longer paying attention but she keenly listened. 'Max, it is not your decision – as you know,' Giselle continued. 'Now, for your sake, don't question this. I'm begging you.' There was no plea in her voice; it sounded rote. 'I'll tell you what, I'm authorised to organise some weekends together. Why don't we start there?'

'Giselle, you are holding my son against my wishes,' Max ground out in a low voice.

'We had an agreement. I am simply caring for Jonas on behalf of the authorities. None of this is my decision, Max. And you still have to be debriefed and deal with the repercussions of the, er . . .

business you were doing in England. And if that is all sorted to everyone's satisfaction, then you need to reacquaint yourself with your colleagues and the projects within your division. It's my guess they will have a new role for you.'

Evie returned to Max's side and clasped his hand. She squeezed it and he understood. This was not the moment to press his case, no matter how much it hurt. 'I know none of this is your doing,' he said, hanging his head momentarily. 'Thank you, Giselle, for taking care of Jonas so well.'

The woman gave a cold smile, first landing its chill on Evie, and then Max. 'My darling, I'm on your side, you know that. I am protecting him from . . . anyway, let me work out some weekends for you to be a family.'

Becker loitered by the apartment door, looking eager to leave.

'I don't want to go home with you, Aunty Giselle,' Jonas said, catching on it.

Evie enjoyed watching Giselle's look of dismay before she schooled her features into a vacant smile.

'Jonas, you remember your promise to behave, don't you?' Giselle said, her tone smiling yet threatening. 'Come along now. We shall be back, I promise.'

'When?' He took his father's hand, and Evie was delighted when he grabbed hers too. 'I want to be here.'

Despite her rising sense of offence on behalf of this family, she knew they had entered a cat-and-mouse game. Leadbetter had warned her to give the impression she was easily flustered or compelled. This was not a moment to be showing any sign of strength or cunning. So, in spite of her internal revolt at having to do so, Evie urged Jonas with a gentle push. 'Your papa and I are going to sit down this moment and work out a wonderful few days together. Isn't that right, Max?'

He nodded miserably.

'And your Aunty Giselle is going to help us to organise a time when you can come back very soon.'

'That's right, we shall be back soon,' Giselle said in her best impersonation of a caring aunt. 'We have the Night of the Amazons to attend, Max, and then Streicher's party.'

Max ignored her remark and kneeled next to his son.

Jonas, defeated, flung his slim arms around his father. 'Why can't I be here?' he said, sounding like he was going to cry.

'I'm still working, Jonas,' Max said in a thick voice. 'I can't be here with you but I shall work it out soon to be here every evening.'

'Can't I stay with Evie?'

'Not yet,' Max said, and his tone told everyone in the room how much he loathed denying his son. 'Evie has to learn her way around Munich, and she's got to get herself settled because everything is so new for her. Then she'll be ready to have you with us all the time.'

Evie's eyes misted as she watched the young boy bury his face into his father's neck. Golden head met golden head and they hugged, the youngster making soft sobbing sounds engulfed in his father's strong arms. The scene and the emotion were threatening to break her heart and she could only imagine what it was doing to Max as he stroked his son's head and made soothing sounds as he prepared to let his son be taken away for a second time.

It was in this moment that Evie understood that this was why she was here. All the angst at Max's betrayal fled, all the despair at leaving her family dissipated, and all the fear that had been building was stared down. Everything about this situation was wrong. Jonas was a pawn. And for Giselle and the ruthless authoritarians she followed, his life, as if he were a small chess piece, was dispensable and wholly subject to their collective whim. The wrong blood had flowed through his veins since he first quickened in his Jewish mother's womb; that was this innocent's crime. And they were still using the infant to coerce the father they needed.

Evie could tell that Giselle was enjoying watching Max suffer. Her glacial expression held amusement without warmth . . . perhaps 'satisfaction' described it better, Evie thought. *Well, I'm going to beat you, Giselle, at your own game,* she promised. *This boy is escaping to England with me, one way or another, and with him his father. You will have neither of them at your mercy by the time I'm finished.*

The words sounded molten in her mind, flowing like lava to scorch themselves into her heart as a promise. The white-hot fury hardened into a cold, crusty nubble of black rock that sat angry and brooding in her chest.

Evie bent to kiss the apple of Jonas's cheeks, loving the smell of sugar on them and the plump silkiness of his infant skin. 'We shall see you next week, Jonas.'

He obediently followed Herr Becker, and Evie sensed her stepson was tasting a similarly sour note as herself.

'We will be at Streicher's event but not the festival, Giselle,' Max confirmed.

Giselle sneered and looked to Evie. 'I think he's protecting your modesty, my dear. There's a lot of nudity at the Night of the Amazons but you are going to have to open up your life. I gather you've come from a tiny village in provincial England but you are now in a big and important city. You can't be, how they say, a shrinking pansy.'

'Violet,' Evie corrected, wanting to laugh in her face. 'No, I will train myself not to be a shrinking violet, Giselle. But the cocktail event sounds wonderful. Time for me to socialise and make some new German friends.' Evie beamed a smile of saccharine delight at Giselle.

As they saw their guests out and finally closed the door, a knowing look passed between them, acknowledging that Evie had just made her first enemy in Germany. Evie hurried to the window, standing just far enough back from the lacy curtain that she couldn't be seen. Luckily so, because her guests had emerged on the opposite side of the street, where a glum-faced Jonas was clambering into a black car, and were glancing up at the apartment.

She focused on their mouths as she'd taught herself since childhood, watching people over the scream of a railway whistle, the screech of wheels and the other noises of a steam train that could drown out all other sounds.

Do you trust her? she watched Giselle say.

Becker frowned. *What's not to trust? A pretty new wife with nothing important on her mind.*

Evie smiled in the shadows, not only pleased that her play-acting had worked but that her lip-reading of German had lost none of its power.

Giselle seemed to look to the clouds for enlightenment of something her mind had snagged on. *Except vacant is not Max's style.*

I did not say she's vacant. I suspect she's quite intelligent in her own way.

What do you mean, Eric?

I mean, quite simply, Giselle, that she's no threat. Evie felt a soft cheer in her mind. *She's in love*, Becker continued. *Can't you see it? That's all that's filling her head right now. And she's nesting.*

Evie hoped she'd translated that right.

She's trying to show him what a good mother she will be, and for the time being she's happy to be mother to some other woman's son. We should be pleased for Jonas. He's going to be raised in the right way finally. The Jewish influence is out of his life.

That's if we ever give him back.

Evie gasped quietly.

The Jewish influence might be out of his life, Eric, but the mother's loathsome blood still flows through the boy. I doubt our people can remedy that. For now, he's a weapon to keep his father in line.

It didn't seem possible that she could hate Giselle any more than she had a few minutes ago but Evie felt her resolve harden.

There's something else there. Evie watched Giselle shake her blonde head, looking perplexed.

Well, I don't see it. This wife is perfect. She speaks German like a local. Eric gave an expression of helpless wonder. *She's even golden-haired – they look like family.*

Evie swallowed with relief, her attention flicking with care to Giselle, who clearly wasn't yet convinced.

I know, I know . . . she said, looking back at the apartment in what seemed to be frustration. *But I don't trust her yet.*

14

Evie decided not to share with Max what she'd gleaned. It would do no good telling him what Giselle had said to Eric. It risked angering Max and threatening their plan, which was for him to return to work while she lived as a housewife and worked out how she was going to fulfil her role for Leadbetter.

But she needed to know more.

'Is it the debrief tomorrow?' she said, handing him a mug of coffee. She liked these lazy weekend days at home with him, but she knew his mind was always reaching towards his son. She couldn't hold a grudge; she understood.

He blew on his breakfast coffee, relaxed after the previous day's tense visit. 'I'd hoped this week would be more about settling back in behind a desk. I presumed wrong.'

'Will Giselle be involved in the debrief?'

'No,' he gusted, vaguely amused. 'She's not that important. She's a minion, that's all, and a dreadful sycophant for Hitler and anyone in the hierarchy who gets close to him.'

'Has she ever met him?'

'I have no idea. I doubt it, though, or she'd be even more

high-handed, if that's possible. She wouldn't be able to stop reminding anyone and everyone that she's in Hitler's private circle.'

'What a ghastly woman Giselle is,' she said, moving the net curtain back to stare out at the empty street. It was still too early for people to be out and about. It was her favourite spot to absorb the rhythm of this city. 'But I don't think her guardianship has had any negative influence on your son. I want you to know that even in such a short meeting I think Jonas is beautiful in every way,' she observed.

'He takes after his mother,' he said, his tone brightening.

She looked back at him. 'In my ignorance I think your son is a carbon copy of you. He has your reticence, your composure, your looks, your interest in all things that move . . . and he hugs hard like you do.'

He found a sad smile. 'Well, I do love that you think he resembles me. That's reassuring. Yet I see Rachel in him all the time, and that allows her to live on.'

'Do you miss her?' She'd not had the opportunity to ask him this before and it came out before she could judge how insensitive her question was.

'I don't know how to answer that. When I was in prison in London, it was you I missed; it was you I thought about, not Rachel. She is a memory – a painful one because I failed her by not urging her to flee to America with the rest of her family, and I failed our daughter in . . . well, in every way. I wanted to name her Sarah after my mother. She barely had time to draw breath.'

Evie shifted him away from that pain back to her mission. 'Tell me more about Giselle. I need to know what I'm up against.'

'What can I say? She hasn't a maternal instinct, to my knowledge. She's so cold that she's arctic in her emotions.'

'Not to you, I note.'

'No, that's true. I'm the one who got away. Giselle isn't used to not getting what she sets her sights on. Giselle is positioning herself.'

Evie felt sickened at how true his words were.

'She can see that Nazi power is going to be an unstoppable force. She seems to agree with all of the party's politics and right-wing visions. Rachel's family wanted to take Jonas with them. I should have let them.'

'Why didn't you?'

'I regret my hesitation. He was all I had left of her and I convinced myself that he fitted the mould that Herr Hitler insists is the true German but . . .' He sighed. 'It was an error not to consider his safety.'

'What about yours?'

He gave a soft snort of scorn. 'Evie, I'm destined for Dachau.' At her frown, he explained. 'The government is setting up what are known as concentration camps around Germany, for everyone from political dissidents to those Hitler's people consider undesirable. Of course, there is no definition of "undesirable" – it's all very subjective. Rachel and her family would definitely have been sent there. But the gypsy folk are equally undesirable because they are itinerant; disabled people certainly do not fit the ideal, and so it goes. Politically motivated people who speak out against all the new rules and regulations are undesirable and will quickly find themselves inmates of a concentration camp. From what I can tell, there are no laws governing those camps other than a sort of private formulation for how they should be run, and their purpose, dreamed up by Theodor Eicke, an SS lieutenant-general at the time but these days I hear he is the Concentration Camps Inspector. It's all secret and coercive.'

'But why you? You don't fit the mould of being "undesirable", surely?'

'Potentially me,' he corrected her. 'I feel I'm an awkward problem suddenly. What are they supposed to do with me – this failed spy with knowledge that could compromise the government?'

She put her mug down and hurried to his side, taking his hands in hers. 'You play along, Max. Follow the script. Act loyal. Lie through your teeth. As soon as we have the opportunity, we jump ship, but it has to be seamless. We have to lull any critics of yours and anyone watching me into a false security. We need them to let the scrutiny drop, and once we sense it, we take our chance.' She shook her head. 'I had no idea,' she breathed, 'about that camp you talked about.'

'Dachau is the Bavarian camp – not too far from Munich.'

'But Jonas?' she appealed. 'Surely not?'

'I don't know about children, but I'm not prepared to test it.'

'Does Britain know all this?'

He shrugged. 'Of course. But does Britain care?'

She looked back at him with confusion and realised she had no answer for him. The Germans had blackmailed him using his child and now Britain was using identical tactics. Her heart and mind were polarised in that moment, like two magnets bouncing fiercely away from each other.

'This is not a conversation for now. Let's get ready. You said the traffic and the crowds will be immense.'

He nodded and sensibly left the previous topic alone.

'I might just write a quick note to my sister that we can post on the way.'

'I'll shower while you do.'

They moved into the bedroom together and she watched him undress, enjoying the process. He cut her a knowing grin. 'It will be your turn soon,' he warned.

'Already showered. I just have to dress.'

'Then I shall watch you undress tonight.'

'Be my guest,' she said, letting her gaze linger on his nakedness as she watched him walk towards the bathroom but not before he struck a strongman's pose in the doorway to make her gush a laugh.

She felt guilty for the laugh, for enjoying him, for already anticipating their lovemaking tonight and rather helplessly hugging herself at her fortune in finding someone this late who loved her back as much. It didn't seem fair to be in such a content mindset when she was here on a mission that might add more evidence to the fact that war and death, misery and destruction, were coming into their lives again.

And Jonas was in the midst of it. Maybe Rachel was the lucky one. She banished that thought. If Rachel had loved Max as much as Evie did, then there was nothing lucky about how life had dealt with Rachel.

Soon after Evie heard the rush of water splashing in the bathroom, she reached for the scarf that Max had given her from her dressing-table drawer. She kept it there, safe at hand, recalling her fear as Giselle had touched it, frightened the woman would discover its secret and the reason why Leadbetter had asked to borrow it.

She got a waft of perfume from the scarf as she handled it. The fragrance was not hers and Evie hated that Giselle had left her mark on Evie's property. That was the point of that whole charade, she now realised. Giselle was fully aware of what she was doing when she'd reached for the scarf. Oh, how cunning a woman can be. She had wanted to leave her smell behind on something she knew Evie treasured – why else would she go through the theatrics of tying on the scarf around herself? No one else would be that presumptuous or impolite. But Giselle was passing a private and powerful message: *everything you have is mine, if I want it. Smell me on what you think is yours*, she was saying to Evie. And then the voice continued, much to her anger: *and I'll take him from you too.*

Never! Max would never betray her for Giselle.

She heard the water again, cutting through her thoughts. She needed to get on.

First, she wrote a brief letter to Rosie, making sure she used two pages of notepaper and only wrote on one side. It was newsy: how much she was enjoying Jonas, that Munich in the summer was lively and fun, that she missed the railways but was a regular on the trams now, and other chatty nonsense to do with a Bavarian cake called blueberry kuchen that would stop traffic if everyone could taste it at once.

She signed off in her usually affectionate manner, promising to write again soon and that one to her father would follow on the heels of this note.

Evie tiptoed to the door and checked that Max was nowhere near; she could still hear the shower going but she knew it wouldn't last much longer. She would have to move fast. She returned to the desk and flipped over the letter to Rosie, placed a corner of the scarf over it and then sandwiched the scarf between it and a fresh sheet.

She wrote an entirely different note, to a different person this time.

She heard Max whistling from the corridor. He would be in the room in moments.

Evie flicked the scarf away, draping it quickly over the back of her chair and flinging the second sheet behind the curtain. She would burn it later. As Max arrived in the bedroom, she was neatening the letter, folding it carefully on the polished oak of the desktop.

'There,' she said, covering her tension. 'I owed her one, not that I had much to say.'

Deliberately, she left the note on the desk and in a breezy tone said, 'My turn in the bathroom.'

Evie felt sure Max would read the letter and conclude she did have nothing important to say to her sister, other than that she was generally enjoying Munich. He knew nothing about the invisible ink that the beautiful Hermès scarf had been drenched with before she left England.

'Walk me past where the Night of the Amazons is happening,' she suggested as they left the apartment building.

'Are those shoes comfy?'

'I can run in them,' she assured him.

Evie caught her breath at the sight of the Nymphenburg Palace, which had served as the summer residence of the old rulers of Bavaria.

'Wow!' she helplessly exclaimed, as they dodged the crowd of festival-goers on the walk up to the palace.

They paused and Max explained. 'It was built in the seventeenth century in the Italian baroque style, but the palace has been tinkered with continuously for more than a century.'

'It's huge,' she breathed.

'It's wider than Versailles, apparently.'

'Not that I'd know if you were lying.' She grinned.

Max kissed her hand. 'I'll take you one day.'

'You said it's a Nazi glamour show?' she queried quietly. 'I don't even know what that is.'

He grinned. 'I don't either – this is the first, but they promise it's going to be an annual event for Munich. Reichsführer Himmler has touted it as healthy eroticism, but this is the brainchild of a paunchy little man called Christian Weber. He's a nasty piece of work and a staunch Nazi; a member of the SS. I've told you about the SS?'

Evie nodded, her heart sinking. Max had explained to her that the *Schutzstaffel* was Hitler's protection unit, which had its origins as a small paramilitary unit. She remembered Max's warning: *The SS is to be feared. It's the agency for terror as much as security.*

'Meanwhile, Munich is Hitler's playground,' Max said. 'Whenever he's here, he has fun.'

'Is Hitler coming?'

He frowned as they were swept along with the crowd. 'There are rumours, but I doubt this rather grand and tasteless erotic show is to his taste. Wagner's operas are more his style. Besides, we'd have seen a guard outside his apartment building on Prinzregentenplatz.' Max gave a small shrug. 'A sure sign the Führer is in residence, and probably a Mercedes parked right outside, black and shiny as anthracite.'

Max turned to her. 'Let me take you for a quick light meal before the necessary rendezvous for cocktails. Best we don't drink alcohol on empty bellies.' Evie felt Max's mood become serious. 'We'll go to Hotel Bayerischer Hof. It's in the old town, not too far from Marienplatz. Some of the top brass will be there. We need to be seen.'

'Then we shall.'

'Evie, what do you hope to learn?'

'Well . . . why, for instance, you were sent to spy on our railways. Why would that interest Hitler?'

'I was never told.'

'So you say.'

He paused, gripping her elbow just firmly enough to ensure she paid attention. 'I was never told,' he repeated.

'Then maybe at your debrief, you can ask why and learn more. We work to give Whitehall what it needs so we can get out of Germany and . . .'

'And what, Evie?'

'A new life,' she finished, knowing it was not what he was asking, but she really didn't want to confront *afterwards* . . . not until they'd solved their present dilemma.

The old town was busy on this summer night. The festive atmosphere of Munich at this time of year was clearly infectious. People were enjoying the warm evening, eating, drinking beer, sharing ice creams or simply strolling along the cobbled streets.

'You have to promise me you'll take no chances.'

'Max.' She looked up at him to allay his concern. 'Get rid of that frown. We're on a lovely night out together. I am simply going to be watching.'

'All right,' he said, uncertainty still in his expression but his tone cheerful.

It took them about ten minutes of pleasant strolling towards the north-west corner of the old town, entering its square, before he pointed. 'This used to be the site of the town's salt stalls,' he explained. 'Then it was designated as a parade ground in the late nineteenth century. Palaces abound. And there is the Hotel Bayerischer Hof, our destination. It's been around since the mid 1800s, bought in 1897 and owned by the same family since, called Volkhardt. Rumour has it the Nazis wanted to take it over as a guesthouse, strongarmed the owners, but they held out.'

'Good for them. Oh, it's splendid,' she said, taking in the sweep of palatial windows and the row of gables at roof level.

Inside she was entranced by Gothic-looking vaults in the main foyer with its highly decorative plaster ceiling; leather sofas and chairs formed cosy clusters through the vast atrium. Rugs covered the stone floors and mirrored doors made the space feel twice as large.

'We've got a private event in the Reading Room, apparently,' Max said, guiding her deeper into the hotel.

Tinkling laughter and deep, amused voices blew like a summer breeze down the hallway and drew them towards a spacious room with a heavily decorated plaster ceiling and a cornice cove she could lie in. Massive, ornate mirrored doors threw light from the chandeliers back into the room, and a Persian rug of busy pattern and deep colours accentuated the richness of their surrounds. Velvet upholstered chairs placed around the room sat mostly vacant as the gathered partygoers preferred to stand, mingle and watch one another from the best vantage point. Smoke hung like a wispy wraith above heads tilted back to blow more into the cloud, or to laugh at remarks that may or may not have been amusing.

As far as Evie could tell, this was a place to be seen. Presumably plenty of the local party faithful were in attendance. It was crowded, so that made it hard to focus on anyone in particular.

'You must be wondering why we're here,' Max suddenly muttered.

'I am,' she remarked.

He leaned close to her ear. 'Because of Julius Streicher, who is Hitler's close friend. He is the incarnation of the devil, in my opinion: the country's number-one Jew hater. Very powerful in Bavaria's north.'

'Why us?' She gave him a dazzling smile as though he'd just told her something intriguing.

'No one ignores his invitations or his gatherings, and I suspect we need to be here so he can lay his lascivious gaze upon you.'

'Me?'

He nodded and leaned in again so they were not overheard. 'I'm a failed spy who has returned with a new English wife. I won't say they're immediately suspicious, but they're certainly wanting to take their own measure of you – of us. He's a nasty piece of work and cruel. Be careful.'

'Up to performance level, then,' she warned, smiling at him as though he'd said something affectionate.

Max kissed her hand. 'Exactly.' he murmured.

A waiter arrived with a tray of effervescing champagne coupes.

'Looks delicious,' she said to the harried man, who was being pulled by the fat, bejewelled hands of a woman trying to win his attention but probably mostly his tray of drinks.

'One moment, madam,' he said to the needy patron in English and turned back to Evie.

'Thank you,' Evie said in her mother tongue, surprised he was a Brit. She took two glasses, passing one to Max, who was being whispered to by a man in uniform.

Her waiter did a double-take that someone else had spoken English to him. 'You're welcome. It's from grapes grown in Avize. Only the best.'

She laughed. 'I'm not that knowledgeable.'

'Some people here insist on knowing,' he said, raising his eyes to the ceiling as though those people were pretentious, but his attention was dragged back to the enormous woman who was quickly turning tetchy.

'You'd better get on,' she said, raising her glass to Max, who didn't look as delighted as she. The waiter turned reluctantly away, and she frowned. 'What's wrong?'

'It didn't take long. Julius Streicher wants to see me.'

Max leaned in close, smiling as though he was going to whisper something wicked. 'I want to impress upon you that this is a dangerous individual.' When he leaned back, he gave a convincing attempt at a grin that she knew to replicate.

She added a soft chuckle as though he was most amusing, even though she felt like someone had just sprayed iced water over her. 'Let's see what he has to say.'

He took her hand and kissed it, whispering: 'He calls himself the northern Führer . . . be careful around him.'

She took Max's arm, balanced her champagne, and let him lead her to where a short, slightly paunchy man held court. He was perfectly bald, and his lips had little definition, bleeding into his jowls to give the impression of an almost featureless balloon of smooth skin, his close-set eyes hooded by slanting brows. She noted Giselle was already in position, tinkling a laugh at something

Streicher was saying. They were surrounded by other, presumably lesser, party officials with a sycophantic look about them.

'Max,' Streicher called out, spotting Max shouldering them gently through the crowd.

'*Sieg Heil*,' Max said, surprising her as he gave the outstretched Nazi salute to Streicher, who returned it casually.

'Don't you mean "Heil *Hitler*", Herr Hall?'

'I'm out of practice,' Max admitted with a grin. 'Too long on my travels. Good evening, Julius.' Evie realised they were more than just known to each other.

'Is this the lovely new wife I've been hearing about?' Evie felt herself being undressed by the Nazi powerbroker's beady gaze. 'You certainly are a catch, my dear.'

'Evelyn Hall, sir,' she said, holding out a hand before Max could introduce her, or Giselle take the front foot with introductions.

His smile did not reach his eyes, but he was busy feasting on her with his gaze anyway. He surprised her by laying his oddly shaped lips – which reminded her of a fish – against the back of her hand. 'Enchanting,' he murmured. 'You've done well, Max,' he congratulated him, as though looking over a prize acquisition. 'Much prettier and far more appropriate than the first, eh?' he jested, flipping the back of his hand at Max's taut belly.

Evie blinked with shock but quickly gathered herself as she noted Max wasn't reacting.

'The other one is best gone,' Streicher continued. 'Wasn't doing you any good. And I'm glad we didn't have to tease her out of your hold like a stick at a grub.'

Evie glanced with deep consternation at Giselle, hoping she might weigh in and stop this. What a vain hope. Instead, she received a condescending smirk.

Streicher was still talking. 'How's your boy?'

'I'd like to have him home,' Max replied, his voice tight but his tone neutral, and Evie couldn't help but admire his composure. She was beginning to get a true inkling of what Max had been up against.

'He's such a lovely little chap,' she chimed in, to spare Max. 'I think I'm quite in love with Jonas already.'

'Not his fault he is half Jew, but he doesn't look it, thank heavens, and we all like his father,' Streicher quipped. 'However, I hope you will give us strong sons and golden-haired daughters of your own.' Now he tapped Evie on the belly in a horrible breach of good manners. But she had been warned, and taking Max's lead did not overreact, instead pasting on a lukewarm smile, making sure to crinkle her eyes as Leadbetter had instructed her.

'Oh, I intend to, Herr Streicher. Max and I are already working hard at it,' she risked, and got the laugh she wanted from Streicher – but more importantly to her, the slit-eyed jealousy from Giselle that the woman could not fully disguise.

Streicher was still grinning. 'Well, with you two fine specimens as the breeders, Germany will thank you.'

Breeders? Hateful man. 'I love Munich and hope to see plenty more of this magnificent country,' she lied.

'And your German is very good too. Is that a Franconian accent?'

She laughed. 'I have no idea. I was taught by a woman from Bamberg.' Another lie. Lotte had been from Strullendorf, but it was close enough.

'Oh, my dear, what a pretty place it is too, in northern Bavaria, the region I control. You must visit sometime – as my guest. And Max, you'd better teach your wife the Heil Hitler, now she's a German resident.'

Max laughed. 'Yes, you're right. Training begins tonight, darling,' he said, wagging a finger, but his glance conveyed his apology to her.

'Why were you not at my Amazons night?'

Evie answered for him. 'My fault, Herr Streicher. Forgive me, I'm a country girl – never been much further than the next village. I didn't think I would cope very well with the crowds.'

'I see,' he said, his small eyes reminding her of a pig. And she felt immediately that this was an insult to pigs. 'That will have to change, as you will both be required at the rally in Nuremberg come August.'

'Of course,' Max said.

August? Hope we're long gone, Evie thought. She smiled. 'I will definitely look forward to that. I have listened to previous orations from the rallies on the wireless.'

'And what did you think?' Streicher said. She shouldn't have given him the opening, and she could feel Max's body stiffening with tension next to her.

'I found them mesmerising,' she lied fluidly, placing down her glass on a nearby table. 'Utterly absorbing.'

Streicher regarded her as one might study an insect. She couldn't read what he was thinking, but finally he smiled. He looked to Max. 'There are a couple of things I'd like to discuss with you, Max.'

It appeared to be a cue because suddenly Giselle was in motion. 'Evelyn – shall we?' Giselle was taking her by the arm in a firm but friendly fashion. 'We should let these men talk.'

'Of course,' she said, unhappily allowing herself to be removed. 'See you soon, darling,' she said, reaching back to peck Max on the cheek. 'Good evening, Herr Streicher, and thank you for inviting me to my first party in Munich.'

'Many more to come for you, I hope,' he said, his glinting eyes enjoying a final roam of her body.

I hope. What did that mean?

15

Giselle led Evie to a quieter corner, lifting a pair of effervescing champagne bowls from a passing waiter's tray. 'Here, my dear – good champagne like this is not served at every party, but Streicher does enjoy showing off.'

'He's the host?'

'Yes. He's also what we call a *Gauleiter*.' At Evie's frown she explained. 'That means high political clout. He's the governor of Bavaria's north. Streicher's always trying to outdo his counterpart from the south, who I think holds the balance of power. You'll meet Wagner in good time.'

'Do I need to? I'm just a housewife.' Evie casually turned her body so she could see Max and the hateful party official; watch their mouths.

You failed, I hear, Streicher said.

I don't see it that way. Depends on how you view it, sir.

'Is that how you see yourself?' Giselle enquired, trying to show interest in her, but Evie noted that she too was looking towards Max.

How should we view it? Streicher asked.

'I'm not qualified in anything.' Evie laughed, glancing at Giselle but noting her attention was still riveted, not on the distant conversation but on the handsome man being pummelled by it.

I sent back a lot of useful information, Evie watched Max insist.

You panicked.

'Germany doesn't need you to be qualified in anything, my dear, so long as you give it lots of brave sons,' Giselle said condescendingly.

No, I was cautious. My instruments were discovered and the Secret Service had already informed police of their suspicions that there was a spy in North Yorkshire. I couldn't risk being found. You know that.

We needed more. If we're going to invade Britain as planned and—

Shock trilled through her like a startled bird.

'Who's catching your attention, Evelyn?' Giselle said, straining to follow her line of sight. In the same moment, people shifted and blocked Evie's view.

'The same person who has yours,' she said. She shouldn't have fallen prey to her own vexation, but she was frankly traumatised by what she'd lip-read. Giselle's attention snapped back to her with a narrowed gaze, her nostrils helplessly flaring.

'I beg your pardon?'

'You seem inordinately intrigued by my husband.'

'Heavens! What an accusation.'

'Is it false? I mean, I understand. He's desperately handsome and such a wonderful man.' She smiled, making it smug, so Giselle would immediately believe this was a tousle between jealous women.

'Evelyn, I've known Max since we were teenagers.'

'And?'

Evie enjoyed watching Giselle look momentarily flustered as she fluttered confused eyelids, trying to get purchase on Evie's point. 'I don't know what you mean,' she said, sounding lame and unconvincing.

Evie sighed as though slightly lost. She had to divert Giselle's attention, already aware that the German woman would love to know anything about her weakness, even if it was a ruse. 'I could use your help, actually. Max and I are very much in love but our marriage is new and there are pressures on it – moving to Germany, me leaving my family behind, Max needing to build a secure life for Jonas, me suddenly being thrust into motherhood of a young boy. Now.' She paused for emphasis. 'I'm ready to take on all the challenges ahead but I'd prefer it if an old flame from Max's past wasn't nibbling away at us.'

Giselle had the composure to look affronted. 'Me?' She gusted a sarcastic sigh. 'You have nothing to fear,' she said, and Evie heard only insincerity.

Evie sensed pleasure in Giselle's audacity, like a cat toying with a mouse. Well, this was not the moment for the timidity of a mouse, but neither was it a good idea to give open offence. She rearranged her expression to appear chastened. 'Then forgive me. I apologise for the accusation. You'll have to indulge a possessive new bride, filled with jealousy for beautiful women her new husband seeks out,' she said, placing her untouched champagne glass onto a passing waiter's tray. She cast Giselle a breezy smile. 'Where's the ladies' room?'

Evie was surprised to see Giselle awaiting her by the hand basins in the glamorous powder room of the hotel as she emerged from one of the stalls. She noted there was no one else in what had been a busy facility when she entered. Presumably, Giselle had asked to be alone.

She smiled in query. It seemed the simplest gesture and did not require her to lead any conversation.

'Evelyn,' Giselle began tightly with a sigh and a pretend smile. She also chose to speak in English – no doubt, Evie surmised, out of some sort of consideration for the amount of energy it must be taking for Evie to mentally translate and then reply in German. *If only she knew*, Evie thought, *that I think in German when I need to*. 'I fear we've got off on the other foot.' She pronounced 'the' as 'zer'.

Evie met her gaze directly and corrected her. 'The wrong foot?'

'I don't understand.'

'In Britain we say "got off on the wrong foot".' She switched to German for Giselle's ease and realised it was a little show of power; *Be careful*, her inner voice cautioned her. 'Marching out of step, in other words.'

Giselle shrugged in a careless manner and shifted to German, as though she could no longer be bothered making the effort for Evie. 'I would like to be your friend, Evelyn dear, and Streicher is right, you really must learn the Hitlergruss. You don't want people thinking you're a dissident of any kind, or not loyal to Germany.'

'I'm not sure I understand.'

'It's the law, Evelyn. For three years now it's been mandatory that you give the official salute. Children are taught it at school.'

'But I'm English.'

'Evelyn, please be assured that you must relinquish all notion that you are British. In fact, our . . . um . . . authorities may need to have a chat with you to establish that you are genuinely interested to be German.'

Evie hadn't expected this, so the surprise in her expression was authentic.

'You are now married to a German engineer who has his role to play in a government position. Max, as I'm sure you've gathered, has a long and proud line and his very name opens doors in the higher echelons of the Nazi Party. And you must not let him down.

Foreigners are not exempted from German law and there are special courts of punishment that I would hate to see you brought before.'

'What?' Evie couldn't hide her astonishment now. She stopped just short of derision.

Giselle halted, then drew her to the side. Her expression was not one of amusement. 'At the moment we are being generous. The world is watching and people will be visiting soon for the great Olympics in Berlin, so'—she shrugged—'the laws are relaxed for visitors. However, Evelyn, you are now becoming a local and, if you love Max, I suggest you conform to our Nazi laws. Two years ago, some performers trained their monkeys to give the salute and the punishment for such scorn was the destruction of their animals and terrible shame for them. Make no mistake, this is serious. There are signs all over Munich, all over Germany, that you'll see reminding you to make the formal salute. It's part of everyday life now. Some slack has been granted you tonight, for instance, but you heard Streicher's caution to your husband. I suggest you practise and then display your commitment to Max and his country from here on . . . or Jonas may suffer for your carelessness.' She smiled. 'Enjoy your evening, Evelyn.'

They'd not lingered, and she got the impression that Max had hurried their attendance. Outside the apartment building, after seeing the taxi leave, she understood why.

'Streicher wishes to have you interviewed,' he said without any preamble.

She frowned. 'Interviewed?'

'Polite way of describing what will essentially be an interrogation.'

'Oh, Max, no!'

He looked around, hushing her. 'We may be being watched,'

he said, pulling out cigarettes that she'd not seen him smoke previously. 'This is for show,' he explained softly and lit up.

'What do you mean?'

'I can't be sure the apartment hasn't been wired in our absence, so I'm taking some precautions. I want to have the apartment rechecked by a second friend, just in case.'

'Is Herr Streicher suspicious of me?'

He shook his head as he blew smoke out. 'Not especially, although suspicion is the natural resting mindset of all fervent Nazis. Right now I think you'd call it due diligence.'

'I have nothing to worry about?'

He sighed. 'Of course you do. Because you are here under false pretences. Stay focused on being the charming new wife and you'll be fine. He's making sure that he has taken all the right precautions in case the Gestapo check.'

'Gestapo?'

'Evie. Just go for your interview and nothing more will come of it.'

Max was at work, facing his debrief, no doubt, and Evie felt like ten o'clock couldn't come fast enough. She had slept fitfully, waking often to turn over in her mind what she'd seen Streicher say to Max the previous evening. She hadn't mentioned anything to him, though. This would always be her dilemma: Leadbetter had won Evie's firm promise that she would report only what she saw, what she knew, what she suspected, and that she would not allow Max to interpret anything.

'He'll want to, Evie,' Leadbetter had said. 'He'll want to prove his innocence by aiding your effort. And we simply can't trust any information he provides.'

'What if I decide he is trustworthy?' she'd asked.

'We cannot indulge our trust in someone who has admitted to spying. Even if he has twisted the truth going back to Germany, and even if he is being blackmailed, the fact is that he's been compromised. And he could be compromised again if his son is threatened. You have to be an island, Evie. Promise me.'

She had given the promise but in her heart she felt it was an empty one, knowing she would be relying on Max simply to cope with this new life – but she was, in reality, juggling both options. Today she was torn, still keeping that barrier up. Without Max realising, she had hung her precious scarf in the window overnight. When he'd queried it, she shrugged. 'Oh, I just wanted to air it out. Giselle tried it on, and I don't like it smelling of her perfume.' It wasn't a lie, but it seemed her innocent scarf had become her major tool for espionage. Not only was it loaded with invisible ink for her letters to Leadbetter, but now it was being used as her code for a meet with one of his people.

She hoped it had been seen, and shortly she'd know if it had been. It was quarter to ten and she couldn't linger in this flat with her harried thoughts a moment longer. She pulled on the scarf but loosely, as it was a hot day, having carefully chosen a light summer frock to match it, and she left the apartment, preferring to go on foot to Brienner Strasse. She had plenty of time.

Evie let her thoughts wander as she walked, having memorised the map between her apartment and the Carlton Tearoom – where she had been instructed to head the morning after she'd used the scarf signal. It was located on another of the grand royal avenues of Munich. She didn't know who she was going to meet except that she would recognise one of Leadbetter's minions by his plain red tie. It occurred to Evie that a red tie was hardly subtle, but then Leadbetter had counselled her that hiding in plain sight would be more successful than skulking in back alleys. So she would greet his man warmly, share a pot of tea, look as though they were sharing gossip from days gone and then part with a kiss to both cheeks and a promise to meet again. They would speak English deliberately, so that if she was seen by chance, or if she was being professionally observed by suspicious Nazi friends of Giselle's, then she could say it was an old friend.

The Carlton Tearoom was a cosier establishment than she'd expected. Everything in Munich right now was focused on summer beer gardens and sitting outside in courtyards, so she was surprised to find herself ushered by a waiter into a spacious, tall-ceilinged room with plush upholstered sofas against the walls, low tables with armchairs, and dining tables with some velvet chairs and some rattan-backed. To Evie it gave the impression of a large formal drawing room, with decorative wall lights and a central chandelier. It was busily patronised, and the clink of china and happy chatter from a well-dressed clientele were clues that she was in an establishment rather than a cafe that saw all sorts.

She cast a quick glance around and saw no gentleman wearing a red tie. She allowed herself to be guided to the back corner beneath an arched half window where two small armchairs were being vacated.

Evie thanked the two women gathering up handbags and shopping bags, adding, 'My timing is perfect,' in German.

They laughed, agreeing. 'Have today's gateau and to hell with the inches,' one woman quipped. 'Enjoy being in the most powerful of company.'

She frowned at the odd remark as the waiter asked if she was meeting someone. 'Er, yes, I am – a friend. Um, perhaps I could have a pot of Darjeeling, please, while I wait?'

'Of course.'

'With lemon, please,' she added.

He nodded. 'The menu is here if you feel like something more,' he said, gesturing towards the printed sheet near the small vase of bright daisies.

She smiled her thanks and he departed. Evie pulled off her summer gloves, which she was glad she'd donned. This tearoom was rather formal. The women were in hats; the few men were in suits. She let her gaze roam, trying not to focus on anyone, and allowed herself to relax into the soft drone of other people's conversations. She deliberately did not look at anyone, or she'd have found herself following those inane discussions about children or husbands, clothes or parties. There was money in this room. She suspected few of the women had ever worked a day.

There was one table close to hers that had only men clustered around it – there were three of them. She glanced over innocently and her gaze snagged on the gentleman who sat closest to the corner, near an indoor palm. She stared, not deliberately, but in consternation, trying to place why he was familiar. When the dawning arrived, it was merely a couple of heartbeats after she'd first noticed him, but to Evie it felt like eternity had passed in those moments.

She met eyes of a hypnotic blue, as though the colour had been carefully mixed on an artist's palette for maximum power. She was briefly mesmerised before she became flustered, recognising that Adolf Hitler was that small gent in the corner, sipping from a china cup and watching her over its rim. Evie felt as though her whole body loosened, like jelly slipping its mould, when he surprised her with a quick smile beneath the famous moustache, and then his attention shifted back to his companions. They spoke quietly and genially, soft bursts of laughter every now and then, as Evie became hotly aware of the Führer's presence and the men's conversation. She could not make out anything and she couldn't risk lip-reading. Nonetheless, her riveted attention obliterated everyone else's chatter in the tearooms. She desperately wanted to look over again but dared not. It was terrifying enough that she was here in the presence of the man who had become a monster in her dreams. And yet there he sat, small and neat in civilian clothes, chatting amiably, his moustache not nearly as comical as it looked in the newspapers, and his presence felt friendly rather than intimidating. She'd intimidated herself, if anything. He'd merely smiled, in an avuncular way rather than leering. She blinked, aware of being watched by the single man under whose authority the most terrible of acts were being committed and upon whose order the country in which she stood may well go to war with the country she belonged to.

Her pot of tea arrived and she nervously busied herself with the tiny silver tongs and a particularly obstinate slice of lemon that didn't wish to leave its companions. It finally came free and she was able to place it in the cup. Evie had always rather enjoyed pouring hot tea over the lemon in order to infuse the brew from the instant it left the pot. It wasn't perhaps the polite way, but no one was watching the Yorkshire spy break protocol. The spy needed to stay calm. She stole another glance his way. The straight, glossy hair was strictly parted on the right and combed in a long flop that wanted to sit forward against his brow. His relaxed face was serious, and beneath the slightly bulging and penetrating gaze were fleshy bags of skin, as though he desperately needed sleep. In that moment, however, he was amused by something one of his companions had said and he chuckled, shrugged and took another sip of his tea with thinnish lips. She would have recognised him faster if they'd all been in uniform; the civvies gave him a measure of disguise but of course he couldn't stay unnoticed for long. Anyone who tiptoed by their table lifted a hand in salute but she noted they murmured their words, obviously trained in not interrupting the powerful head of their nation. He responded lazily, clearly not wishing to be noticed or saluted.

She had to tear her gaze from him and forced herself to adjust her scarf and look across towards the dingling bell of the doorway, where she caught a flash of red arriving and being greeted by the same waiter.

It was a woman wearing a smart skirt suit with a pillar-box red length of silk tied loose and low in an interpretation of a man's tie. Evie adored the masculine look.

'Evie!' the woman called, waving, as though spotting an old friend, totally ignoring the important patron nearby.

Evie, still in slight bemusement, raised her hand in greeting and the waiter escorted her guest to her table; she had no idea of her name but clearly this was the right person. So much for a clandestine meeting: right under the nose of the Führer. The woman suddenly saw him, lifted a hand and dipped her head, moving on quickly towards Evie with outstretched arms and a sigh of pleasure.

Up close the woman was older than she'd first thought. This urbane creature wore her years so well that even her wrinkles appeared immaculately carved and positioned. 'Hello, darling Evie.' It was as though they had known each other all their lives. 'How wonderful to see you in Munich,' she said, and Evie was acutely aware they were performing for any observers and one in particular.

She deliberately spoke in German and Evie followed suit. 'I know – I can't quite believe it,' Evie risked in a bright voice, letting the woman bend to kiss her cheeks.

'Darling! I told you I'd meet you off the train,' her new friend gushed. 'How splendid to see you again. How's your family?'

'Everyone's well. Missing me,' she began, glancing at the waiter who was hovering, determined not to look again to her left.

Her companion pointed at Evie's pot. 'I'll have the same, thank you.' He withdrew. Without breaking her smile or tone, her guest said in a low voice. 'You can call me Jean.'

Evie didn't lose a beat either. 'Thanks for suggesting the tearoom, Jean. It's beautiful,' she said, looking around, admiring the cafe. 'Did you know he'd be here?' she said, dropping her voice but maintaining the smile.

'It's a favourite spot for him . . . but for me too, and I thought you'd like it,' Jean said, leaning in as if she were saying something that only women could share. 'Don't be scared. Hiding in plain sight is the only way.' She sat back and gave another sigh. 'You'll find Munich is a wonderful city, especially in the summer. Now, tell me all about you and . . . Max, is it? Congratulations again, by the way.'

Evie played along, making nonsense conversation for a few minutes, and Jean kept up her side of the charade. When they'd been chatting for a while and everyone had forgotten the newcomer, Jean suddenly pulled her chair around, putting her back to Hitler and his friends. 'I want to show you some photographs,' she said, pulling out an album. 'I hope you've brought me some from the wedding.'

Heads together, Jean began pointing at random photos in the small book she'd opened. 'Here's Wolfgang all grown,' she said, before dropping her voice. 'It must be urgent,' Jean said, 'for you to use the scarf.'

Evie shrugged and knew to keep smiling. 'Gosh, he *has* grown.' She dropped her voice. 'I attended an event yesterday. It was a cocktail evening. Lots of men in uniform, so very much the high-ranking Nazis, including Julius Streicher.'

The slightest lift of Jean's eyebrow clued Evie that she'd made the right decision by signalling for contact. 'Oh, do tell, you mischief-maker!' she chuckled, as though Evie had just opened up a new line of gossip.

Jean's pot of tea arrived.

'Firstly, he wishes to have me interviewed.'

Jean didn't overreact.

'Max says it's protocol.'

Jean nodded, checking no waiter was close enough to overhear. She spoke fast. 'Possibly so. But don't drop your guard or get cornered. Hold the line of whatever backstory London has crafted. Don't deviate from it or embellish it. It's why it's there – as full protection. And here's Franz . . . still so handsome, no?'

Evie nodded and smiled.

'And by the way, if something goes wrong, we met in Paris at the Sainte-Chapelle, admiring the stained-glass windows. We shared a drink at a nearby cafe. I had absinthe. You had a coffee with milk.'

'Max?'

'He had absinthe too. And I said to call me when you arrive in Munich and we'd meet. Now, what else?'

Evie pointed to a photograph and chuckled for the benefit of onlookers while she muttered, 'I observed him saying to Max that he'd failed them. That they needed the information'—she dropped her voice and leaned right in to whisper, as though saying something particularly poisonous—'if they are to invade Britain.'

Jean sat back and laughed lightly. She picked up her cup and took two sips. Evie could tell from her companion's gaze that she was trying to digest the shocking information, as though considering how to respond and not just what to say next but how to proceed. She took some time pouring her tea, adding lemon.

She sipped. When Jean finally replied over the rim of her cup, her tone was admirably light. 'I've suspected as much. You actually heard him say this?'

'No, I couldn't hear it.'

Jean frowned; she had to quickly rearrange her expression from immediate exasperation to interest. 'Oh, do explain.'

Evie bent her head to look closely at a photo as if trying to peer into the background to read something. 'I can lip-read.'

Jean sipped again. 'I see. Is this skill reliable?'

'I might as well have heard it; you can rely on what I saw.'

'In German?' she queried, smiling, impressively ensuring there was no tension in her body language.

Evie nodded firmly. 'And this is your lovely home, I presume?' She stole a glance at the Führer.

'Stay calm, Evie. He's not interested in you. This is simply a preferred haunt. Do you know why?' She smiled wider as if deep in their intrigue about somebody having an affair, or a similar piece of gossip. Evie shook her head. 'He comes here because the whole room of patrons don't stand and give him the Hitlergruss or a round of applause.' Jean blinked. 'He likes the peace and slightly more relaxed attitude towards him of Munich's moneyed people.'

Evie nodded that she understood.

'No need to feel panicky – remain calm and you'll be ignored.'

She didn't appreciate Jean's slight condescension; it hadn't needed to be said. She *was* calm. What's more, she was doing a job for which Jean had likely been given months of training, while Evie had been cast into this because of a threat to someone she loved. Now she was a spy on Germany, and it was no different to why Max had been spying on Britain. At least he had lied. Why could Whitehall not appreciate that? Disguising her annoyance, she smiled, surprising herself at how well she could pretend around anyone and everyone these days. 'What are you going to do with the information?'

'Pass it forward and await a response.'

'How will I be told?'

'Probably me, or . . .' Her volume lifted slightly. 'Oh, you must try my hairdresser, then,' Jean said, full of enthusiasm as she leaned forward and touched Evie's hand. She dropped her voice. 'Have a new style done that suits a fashionable Nazi hierarchy's wife; it will suit you and embed you further in the elitist company that Max can show you around.' She reached into her bag, speaking more loudly now. 'Here, darling, I'll write down the name of my salon.' Jean took her time. 'There you go. Ask only for Hannah. She'll make a new woman of you.' She giggled, draining her china cup.

'When?'

'I'll have a word – I imagine even though she's terribly popular that she'll make an exception and get you in for, oooh, maybe midweek?' Jean said. 'Well, off you go, darling.' She stood and Evie had to follow suit. They kissed. 'Let's go to the park next time,' Jean gushed, answering her question. 'I'll send a message.' That was code for the dead drop not far from her apartment.

'Lovely,' Evie agreed, feeling edgy for all the intrigue and play-acting. 'Until then. Er . . . let me . . .'

'No, no, Evie. This is my town. I can cover it. Your turn next time.' Jean waved Evie away, shooing her towards the door as she called for the waiter to bring the bill.

Evie was determined not to look his way, not to be forced to give the salute that she really did need to practise, or risk being singled out and potentially humiliated. And yet her treacherous eyes caught movement to her left and dragged her gaze to Adolf Hitler, who was moving out of his chair and standing. He was staring at her, the slightly bulging eyes like two brilliant spotlights upon her. Her insides felt as though they were rearranging themselves. She'd barely got started and had been found out, by none other than the Führer! It was as though there were no other people in the tearoom except the pair of them. He began to raise a hand and she knew he was going to call her out, have her arrested, and—

He pointed to the ground, though, and she couldn't help but notice the tremor in his hand as he did so. Hitler saw her register it and he quickly returned his left hand to his pocket. 'You left your scarf,' he said in a soft voice, the smile curling oh so briefly upon his thin mouth.

'Oh?' she said, startled, not just by him but by her carelessness in nearly losing her extremely precious accessory. 'Thank you, sir,' she said, not knowing how else to address him. 'Er, Heil Hitler,' she mumbled, surely blushing, as she raised a hand slightly and self-consciously.

He returned it with a limp gesture and the smile faded and she was forgotten as the waiter fetched the scarf and Evie fled, cheeks burning with guilt, feeling sure that his singular and searching stare saw right through her.

16

In Whitehall, Hugh Leadbetter leaned back in his chair and absently heard the familiar creak of its comfy seat. The gentle knock told him Mary was back.

She opened the door, arriving with a small tray. 'I took the liberty of bringing biscuits, sir.' She smiled, setting down a Queens Green Solian Ware cup holding a strong brew. Next to the saucer she placed a matching quarter plate with his favourite Garibaldi biscuits.

'Not good for my girth, Mary.'

'But good for when you're pondering something tricky, sir.' She gave him a knowing but affectionate glare. 'You do look worried.'

He sat forward, sounding suddenly exasperated. 'She's out there in the field with zero experience and next-to-no backup. She could be walking into a trap at any time.'

'Drink your tea. I think she's been underestimated too many times, if you don't mind my observing, sir. From a woman's point of view, I found her most impressive. She certainly had the measure of all you men who could only see the pretty, innocent Yorkshire girl rather than the simmering intelligence within. I got the distinct feeling that she deliberately hides her perceptive ability.'

'How do you mean?'

'Well, forgive me, but she certainly outwitted all of you putting obstacles in her way. I think that quality will serve her well. I understand your anxiety but you made the decision to send her there and gave her an ultimatum.' She softened her point with a smile he trusted. 'No point in feeling regret, sir. Your instincts are rarely off the mark.'

He nodded as he sipped. 'Do you know something, Mary?'

She raised an eyebrow.

'No one likes a woman who is always right.'

'Enjoy your tea, sir,' she said with a grin, withdrawing and closing the door behind her.

Leadbetter sat back again, biscuits forgotten, and absent-mindedly ran a hand through his thick silvered hair as he pondered the latest news from Evie that had arrived via the agent Jean. He'd received Evie's recent correspondence, written on the back of the innocent waffle she'd sent to her family; they were allowed an hour or two to read her letter before it was scooped up and removed. There was a messenger on hand to take any letter from Evelyn Hall to her family and rush it straight to his office, where he would place it under a handkerchief and heat up the invisible ink using an iron.

At the sight of the small ironing board his secretary had cackled, hugely enjoying its presence. 'May I bring in some small items, sir? Tea towels, perhaps? We can do them over a morning cuppa.'

He couldn't risk accessing his new spy's knowledge in anything but a secret fashion, so they were disguised within everyday family letters. And the invisible ink ensured that if for some reason Evie's messages accidentally got out of her family's clutches, no one would be wiser to the hidden correspondence. It was cumbersome but it worked and she was good at brevity. He read her note again.

Dachau. Some sort of prison or locked ghetto for dissidents and anyone the Nazis consider undesirable from homeless to those who speak up against the regime. Talk of torture and death. Especially the Jews in its sights. Britain must step in! These are innocents. Please talk to govt. Max and Jonas could be next . . . or me.

The news about the Jewish persecution was not new. It was shocking, of course, but it was not in his remit to focus on it. That issue was someone else's problem at Whitehall.

He cleared his throat audibly, sensing in himself the duck-and-weave of his rationalisation, as an inner voice reminded him that it was everyone's duty as a member of humankind to look out for the vulnerable. Evie's terse message made it clear that young and old were being treated with similar brutality. *Britain must step in!*

'You naive child,' he murmured, looking away from her letter. He turned his attention to his scribbled note from just half an hour ago. Jean had telephoned him with some shocking intelligence; it had come from Evie's lips and he wasn't sure he could trust it – not because he didn't trust Evie, but because he felt she was potentially overwrought.

And yet deep down he knew he was being unfair. In the time he'd spent with her, he'd never had the impression that she could not control her emotions. If anything, he was filled with admiration at how well she had conducted herself through his hurried sessions, during which her mind had been crammed with advice on how to spy, what to look for, what to pay attention to. She hadn't cracked, she'd never complained, she'd always been quick to grasp his meaning. Mary was right – Mary usually was – that Evie was the perfect material from which to mould a cunning spy.

But this? Invasion of Britain! Unthinkable, surely?

And yet this was precisely the conversation that was being had in the halls of Westminster right now. And even though the politicians and policymakers might query how Germany could possibly be considering another war, Hitler's expansionist attitude was being tolerated by a British government aiming for appeasement. However, some visionaries were taking steps. The director at the British Museum was already moving valuable pieces out of London.

As Leadbetter thought this, he felt the spangles of truth exploding: Hitler had marched into the Rhineland in March, but given the general consensus that the Treaty of Versailles had been overly harsh on the German people, the British government had taken no action. Was it looking the other way? Or was it fearful that to act was to incite the very situation everyone wanted to avoid? Here was Evie telling him outright that someone as senior, as loyal and as close to Hitler as Julius Streicher was openly talking invasion at a cocktail party. He really should be as alarmed as she.

But Leadbetter knew that to take this any higher was to risk ridicule. He had no proof. He had only the word of a young woman with no experience in the field. And now she was about to be interviewed by Streicher's people. He trusted Evie but no one else would. He gave an audible sound of exasperation and swallowed his cooled tea.

The phone jangled on his desk. His time was up.

'Yes?'

'It's Munich.'

'Thank you.'

'Sir?' the woman said politely as if answering a call.

'Yes, thank you for calling back.'

'It's a busy day at the switchboard,' she admitted. He was impressed that this agent had got herself hired as a senior telephonist at the Munich exchange. 'How would you like me to place that call for you?' asked the woman Evie knew as Jean.

He knew to keep it brief, especially from the clipped tone of her voice. 'I must insist on proof. If she can get firm evidence to corroborate her claim, she can come home.'

'Thank you, sir. Glad to help. I'll put that call through now.'

The line went dead and Leadbetter hoped he hadn't just signed Evie's death warrant with his demand.

Evie leaned around the door of the kitchen where she was contemplating what to make for lunch, to watch Max and Jonas building a railway track on the short hallway floor. They were making the most of a weekend together. Max sensed her presence and looked up with a sheepish expression.

'There's no space.'

'And how long do I have to keep stepping over your tracks?'

'Just today, Evie.' Jonas crossed his heart. 'I promise.'

She found it hard to resist Jonas. Those huge eyes were all blue innocence, like blackbird eggs. They were quite unlike the eyes of the man who would gladly see the little boy swept up into a ghetto, forgotten about, even got rid of. She hadn't told Max about seeing the Führer because then she'd have to explain about Jean and why she had gone to the tearoom in the first place. She didn't want to lie to Max. Somehow withholding information felt less upsetting, so she held her tongue.

'All right,' she said, sighing theatrically. 'Just today, then, because it's raining. Coffee, Max?'

'Mmm, yes,' he replied, testing an engine and then putting it back on the track. She watched him look at his son with triumph and couldn't help but smile. They were so similar, and she hoped the bond they shared would never be broken.

Jonas clapped with delight. 'Victory!' he yelled, and took the controller. 'How long before we go out?'

'Shall we say a couple of hours?' Evie offered.

'How long is that?'

Max laughed and scooped up his son. 'Just long enough for me to do this,' he said, beginning to land loud smacking kisses over Jonas, who became quickly hysterical in his laughter at being tickled.

Evie couldn't help feeling the joy of that moment. In that instant, there was no Roger the fake – there was only the man who owned her heart, the one who loved his son. It triggered yearning thoughts of wanting this to be her family for real.

'Help!' Jonas called, cackling with laughter. 'Evie, help!'

She couldn't deny him and in truth had constantly been surprised over these past two days how easily she'd fallen in love with Jonas. She had tried to avoid the word 'love' in her mind but he'd burrowed deep into her life with such speed it was already too late.

Like father, like son, a small voice sighed in her mind. It was true: she'd fallen for Jonas just as hard, just as fast, as she had for Max.

'Evie!' he squealed as his father locked him in a bear hug and made roaring sounds.

She dissolved into laughter with him. 'Come on, you two. I don't think we can coop ourselves up much longer. Rain or not, I think we should go for a walk.' She gathered a grinning Jonas onto her lap and hugged him, feeling his warmth – sweaty now from all the wrestling – and smoothed his hair. She kissed his round, angelic face. 'Go and fetch your shoes,' she said. 'Then we'll have some food and go out on fat bellies.'

Her stepson giggled.

Evie and Max both watched Jonas obediently disappear.

'I never did ask you about the conversation you had with Streicher at the cocktail party,' she said casually.

'How did you find him?' he replied.

'Every bit as unpleasant as you warned me.'

He nodded. 'There's so much jostling and grasping for power in the Nazi ranks. Everyone wants to be close to the main man. I am happy being as far away as possible.'

'Well, he's in Munich so you may not be so lucky.'

He frowned at her. 'How do you know?'

'Oh, er, I overheard a couple in Prinzregentenstrasse,' she said, deftly covering her error. 'I saw them pointing out a guard in the doorway of his building.'

'He all but commutes here,' Max groaned, having sensed no guile, and Evie hid her relief by sipping her coffee. 'How did it go with Streicher? Awful,' he said. 'He reminded me that I'd failed the Führer and my brief.'

'Did he say how you might redeem yourself?'

Max sighed. 'He didn't, but during my debrief I learned that I'm to spearhead the building of some new railway sidings.'

'Where in Germany? Will you be going away to—'

'Not Germany. Poland.'

Their gazes locked in a frigid silence. He put a finger to his lips. And she frowned, because he'd told her he was having the apartment checked. But she was cautious.

'Well, that's all very exciting,' she said breezily. 'But don't bore me any more with talk of railway tracks. Remember, I ran away from Yorkshire and my life on the railways.' She bent down and made a kissing sound near his cheek, whispering, 'Bathroom.'

As she moved through the bedroom, she turned on the wireless. Hitler's voice boomed from the speaker. It was a repeat, she noted – another of his persuasive speeches, which he had delivered earlier this month. It was more of his usual rhetoric about the struggle of the previous decade to take power and how that power was now absolute . . . leaning hard on loyalty, commitment, and how important his leadership was for the Reich. Nevertheless, she had decided that these orations had the power to captivate an audience – his ability to bewitch was real.

Max arrived and cast a silent sneer at the wireless. Again, he hushed her and mouthed the word 'look'.

She frowned as she watched him undo the back of the wireless set to reveal its inner workings. Hitler yelled over them but Max gestured to some gadget within and then pointed to his ear.

She understood. Her mouth opened in surprise and gave him a questioning look.

He pointed to the bathroom. Then he spoke aloud and brightly. 'It's as if our Führer is in the room,' he remarked, as though listening in on her thoughts. 'Impressive, don't you think, darling?'

'He's mesmerising,' she said, feigning excitement at the powerful words. 'Well, you listen. I'll have a quick shower.'

They moved into the bathroom.

She turned on the shower and opened the window to let the sound of the trams and the general activity of the street below add another layer of noise. Evie gestured for him to close the door. 'Jonas?' she whispered.

'Lost to the make-believe steam he's probably choofing around the hallway. I know I said the apartment was safe but I'm glad we checked again – this device has been added since our arrival. Who would have thought they'd be quite so cunning?'

'We're safe in here?'

'I've checked every nook and cranny. I've even dismantled some of the pipes to check they're not listening through the basin.'

She wasted no time. 'Poland?'

He nodded before shaking his head in a way that looked helpless. 'I don't know what it's about.'

'But for you to build railway sidings, that would mean moving into another sovereign territory.'

'I agree. Invasion is the only deduction one could make.' She sighed with disbelief, while noting how he held her gaze. 'But can you trust what I just said?'

Evie blinked.

Max gave a shrug. 'Don't report it, and risk Britain not having this inside knowledge, or report it, and risk that I'm deliberately misleading you.'

She watched him, feeling trapped.

He took her by the shoulders and she flinched. 'You know sometime very soon, Evie, you'll have to choose. Either you trust me, and I will help, or I will not give you any further information.'

'And risk Jonas?'

'I already have. If you don't trust me, then Jonas and I are as good as dead anyway.'

Dead. The word hit her like a bullet.

'Because giving you information achieves nothing but more suspicion. Perhaps I really must just go along with this charade and let you get what you need by whatever methods you can, and that way I haven't tarnished any of your intelligence gathering. Anything I say or do puts doubt in your mind – and all because I withheld the truth of my fear for my child. But what I couldn't withhold, Evie, was how I felt about you. That was my error and I regret ever stepping off that train at Levisham the first time.'

She swallowed. 'I don't regret you, Max.' He didn't overreact to her comment. He waited as Hitler yelled on in the background. She could imagine the German leader, pounding his shaky left palm with his emphatic words. 'And it's Leadbetter who doesn't trust you,' she said.

They were standing so close, and she wished she'd turned on only the cold tap in the shower because the steam was making her feel too warm . . . or was it him who was doing that?

'Do you know any more?' she pressed.

'It will cost you.'

She looked back at him, surprised. 'How much?'

'More than a kiss, but a kiss will get you some knowledge.'

She gave a soft snort. 'Is there more?' she demanded in a low voice. He nodded. 'Go on then,' she relented, closing her eyes and all but puckering her lips.

'No. You have to kiss me.'

She mock glared at him. It was Max's turn to close his eyes and he leaned back against the basin, patiently awaiting her touch.

She took in the golden glow around his hair – like a halo, as the sun emerged from behind sodden clouds in that moment to light him. She knew it was a crazy thought, but she took it as a sign. She knew this man; she loved this man and her instincts had not steered her wrong through life thus far.

As the sun lit the droplets of vapour in the room it was like a new dawning, after weeks of her mind being blurred by anger, fear and other people's opinions, mutterings, conclusions. Yes, she'd been angry, and she could wish now she hadn't been quite so impetuous; perhaps if she'd given him that chance to explain, things might be different. The spy had lied for all the right reasons, not the least of which was not letting down Britain.

Max Hall was quite simply the terrified father of a German Jewish boy, whose future was in doubt if Max didn't respond to the coercive behaviour and threats of the German government. Was her government much better? They'd coerced her, forced her into a corner as she was torn between patriotic duty and her love for a man. And now they were using her in a way that was not dissimilar. The Nazis threatened his son's future while Whitehall threatened his life.

All of her brimming emotion found its way to her lips as they landed gently on his. Max let her kiss him and without meaning to she intensified it. It was her muscles moving, her arms reaching around his neck, pulling him deeper into the kiss. Evie placed her hands around his face, cupping his cheeks, loving the rough feel of his jaw. In that heartbeat he surrendered. She felt Max's arms around her body, one hand at her shoulder, the other in the small of her back and he was pulling her closer. He leaned to switch off the shower tap and as the steam was sucked out the window they kissed until her lips felt swollen and she'd lost all sense of time. Hitler had stopped shouting and Jonas was banging at the door to say he was hungry and only then did they separate.

'Coming, Jonas,' she called, her gaze locked on Max.

Max pulled her back. 'Let me help you,' he whispered.

She searched his anxious face. More than Max, more than Leadbetter, more than anyone, Evie trusted herself and she made a decision. She nodded with a small smile before easing out of his embrace and did not give Max a chance to reply, although she heard his sigh of relief as she opened the door a crack and turned to him. 'I'm going to trust you, Max.' That statement riveted his gaze. 'I can lip-read.'

He stared back at her, trying to make full sense of her admission. 'How well?'

'I can tell you word for word what I saw you say to your colleague on the train from Goathland that day, when you were supposed to stop off at Levisham.'

'Bloody hell,' he murmured, recalling the conversation now and how angry he'd been. 'That man made awful, blatant threats.'

She nodded, dropped her voice, although they were seated alone on the edge of the bathtub. 'I didn't understand it then, but I do now. I also understand, with no little despair, that Germany has plans to invade Britain.'

'How did you come by this—'

'Max, I know exactly what Streicher said to you.'

He shook his head with awe. 'What a dark horse you are, Evie. And what a talent. Then you'll know how precarious our position is.'

She nodded. 'I promise to be very wary.' She left Max to find his son who had been alone for too long.

Evie discovered Jonas had tired of playing with the train set and had moved into the sitting room. He had a board game that he was setting up. She glanced out the window and could see the sky was brightening considerably. Evie was still tingling with desire, wishing she could have consummated it with Max.

'We'll definitely get out this afternoon, otherwise I think you'll leave a trail of destruction in every room.' She laughed.

'What's that?' he asked.

'This mess,' she explained, smiling. 'What would you like to eat? A sandwich?'

He nodded, distracted. 'Will you come and play this game with me, Evie?'

'Yes. Let me just get you some food.' She tried not to sigh, thinking of his frustrated father, still in the bathroom probably and waiting for his desire to dissipate. It actually made her laugh quietly. 'Give me a couple of minutes.'

She busied herself in the kitchen, and accepted another quick kiss from Max when he finally emerged looking sheepish but galvanised.

He annoyed her by stealing half of the sandwich she'd made for Jonas.

'He'll only eat that much.' He gestured at the remainder, chewing greedily on the stolen sandwich.

'You've got salad cream, just there,' she said, pointing to the corner of his mouth. 'A testimony to your greedy gorging.'

'In this country we call it mayonnaise,' he said, following her over to where Jonas had set up his board game.

'Ready to play?' Jonas asked, wide-eyed. 'It's a new one.'

'Who gave you this?' Max said, still chewing, frowning as they flanked him on the sofa.

'It was a gift from Aunty Giselle.'

Evie too frowned at the board. It was an ugly-looking game on first impression, and she watched Max pick up the lid and stare at it, perplexed.

'*Juden Raus*,' he read out. He turned his horrified expression to Evie. 'Jews out!'

Unaware of the game's offence, Jonas explained it to them. 'We have to move around the board, rounding up these ugly people.' He pointed to the cones with sinister-looking images on them of men with cunning expressions and large noses. The enemy characters were standing on points of the board with names like Lowenstein Shoes or Rosenbaum Confectioner. 'And then you place them on top of your player, like this,' he said, putting one of the cones on the head of the sweet, smiling character depicted on his piece. 'And you put them outside the city's walls. Aunty Giselle showed me that you win the game when you get rid of six Jews.'

Evie read more of the board in deepening despair. She could see how the players would deposit the Jewish caricatures at the walled city's gates, labelled *Auf nach Palästina!* Off to Palestine! She could feel Max's rage as he read from the leaflet by Dresden toymaker Günther and Co, which was clearly cashing in on the fascist ideal being seeded around the country.

'. . . up-to-date and outstandingly jolly party game for grown-ups and children.' He was careful to translate it into English to keep Jonas out of their conversation. 'My so-called friend is brainwashing my son. This is just another couched threat.'

She nodded. 'Jonas, eat up and then let's get out. It's turned into a reasonable day. We can play this later,' she said, then whispered to Max in English, 'Throw it away.' She paused. 'Better still, burn it,' she mouthed.

Her decision was cemented. She and Max were now in this together. Getting all three of them out of Germany was all that mattered.

17

Max had thought about Evie's admission that she could lip-read in both her languages. He couldn't think of a better way to use her skill or allow her full access to his work without either of them acting suspiciously, so he set it up.

'This is a lovely idea,' Evie said, arriving at the Reich Ministry of Transport's offices in Munich. They were housed in the back of the old town hall on the eastern edge of Marienplatz, which had recently undergone renovations to add pedestrian tunnels that swallowed its ground and first levels. 'I'm glad you're not in one of those new Third Reich buildings,' she whispered.

He couldn't agree more. With his architect, Albert Speer, Hitler was redesigning Berlin with monumental buildings that were a weapon of propaganda – to promote strength, power and adoring admiration of the man behind the vision. Their Führer was a frustrated, failed artist who yearned to be an architect but didn't have the skills, only the grandiose ideas. Max helplessly admired Hitler's use of height and massive spaces with minimal decoration to humble the visitor. It was, in a way, how the Catholic Church of centuries past had built enormous cathedrals to make the pilgrims quaver and bow down in their shadow. Evie was right, though: to work in the slightly cramped but noble space of the neo-Gothic structure first built in the late 1400s eased his mind somewhat.

He took Evie's elbow and escorted her across the gleaming marble floors, smiling as she looked up to admire the polished timber ceiling, its beams perfectly lined up. He guided her up two flights of curving stairs to emerge into creaky offices that overlooked the square.

'Are we in the tower?' she asked, her eyes sparkling.

He grinned. 'We are. The fairytale bit.'

People smiled and began leaving their desks to greet her.

'Er, well, everyone, I promised you'd get to meet her. This is Evelyn, my wife.'

She gave them her most dazzling smile. 'Please call me Evie. I'm so delighted to meet Max's colleagues,' she said in flawless conversational German, once again thanking her stars that Nanny Lotte had insisted her girls learn the colloquial language as much as the more polite version. 'Is this for me?' she asked, sounding amazed, even though Max had warned her they would put on some coffee and cake.

'No, any excuse for cake,' Max answered and got the laughter he'd hoped for.

He began the individual introductions. He'd warned Evie beforehand to listen out for the name Brenner Burkhart. 'My boss,' he'd explained.

'Ah, sir, I'd like you to meet my wife. Evie, this is the head of our team, Herr Brenner Burkhart.' He deliberately didn't emphasise the name or make any specific gesture but he could see the acknowledgement in Evie's glance. She barely broke eye contact with his superior.

'Herr Burkhart, how lovely it is to meet you. Max is so happy to be returned to his team.'

'Yes, we missed him,' Brenner said, and Max was aware of his gaze lingering on Evie for a few moments longer than felt comfortable. It was not a look of admiration – although he didn't doubt the man was impressed by her alluring presence. No, Brenner was one of the party faithful and so his antennae were up and searching for guile, like any devoted Nazi follower. He would find none in Evie. Max had learned to trust her effortless manner that moulded around whomever she met. He watched her now, impressed, as she showed no reaction to the lengthy gaze other than holding her smile.

'Max mentioned you have family not too far from London,' she said, her tone entirely relaxed. He recalled how he'd needed to adopt a similar informal manner when he'd arrived in Britain to begin his mission for Germany. It had sickened him to even step on a train headed north – that's where this man had sent him – and he'd had to coach himself in how to act natural and in no way give rise to suspicion. He didn't think he'd ever have been caught if by chance that equipment hadn't been discovered by the children playing on that side of the moor. Anyway, that river had broken its dam – it was no use thinking over it any more. Right now his single aim was to protect Evie, to help her wherever he could in spite of Leadbetter's warnings. And to get his son out of this doomed country.

He came back to the conversation about Brenner's distant cousin once removed who lived in London and was a well-known tennis player turned coach. '. . . sounds more English than you, possibly, Frau Hall,' Brenner was saying.

An idea occurred to Max. 'Er, Brenner, I wonder if we could have a word. I've had some thoughts on our newest project.'

His boss looked surprised. 'Don't you want to stay with your wife, Max?'

'She's more than capable of helping herself to cake and meeting the team, aren't you, darling?'

'Of course,' she said. 'Please don't let me get in the way of the important stuff.' She beamed Burkhart a charming smile. 'It was lovely to meet you, Herr Burkhart. And thank you for letting me interrupt the morning.'

Max watched his boss give a short bow to Evie before Brenner led him to the other end of the room, well out of earshot. Someone interrupted briefly for his boss to sign a document and Max took a few heartbeats to cast a glance Evie's way. She was watching, smiling and chatting with the others, accepting a slice of cake, but her attention was on them. She'd caught on. *I love you, Evie*, he thought, impressed by her quick wits; other than Giselle he'd never met a woman who possessed such smartness. Giselle's of course was focused on ruthlessness and suspicion, while Evie's was all about acuity. She had a mind like mercury that could slip around her every situation.

'So?' Brenner wondered.

They were facing each other. Max hoped this would work.

'I need a more comprehensive brief about these tracks we are required to build for Poland.'

His boss frowned. 'Why?'

Max gave a soft snort to suggest it was obvious, surely, but his superior came from a background in airfields and had more recently turned his attention to autobahns to connect cities, even countries, with a hurtling stream of traffic. He had little experience in railways and Max leaned on that now. 'Sir, I have to calculate what we're carrying, how often, how heavy. I have to build within all sorts of parameters.' He waited as the man considered this, then pushed. 'I have full security clearance, of course. There is nothing you can't say to me about this project that I am not permitted to learn. And it goes without saying that I do not discuss my work outside these walls.'

'Not even with your pretty new wife?'

Max laughed. 'The usual. A hard day at the office, or the new secretary can't make coffee – that sort of thing, sir. Evie grew up on the railways in Britain, and I am convinced that marrying me was her way of escaping that life. From what I can tell she has zero interest in hearing about anything that involves trains.'

'Unless it's the *Orient Express*, perhaps?'

Max was pleased by his boss's playful note. 'Oh, then I'm sure she'd make an exception, but for now Evie's mind is consumed with making babies.'

Brenner nodded. 'Not just her mind then, eh, Max? I thought you were looking tired.'

Max laughed, as he knew he was expected to. 'Anyway, is there any more you can tell me so I can do this job more expediently?'

'I'll be cleared to give you a full briefing next week, Max, but for now I suspect it's fine for you to learn that we need to build tracks into Poland that can fit the German rolling stock.'

He nodded, schooling his features to be absorbed but not in the slightest intrigued to ask why. 'What are we carrying in, sir?'

'Heavy materials and men to build a munitions factory.'

'All right,' he said, still not reacting. 'How far into Poland?'

'A place called Nowogród Bobrzański. Middle of nowhere, about four hours from Berlin by vehicle. It must service a potential invasion into Russia. As well as the factory there it will house workers, as well as all the support buildings for those workers. So there's people for the train to carry in. And as well as industrial equipment we need building materials to transport to this place via rail. There's even talk of a casino!' He grinned. 'Prisoners will do most of the hard labour.' *Prisoners being Jews and undesirables*, Max thought, horrified. 'But some very large holding tanks have to be constructed to protect explosive material. This is a big project ordered by the Führer and I want our part of it to be seamless. Those rail tracks have to be reliable and fast.'

'I'm looking forward to doing my best work for you, sir, and for the Führer,' he lied, hoping Evie had lip-read this all for herself.

Evie had suggested they take a stroll through the Englischer Garten, saying she'd love to see some German parklands.

'By all means,' Max had agreed. 'It's perfect for Jonas to burn off some energy too.'

He strolled now, flanked by the two people he loved in the world. Anger about the board game Giselle had given his son had dissipated into something cold that congealed around his original grief. They belonged together and they would fuel him. Right now, though, the joy of having Evie's trust was as wondrous to him as it was to hold the hand of his child. He had one arm flung gently around her slim shoulders and could feel Jonas's tiny hand in his as his innocent son skipped along beside him, noticing everything, it seemed, from the shape of the clouds to the way the man in front was weaving around on his bicycle.

'Why do they call this the Englischer Garten?' Evie wondered aloud.

'It was originally a deer park, back in the eighteenth century, and likely a hunting chase. I believe it started out as an idea for a military garden but then the concept broadened to become a public garden. The royal gardener was called in to help with planning the layout and he'd studied English landscaping. A lot of its appearance has that rolling, carefree, informal style of British parkland, as opposed to the stricter, more regulated form of a French or Italianate garden.'

'Yes, I see that now. It certainly feels like one of the huge London parks.'

He paused to lay a soft kiss on her cheek.

'Ugh!' Jonas groaned, much to their amusement.

'When did a six-year-old become so cynical?' Evie said.

Max sighed. 'You'll love girls kissing you soon,' he assured his son, and got an even more scornful response – this time a look of disgust that made his father laugh.

'Max! And Evelyn – how lovely to run into you. Jonas, my darling, give your aunt a hug.'

The good mood fled as Giselle scooped Max into a close embrace. That this was some sort of coincidence was clearly a lie, and he resented her intrusion not only on his family time but also their time out in the open, where he and Evie could speak freely. He wanted to discuss what she'd lip-read at the office. Giselle kissed his son's golden head and straightened, smiling her fake smile at them. She was on the arm of a man he didn't recognise. He pulled Jonas gently back and picked him up.

'Karl, this is my old friend Maximillian Hall and his new bride, Evelyn, who is English. Max and I grew up together – our families were close.' She paused a beat, eyeing Max. 'And this is Munich's police president, Karl von Eberstein.'

Max regarded the man, who matched his own height.

'Heil Hitler!' von Eberstein exclaimed, and Max made a half-hearted effort as though too tangled with Jonas's hand to effect a full salute. He also mumbled the Heil Hitler but ensured it was just clear enough, as von Eberstein offered his hand. 'I know your family distantly – went shooting with your father once,' he remarked. Max frowned. 'I was a youngster, but where my father was gruff and distant like a typical army major, yours was amused by children and took an interest in me that day. I doubt you were born when I met him.'

'I was born in the late winter of 1905,' Max replied, buying himself time as he thought back to childhood days and whether he recalled his parents talking about the von Ebersteins. He didn't.

'Well, well. It was exactly then – 1905! January. Freezing. The trip was part of my tenth birthday celebrations, I seem to recall.

Your mother took pity and quickly baked a small cake for me. She was a warm woman, from memory . . . English too, right?'

Max smiled with care, as he shook the man's hand. 'Yes.'

'So, history repeats itself,' von Eberstein said, taking in Evie properly now. 'You really should give the Heil Hitler, my dear.'

Max glanced at her to see Evie give the older man a charming smile. 'I'm learning how to do it properly. I don't think I'm confident enough yet, sir, but I will soon. It's a pleasure to meet you. I know so little about Max's upbringing. It's like pulling teeth.'

'I can assure you it would have been a happier household than mine, for sure, with his parents. How are you finding Munich?'

'Absolutely wonderful. Everyone is so happy here.'

The man shrugged. 'That's because everyone's in holiday mood – all the children are enjoying their time away from school. Mind you, spring and summer do make us Germans happy, as does our Führer.'

'He's so impressive,' she remarked. 'I suppose you've met him?'

'Of course,' he said, giving a slightly scornful chuckle.

'My . . . I'd consider that an honour.'

'How come?' Giselle leapt in with an interested frown.

Max tried not to tense his jaw. He knew Evie had already proved herself capable of throwing any sniffing dogs off her scent.

She didn't miss a beat. 'Well, how he is making every German so proud, and look how bright and jolly everyone is. It's wonderful,' she sighed, and in a way that made her seem all but vacant. 'I'm just so pleased to be making my home here with my new family.' She gave a sheepish grin to von Eberstein. 'Actually, I was quite thrilled to leave my own. We lived in the middle of nowhere where nothing happens and life is boring. Now I'm in a big city with so many shops – I just can't wait.'

'To spend my wages, you mean?' Max laughed, joining in with Evie's obvious plan to make herself appear as inane as possible.

'Yes, my darling . . . and maybe to kit out a nursery.' Even he couldn't help but mirror Giselle's shocked silent question. 'No, no, not yet. But'—she squeezed his arm and looked at the others with a sugary grin—'we're working furiously on it, aren't we, Max? I think of nothing else but giving Jonas a brother or sister.'

He could feel Giselle's gaze upon him but he refused to return it and gauge what her expression contained – anything from revulsion to despair, he imagined with some delight.

The older man chuckled. 'Another son would be excellent, Max. You come from excellent stock, and while I know Jonas has blood that is . . . well, shall we say, tainted,' he murmured, although Jonas had long ago stopped paying attention, 'I think with Evelyn's contribution we can expect a fine Aryan brood from you.'

Max had to school his features with effort to avoid showing revulsion for the man.

'I didn't know the von Ebersteins and the Halls were friends,' Giselle said, returning to the earlier conversation as if needing to switch topics.

Von Eberstein answered. 'Well, you were probably a twinkle in your father's eye at the time, and then we left the region soon after,' he said, now turning his attention to Jonas.

'Heil Hitler, young man.'

Torn between relief and despair, Max watched Jonas give the man a firm-armed salute, uttering the dreaded words.

'That's the spirit,' von Eberstein encouraged him. 'Mother's blood aside, I think we can lean on your father's to get you into the Nazi Youth Party soon.'

Over our dead bodies, Max thought, but he couldn't risk offending this powerful man.

'Oh, Evelyn, I was asked by Herr Streicher's people to help organise the interview he mentioned. Nothing to worry about, dear, just protocol,' Giselle announced, sounding as insincere as Max could recall.

'Yes, that's fine. When would be convenient?'

'I thought tomorrow at ten. I'll send a car to take you to Herr von Eberstein's offices. The interview will be held there.'

Max watched Evie nod good-naturedly. 'Fine.' She even added an innocent-sounding 'thank you', as if Giselle only had her best interests at heart. He knew it would be the opposite.

'Bring your passport, Evelyn . . . oh, and your wedding album would be splendid too.'

'Really?' Evie said, sounding as surprised as if Giselle had suggested she bring her favourite recipe for lamb stew. 'Why on earth would they want to see our wedding photos?'

Giselle shrugged. 'Gestapo are odd creatures. I have learned never to question their requests but simply to go along with them.'

Evie laughed. 'I shall be very glad to point out all my family and friends to them,' she said. Max was impressed by her composure, especially as she turned to von Eberstein, not showing a hint of the acid taste of fear that was surely oozing into her mouth. 'Good to meet you, sir. Enjoy the sunshine.'

Max followed her lead and nodded at the top policeman. 'Sir . . . . Giselle,' he added in farewell to them both. He linked arms with Evie again. 'Come on, darlings, I think it's ice-cream time, right, Jonas?'

Jonas squealed with pleasure and ran ahead to an ice-cream kiosk, which boasted a long queue. Max refused to look back, although he sensed Giselle casting him a lingering glance.

'That meeting was no coincidence,' Evie said.

'No. We're being followed, or at least observed constantly. I have to hand it to Leadbetter. He was right about having those photographs mocked up so perfectly.'

She nodded. 'What are they looking for?'

'It's my feeling this is a two-edged sword thing. I think they're giving me a veiled message – a warning that I failed them and that I need to perform now, as they can access and persecute all those I love.'

'I see. And the second?'

'Just a reminder that no one escapes scrutiny, not even the new and innocent wife.'

'I am convinced that Giselle has no genuine interest in me, Max.' At his immediate worried sigh, she squeezed his arm. 'No, that's a good thing. She's so focused on you and what you might be up to that she has dismissed me as a threat.'

'You were pretty amazing at disarming any notion either of them had that you might be an equal.'

'I can operate in the shadows behind you. You were very cunning today with Burkhart.'

'We'll talk later. Did you get it all?'

She nodded. 'Chilling. Oh, can you get the ice creams? I forgot to spend a penny before I left, and I've just spotted the public lavatory.'

'Off you go. We'll probably still be in the queue when you return.'

Evie had no idea where the public convenience might be but she had seen Jean lurking and now she followed her, hurrying as she sensed Max still watching her. As she drew level with Jean, she murmured, 'Lavatories. I'll pretend we've met by chance.'

Jean overtook her and led the way. It wasn't far. She could still see Max and Jonas near the ice-cream kiosk. There was a queue too. She stood behind Jean as though they were strangers, looking away into the distance.

Jean was turned ever so slightly as though looking in the opposite direction.

'Jean? It is you!' she said, laughing aloud.

'Evie! What are you doing here?'

'Dancing from foot to foot – I hope this queue doesn't last too long.' They laughed together and immediately dropped their voices.

'What were you doing with the police president?' Jean queried.

She shrugged. 'No idea. I thought we simply ran into them, but I now suspect that Giselle is keeping tabs on us. She was showing Max that she moves with the kind of people who could hurt us.' Jean nodded as if in agreement. Today she was dressed in a pale grey silk and linen summer dress with black-and-white brogues and a large hat that essentially covered her face. 'Why are you following us?'

'I've heard from our mutual friend,' she murmured, allowing a woman and her daughter to go before them.

'And?'

'He wants proof.'

Evie resisted the urge to look at Jean, aghast. 'What does that mean?'

Jean lowered her voice still further, digging in her handbag as though distracted. 'Firm evidence that corroborates what you mentioned about invasion.' The last two words were barely more than a whisper before she gushed a laugh.

'Say the name Brenner Burkhart to our mutual friend and tell him that Max is now working on a railway into Poland where an ammunition factory is to be built, complete with accommodation and support for a small village. Russia is being discussed as a target.'

Jean laughed again but Evie heard only her horror. The older woman clasped her hand. 'I'll try, but please don't forget to mention that to the hairdresser, or you'll never keep up with the times. My turn. Hope to see you again soon.' She strode forward and disappeared into one of the cubicles.

When Evie emerged from hers, the woman who was cleaning the toilets turned to her and said, 'I was paid to give you this.'

She held out a tartan handkerchief. Evie stared at it. 'The woman in the large hat and black-and-white shoes said you need to return this to a mutual friend.'

'Oh,' she said, reaching for the handkerchief. Did she mean Leadbetter?

'Doesn't seem special enough to worry about,' the cleaner observed.

'Oh, it is,' she assured her. 'Did she say anything else?'

The woman shrugged. 'Not to forget that hair appointment next week.'

Evie smiled. 'No, I won't. Thank you.'

The woman returned to mopping the floor but Evie's pulse was racing. What did the tartan handkerchief mean?

Proof! She turned the word over in her mind as she strolled back towards Max and Jonas. She couldn't do this alone; she knew now she had to bring Max fully into her covert activities.

Max greeted his wife with an easy smile that belied the suspicion behind it. He was not enjoying being taken for a fool.

'Finished already?' she said, ruffling Jonas's hair.

'You were gone long enough for us to queue and eat our ice creams, unfortunately. I did buy you one.' He glanced at the bin nearby to make his point. 'I'm afraid it melted.'

Her brightness didn't falter. 'Oh, I'm sorry. It was quite a walk and then there was a long queue.'

'It's fine. We were entertained by an arrest.'

'Arrest?'

He nodded, watching her carefully. 'Von Eberstein wasn't here for us alone, it seems – his henchmen picked up a woman.'

Evie's eyes widened. 'In front of everyone?'

He nodded, watching fear flit across Evie's expression before she schooled her features to neutral. 'Jonas, you can play now. We'll watch you.'

'What about the swing?'

'I'll be there shortly to push you.'

Jonas skipped away to join the other children scrambling over play equipment and waiting his turn to hurtle down the slide.

Max's smile faded and he turned to Evie. 'Police, Gestapo, secret police,' he murmured. 'They have no qualms about making a public arrest, including that of the woman I suspect you were in the queue to meet.'

'Pardon?'

His answer was to blink and wait her out. 'I saw you standing with her. Why did you meet?'

He could imagine cogs turning in Evie's head; somewhere in that clever mind she was trying to protect him while keeping her promise to the overlords in Whitehall.

'If you don't wish to tell me who, fair enough – but at least tell me why.' The cogs continued to turn as he watched her. He felt the search of her gaze like a spotlight. He sensed she wanted to share something but still needed more from him. 'On Jonas's life, I will never betray you.' Their gazes locked. He shook his head. 'You don't trust me entirely.'

'It's not that. I'm not convinced you trust me fully.'

'What?'

'*You failed, I hear*, your overweight friend at the cocktail party said, to which you replied, *I don't see it that way. Depends on how you view it, sir.* He responded, *How should we view it?*, and you, somewhat defensively, said, *I sent back a lot of useful information.* Want me to continue?' she offered, but didn't wait for his response. 'He talked about you panicking unnecessarily. *We needed more. If we're going to invade Britain one day and—*'

'All right, all right – I get it,' he said, resigned and impressed at once. Now it was he who felt obliged to check there were no eavesdroppers.

'Why didn't you say something to me about that conversation?' she asked.

'Because you wouldn't have trusted me if I'd repeated it to you. The only reason you trust it is because you witnessed it for yourself. If I'd tried to warn you at the time, I doubt you'd have passed that on to London. Have you passed it on?'

She nodded and looked down, disappointed. 'It's not enough. They want proof.'

'Leadbetter can go . . .' He chose not to finish what he wanted to say. 'You are not going into danger, poking around Streicher. He is merciless. He would snap your neck like a chicken's. Was the woman in the black-and-white shoes a friend of yours?'

She could truthfully shake her head.

'I don't believe you. Were you meeting her?' He was not going let her off the hook. 'Evie, this is Jonas's life too.'

'Yes,' she replied. 'I was meeting her.'

He cursed beneath his breath. 'Well, now they have her. Did you speak for long?'

'Barely moments and not obviously. No one would know we had communicated anything, to be honest.'

'You can be sure of that or they'd have dragged you in too.'

'There's always tomorrow,' she quipped.

'Don't jest about this, Evie. I won't be able to argue a case for you, or Jonas. They'll consider me guilty too and we'll all be involved in a cosy family execution.'

Her expression told him the words hit her like a handful of stones. 'I'm not a dullard, Max.'

'I'm not suggesting you are. I'm suggesting you are vulnerable and I'd like to be in a small room with Leadbetter for just ten minutes for putting you into this position.'

'*You* put me in this position.'

Max threw up his arms in frustration as he felt himself reach his full level of tolerance, a rare atmosphere for him. 'I can't fight this, Evie. Please just go home – and by "home" I mean Yorkshire – to be safe with your family. Jonas and I will take our chances.' He stood. 'I'll go via the railway station tonight and book your passage. I think it's best that you leave tomorrow. I'm too frightened for you.'

She looked back at him, aghast. 'And what will you say to all your people about your new wife deserting you?'

'Don't worry about that. I'm good at lying, as you've accused me. I'm sure I can work out a story they'll believe.'

'And Jonas?'

He was reassured to hear how uncertain she sounded. He took no pleasure in this approach but the time had come for him to exert himself, to stop being a bystander. He had plenty to lose with this dangerous game they were playing on behalf of others.

'He's lost one mother,' Max growled, surprised he sounded so quietly aggressive. 'He can learn to lose another. Besides, he's got much bigger problems.' He turned to leave.

'Max . . . wait!'

Now she sounded unnerved. Good.

'Just go, Evie. I've explained myself over and again. One day, when you have a child, you might be able to touch a fraction of the fear I have for Jonas's wellbeing as he's used as a pawn. We did nothing wrong except love a Jewish woman. That was our sin. So you can tell Leadbetter to shove his deal, and I ask nothing of you other than that you leave and forget me, forget my plight. It's not yours . . . it never was.'

This time he departed with purpose. Without looking back, he swung Jonas onto his shoulders and strode off.

18

Evie looked on in bewilderment. It was as though time had slowed and she was watching the scene at a quarter of life's normal speed. Max was fighting back. It was a shock, no doubt, but it was also heartening in a way she really didn't want to admit . . . certainly not to Leadbetter. Perhaps she'd been waiting for the moment Max demanded people see him in all his dimensions. She'd fallen in love with a man whose remoteness had attracted her, and it was that very quality in which she'd sensed strength. But since his arrest she'd not glimpsed that inaccessibility; if anything, he had compromised himself by being too open, too fragile. He'd allowed all of them, Evie included, to punish him into submission – caught in the act of espionage that she knew in her heart was never his desire.

She craned her neck to see Max, but he had either changed course or blended into the flow of people enjoying the parklands. She stood on tiptoe, hoping to glimpse Jonas's golden head bobbing above the crowd, but she'd lost them, and in that moment Evie felt a fresh agony. Surprising herself with her speed, she began to hurry, dodging parents swinging laughing children off the ground between them, racing around young lovers, and apologising for frightening an elderly trio, out for a stroll, as she bore down on them. Evie ducked and weaved, pausing only to stand on tiptoe to look for Max and Jonas. She couldn't spot them but she kept moving.

As she hurried out of the gardens, there were crowds of people flowing down the main boulevard that would take her home. She decided to go via the Old Quarter: she was sure Max had said it was only slightly longer but often quieter, with fewer people to dodge. She'd already lost Max and Jonas, so risking a twisted ankle wasn't worth it. What she hadn't counted on was getting disoriented by the cobbled streets of Old Munich. She thought she knew her way back but she became muddled and found herself having to retrace her steps, then tried to find new ways to weave her way back to the carillon. If she could reach the clock, she could get home easily.

Evie hurried into an unfamiliar square that had some sort of guarded monument at one end. She tried to recognise one of the alleyways. She thought something looked familiar and she cut across the cobblestones towards it.

'Halt!'

She glanced around, not for a moment imagining the order was directed at her, but it seemed it was. A granite-faced man in imposing uniform with a rifle and a pistol at his side was pointing at her.

'Me?' she said, filled with disbelief.

'You are breaking the law!'

She shook her head. 'I . . . sorry, I don't understand.'

He advanced on her and passers-by dipped their heads – worried or embarrassed, she couldn't tell.

'Give your salute, you lazy slut.'

She had to listen to the word again in her mind to be sure she had heard right.

'What?'

'You must pay your respects to the fallen at the Ehrenmal, as ordered by our Führer. It is the law.'

Evie felt so bewildered she froze. Presumably he took it to be defiance because he suddenly blew a whistle.

'What's going on?' she pleaded in her most polite German.

'You have broken the law and disrespected our Führer and the memory of the struggles of 1923.'

Other soldiers began to arrive. It was only now that she worked out they were SS – the very unit Max had cautioned her to avoid at all costs. One, quite a lot younger than her, smirked. 'Oh, let her go, Hans. She's pretty. Perhaps she was thinking about her husband's huge—'

'I beg your pardon,' she snapped, her voice thin and high. She was frightened, and although she didn't know what this altercation was about, she was not going to let some pink-faced young lad speak to her so badly. 'How dare you.'

The first soldier gripped her arm. 'How dare *you*. I don't care that she's pretty – her looks do not give her permission to avoid the Hitlergruss.'

She finally understood. 'Look, I'm very sorry. I didn't know—'

'Didn't know?' her tormentor raged. 'Everyone in Munich knows.'

'I'm new to—'

'I'm arresting you for giving offence to our Führer,' he said, not letting her finish. 'Take her to Ettstrasse,' he instructed the junior soldier.

'I was just going on my break—' he began, but sighed when his elder cut him a vicious look. 'Come with me, Fräulein,' he said and nodded at another of the men, who fell into step with him.

'Where are we going?' Evie asked, her voice small and genuinely fearful.

No one answered her.

It took about five minutes of walking and she lost track of which direction. She was escorted into what she took to be a police station in an imposing grey building with dozens of windows in neat rows that glinted at her like eyes gleefully watching her arrival.

It was chaotic inside the reception area, but she was able to establish that she was in the Bavarian State Police office. Beyond that she could make no sense of it all: there seemed to be queues of people lined up in front of the high counter, awaiting some sort of admission. The majority looked either anguished or bored; no one was objecting or complaining. It seemed unthinkable that so many people could be in trouble at once.

She was taken to a courtyard and told to wait until her name was called. Despite her questions, the man who'd escorted her there only stared back mutely. Max would have no idea where she was; no one knew what had happened, so no one could rush to her aid.

It was closing in on three hours of hopeless pondering when she finally heard her name. 'Over here,' a policeman said, beckoning at first and then came just short of manhandling her. He pushed her towards something he called the *Vorführzimmer*.

In this so-called 'presentation room' she was one of dozens being registered and searched. She was checked over by a woman who found nothing of interest on her. Next, her bag was emptied onto a desk and her purse rifled through. Her lipstick was picked up and she did feel a momentary clench in her belly when the woman opened it for an officer and he stared at it. Her mind was already scrambling to say something to distract him, but before she could demand to have this all explained, he lost interest in her lipstick and other belongings, which included the most incriminating item of all, she now realised – the handkerchief from Jean. How cunning that Jean had used something so ordinary. Evie still didn't understand what the signal meant and presumed she'd learn . . . if she ever got out of this place. The officer said nothing; he simply flicked a finger as some sort of command for Evie to be summarily moved along to where a weary-looking pair of uniformed men were recording names and sorting people. From there she was escorted to a cell that was already overcrowded. Some women were crying, others yelling; some huddled in corners and stared at nothing from out of red eyes and tear-streaked faces.

She stood to one side as shock crept in and reminded her that no one knew where she was and that she was a spy in a foreign land. Her situation was precarious, no matter how innocent she appeared.

'What are you in here for, pretty youngster?' an older woman asked. Her lipstick was thick, scarlet and wider than her lips; her clothes were tight and risqué. Evie wondered if she'd been arrested for soliciting but dared not ask. There was nothing else to do, and Evie realised the conversation on offer was like sport for the more experienced.

'I didn't salute,' she murmured, feeling ridiculous to be in a prison cell for something so pointless.

'You didn't salute who?'

'No . . . it was some sort of monument to fallen soldiers.'

The woman gave a snide chuckle. 'Drückebergergasse?'

'What's Drückebergergasse?' she asked.

A much younger woman strolled over. She was flirtatiously dressed too with a daring neckline to her frock – but the quality of her clothes couldn't be disguised – and she sounded a little drunk. Her gaze swam slightly. 'Good evening. Let me help. This is the name given to a small side street whose correct name was Viscardigasse.' Her education couldn't be concealed, either: she spoke in a cultured manner.

'I wasn't in a side street,' Evie assured them. 'I was in a square.'

'Ah, yes,' the younger woman continued with a tight smile. 'Our Führer declared the Feldherrnhalle a national landmark and erected a memorial to the sixteen Nazis who lost their lives during his Beer Hall Putsch,' she explained, swaying slightly on her feet. She pointed but ended up prodding Evie. 'The rule now is that anyone who passes the memorial must give the Hitlergruss. It's guarded by SS officers to ensure no one is wicked enough to defy the Führer and fail in their duty. Make sure you give a crisp salute, like this!'

Evie watched the woman effect the Hitlergruss in a most exaggerated fashion.

The older woman looked disturbed and melted away, muttering that she couldn't risk any more trouble.

'See how scared everyone is of him,' the plucky one said and gave Evie a drunken grin. She shrugged. 'It's so trifling and sometimes they wave you away, but at other times the guards are petty and probably have a very small *schwanz*. So they have to remedy that by appearing spectacularly important while actually being spectacularly pathetic. They especially like to arrest the pretty ones. Makes them hard.' The girl gripped her own groin momentarily.

Evie blinked and the young woman gave a gust of laughter before staggering away to collapse against a wall and slide down it to the floor.

Evie felt a fresh trill of helplessness. She found a vacated corner and faced it rather than stare at the hopelessness around her. Another two hours passed. She stayed silent, lost in her thoughts, until she was called again. This time she was taken to an airless room and sat with another official who turned a desk fan towards himself.

'You failed in your duty, Frau Hall.'

She was ready for him this time. Evie cleared her throat and pushed back her hair. 'Yes, I did, and I realise that now. May I just explain—'

He held up a hand to stop her talking and murmured what he was writing. 'Prisoner admitted to her crime.'

'Crime?'

He blinked and looked up through the thick lenses of his large round glasses, regarding her with a magnified suspicious gaze. 'What would you call it?'

She shook her head, aghast. 'An oversight, surely?'

'It is law. You cannot overlook a law.'

Evie stared back at him, feeling helpless. 'Am I allowed for someone who is German to speak for me?'

'Yes. I presume you mean your husband?'

'Maximillian Ryker Hall. Yes.' She proceeded to give their address and the telephone number.

'Right, Frau Hall. We shall contact your husband. In the meantime' — he smiled — 'this officer will show you back to your cell.'

Evie had given up hope of being given any further explanation, so she no longer asked questions. She followed the policeman meekly, to a different cell this time, which contained a row of cots. There were fewer women behind these bars. Some slept on sheets, while others lay directly on stained straw mattresses, and she gleaned that sheets were for the long-term prisoners. So she was now mixed up with convicted criminals as well as casual wrongdoers. There were no mattresses left so she leaned against the wall and slid to the floor; dust from the straw had become glued there, it was so rarely swept. Women nearby itched and scratched, probably from lice in the uncleaned, unaired mattresses.

She recognised one of the women from earlier slinking towards her. It was the younger one, who appeared to have sobered up. 'How did that go, Pretty?'

'My name is Evie.'

'No one in here cares – unless of course Pretty Evie is well connected, and then you should be let out soon with a slapped wrist.'

She had to pray that Max's name did carry the weight that others had led her to believe it did. She shook her head at the woman as if to say she didn't know that she had that sort of clout.

'I'm Carla,' she drawled, and smiled.

Beneath smudged mascara and lightly rouged cheeks, Evie could tell that Carla was a lot younger than she projected.

'Why are you here, Carla?'

'I was drunk – at least, I remember drinking a lot. And then, I'm assured, I spat in the pathway of a soldier.'

'Good grief, why?'

The narrow-shouldered girl shrugged. 'Why not? I remember one tried to touch me but no one will listen to that. Any girl out drinking or dressed like me is clearly asking to be raped, I gather. They're all swaggering idiots. They get their uniforms on and stop being respectful – they become arrogant and think they can treat women like playthings. Meanwhile, far worse, the men in power want the women of Germany in plain clothes with our hair tied back and big bellies full of children, cooking at the stove all day. No lipstick, no fashion, no hair flowing free, no flesh exposed, no fun. Unless it's behind closed doors when they can treat us all like their whores. I refuse!' She grinned. 'It will probably get me thrown into Dachau but I'd rather die young with my head high than bowed low to an insane leader.'

'Hush,' Evie cautioned her, looking around and feeling relief that everyone was either asleep or dozing, or at least lost in their own despair. 'Even if you think it, don't say it aloud.'

'I'm not afraid,' Carla boasted. 'Everyone cringes, bows to him, salutes him. I think he's a madman – a psychopath, even, but I seem to be in the minority of brave people who will speak out.'

'There are other ways to rebel, Carla, without risking your life.'

Carla gave her look of disdain. 'I refuse to sleepwalk like my wealthy parents, who are like sheep simply following the farmer to slaughter,' she admitted in a whisper. 'I would love to see my mother's face when she hears I'm in the local lock-up.'

'I admire your courage, but you're no use to the dissenters if you are sent to the camp.' She hoped she had found the right word in German for rebels. Carla seemed to catch what she meant. 'Find more subtle ways to defy the system.'

'Not saluting isn't enough, Evie,' Carla said, sounding dismissive. 'And incidentally, if you're very brave and wish to make a silent protest against the regime, then you take the tiny side street we spoke of earlier – Viscardigasse, nicknamed Shirker's Alley in your English – as a detour to avoid the Feldherrnhalle, which means you can avoid giving the salute. The SS are aware of this defiance.'

'If it's known about, aren't people caught?'

'Of course!' Carla laughed. 'But that's the point. Defiance is taking the risk of being caught, just to avoid saluting.'

'What happens if they are caught?'

'There are severe punishments because, unlike your mistake, their behaviour is deliberate.'

'And people do this?'

'People like me, yes. All the time. But it is getting very dangerous now.'

Evie couldn't help herself, whispering: 'I'm a lot more rebellious than you think.'

'You'll have to prove that.' Carla waggled a finger. 'I fear you're one of those adoring wives, encouraging their husbands to contribute to the Volkswagen fund, believing all that rubbish about every family having a car. You'll disappoint me if you are one. He is so deluded, and the women of Germany at the very least need to wake up.'

'I've only been in Germany for a few weeks.' She told Carla her story, carefully curating it to be consistent with the background everyone had agreed to in London.

Carla's eyes lit with fascination. 'Well, now you're a lot more interesting. English? But your German is so good.'

Evie explained that as well.

'Lucky you, finding Mr Right – but turn around and go straight back to England. Germany is headed in the wrong direction.'

Evie was glad that they were finally whispering. 'Tell me about the fund you mentioned.'

Carla obliged, nibbling on nails whose polish was chipped. Her fingers were small and her hands without blemish, attesting to her youth and a lack of manual work. As she talked, Evie guessed that Carla might be eighteen or nineteen at best. Either she possessed an amazing political motivation for her age, or someone she admired had drenched her mind with the 'other truth', holding a mirror to Germany's positivity and reflecting back its underbelly, revealing what Hitler might be dragging his nation towards.

'It has a pet name of Volkswagen,' Carla explained, 'and our Führer has promised that every family will have one for under one thousand Reichsmark. Germans are already depositing their money in a national savings plan that invests in this new automobile industry, but there are some who believe the funds are being accumulated so he can build his army, his tanks, his aircraft.'

Evie's ears pricked but she didn't react, so that Carla would keep talking.

'Herr Hitler has commissioned the Volkswagen through Porsche.' She frowned. 'You know this family empire?'

Evie frowned. 'I've heard of the car.'

'Yes, well, Porsche is responsible for many cars. The family has built its wealth designing cars most can only aspire to. I do admit, they're beautiful.' She gave an embarrassed shrug. 'He's a genius. An Austrian who is fast becoming a German.' She grinned and pretended to shake her belly. 'Getting fat and rich on Nazi grants.'

Evie frowned. 'Carla, how do you know all of this?'

Carla gave a sour grin. 'My father's an industrialist and jealous of Herr Porsche. Porsche has a son he's close to, who is involved in design and also drives racing cars that win a lot of races. He's quite handsome, actually. My father has no son, only me. I can't say this to him but I'm happy that my family has no grants from Berlin. I would have to run away from home if my father felt obliged to design bombers and tanks like the Porsche family have.'

Evie blinked. 'You know this?' She made it sound perfectly casual, as though they were making conversation to pass the time.

'Actually, I don't know if they're obliged or simply grateful for all the money they earn from Germany's government; they're certainly favoured. It's all meant to be secret, but I've heard my father blustering to his business cronies and watched him wringing his hands with envy. He thinks I am empty-headed and can't put the pieces together. He wants to win one of those contracts, but I swear if he does I'll run away to America or something. He had to see the doctor about his blood pressure yesterday.' She actually laughed. It sounded cruel, but Evie thought the laughter had no mirth and in fact sounded sad.

'His blood pressure is bad because of the contracts?'

'No, because Porsche's son is in Munich. So is our Führer, my father said, so I think he's presuming there must be meetings and talk of more contracts.' Carla snorted her disgust and hauled herself to her feet. 'Look at everyone, asleep even when they're awake! They should be banging on the doors, demanding release, protesting any way they can. We shouldn't be kept like animals.'

Evie nodded, wishing she could muster the sort of juvenile energy that Carla exhibited. It was being directed the wrong way, she felt, but it was not her place to say anything that might risk damaging her cover story. Carla walked away and started yelling for a guard.

Evie turned back towards the safety of the wall, where there was no possibility of eye contact. She thought of Leadbetter and what he'd think of her already falling into the clutches of the German police. She thought of Max's fury at learning what had befallen her, and she thought of a railway station in Yorkshire and its simple life that she would give anything to return to. But mostly she thought about the son of Herr Porsche and whether she had been thinking too directly about finding this revelatory evidence; maybe it needed a more oblique approach, via a family like the carmakers. It was a new thought that occupied her until she fell asleep looking like a vagrant, propped up against a grimy wall.

19

Max sat across from a hard-faced officer. He wondered if they went to some special academy that trained them in this sneering expression.

'Why have you not schooled your wife in the salute, Herr Hall? Surely this is fundamental?'

'It is, I agree,' Max said smoothly, not rising to any bait thrown his way. 'My son effects a perfect salute and was commended on it only today by the chief of police.' He watched the man's gaze narrow.

'You were with the Police President today?'

Max nodded. 'Yes. Karl von Eberstein and I go back. Our families were close,' he said, affecting a slightly breezy tone as he bent the truth. 'He was introduced to my wife and passed a very pleasant conversation with us. He has in fact invited her to join him . . . Oh, anyway, you don't need to hear all of that.' He waved a hand. 'Forgive me,' he said, hoping it was setting off all the right internal alarms within this young officer, who had just minutes ago looked smug. Not so now. Max waited.

'Your wife broke the law, Herr Hall.'

'My wife, as I gather, was lost, Herr Schulz. She has only been in Munich a very short while and is making a solid effort to learn how to get around this city. But she has not explored the Old Quarter much. It was next on our to-do list. All that history, you know.' He smiled. 'I wanted to share it with her and show off this beautiful city.'

The youngster nodded.

'And, of course, if I'd had the opportunity, I would have impressed upon her the sanctity of the monument and the importance to the German people for showing the right respect at that square. I would have made it very clear that she must salute every time she happens to pass . . . as I do, as all Bavarians do.'

'Not all of them, Herr Hall. We catch many and prosecute all of them for deliberately avoiding the square and Feldherrnhalle, in order to avoid the salute.'

'Oh, now you see – that's my very point,' Max enthused. 'There was nothing deliberate about my wife's actions. She'd never encountered that square or knew the law attached. She's English.' He shrugged, and tapped his temple. 'Her head is full of whatever it is that fills women's heads. All she wants is a baby. It's consuming her and exhausting me.' He grinned.

The young man's mouth twitched. 'Not a bad problem to have.'

'No, indeed.' Max laughed, pulling out his cigarettes and offering one.

'We shouldn't,' the man said, reaching for an ashtray from a table behind him.

Max gave a careless lift of his shoulders. 'I'm not going to say. Blame me.' He lit the man's cigarette with a flick of his lighter and drew back on the glowing tobacco. 'One more drag and I'll put mine out,' he promised, eager to get rid of it. He sucked back, sighed and pressed the three-quarters of the cigarette still to burn into the ashtray, bending it in half. 'So what are we going to do about my wife? You seem awfully busy out there.'

'There are a lot of women to process today.'

'And I have a baby to make,' Max quipped, which brought more than a twitch of a smile this time. 'Listen, Herr Schulz. Let me help one of those problem women go away from your long list. I am really most apologetic for not having ensured my wife knew the protocol of that special place – she's a foreigner and I won't allow her to make that mistake again. And, I'd like to make a suggestion to you.'

'Oh?'

'What if she and I go back later this week? We'll take a wreath and she can make a public demonstration of her contrition by saluting the fallen? And for my part, I'd like to let my friend Herr von Eberstein know of your sensitive handling of this matter. He is very well connected, and a word in the right ear about you . . .' Max shrugged, playing the only ace he thought he might have in this situation. Schulz looked young and Max had sensed ambition; maybe pandering to that might help, or it could go the other way, but the risk was taken – he felt it was the only chance he would have before older, more petty and by-the-book people became involved.

'You'd do that?'

'Of course. I appreciate your wise and measured approach,' Max complimented him. 'You've seen to it that my wife will never make that error again, so you've done something that your office stands for,' he continued, hardly believing his own oiliness.

Evie was dreaming of the signals room. She was waiting for a train to pass before she changed the points that would send another one – which was full of soldiers in Nazi uniform, giving chase – in a different direction. The first train only had two passengers: Max and

Jonas. They were speeding towards Levisham, needing to get through to Goathland and hide on the moors from their pursuers. The steam trains suddenly began to shift their shapes, twisting and folding into racing cars with numbers on their sides, made by Porsche. Carla and a man who Evie knew must be her father were standing at the side of the tracks hurling stones at the cars.

She was woken by a rude shaking of her shoulders and the dream evaporated.

'Get up,' was the abrupt instruction, and she realised with a glance at her watch that she had been leaning against the cold wall for nearly four hours. Stiff and bleary, she cast around for Carla, but the teenager was gone – she hoped retrieved by a pair of agitated parents who had assured authorities that they would take their child in hand.

Evie didn't ask why she was being roused. She half expected to be led back into the interview room but, no, she was taken out into the main reception that had emptied somewhat. There stood Max. Unmissable in his tall and imposing shape, he was running his hands around the edge of his trilby, obviously waiting unhappily but keeping his impatience contained.

She had no idea how long he'd been here advocating for her or waiting for her to be brought out. She didn't even know yet whether she was to be released. But his presence was like an ache disappearing. The hackneyed notion that her gallant knight had galloped in to rescue her didn't feel corny in the slightest; she had never been so glad to lay eyes on anyone, but especially this man, whom she helplessly loved more than any other. In that heartbeat she knew she would never wish to be parted from him again . . . and wouldn't, she decided.

The slight slump of his shoulders at the sight of her told her how much anxiety he had suffered since she had ostensibly gone missing. She knew he would have felt only dread, and Jonas might have even picked up on that feeling and perhaps been upset that she'd deserted him. Suddenly the thought of letting the little boy down felt overwhelming, rolling into a ball of different pressures; Ron's fervent desire for a boy, her aching need for a family, and Max's more desperate need to protect his son all coalesced to make her feel so unhinged that she staggered slightly, tears escaping.

'Max,' she wept, feeling pathetic but unable to stem the outpouring. 'Thank heavens,' she quavered, voice catching.

But he was there, closing his arms around her within two strides and holding her upright. She knew he wouldn't appreciate a scene, and was relieved that she found her footing and regained her composure promptly, quickly drying her eyes and even apologising for being emotional.

'I didn't know how to argue my case.'

Before he could say anything, another voice interjected. 'Frau Hall?' It was the interviewer, beckoning to her.

Feeling stronger with Max at her side, holding her arm, she moved to the high counter where the SS officer looked down at her; he'd never given her his name and didn't do so now.

'Your husband has argued eloquently that you have only been in Munich for a short while.'

'That's right,' she said softly, determined to present herself as contrite. 'I am deeply sorry for all the nuisance,' she said, finding the right words but hating that she was the one apologising.

The man stared at her, clearly wanting to exert his authority, but she watched his gaze flick beneath a hooded brow to Max, who was yet to utter a single word. Something in the man's eyes looked cowed.

'You may go,' he snapped. 'I would urge you not to make the mistake again.'

She shook her head and glanced at Max, but he was already moving away.

'Sign here, please, Frau Hall,' the officer said. She did so and he turned away to call the next person and did not look at her again.

'Max?'

'Let's get out of here,' he said, guiding her towards the main doors.

Outside, the evening had closed in and she inhaled deeply, realising how stale the air had been in the holding cell from the stink of sweating, nervous bodies. 'Where's Jonas?'

'With Frau Speigel. We're lucky to have her as a neighbour.'

She nodded. 'I'm sorry, Max.'

'Not here. Let's get home. We have things to discuss.'

Jonas was waiting for them on the stairs outside Frau Speigel's and surprised Evie by flinging himself into her arms. He smelt of soap and sugar, which she was beginning to recognise as the fragrance of Jonas. Holding him tight made her feel safe. She didn't know when he'd transferred so much love to her but it prompted a ball of emotion to find its way to her throat and stick.

'I thought you'd left us, Evie,' Jonas admitted, his large eyes looking round and scared.

Dampness stung at her eyes but she dabbed at them quickly with the tartan handkerchief she dug from her bag, the question again flitting through her mind as to why Jean had paid a woman to give it to her. The answer arrived as she unfolded the hanky; a tiny piece of paper fluttered out. She and Max stared at it, unmoving. Jonas was the one to reach for it.

'Thank you, Jonas,' she said, taking it and glancing briefly at it. She blew her nose and dried her cheeks. 'You should go to bed now.' She hugged him, kissing his face. 'I'll be there when you wake up, I promise.'

'Come on, Jonas. Evie looks like she wants to take a bath.' Max guided him. 'Go and choose a book we can share.'

She saw him glance at the note and they both knew she would be reading it before the tapwater had hit the bottom of the bathtub. What he didn't know was that she had every intention of sharing its contents with him.

In the tub, Evie submerged herself to her chin in the cocoon of warmth until her fingertips wrinkled and the water became unpleasantly cool. It was time to face Max, tell him everything and hope that her judgement had not deserted her in doing so. She emerged from the bedroom in her dressing gown to see both Max and Jonas waiting for her, despite their plan to get Jonas into bed.

'I want to say something important,' Evie said. 'I want you to know that you, Jonas, and your father are the two most important people in my life now. I will never leave you, Jonas.' She sat on the bed next to him and knitted her fingers through his. 'See this?'

He nodded gravely.

'This is like a lock. No one can unpick it. Only you and I have the key. You and I will never be parted.'

'And Papa.'

'Yes, and your papa.'

'Right, son. You've seen Evie and she's promised she's not going anywhere. Trust her now. It's long past your bedtime.' Max stood and picked up Jonas, who clung to his neck, and Evie felt a pang of love watching the father and child that should have never been parted as they had been. Only she could fix it.

'Will you tuck me in, Evie?'

She stood, followed them into his bedroom and, while Max closed the curtains and switched on a tiny lamp, snuggled him into bed and kissed him with a loud smacking noise to make him giggle. 'I love you, Jonas. You have happy dreams.'

'I don't want to go back to Aunty Giselle's,' he said suddenly.

'I know, darling,' she said, not missing a beat. 'But we'll be together again soon. Just one more visit with Aunty Giselle,' she said, winning a look of admonishment from Max. 'I know, why don't you take one of your special things with you?'

He was diverted by her suggestion and his tone brightened. 'Just one more visit then, and I'll take my silver Märklin zeppelin train.'

'Well, let's pack that one up,' she said in a gentle voice. 'But first, a butterfly kiss.'

'What's that?' he asked, his tone filled with wonder.

'Let me show you.' She pulled him so close she could smell the toothpaste on his breath. 'Now'—she pointed at his right eye—'we have to put my eye and your eye as near as we can.'

He began to giggle.

'Like that, perfect. Right . . . be still and wait for the butterfly wings.' She fluttered her eyelashes, the action tickling his golden lashes, which sat long and glinting at the top of his chubby cheek, and prompting an explosive laugh from Jonas. 'And that is called a butterfly kiss. My mother used to give me butterfly kisses when I was your age.'

'Where is she?'

Evie didn't hesitate. 'She's in heaven with your mummy. Two mothers watching us laughing.'

Jonas looked delighted. 'And my baby sister?'

'Oh, she's there, of course, in your mother's arms,' she said, standing up to disguise the surge of sorrow she felt for the sunny child she was now responsible for and was making promises to that she wasn't sure she could keep.

'Night, night, son,' Max said, taking Evie's spot on the side of his bed. He bent low to whisper something and she watched the little boy's arms snake around his father's neck again and give a tight hug. 'Sleep soundly,' he said and stood to switch off the overhead light.

After pulling the bedroom door not quite shut, Max put a finger to his lips and pointed to the bedroom. 'You look too tired to talk and I'm going to take a shower,' he said, deliberately enough for her to understand his meaning.

She gave a yawn, loud enough for any listeners to pick up. 'Thank you. We'll talk tomorrow. I'm going to put the wireless on and let the music see me off to sleep.'

She made all the right sounds of someone getting into bed, ensuring the bed squeaked a little, sighing as she settled in as though allowing herself to drift. Instead she silently got out of bed and tiptoed, following Max into the bathroom. The wireless was on, playing classical music, and he turned on the shower and closed the door.

'Well?'

She took a deep breath. This was it. All in. They were either going to work as one, or Max was right – she should leave, and while leaving Germany was her aim, giving up on him was not. 'I was trying to find you but I became hopelessly lost. In my muddle I thought if I could find my way back to Marienplatz, I would know my way home. But I crossed that square and . . .' Her shoulders dropped and she leaned against the sink. 'You know the rest.'

He nodded. 'Did they find anything?'

'Nothing,' she answered firmly. 'There was nothing to find.'

'What about the note in the handkerchief?'

'I'm going to tell you everything, Max, because I trust you, even though your detractors don't.'

'Go ahead.'

She couldn't tell if he was angry or simply frightened for her. 'The woman I met in the gardens this morning is called Jean. She's my contact to L,' she said carefully.

He nodded.

'I told her what Streicher had said to you. And I've told her what your boss briefed.' He raised an eyebrow. 'I also mentioned that you looked as shocked as I felt while observing you both.' She blew out a frustrated breath. 'Anyway, L wants proof. If I can give it, then we're off the hook. That's all of us, Max. I'm not going without you both. However, I have to magic up some sort of proof that corroborates what I've told L. But Jean being arrested adds a new deadline.' She held out the tartan handkerchief. 'She left this for me, presumably as a signal that she's been compromised.'

'And the note?'

'She scribbled that she'd seen Gestapo and had to presume they were there for her. This means she has not had an opportunity to tell L about my visit to your work. There's another way via a hairdresser and I'll be visiting her this week. I suppose she must have spotted her followers and just had time to pass on a message to me. Will London help her?'

Max shrugged. 'I don't know. Germany didn't help me.'

'I don't think they have anything certain on Jean. They might just be probing.'

'Suspicion can be triggered over the slightest misdemeanour or even just a hunch. Gestapo are capricious and sadly have been given the power to exploit their suspicions that are rarely based on fact.'

'What will they do to her?'

'Interrogate . . . They have methods,' he said, looking uncomfortable.

'But she's been trained, presumably.' Evie slumped with dismay.

'Well, they'll likely start gently . . . days of questions, and then the treatment will intensify. Everyone has their cracking point, Evie.'

She tried to disguise the horror she felt. 'Then we have a new deadline before she hands over my name. I think we give ourselves a week, tops. I have to find proof in days.'

'That's ridiculous. How and where do you start?'

She shrugged, but her mind kept returning to the Porsche family that Carla had mentioned.

'Show me the note.'

She did so. 'As you can see, it's a hairdressing salon. A safe place to get a message to and from L if I can't reach Jean.'

Showing Max her secret note seemed to break through the dam he'd built. He took her hand and squeezed it, then lifted it to his face to kiss it. 'We'll find the proof you need, I promise.' He rubbed at his chin in thought; she could hear the rasp of his beard. 'Do you think telling them about my project to build a new railway track into Poland for an explosives site is sufficient?'

'It should be. It certainly frightens me – and you, I can see – and I can't imagine they need much more evidence of the intention for war, but . . .' She shook her head.

'They won't trust it?'

Evie nodded. 'If I even mention your name, they won't take it as seriously as if I gave them something that had no connection to you. No, we're going for the obvious. Let's not talk about it and just relax – let our minds do some unconscious thinking.'

'Unconscious thinking?'

'Yes, I subscribe to that. The pathway to solving a problem often feels clearer when I'm not deliberately worrying about it. If I bake a cake, or go for a walk on the moors, or focus on creating an artistic layout for some wildflowers to frame . . . somehow ideas seem to filter through in that quiet distraction. So, you'd better shave that rough stubble if you're hoping to capitalise on how affectionate I'm feeling,' she offered.

Max looked back at her in disbelief. 'I figured you'd be exhausted.'

'Not too fatigued for loving you, though.'

'Hold that thought,' he said, allowing her to lighten his mood as, for the first time in a long time, they laughed together in the way that only lovers do.

They were in no hurry for this interlude to end, to reach its culmination . . . to ever require them to let go of each other. But it was over too fast and together they soaked in gratification over the quiet minutes as their breathing deepened.

They didn't speak but Evie was sure that as she listened to his heartbeat, the beats slowing until it found its resting rhythm, he was listening to hers.

She finally broke the silence. 'Max, do you know any Porsches?' she whispered below the covers, shifting to English for an additional layer of protection. It had only just occurred to her, given his family connections.

'Porsche!' He laughed. 'What on earth made you even ask that, right at this moment?'

She hushed him, nodding towards the wireless, which was now playing a stirring piece from Wagner with lots of cymbal clashes that would help.

He dropped his voice to match her whisper and replied in English. 'Good timing, Evie. I'm so glad you mentioned Porsche,' he said, not disguising his sarcasm.

She grinned, waiting.

'I have sat in a domestic vehicle, but my fanatics assure me it is the car of cars when it comes to racing.'

'Go on. Tell me what you know about the family itself.'

'I hope this is worth it,' he warned. Max rolled onto one elbow, placing his other arm beneath the sheet to cup her hip. His hand felt large and warm, and strong around her. 'Ferdinand Porsche is probably around sixty or so now and is the genius behind the car.' He grasped that they needed to keep whispering; that her question had purpose. 'He's also, as it happens, close to Hitler. Porsche is originally Austrian.'

'Like the Führer.'

'That's one of the links. But our Führer is as crazy for cars as Jonas and I are for trains. It's a passion for him.'

She gave a nod. 'And . . .'

'So, they're really quite friendly. As I understand it, Hitler holds his fellow Austrian in high esteem. Just a few years back now Porsche was commissioned by the Führer to design something called the "Volkswagen" for the German people.'

'The People's Car,' she repeated in English. 'Yes, I've heard all about it.'

He nodded. 'Every working German was promised a car if they put in for the savings plan for the good of all Germans. It would not be a crude vehicle, but a genuine four-wheel drive, with a three-cylinder, air-cooled diesel engine.' He sighed. 'I always thought it had a military quality to it with that description, but that's what Hitler wanted for his people and he made the promise that it would not cost more than one thousand marks.' He laughed. 'Imagine that. One thousand Reichsmark – what an impossible design feat to be landed with. Porsche was torn, no doubt. It is one of the most prestigious contracts to be assigned.'

'Why was this car so important?'

He shrugged. 'Hitler was jealous that one automobile existed for every six Americans, every twenty-eight French but only every one hundred Germans. He wished to change that ratio, to promote Germany as being ahead of all other nations with its technology.'

'But Germany's money had lost so much value with its inflation. How did he think he might achieve this?'

'The Reich cunningly introduced the lay-away scheme so workers regularly contributed money from their wages as savings for their own car. The people's savings funded the project but that increasing well of money also funded other projects in the meantime.'

'So I hear.'

'Through whom?'

She told him about Carla.

He nodded. 'There are plenty of engineering firms vying for Hitler's attention.' He stopped talking, frowning as though moving through some tangled thoughts.

'What are you thinking?'

'That you've definitely stumbled onto something.'

'Tell me,' she urged, pulling the covers above their heads to muffle their voices further still.

Max continued. 'Her father would be jealous, because it was always hoped that Volkswagen would have a field-service capability. It's my understanding that Porsche was ordered by the Reich to ensure his new car would have space for three men, one machine gun and ammunition.'

That caught her attention.

'There's more. The plant where the car was to be built and produced in big numbers was in Fallersleben, near Hanover. Porsche's bonus from Hitler for his efforts was rumoured to be around six hundred thousand marks, which by then was worth close to a quarter of a million US dollars.'

Her eyes widened with awe. 'I can't imagine that much money.'

'No, well – you can at least imagine how much in Hitler's debt Porsche felt. I mean, he's already a wealthy man and he needs no more awards or praise but even so, that's big and irresistible money. And so, when Hitler asked his friend, now feeling very warm and appreciative of the Führer, to also push forward with a plan to build aircraft bomber engines, he could hardly say no.'

Evie felt a click of tension in her throat at this revelation.

'So Carla wasn't lying,' she said, her mind turning over as to how she could use this to help their situation.

'No, I doubt that, and she's obviously in a privileged position to know it. I gather through gossip around the transport division that it was always understood the enormous plant at Fallersleben would shift its priority from cars to a war-production site in a blink when required.'

'Not *if* required?'

He shrugged. 'Luftwaffe Chief Hermann Göring has only praise for Porsche. They're all in bed together.'

'How far advanced is it?'

'I don't know. The plant was being built when I left for England. It's over two million square feet.'

'And the engines for bombers?'

'I've not been among the right people for a long time to be able to answer that, but Porsche is no stranger to aviation. He's been designing aircraft engines for a couple of decades. And he won the 1910 race for touring cars over two thousand kilometres at a sensational top speed of one hundred and sixty kilometres per hour. I was a lad when he achieved this, but I remember my father's ecstatic praise, and everyone was talking about how the next dimension for that engine had to be for aeroplanes. Only last year he launched the Type 55.'

They emerged from beneath the covers to stare at each other silently with only the moonlight to illuminate the room as Wagner roared on.

'How can you make use of this, given you believe we only have days?' he mouthed, testing her lip-reading. It was easy in English for her.

With her lips next to Max's ear she murmured, 'By telling me you know Ferdinand Porsche.' She swallowed. 'He's in Munich, according to Carla.'

He looked impressed. 'He's not my generation, of course. We've met on a few social occasions – he's greatly admired – but our paths don't cross easily.'

She shook her head. 'I don't mean Ferdinand Porsche senior, I mean the son. Are they all called Ferdinand?'

Max grinned. 'His son is known as Ferry and I happen to know *him* quite well. If he's here, then I can probably arrange to meet him.' He kissed her.

Evie clasped his cheeks with rising excitement. 'When?'

'Tomorrow, I suppose.'

'No one will suspect anything?'

He shook his head. 'Why should they? We've known each other a long time – old acquaintances. I can express an interest in the Volkswagen design . . . We're all in engineering, after all.'

Evie kissed her husband long and hard. 'Why didn't you think of this before?' It wasn't a fair question and she knew it.

'You wouldn't let me in. Now you have and now I can help. Until this moment I didn't know how.'

'We're going to find our proof, and we're going to leave with Jonas.'

He smiled. 'Except I don't know how to get him away from Giselle.'

'Leave that to me. We're taking him to Yorkshire and we'll live a quiet life on the railway, among the cherry trees.'

'You can make your jams and cakes, press your cherry blossom and greet your guests in the spring when they come to see Levisham's confetti-dusted platform.'

'Promise me you believe in that.'

'I do promise you, Evie,' he said solemnly. 'But tomorrow you have your interview with the kriminalpolizei and that's the first pressing hurdle to get through.'

'Should I be worried?'

'I wouldn't think so, but these interviews are hardly comfortable. They seem to want to trip everyone up . . . As I warned you, they are all suspicious,' he remarked. 'So expect awkward questions, but don't fall for it. Be direct, be puzzled by them, answer with all innocence. I've watched you reduce a roomful of Whitehall men to bafflement so I'm confident you'll come through.' He gave her a wicked smile. 'Now, where were we?' he said, sliding down her body beneath the sheets.

20

Giselle had sent a car and escort for Evie, and a second one to take Jonas away. Each time he left, it felt harder, more painful. This time he cried, and she cried with him. Max was strong, though.

'I swear to you, Jonas,' his father said, not a tremor in his voice, 'we're bringing you home soon.'

The boy didn't understand and there was no point in trying to explain in any roundabout way that he was the hostage until his father made good on the ransom. As the car taking their son drew away, Max guided Evie to her escort. 'This has to end,' he promised. 'I have to find a way.'

'I'll find it,' she assured.

'You just focus on answering all their questions. It's routine.' He stepped back and let the driver close the door between them. He waved as the driver started the car and then Max turned to leave for his office.

Evie was dressed in a soft linen suit in a silver grey, with narrow sleeves that dipped just below her elbow. Beneath the jacket was a pale lemon blouse in a lightweight cotton. Leadbetter had organised for her to be dressed by a woman at Selfridges in London. Both he and Mary had accompanied her to the grand store; they had looked like a pair of proud parents as she stepped out in various outfits.

'Well, I do rather like that red one,' he'd remarked but Mary had given him a look that Evie suspected she'd given him many times in private during their long working relationship.

'All very well for the single woman, Hugh,' she admonished him, using his first name now they were out of the office. 'But you don't want Evie to appear like a siren. She needs to look like an incredibly happy new bride.'

'Well, what does that look like?' he asked, sounding equally exasperated.

'That looks provocative. The very colour screams *come to me*.' She smiled indulgently as Hugh all but choked on the wafer biscuit he was nibbling. 'Put the silver grey suit on again, dear. I think try that . . .' Mary uncrossed her stocky legs and feet, which she had pushed into sensible shoes, as elegantly as if they were long and shapely pins teetering on stiletto heels.

Evie had come to love Mary, whose confidence in herself was infectious. She didn't think anyone would ever have the final word with Mary around . . . although Mary probably allowed her boss to think he always did. Evie watched Mary flick through the rack that had been filled specially with options for them. 'Yes . . . try that. Now this, Hugh, is elegant and extremely pretty in its minimal simplicity. Beneath that jacket, Evie, it's going to look fresh, dutiful – perfect – but there's no compromise on style or quality.'

Hugh picked up the conversation as he sat back on a velvet chaise longue, sipping tea from a china cup that the assistant had poured for him. This was an altogether private consultation. The three of them, together with Sylvia, their dresser, had the entire dressing room to themselves, which is why Hugh had been allowed within the inner sanctum, as Mary had termed it. 'You have to look the part of Hall's wife. You might be a stationmaster's daughter from York, who doesn't set much store by fashion, but the people who know him in Germany would also know that he wouldn't fall for someone without sophistication. If it's mentioned, you should admit that you dream about fashion . . . Let them believe that's all you aspire to, Evie. They are not to know how politically savvy you are or that you keep abreast of world events.'

'What Hugh is trying to convey, Evie, is lean into the silk, the lace,' Mary continued. 'Wear gloves, match your handbags that we'll choose shortly, keep your shoes polished, groom your hair and wear a touch of rouge and lipstick. Fashion, shopping – that's what fills your head, and your new husband has purchased a wardrobe for you and your new life.'

Evie had taken their advice so lightly at the time as to be hardly felt but she understood now, leaning back against the car seat, just how cluey Hugh Leadbetter and Mary were in this game of spying. She smoothed her skirt and willed her hands to lose their clamminess, even finding a smile that Hugh had won the debate in the end and the red dress had been purchased.

When she arrived, Evie was shown into a vast office space and seated before a grand desk with nothing on its surface but a lamp, a pen and a single file. No photographs, no books or signs of other work. Seated behind the desk was a man in plain clothes, who stood as she arrived.

'Frau Hall? Welcome. Please, have a seat.' He extended his hand courteously. 'I am Hans Frick.'

'Herr Frick.' She nodded and beamed at him, grateful but puzzled at the lack of saluting. 'Er, I was asked to bring these items in,' she said, trying to sound especially cooperative as she dug in her linen bag and dragged out her wedding album. She didn't have to fake nervousness; her body was doing a fine job of showing it already. With deep trepidation, Evie placed her new British passport on top of the album. Leadbetter had had it made up in her married name, assuring her that it would be destroyed and regenerated, if required, in her maiden name when she returned.

'Good, good. Please . . .' He gestured again to the chair. 'I have ordered coffee,' he said.

'Thank you,' Evie replied, noting that his pale eyes behind his glasses had a deadened quality to them, as though he wasn't the slightest bit interested in her facade. Their direct gaze was like the lens on a microscope that had been twisted until the focus was sharp and able to see all the tiny nuances and signs of lies, and it felt determined to pass through her defences to where she was hiding beneath her carefully selected outfit. Evie tried to shake off the fearful thought of being found out by tossing her hair slightly. She needed the fear of Frick out of her head.

The interviewer's skin was pale, his hair so short that the light from overhead and the bank of windows shone through its translucent, reddish hue to the pale dome of his skull. He was neither tall nor short, thin nor fleshy. 'Undistinctive' was the word that came into her mind as he thanked a grave-looking secretary wearing thick-rimmed spectacles for bringing in the tray. She removed Evie's passport as she left; Evie was sure her heart paused in that moment.

'Why . . .?' she began, dry-mouthed.

Frick made a *tsk*ing sound. 'Routine,' he soothed her. She loathed the word, which sounded like a lie. He took his time pouring the coffee with smooth, slightly freckled hands that had never seen rough work. 'Milk and sugar?'

'A dash and no sugar, thank you.'

Frick offered the cup and saucer and took a sip from his own. 'Ah, lovely.' He leaned forward, finding a smile that seemed to stop halfway across his mouth and freeze itself there. 'Frau Hall, I am from the kriminalpolizei. We are often shortened to KriPo.'

She nodded, frowning and pretending that its very mention had not made her insides feel watery. She waited, forcing her features to offer up nothing but neutrality. Leadbetter would be proud . . . although not if she vomited, as her belly began to threaten vaguely.

'Herr Streicher said this was simply protocol,' she offered, desperate to wet her mouth with the coffee but terrified she would tremble and miss her mouth . . . or worse, find that it worsened her nausea.

'Yes, yes, indeed,' he agreed. 'Ticking little boxes, as they say.' He tried to smile again and still it froze as though it had reached some sort of invisible barrier.

Evie didn't know who *they* were, but she smiled acceptance.

The secretary returned. Frick was given a curt nod of approval and Evie was relieved to see her passport delivered back to the table. She knew she had to calm down if she was going to walk out of this office unscathed and with her cover intact.

'How can I help?' she said, sitting forward in an effort to alleviate the tension that had crept into her shoulders.

He reached for the passport before him; his long pale fingers caressed the gold embossed on the blue leather before tracing the typed, four-digit number in the oval window at the top. Then he touched her name, handwritten in black ink in a similar, larger window at the bottom. He scrutinised the book, turning each page carefully as he studied. 'Your passport is in your married name; that was rather quick work by a notoriously slow government department,' he observed, glancing at her. It seemed he'd given up on trying to smile.

'I wouldn't know, Herr Frick. I've never had a passport before now. I've never travelled very much further than London from my home in Yorkshire, so my first passport was made in my married name.'

'I see. And you came via Paris, I note?'

She smiled. 'Our honeymoon was in Paris.'

'You weren't there very long, though?' He'd turned a statement into a question.

'No . . . Well, Max – er, that's my husband – he had some pressing work but I do think he wanted to get home to his son, Jonas.'

'And how did you feel about that?'

She looked back at him with feigned confusion. 'Feel?'

'Being asked to raise another woman's child? A Jew's child.'

Evie sensed the first trick question; no more easing in, then. She nodded passively, then feigned a soft shrug. 'I love my husband. He didn't leave his wife for me, so I feel no guilt. I met him after all of that trauma. I was an entirely different woman, from a different background and a wildly different upbringing. I suspect that difference suited him.'

He raised an eyebrow slyly. 'You deflected my question, Frau Hall.'

She managed to smile. 'I apologise. I didn't mean to. I'm trying to give context to my relationship. I knew nothing about Max when I met him,' she said, for once telling the whole truth. 'I think I'm still to learn plenty about him. But I'm a widow myself and the opportunity for a second chance doesn't come along often. When I found myself falling in love – something I didn't think I'd experience again – I didn't want to let that go. I'm not in any way concerned with what's gone before in Max's life. Jonas is an amazing little boy. He looks like his father; acts like him. He's obsessed with trains, like his father.' She smiled. 'I see only Max in him, and because I love Max so much, I find myself helplessly in love with Jonas too.'

'Bravo, Frau Hall. I believe you,' he said, although she was certain he did no such thing. 'You say you didn't know anything about Herr Hall when you met.'

'That's right. I knew him as a regular rambler in our region of Yorkshire.' She used the English term, unsure of how to say rambler in German but also deliberately to confuse. He frowned and she explained. He nodded. 'He was also a regular at the teashop at our station and that's how our friendship began at first.'

'I see. It seems you fell for each other quickly.'

'Yes.'

'Did you discuss his work?'

She shook her head. 'Not really. He described himself as an engineer and as I'm not particularly interested in machinery and how it works, I found other interests. We mostly talked about the Yorkshire landscape and rambling, and more about my life and duties at the station that interested him.' Again, at Frick's puzzled look she elaborated on the topic of her work, detailing her wildflowers and plans to expand the kiosk. Some of it was fabricated but it sounded plausible.

'Go on.'

'Er, Max told me he was doing some work in London for an engineering firm and using the short period in Britain to visit some family in the south . . . and I didn't think anything more about that.'

'Did you meet them?'

'No, actually. I feel badly about it too. His cousin, whom he's close to, couldn't come for the wedding. Anyway, I hope we shall have the opportunity to meet soon. I think Jonas should know his family.'

'Why?' He pushed his small, rimless glasses higher up his nose.

'Well,' she began patiently, 'his mother's family are in America, as I understand it, and that's probably a good thing.' She watched his dead eyes glitter to life; she'd said something he wanted to hear so she gave him more. 'How can I say this delicately? Er, it's probably best that we focus on Jonas being his father's son right now. He's very proud of his Prussian grandfather too,' she embellished, 'and to be honest I think he's a little torn between growing up to be a railway engineer like his dad or joining the German military and following in his grandfather's footsteps.' She hoped they never questioned Jonas on that whopping lie.

He nodded. 'Good, good. I'd like you to tell me if you know this person, please?' He opened a file, took out a photograph and placed it before her.

The change of topic was so fast her mind felt as though it was being stretched like a rubber band. Evie kept her features in neutral. Should she lie? How much did they know? Leadbetter had always said to skim as close as she dared to the truth in every situation.

'I do. Her name is Jean.' Evie tried not to look as though she was holding her breath with the tension that was gripping her chest.

'How well do you know her?'

'Not well at all. I . . . we met her in Paris at Sainte-Chappelle. We were all admiring the incredible stained-glass windows.'

'I see. But you seemed like great friends.'

'When, Herr Frick?' She needed to challenge him, show him she was confused by all these questions.

'At the cafe.'

She frowned as if consulting her memory. 'In Paris? Oh, at the Carlton Tea Room, do you mean?' she offered innocently.

'I do.'

'Was I being followed?'

'Just go ahead and answer my question, Frau Hall.' He was polite but there was nothing friendly about his tone.

'Er, we are friends. But I wouldn't say good friends, because we hardly know one another . . . but she lives in Munich and now so do I, so I hope we will become closer.'

'Did you know she had been arrested?'

Evie stared back at him in shock, impressed at her performance but sure it had a lot to do with the waves of anxiety she felt from being pinned down by the unsmiling Frick. 'How would I know that?'

'Because you were with her when it occurred, Frau Hall.'

'What?' *Don't say 'what', say 'pardon'*, she heard Rosie say in her mind. *Oh, Rosie, I'll never gripe at you again if I can make it out of this room*. She heard Leadbetter call out alongside Rosie: *Skim the truth*. 'Herr Frick, I saw Jean for a pot of tea and then the following week I happened to run into her in the queue for the bathroom in the Englischer Garten. I was there with my husband and Jonas for ice cream. It was a chance happening but it was also a lovely day and I think half of Munich was there. I had hoped to bring her back to say hello to Max again, but she'd gone.'

'That's because we arrested her.'

'In the parklands? But what for?' She kept her voice small and tight. It wasn't hard.

'Routine questioning,' he said, deliberately vague.

Evie shook her head. Time to distance herself. 'I don't know anything about that or why you would want to question her. I don't know much about her life.'

'What did she say to you while you queued?'

Evie looked to one side as though trying to recall the conversation. 'We said hello, had a bit of a smile about bumping into each other. We mentioned the weather, we talked about the Olympics, as I recall, and I think I told her that Max and I would be going to the rally in Nuremberg after that, because I would love to be a part of the spectacle and experience it for myself.' She hoped that sounded appropriate. 'I don't remember saying much else. Jean went into a cubicle, I waited in line for the next available and when I came out, Jean had left.'

'Did you make plans to meet again, as friends do?'

'No. I suspect we might have if we'd met outside again but I just figured she was in a hurry or had to get back to someone as I did, and we would telephone each other at some stage. Herr Frick, is Jean in trouble?'

'I don't want you to worry about that.'

'Well, I do. I mean, I hope I'm not in any trouble for knowing Jean. As I say, she's still much of a stranger. I have no idea where she lives, or if she has family. Whatever she's done, I can't help you with—'

'That's fine, Frau Hall. So, you will go to the Nuremberg Rally?'

She blinked at the change of topic again. 'Of course. Max wants to take me. I'm very much looking forward to the Rally of Honour.'

'I'm impressed you know this year's theme.'

Evie smiled. 'I want to learn more about my new country. Max assures me the Nuremberg Rally is a glorious spectacle and a chance to witness enormous pride in being German.'

'It certainly is.' He actually looked pleased in that moment. 'And how are you finding Munich?'

'It's very beautiful and I'm looking forward to getting out into the countryside. We hope to start taking some train journeys soon. It's my new home and I feel lucky that I liked it instantly.'

'And how did you feel about being arrested yesterday, Frau Hall?'

He caught her out and she faltered. 'I . . . I . . .'

'Did you not think we would know?'

'Herr Frick, I don't even know why I'm here or who you all are. I was not arrested, as I understand it, but I was taken for questioning for failing to give the Hitlergruss before a monument that I didn't know existed. I was lost at the time and confused, trying to work out my way back to Marienplatz. I didn't know about the rule.'

'You didn't know about the Hitlergruss?'

'I didn't know about the rule in front of the monument. I was just trying to find my way back to our apartment. I was distracted.'

'But you didn't give the Hitlergruss when you met me either, Frau Hall.'

She wanted to accuse him of the same. 'No . . . no, that's right. I'm nervous, that's why, but I am learning, Herr Frick. Max is coaching me. I was practising last night. And I planned to salute before you, but I'm not sure about the timing. I have to ensure I salute immediately. Forgive me, I tend to wait for the other person so I know when it is appropriate.'

'It is never inappropriate, Frau Hall. That's what you need to keep in mind.'

She nodded, looking chagrined.

'Where do your loyalties lie, Frau Hall?' There was the switch again.

She looked back at him, deliberately bamboozled by his enquiry.

'It's a simple question,' he said.

No, it was loaded with meaning. Evie didn't answer immediately, letting him believe she was considering his question seriously and there was not a rote answer. 'Let me say this, Herr Frick,' she said finally after an uncomfortable pause. 'My loyalties are to Max and to Jonas. They're my life. And my life is here in Germany with them, particularly in Munich, and I wish for it to be a happy one. I will be a loyal wife to a German man in the eyes of authorities, but to me I am simply loyal to a good man, no matter his nationality. We live here and we are hoping to increase our family soon, so my children will be German.'

'Good. We would encourage that.'

We? 'Have I answered your questions sufficiently, Herr Frick?'

He reached for the wedding album and she felt ill at the thought of him asking her questions about all the guests. Leadbetter had told her to memorise the names. Right now, she was sure her mind was going blank as she watched him open the cover. He turned each page, scanning the photos and, to her relief, finally closed the back cover.

'You make a handsome couple.'

She dipped her gaze modestly. 'Thank you. It was a beautiful day, though not the day I'd planned in my mind's eye for my wedding.'

'No? Why's that?'

She shouldn't have given him the opening. She was breaking one of Leadbetter's golden rules of not giving information when it wasn't asked for. Even Jean had cautioned her against embellishment and yet here she was, about to spin a tall tale. But it seemed the moment needed it. He was judging every word; they needed to sound like hers, not something she'd rehearsed. 'Max needed to get back to Germany in a hurry, as I told you. I tried to persuade him to hold off so we could have the wedding at the start of autumn, which would give me time to plan it properly, but he was determined.'

'Did you ask him why?'

'Yes, of course.'

'And his response?'

She groaned. 'Work. He'd received an urgent message about a new railway track that the German government had agreed to build and they needed him on the project immediately.'

'Where is this track for?'

Evie shook her head in a way that said *don't ask me*. 'I really have no clue, sir. He knows I wouldn't know one city in Germany from another. I plan to remedy that, of course, but I had stars in my eyes and was just so thrilled to marry the man of my dreams, so I agreed to the hasty wedding and the short honeymoon and the quick return to Germany.'

Oh dear, Leadbetter would surely gag if he heard that schmaltzy reply. But Frick seemed to accept it.

'I wanted him and our happiness more than a lavish wedding, so we kept it very small with only my closest family.' She opened the cover, pointing to the photographs of strangers Leadbetter had rounded up. 'My father, Alf. My sister, Rosie. The rest are just a few friends from the village of Levisham,' she lied. The man posing as her father was called Brian-something.

Frick pointed to the small flower girl and Evie smiled. 'I used to help out at the nursery school when I could,' she said. 'That's

Emily, one of the pupils, whose mother is a friend.' She tapped another figure. 'There she is. That's Lizzie. She spent ages gathering cherry blossom and fresh rose petals to use as confetti.'

'All very lovely,' Frick said, unable to hide the tedium in his voice. She'd bored him into closing the album of lies. He handed it back, but not her passport. 'Well, thank you, Frau Hall. That will be all. Can I arrange for a car to return you to your home?'

She needed that passport. *Hold your nerve*, she told herself. 'No, Herr Frick. That's absolutely fine. I was actually planning a visit to the hairdresser after this appointment, so I'll find my way there.' She made a show of checking her watch. 'Oh yes, I should make it just in time.'

He stood. 'I wish you a happy life in Germany, Frau Hall.'

She beamed and hoped her knees, which felt as though they may have liquified, would somehow hold her up as she stood to shake his limp outstretched hand.

Don't ask again, she pleaded with herself and still she did. 'What about Jean, Herr Frick?'

'My best advice to you is to forget your acquaintance Jean.' He shrugged. 'Good day, Frau Hall.' He pressed a buzzer on the desk.

'Oh, I nearly forgot,' she said in the voice of a distracted person. 'My father always says that I'd forget my head if it wasn't sewn on.' She chuckled.

'Pardon?' Frick said.

'My passport,' she said gently, pointing, as though he may have forgotten.

'We might hang onto this a little longer, Frau Hall. Just doing our due diligence.'

Evie gave him a smile that she hoped didn't look like a rictus of terror and turned to leave, her heart pounding. Without her passport, she was captive in Germany.

21

The trembling was beginning to abate. Now it felt like a vague electrical current running through Evie's body. She didn't think she should take the tram, so she made her way to the nearest taxi rank and waited until a car could drive her to the salon that Jean had noted in spindly ink – under the very nose of the Führer. She needed to be as brave as Jean.

The hairdresser, Hannah, was not expecting her today but time was now of the essence. Leadbetter needed to know about Jean, and Evie felt certain that Frick had not been entirely convinced by her performance. No longer having her passport was a very real problem. But with only days to get the proof that London demanded, Evie told herself that to start tying herself up in knots over something she couldn't change was pointless. Come the opportunity, she would be fleeing anyway and would have to think on her feet, plus Leadbetter would help – he'd promised he would get her out . . . She had to count on that.

The driver dropped her outside Hannah's Hairdressing Salon, which had net curtains in the windows and pictures of the latest hair trends in the shopfront. Evie scanned them briefly, trying to use the reflection to check if she was being followed. Everyone behind her looked to be going about their business; she couldn't see a single person lurking, but then, if they were good at their craft, she wouldn't spot them. Evie took a steadying breath before entering the salon, a little bell tinkling on her arrival. Women were seated around the shop in various stages of having their hair attended to, one seated under a rather complex contraption that looked straight out of a horror film. She stared at the woman nonchalantly reading a magazine as one of the uniformed hairdressers unrolled curlers that were each attached by a thick black wire. It was like a giant octopus, tentacles reaching down to the woman's head as though preparing to steal her thoughts or deliver some terrible electrocution.

Others sat quietly reading beneath silver helmets, which blew hot air around the sheer scarves wrapped over their curlers. A couple of the customers were enjoying manicures. Evie realised in this moment how sheltered her life at Levisham had been. She had heard about salons but never visited one; her hair was cut by one of the village women and it had always been wavy enough to not need curling. She was so entranced by the scene that she didn't see the assistant approach.

'Good morning. Are you Frau Fischer for eleven o'clock?'

'Er, no.'

The young woman smiled. 'Do you have an appointment?'

Time to lie. 'Yes, I believe I have one with Hannah. I'm Frau Hall.'

The assistant frowned as she looked through her appointments book. 'I'm so sorry, I can't see your name written down in our bookings today, Frau Hall. Could it be another day, do you think?' She began flicking pages in the large book.

'No, definitely today,' Evie pressed. 'Is Hannah here?'

'She is. She's in the office for the next half hour while Frau Neumann dries.'

'Could you possibly let her know I'm here? I'm a friend of Jean's. That's how she may remember me.'

'Take a seat, please,' the woman offered and disappeared.

A minute or so later a slim blonde arrived with an anxious expression she was trying to disguise with a smile. 'Frau Hall?'

'Yes. Hannah?'

The woman nodded. 'I wasn't expecting you until later this week, actually.'

'Oh, my mistake.'

'Thank you, Anja. Get back to Frau Muller's nails.' Hannah returned her attention to Evie as the woman she'd called Anja hurried away. 'Come through.'

Before she could protest, Evie was gowned with her head back in a sink having her hair washed by Hannah's strong fingers. Luckily no one else was at the basins so they could talk.

'Why are you here?'

Evie didn't waste time explaining. 'Jean's been arrested.'

Evie couldn't see Hannah's expression from the position she was in with water flicking into her eyes, but she presumed by the sudden halt in movement that Hannah was predictably shocked. Evie reached beneath her gown into a pocket and withdrew the handkerchief. 'She asked me to pass this onto our mutual friend, but I don't know how to do that or what it means.'

'It doesn't have to physically be sent. I've sighted it now. It signals that she's been compromised. How did she get this to you?' Evie explained and about Frick. 'You've been with the KriPo.' Hannah cringed, her voice taut. 'You could have been followed.'

'Maybe I was. But I'd already told him I had an appointment with a hairdresser. They can hardly suspect anything.'

'Frau Hall. Gestapo, KriPo, SS . . . they all suspect everyone.'

'Will you get a message to Leadbetter, please? He has to know what's happened to Jean, but also that I need some sort of escape plan. The authorities have kept my passport. I have no documents that can get me safely into another country.'

'I don't communicate directly with London,' Hannah whispered, pretending to bend down and pick up something so she could lean close to Evie's ear. 'Messages go through a third party.'

'Well, get the message to London.' Evie's manners were failing her in her fear.

Hannah didn't seem to notice. 'I'll get the message through. And I'll call you to make another appointment. Whatever that day and time is, that will be your getaway date and train. If I have no escape day for you, then I'll make the appointment for a Friday and it will mean you should come back here.'

'All right. I understand. Thank you.' Evie made to get up, but Hannah reached out a hand to stop her.

'Well, you're probably being followed or watched, so let's do your hair properly. What would you like?'

'Could you make me look like Loretta Young?'

'With Cary Grant, or the Clark Gable movie?'

They shared a small laugh that released tension.

'Did you see *Born to Be Bad*?' Evie asked.

Hannah nodded. 'It wasn't very good.'

'No, but I liked her hair in it.' Evie chuckled.

She left the salon feeling every inch like Loretta Young as requested; she hoped Max would approve. The long process of having her hair washed, cut, reshaped, dried and styled had eased her fears and calmed her. It had given her quiet time in her mind to plot. She was at the mercy of Giselle, Frick and the Gestapo, who were presumably now interrogating Jean – which meant they likely would come looking for her, too. But she was so close to seizing the proof Leadbetter demanded that something akin to stubborn pride refused to let her do anything but press forward with her plans to meet Porsche and hope to uncover some state secrets.

Max had been as good as his word and their luck was running. An early dinner meeting had been organised with Ferry Porsche for the following evening.

Evie had never seen anything like this place – couldn't have dreamed it up if she tried. The Hofbräuhaus was like a party all on its own; it didn't need the dozens of happy, chatting diners to add atmosphere, although in truth, she was glad there were so many. They made it noisy and casual and she was privately enjoying Giselle's obvious awkwardness at finding herself in such boisterous surrounds.

'Why does she have to come?' Evie had asked in frustration when Max admitted inviting her.

'To balance the table, but also to throw her off the scent.'

She'd frowned at his reasoning.

'Your interview with this Frick fellow shows we are being watched carefully and Giselle remains ever suspicious, but at least no one can come up with anything against you . . . or us,' Max explained. 'Inviting her makes us look all the more innocent. If we avoid her, it will only make her more determined.'

'How am I supposed to charm this fellow if she's watching my every move?'

'That I don't know. But I'll think of something.'

'Where are we going?' she had asked.

'The Hofbräuhaus is the place where Hitler initially showed his true colours, where his first genuine attempt to rally people to his cause and to seize power took place. It was this failure at what we all know as the Beer Hall Putsch that had him imprisoned.'

'And that's when he wrote *Mein Kampf*,' she said, letting him know she had paid attention to topical events. 'Then why would you choose this place? Doesn't it make your spine tingle a bit?'

He nodded. 'I hate it.'

Her eyes widened with surprised query.

'But because this dining room is so beloved by Hitler, Porsche will feel comfortable. Actually, it was his idea.'

'Really?'

'Yes, he has a longing for a Munich bratwurst and this dining hall's famous pretzels and cheese dip.'

She grinned, trying not to show the nervousness she was feeling. 'Right. What should I know about him?'

'He follows firmly in the old man's footsteps, but he's like a carbon copy anyway. When you meet Ferry, you're meeting the young Ferdinand. They work very well together and collaborate closely on engineering designs, although I understand that Ferry is now heading up the sports car section. But I'm fairly certain he'd be privy to everything his father is, and he will no doubt know about any project for the military and have access to designs. He'll be involved up to his neck.'

'And he knows Giselle?'

'I wouldn't call them genuine friends, although outwardly they would present that way simply because they frequent the same society events. Never forget while we're in their company, Evie, that these are both Nazi Party faithfuls – paid-up members. Giselle believes very much in the Nazi doctrine while Ferry is working hard to fulfil Hitler's ambitions with engines, whether on the ground or in the sky. Whether he is politically motivated by the Nazi creed is questionable, but your young jailbird friend is right. Ferry's family is getting wealthier by the day on Nazi grants, bonuses and commissions.'

'I won't forget. I'll just find out what I need.'

Max looked dubious. 'What you need are blueprints or formal schematics.'

She knew he was right, and his remark put a dampener on the day before it had even begun, because achieving that felt like a river too wide to cross.

Max must have realised that his remark not only stated the obvious but undermined her resolve. 'Look, if anyone can get Ferry to talk, you can with your disingenuous manner. Just see where the conversation leads you. There can always be a follow-up get-together and'—he shrugged—'who knows where that could lead. Just tread carefully with this initial meeting. Now, cheer up. You look very beautiful.'

Having heeded his warnings that this beer hall was far from elegant, she'd chosen her outfit with great care. Max had warned her that Hitler was moving Germany away from the sartorial sophistication of Paris and London and had set up the Aryan-German Manufacturers in the Garment Industry to encourage Germans to buy locally made garments. The Führer's was a twofold objective, Max explained; not just moving towards a wholesome, 'homespun' style but to ensure that Germans would now wear clothes touched by 'Aryan hands only'. It was a veiled threat at the Jews who had long been associated with tailoring. In Germany these days, it seemed, to flaunt the fashionable hedonism of Hollywood was in direct opposition to National Socialism, which wished to promote frugality, respect for natural beauty, service to the nation and other lofty ideals.

'Enemies to this theory, as far as women go, include everything from eyebrow plucking and dieting to wearing trousers and perfume,' Max explained as Evie shook her head. 'The wealthy and fashionable still do all those things, of course,' he said. 'Even so, you can feel the changes coming.'

Evie wore a pale blue summer dress in a linen that was all the rage this summer. While it smacked of a uniform to Evie, Max assured her it was fashionable and did nothing to hide her smart figure. It was he who had found it in a local women's dress shop not far from their apartment and bought it, knowing how determined the Nazis were to force women to see themselves as good wives and good mothers. There was no need for bright lipstick or flashy clothes. The sleeves that sat above her elbow were slightly puffed but the rest of the dress could only be described as just short of a nursing uniform.

'Look, I know it looks matronly, but your youthful and very delicious body will defy its conservative approach. All we want is approval from those who see intrigue around every corner.'

That had made her grin. Together with the large, square buttons down its length, which seemed to be the only frivolity in the starchy outfit, she managed to give her appearance a playful spirit through her new hairdo. Max had admired its short tumble of flicks and licks – it was clever and quietly provocative. Ignoring his advice, she did sweep some lipstick across her mouth, in a carmine colour. The sun had bronzed her skin to give it a healthy sheen, so she added only a light hint of rouge for added glow. She wore no jewellery other than her watch and wedding ring, and before they departed the apartment, she tied the belt a fraction tighter to show off her small waist and stretch the non-creasing fabric just a bit more firmly across her breasts. She had to catch Ferry's attention.

They'd taken a tram part of the way before walking through the old town, enjoying the contact of holding hands and feeling closer than ever on this balmy evening.

She heard the happy Hofbräuhaus before she saw it with the rhythmic and jolly sounds of an oompah band. Men were laughing and yelling '*Prost*' repeatedly. The lighter voices of women were drowned, confined to the odd shriek of laughter that pierced the cacophony of male sounds and brass instruments.

Inside, it was all action. She marvelled at the vast main hall as they stood patiently while the waiter worked out where their table was. The ceiling alone was a riot. Frantic frescoes in the bold baroque style were picked out with the contrasting paint colours. Flags from the House of Wittelsbach were depicted, waving at the top of each glittering lantern chandelier in the wind, and it wasn't lost on her that they formed the shape of a swastika. Long wooden tables stretched for as far as she could see through a line of arches, packed with happy diners, and she looked, slack-jawed, as waiters carried around massive steins of the famous beer of Munich.

Max noticed her surprise. 'You need very strong hands to work here. Each of those carry a litre of beer.'

She gasped. 'But he's carrying three in each hand.'

He laughed. 'He probably thinks that's easy. In older days, the mugs were made from stone or pewter.'

'Makes our pint of bitter at the local pub look almost puny.'

The waiter cleared his throat. 'Sir, if you'll follow me, your party is already here and have chosen to remain indoors rather than in the beer garden.'

'Fine. Lead the way.' Max thanked him with a nod.

Evie and Max trailed behind the waiter, who led them nearly the length of the main dining hall.

'They used to make the beer on the premises,' Max said, looking over his shoulder at her bemused expression. 'There was a purity law that is still valid today as it was in the Middle Ages. So the quality is high.'

'No wonder everyone's drinking . . . including the women, I see.'

'They'll all be singing soon.'

'Surely not?'

'Oh, yes. It's all part of the Munich beer scene. Singing is obligatory. Giselle will hate it.' He winked as they arrived at their table, almost at the centre of the crowded room, Giselle in its midst looking about as comfortable as a rat who'd accidentally strolled into a roomful of cats. As her darting gaze found Max, Evie saw relief relax her shoulders. She couldn't help but take private delight in how out of sorts Giselle appeared, especially having made the wrong choice of clothes for the occasion; they were far too European and glamorous.

Next to Giselle sat a man around Evie's age. His hair was coal-dark and wavy, with a strict parting, and he watched her with eyes she thought were brown until she was seated opposite him and concluded they were the blue of midnight. She could tell he was already struck by her arrival, which was helpful. His full, rosebud lips sat above a distinguished cleft in his chin and they flattened now into a smile as he stood to greet them.

Max spoke first. 'Ferry, you seemed determined to meet her, so I'm delighted to introduce you to my wife, Evie Hall.' He turned to Evie with twinkling eyes. 'He wasn't at all interested in dining with me until I gave a promise to bring you,' Max said.

Ferry lifted his hands in the way of a supplicant. 'Can you imagine what Dodo would say if I didn't come home with a full rundown on the woman everyone is intrigued to meet?' He winked at Evie and she found herself helplessly liking him immediately. 'Dodo's my fearsome wife,' he explained, reaching a hand towards her.

'Hello, Ferry,' she said laughing. 'I hope you'll take back a good report. Max has told me you two are old friends.'

Ferry kissed her hand briefly and then gestured for them to sit.

'Yes, Max used to visit our home when I was a child. I was always envious of him because he was so good with machinery. I looked up to your husband, even though he was barely ten.' They shared a laugh. 'And now he is surely the envy of all with his beautiful new wife.'

'You're an old rogue, Ferry. You know Dodo is admired by all.' Max helped Evie into her chair. 'You'll fall in love with Dorothea when you meet her, as we all did.'

'Ah,' Evie said. 'Why isn't she here?'

'Our son is very young still. You can't tear her away from him,' Ferry admitted.

Evie put down her bag and turned to the woman who'd remained seated during this exchange. 'Good evening, Giselle. How are you?' she said, brightly, making sure she looked utterly comfy among the cacophony.

Giselle didn't have the opportunity to answer – though her sour expression told Evie all she needed to know – because the waiter arrived with beers.

'I took the liberty,' Ferry said, all but licking his lips. 'I'm parched.'

'Well done,' Max said approvingly. 'I think our waiter would like us to order.'

The man shrugged apologetically. 'It's busy this evening. You risk a long wait if I don't take your order now.'

'Darling?' Max nudged Evie.

'I haven't a clue. Shall I just leave it to you?' she said, sounding deliberately daunted and as though she might always defer to Max for decisions. She could almost feel the heat of Giselle's sneer but didn't turn her way.

Ferry piped up, his smile small and cautious, but it was all for her. 'May I suggest the cheese dip and pretzel?'

'You're so predictable, Ferry,' Giselle drawled with a sigh. 'I suppose you'll have those pale weisswurst and start sucking them out of their skins?'

He affected mock offence. 'Why not? I may be predictable – although frankly what else does one come to the Hofbräuhaus for, if not its sausage and beer? – but you're much too prudish, Giselle. You need to relax like Evie here. You don't come to this place to be all purse-lipped and frightened of some pork fat.'

Giselle gave a groan of disapproval. 'I'll just chew on a pretzel.'

'Well, I'll have whatever you suggest, Ferry,' Evie said brightly. She fixed him with a gaze across the wooden table as beer steins were slammed down. Her beer and Giselle's were in smaller glasses.

'To old and new friends,' Ferry said, lifting his stein towards the centre of the table.

'*Prost!*' they chorused. Max immediately started talking to Giselle as Evie took a sip, deliberately making sure she left foam on her upper lip.

'Oh, here,' Ferry said, digging a handkerchief from his pocket. 'You've got . . .'

'Have I?' She giggled in a way she felt sure Rosie would be proud of. She took his square of linen and carefully dabbed at her mouth, deliberately staining it with the shape of her lips. 'Oh, dear, I'm sorry about the lipstick.'

He laughed. 'Don't be. It's like I've stolen a kiss,' he said, exactly as she'd intended.

'So, Ferry, Max tells me you build cars, and all sorts of other engines . . . just about anything that goes fast and makes a lot of noise.'

He grinned, dimples forming in his cheeks to give him a cuddly appearance. 'Max builds railways and yes, I build cars alongside my father.'

'What else?' she said lightly.

'Well, an engine is an engine, Evie,' he fielded.

Right. He was being coy. She would try again with a different tack. 'Tell me about your lovely family.'

He nodded. 'I married my darling Dorothea last year and we have been blessed with a son, named for his grandfather.'

'Another Ferdinand?' She smiled widely with pleasure to lure him.

'You don't know real love until a child is involved.'

And yet he and his kind were happy to coerce Max by using a child for blackmail. Evie resisted a grimace. 'Yes, Max said something similar when we met. I have to say I'm in love with Jonas, so I can only imagine how it will feel when we give him some brothers and sisters.'

'How did you two meet?' Ferry asked.

Max, she noted, was still deliberately turned away, engaging Giselle in conversation. Evie gave Ferry the potted version while layering in the romantic detail. 'I was in love with him on sight,' she finished, 'but don't ever tell him that.'

He put a finger to his rosy lips. 'Our secret. I'm glad Max has found happiness. And you, of course, fit the bill perfectly.'

It was an odd remark, but she let it land and feel like the compliment that was intended, rather than the insult towards Rachel that was buried beneath it. 'Yes, I've been assured by others, like Giselle. That makes me happy to hear. We want to build a life in Germany together. It's very different from my birthplace of Yorkshire but I'm looking forward to it.'

'You will build a good life here. Max is too talented in his field not to be considered essential . . . especially with the way the world is going.'

It was the opening she needed. She frowned. 'Do you mean war again? Max has been muttering much the same. He hates it getting in the way of all our plans. I mean, he can't tell me much and I respect that, but even so, it makes him glum from time to time . . . how you look right now.'

He hesitated, as if taking stock of her. 'Yes,' he finally agreed, looking wounded. 'I wish it weren't so.'

'You sound wistful.'

She watched Ferry shrug. 'Takes me away from what we all love, which is cars and racing. I don't want to focus on tanks or bomber engines.'

'I know,' she said seamlessly, as though hardly hearing his slip. 'Max doesn't want to think about new railways heading east out of Germany and I hate him even mentioning it.' It was a stab in the dark but she'd let it out to show that she was in her husband's trust.

He nodded. 'My wife has asked me not to discuss war plans in our home. *That's for the office*, she scolds.'

'I couldn't agree more,' Evie said, smiling sadly.

'Forgive me, I don't mean to spoil your mood.'

'What are you spoiling, Ferry?' Giselle said, leaning back into their conversation. 'You both sound maudlin, while Max has been telling me about the day he lost his trousers.'

Evie gave him a droll smile. 'Is that so, darling?'

'All very innocent,' Max bleated. 'Giselle is reading far too much into it.'

The food came and the discussion shifted to the forthcoming Olympics.

'Our Führer is determined that our German athletes will run faster than the African Americans,' Giselle said.

'Oh, they will – probably out of fear of letting him down,' Ferry replied with a grin, cutting into a sausage, which was horribly pale and looked uncooked to Evie. 'Normally, Evie, a Munich dweller would take one of these sausages and suck the calf meat straight out of the skin.'

She looked at him in horror, doing her utmost to keep it light-hearted and full of mock awe. Inside she felt ill at the thought.

'If you look around, everyone is, but given you are English and still learning the way, I will peel the skin off and slice it up.' She watched him daub mustard onto the equally pale meat that emerged from the white skin.

'Ferry's a heathen,' Giselle said. 'These sausages are for breakfast . . . at worst, lunch. Never after the clock strikes twelve,' she counselled.

Evie laughed. 'I think you should eat your sausages whenever you want, Ferry,' she said, and he nodded his head in a bow of thanks. 'We have something called black pudding in Britain that can make many feel quite squeamish.'

Ferry laughed. 'Ah, the sausage made from pig's blood. I'm yet to taste that. Is it a Yorkshire delicacy?'

'I think the people of Lancashire tend to hold that honour, although I believe it was brought to our shores by the Romans.'

'My, my,' Ferry said with a grin. 'Impressive.'

She knew she was simply making conversation but she needed this time to draw him in, make him feel comfortable around her. It seemed talk of sausages was the way to go.

Max was impressed with how effortlessly Evie was building her trust and friendship with Ferry, but he suspected only he could feel the anxiety building within her. She was getting too far away from where she needed to be. He knew this sensation all too well from his own lonely days as a new spy: no training, no desire, no experience from which to draw. Just one's own presence and wits in the moment. She was better than he had ever been, though. Evie's mind was like quicksilver, he'd come to learn; able to slip away in any direction in the moment where speed of thought was paramount. And while he was enchanted by her prettiness and found her no-nonsense manner refreshing, if he was pressed to pick one aspect of Evie that he loved more than any other, her sharp, intelligent mind would always win. He'd never met anyone with her clarity – she saw life and its situations so clearly. Max imagined she was also aware of the drift in the conversation, and he didn't want her anxiety to creep through and show itself to the snake in their midst.

He needed to do something fast. Either he could refocus the discussion back onto work, although that would feel clumsy, given they were now on the subject of food. He was about to mention how much he was looking forward to eating some Prinzregententorte again, ready to explain how it symbolised the seven Bavarian districts with its layers of sponge and chocolate cream, when Giselle cut across his thoughts and his line of vision.

'Of course,' Giselle said, leaning across Max to interject into the conversation but perhaps especially so that he might get a clear view of her cleavage and what he'd been missing all these years, 'Max can now eat sausage without guilt.' He realised she had a third aim – to insult. For some reason Giselle thought her cutting tongue was somehow a way of showing her interest and affection. He saw Evie glance towards him in defence, but the frown was already forming on his face and had given Giselle her opening. 'He doesn't have to fear the meat of swine any more.'

He was tired of the veiled insults to Rachel, who deserved to be remembered for her generous spirit towards everyone. 'I never did, Giselle. I was simply respectful of my first wife's habits.' Could he? *Yes! Do it!* 'Darling, could you pass . . .' he began but never finished because he managed to make a deliberate distraction look like an accident as he knocked a half-full stein of beer into Giselle's lap.

She actually shrieked, much to his private delight, and he could tell Evie had to restrain herself against tipping back her chin and cackling with delight.

There was no such dignity from Ferry, who roared his laughter.

'Giselle,' Max began, exaggerating the beginning of his stuttering apology.

'Max, you oaf!' Giselle said, breathing through the cold shock of the beer that was still pooling in her lap and dripping beneath the hard wooden chair. 'Oh, shut up, Ferry!'

'I'm sorry,' Ferry began, still laughing, 'but you should see your face.'

'Let me—' Max started again.

'Leave me alone,' she warned as she stood, nearby diners watching with unguarded amusement. 'Waiter!' she shrieked this time.

A man skipped over. 'Fräulein? Ah, let me show you to where

you can . . .' He led Giselle away. Ferry was making an attempt to hide his laughter, leaning back to say something to another diner.

Max winked at Evie. This was her moment. He needed her to take it and make it count.

22

As Ferry turned back to smile at Max, who was sheepishly following Giselle, Evie gave a small, embarrassed laugh too. 'I don't mean to,' she said, covering her mouth with her hand.

'Giselle deserves it. She's always so vitriolic and makes everyone feel uncomfortable.'

'She's a bit mean-spirited too.'

'Has she been unkind to you?'

Evie shrugged. 'It has to do with Max, I'm sure of it.'

Ferry nodded. 'You would be right,' he said, popping another bit of sausage into his mouth. Mustard was glistening from his chin, finding the deep cleft a welcome vessel.

She pointed. 'You have . . .'

Ferry gave a grin. 'Tends to happen when I'm greedy. I should stop now.'

'The food is delicious,' she agreed, tackling her own meal and keeping her tone conversational. 'What did you mean about Max and Giselle?'

'She's jealous. Why wouldn't she be? You're a gorgeous woman and you fit Max perfectly . . . even though she thinks that she does too. What's more, you wear his ring, and we all know how loyal he is. It must be driving her insane.' He laughed again. 'Which pleases me.'

'You don't like her?'

'Not especially. I think she's cruel. This is not a quality I can admire in any woman.'

'How about in the Nazi Party?' It was a clumsy segue to where Evie wanted to take him. Fortunately, though, Ferry didn't seem offended; he kept happily chewing.

He shrugged. 'There are cruel people everywhere, Evie, but you know this. Are you a sympathiser towards the Jewish people?'

She had to curb her natural response and instead frowned as though considering his question. 'I've never thought about it,' she lied.

'Forgive me. I thought your remark referred to the alienation of some people.'

'No,' she lied. 'I have the impression that persecution can befall anyone who speaks out against the regime.'

'No one does any more,' he replied evenly, finally pushing knife and fork together. 'Or if they do . . .' He dabbed his mouth neatly and horrified her by dragging a finger across his throat.

She blinked as he dabbed his mouth again and looked at her expectantly to check his face was clean. 'All clear,' she said, amazed that she sounded almost affectionate – certainly like they were old friends.

'Good,' he said, putting down his napkin. 'All of us in Germany are feeling optimistic. We've had fifteen or more years of living like pariahs, and now we have someone at the helm who is steering us, leading us . . . We're feeling strong about our future, making decisions that give our children the prosperity we crave for them.'

It was time to back down. 'Please don't misunderstand me. I admire all that Germany is doing,' she lied. 'You only have to look around to see how happy people seem.'

He grinned. 'Summer does that to us, of course.'

'So, what's your role, Ferry? I mean in the party,' she said, quickly qualifying her question to dilute how pointed it might feel. 'Max says he doesn't really have one, even though he's a member.'

'He will – if not now, then imminently. He's an engineer. They'll be making very good use of Max soon, as I understand it.'

'Really?'

Ferry nodded. 'You said it before. Railway expansion east out of Berlin, I hear.'

Evie knew her geography but played dumb. 'Oh? Where to?'

'Lots of places east of Berlin.' He laughed. 'Into Poland to begin with.'

'Do we want to travel into Poland on holiday?' she mused softly, quite impressed at how clueless she sounded.

'Not on holiday, dear Evie,' he murmured. 'Shall we say . . . acquisition.'

'Oh,' she said, grinning. 'I'm not sure I know what that means except it sounds secretive.' She leaned in, sipping her beer. 'Tell me more. Max is so reticent.'

'That is his nature, but given what he is working on, it's a helpful quality.'

'Is he important? He's always so modest. He tries to explain what he's allowed to, but you make it sound more thrilling than he does.' She gave a small, dim-witted chuckle.

'He is important now. The tracks to new depots in the east are vital, as are the engines we're designing at our workshops for aircraft.'

She didn't overreact. 'That sounds exciting.'

'I don't know. I think I was born in a car! I'd rather be working on car engines – racing cars are the most exhilarating engines in the world. I am finding all this special work being demanded for the Luftwaffe is getting in my way, but I have no choice. Our company is committed.'

'I think aircraft engines are romantic,' she remarked, wondering from where on earth she'd dug up that curious sentiment. But she didn't think Max could hold Giselle off for much longer, wherever they were. She needed to push Ferry, though she wasn't sure into what – but it needed to be something of substance she could send back to London.

Ferry laughed. 'Do you really?'

'Yes, flying off into the great dome of the sky . . . Where to?' She shrugged with an almost whimsical expression.

'Straight over London in this case, I would imagine,' Ferry said, sounding heartless.

She blinked with concern she couldn't hide fast enough.

He reached for her hand. 'I'm sorry. That wasn't very kind, given where you're from. I was born Austrian . . . and I love Austria but my life is here and everyone I love is here. It's fine to hold affection for the country of your birth as I do, but I am now German and everything I do is to advance Germany. You should take the same approach.'

She wanted to ask if that was because the German Reich paid him so much money, but she said instead, 'Yes, I feel exactly the same. I hope it won't come to war, though. Life is perfect right now.'

'If I showed you the designs in my office at home, I think you'd accept it is coming. You and I can't stop it, so we might as well stick with the winning side.'

Once again, she kept her response neutral, although what he'd just said about the home office made her want to leap to her feet. 'You're that confident?'

He nodded with a sly smile. 'With our bomber engines and our fast-moving tanks, no one will be able to withstand us.'

'Are you that far into your designs?' She could see Max at the far end of the restaurant, Giselle just ahead of him with her scowl still in place. 'I'd love to see them.'

He looked genuinely surprised. 'Surely that sort of thing doesn't interest you?'

'Machines do, I have to admit. I've married an engineer, haven't I? I always wanted to be a designer of things – I just didn't know what.' She laughed through her lie. 'I think you engineers are so clever the way you can visualise something extraordinarily mechanical and then draw it to specification.'

'Wow. I wish my wife admired that in me.'

She laughed again. 'I'd so like to meet her.' Max and Giselle were nearly back at the table; this was it.

Ferry shrugged. 'Well, Stuttgart is a mere train ride away. I'm sure you can twist my arm to see the latest racing car in design.'

Evie felt her hopes rise as she leaned in. 'Is that an invitation?'

'Of course.' He grinned. 'You must visit. In fact, we're having some people over this Saturday for lunch. A picnic day. You and Max are very welcome. Bring Jonas; there will be plenty of other children to play with.'

'Oh, we'd love to.'

'Good. That's a date. I'll organise it with Max. I think you and my Dodo will get on very well.' He stood to welcome back Giselle to the table and held out a chair for her.

'Hello, you two,' Max said, glancing towards Giselle, who now had a damp stain on her dress that she was trying to cover with a scarf.

'I'm only stopping to say farewell,' she said curtly, gesturing towards the offending mark. 'Please don't say sorry again, Max,' she said, raising a hand to ward off whatever he was about to say.

He sighed. 'All right, let me at least get you a taxi and kiss you goodbye.'

Evie mentally shook her head at how Max was turning on the charm, but they'd got what they came for. When he returned from seeing Giselle on her way, he found her alone. He frowned.

'Ferry?'

'Insisted on paying. He's finished – you haven't. Yours has gone cold.'

'I'm not especially hungry. Did we achieve anything?'

'Your antics were inspired. We're off to Stuttgart because of them . . . *Shhh*, here he comes.'

'You didn't have to do that,' Max said, smiling at Ferry. 'Thank you.'

'My pleasure. I'm sorry our meal was interrupted, and you barely ate your food, but it did mean I had your lovely wife all to myself.'

Max's smile widened. 'I'll finish it now. And it's our turn next time. Bring Dodo.' He grinned at Evie.

'We'll do better than that. I've invited Evie and yourself to come to Stuttgart at the weekend.'

Max delivered an appropriately surprised and delighted expression.

'We're having a bit of a thing for friends – you'll know most of them, Max – so it would be lovely for you all to join us. Evie said you'd love to . . . so it's not a question, old chap, it's a deal. See you at the house. You know where to come. Be there Saturday. Don't be late.' Ferry leaned in and kissed Evie's cheek. 'I'm sorry to leave so early but I want to let Dodo know you're coming and have a chance to wish my son goodnight. He's too small to know, but Dodo says it's important for him to hear my voice.'

'Oh, that's sweet,' Evie said, squeezing his hand.

'Thank you for keeping me company when my two friends abandoned me.'

'I'm glad they did,' she said, and he could never know how she meant her compliment.

Ferry shook Max's hand but was still gazing at Evie, dimples deepening at his smile. 'Bring swimming gear. You,' he said, turning to Max, 'bring tennis whites.' He took Evie's hand and kissed it. 'Ask Max to take you back via Viscardigasse. Live dangerously.'

She pretended to be amused as though she couldn't wait to learn what it meant, but felt immediately sickened after he'd left. 'Ugh, I never want to pass through that square again.'

Max sat down again. 'Tell me everything!'

She summarised her conversation with Ferry while he finished his beer, which had lost much of its effervescence, leaving his meal untouched; it had become cold and glutinous in his absence. 'Very good, Evie. I don't know what comes next, but the door has opened.'

She clasped his hand. 'I couldn't have done it without you. That was a masterstroke.'

'Giselle was livid, but I rather enjoyed it. She's had that coming for years.'

'I hope Rachel was watching.'

He looked back at her, his smile dying, but it was with tenderness. 'I do too. The first of many blows I hope we can strike in the very short time we have.'

'So you'll organise tickets to Stuttgart for Saturday?'

He nodded. 'First thing. What do you plan to do?'

'I plan to steal Ferry's designs and get them to Britain.'

Max blinked in astonishment; it seemed that if she'd said she planned to sprout wings and fly to the moon, he might have accepted that more easily. 'You can't be serious.'

'I am deadly serious. I want us out of here.' She dropped her voice. 'War is coming faster than we can imagine, Max. He's boasting about it. I realise nothing we do can stop it, but we can help Britain be more prepared. What's more, I don't wish to spend another second more in Germany than I have to. I'm going to earn the right for the three of us to leave.'

He looked down.

'What does that look mean?'

Max shrugged. 'I do admire your confidence but the chances of seeing anything incriminating is slim. I doubt he's going to offer them up.'

'I'll have to persuade him.'

Max regarded her with a stare of incredulity. 'And if you can, how are you going to steal these designs? They'll be under lock and key – if they're even there.'

'Oh, they're there. He told me as much. I just have to work out how to get to them.'

Max shook his head. 'Evie, I can't let you do this. Really. I thought you were just going to pump him for information.'

'It won't be enough for Whitehall to buy your freedom. You have to understand this.'

'Then don't worry about my freedom. You and Jonas . . . If you can both get out, it's all that matters.'

'It's all of us or none of us, Max.'

'Where do you get your confidence? Listen, I'll take every risk you ask of me if it means saving you and Jonas. I couldn't care less what happens to me, but if you're caught, you know what faces you.'

'And if I don't try, I also know what's ahead. A life of loneliness and regret – not to mention the sickening guilt of not saving a little boy's life or his father, whom I happen to love. Let's agree now, this is for Jonas. Everything else is a bonus.'

'Together, then, we'll find a way,' he promised.

She linked her hand in his. 'We are never going to be parted. We succeed together or . . .' She shook her head. 'We'll pull this off, Max.'

Giselle, who seemed to be her own authority, had grudgingly granted them Jonas for more than just the weekend. Evie had asked

Max why they weren't arguing more ferociously for Jonas to be returned permanently.

'Giselle needs to feel she has power over us – it may keep her distracted, plus I want her to think us helpless – she thrives on knowing she has her mouse cornered. And . . .' He hesitated. 'I'm fearful of pushing too hard and having her tell me what I don't wish to hear, which is that Jonas will never be returned. As long as he's with her, he's still within my grasp and just maybe you can get him away.'

'*We* will get him away, Max,' she asserted and he nodded. 'I suppose it's a heartening step forward to have him for five days now that the summer school holidays have officially begun. Let's give him a happy time.'

They were commencing Jonas's stay with the trip to Stuttgart on the train, which pleased the lad enormously. The train journey was a couple of hours headed west, through lush meadows with drifts of wildflowers that lifted their spirits and towns straight out of fairytales of half-timbered houses, the odd castle and tall church spires. She caught glimpses of hilly, cobblestoned streets and long-poled boats that bobbed on small rivers before she understood that they were roaring by the mighty, glittering Danube at Ulm. They left it behind as they continued snaking their way across the verdant countryside, which shifted to alpine in the distance; Evie could see the rich green of the valleys turn to the cool darkness of forest at the foothills. She imagined those alps would be snow covered in a matter of months and even more breathtaking.

The journey clattered on over cups of coffee and snacks to keep Jonas occupied, and she watched the terrain ease into vineyards as they drew closer to the important city that was their destination. She loved Yorkshire but if she had to swap it, it would be for this romantic Bavaria, which seemed to offer everything from mountains to picturesque meadows, river life to walled medieval towns and terraced vineyards. She longed to visit the Black Forest and its picturesque villages made famous by the Brothers Grimm, whose stories she'd grown up on, but she knew in her heart she never would: all she really wanted to do now was escape this place of heartbreaking beauty.

As they alighted, carrying their sports clothes for their day with the Porsches, Max gave her a short history of what he knew about Stuttgart.

With Jonas skipping between them, licking a lollipop, Max explained, 'This used to be a regal city; now it's an industrial one, making its name as the premier car manufacturing capital of Germany. Daimler, for instance, and Benz.'

'As well as Porsche,' she said.

'Exactly. When Ferry left school, he began working for Bosch here, while I moved to Berlin to study physics and engineering at university.'

'Did you always intend to work for the railways?'

'Always.' He laughed. 'I was fascinated by trains.'

'Like me, Papa,' Jonas piped up, making them smile.

Max put a hand on her arm to stop her at the taxi rank. 'Evie, what are we going to do?'

There was no one waiting around them, so they could speak openly. She knew she'd been far too cavalier refusing to plot with him or even discuss options, but she trusted her intuition. 'Max, I know this probably goes against your inclination, but I think we have to improvise in the moment. My father always says the best laid plans go wrong. I don't think we can hatch any sort of idea not knowing the house, or the situation.'

'But we need *some* plan,' he appealed.

Evie shrugged. 'We work together and contrive a way to get me into Ferry's study, or as close to as possible. And then I shall be relying on you to keep watch or, at worst, to keep others occupied while I try to get my hands on those plans. At worst, if I can glimpse them, I can pass on what I've seen.'

'Will Whitehall trust that you've seen them?'

Jonas was staring at a butterfly, entirely disengaged from their conversation. She dug into her bag and lifted out the Minox. 'Do you know what this is?'

He frowned. 'Nothing I've seen before.'

'It's called a subminiature camera. Leadbetter gave it to me. I'd say it might be helpful if I could get some snapshots to back up my claim.'

'On that?'

She nodded, actually grinning. 'It's very impressive. I've seen photographs taken with it.'

'Bloody hell. All right, don't for heaven's sake let that be seen by anyone.'

'I won't.'

'Evie, that alone could get us both executed.'

'Max, can you not make me any more frightened than I already feel?' she muttered.

He nodded his apology. 'Right. Sorry. This should be me, not you.'

'If no opportunity arises, we try again another way, or perhaps I find a new target. Jean obviously hasn't cracked – not yet, anyway. We have to count on her not saying anything, so just go about your day, Max. Don't focus on me. Play tennis, swim . . . If I know you're feeling anxious, I'll lose my nerve. Besides, I don't see we have a choice.'

He looked mortified. 'That's not true. We can go home now. Say Jonas felt ill or something. We could—'

'Stop,' she warned. 'I want to go home, and by home I mean Yorkshire. So help me do this, or get back on that train and get out of my way.' Her words must have felt like a slap. 'This is why we're here. This is a chance we've been given and we have to take it and ruthlessly exploit it.' She stared furiously into his face, searching his eyes, needing his wholehearted support.

He nodded. 'Let me lead. I can read these people. It's a taxi ride from here,' he said, sounding beaten.

The Porsche villa was a long, triple-gabled house with shuttered windows and brightly coloured window boxes spilling geraniums, their scarlet glory entwining around ivy and other climbers to make a gloriously pretty welcome. Evie had already sighed at the attractiveness of the Feuerbacher Heide region, an extensive park-like area in the north of Stuttgart. Here meadows were being grazed on by cows and they reminded her painfully of the Yorkshire she missed. Their taxi had climbed up the northern slope to the highest foothill, which the driver informed them was called Killesberg. After rounding several bends, the Porsche villa had sprawled before them among sumptuous grounds.

It spoke strongly of wealth. Evie was left in no doubt that the Porsche dynasty was growing richer by the day from its Nazi connections. As if hearing her thoughts, the taxi driver continued.

'This is probably the most expensive address in Stuttgart. It has wonderful views of the city. All the houses here belong to important people. And this family you are visiting . . . well, they are perhaps the most well known. The Führer himself has visited twice,' he said proudly. 'You are obviously important people too.'

They fended off his gushing observations with a smile and a large tip on the fare. The driver's eyes widened with pleasure before he leapt out to open doors and the boot to take out their bags. 'There you go, young man,' he said, tipping his cap at Jonas as he handed him the smallest bag.

'We're going swimming,' Jonas told him.

The man grinned. 'Perfect day for it.'

At the door a housemaid greeted them and showed them through to where the 'picnic day', as Ferry had called it, was in full swing. A blonde woman smiling broadly from a heart-shaped face welcomed them. She was dressed rather gloriously in what looked to be the latest style in pantsuit – probably designed for a beach visit – with floaty white trousers and a matching cropped top, beneath which Evie spotted the unmistakable shape of a swimsuit.

'Max!' she called, approaching with outstretched hands. 'And you must be the beautiful new bride, Evelyn, that I've heard a lot about?' She clasped each of their hands. 'I'm Dorothea – Dodo – Ferry's wife.'

'I'm Jonas.' He smiled up at her.

'Welcome, all of you, especially Jonas,' she said, dropping Max's hand to ruffle the hair of his son affectionately. Evie noted it was the gentle touch of a mother. 'All the children are outside playing, Jonas, and we shall be serving lots of lovely food shortly. Why don't you go and join them in the meantime? Er, Helga, perhaps you could take Jonas out to the children, please?'

The housemaid smiled at Jonas. 'Shall we go?' she offered, holding out a hand.

Jonas glanced at his father. 'Go on,' Max encouraged, and Evie bent to give Jonas a kiss, sensing he wasn't shy so much as uncertain about strangers.

'I'll be out shortly,' she assured. He went with the maid. 'Please call me Evie,' she said, matching Dodo's smile as she handed over a bright bouquet of summery flowers that they'd brought from the Munich markets.

'How could you know that yellow is my favourite colour?' Ferry's wife cooed. 'Unnecessary but lovely, thank you, Evie. You have brought swimming stuff, I hope, or Ferry will nag me to find something to fit?' she said. Raising an eyebrow, she added, 'And you're tiny, my dear. Anything I put you in will swim right off you!'

They both laughed. It wasn't true; Evie thought their hostess possessed a lovely figure, but Evie liked her modesty. She held up her bag where the treacherous camera hid. 'We were warned and came prepared.'

Dodo smiled. 'You can change as soon as you please – everyone else is already dressed for swimming. But let me show you through so you can meet everyone. Ferry's drinking beer and barbecuing, Max. I'm sure you'll find him. Just follow the noise.'

He pecked Evie on the cheek. 'See you later.'

Dodo watched Max leave and then glanced back at Evie. 'He looks well. I'm thrilled he's found you. I hated to hear that he was widowed.'

'Sadly, I've met some people – including someone he considers a friend – who celebrated Rachel's death,' she risked, needing to take a measure of the Porsches.

Her companion's features straightened. 'Mmm, and I think I can guess exactly who that is.' She lowered her voice. 'While all of us wish to see Germany advancing itself, we don't all necessarily share the identical philosophy on how.'

A fence-sitter, then, Evie decided. Her host wasn't taking a clear position, perhaps allowing herself the excuse of that old helper – the blind eye. Dodo could hardly deny the lifestyle that the Nazi Party was affording them through all the orders, grants and general support, and she couldn't have a loud opinion on how the German government went about imposing its vision. It was no use probing further.

Dodo was still smiling kindly at her, unaware of Evie's misgivings. 'I'll have Helga take all that upstairs for you.' She gestured at the bags, then squeezed Evie's arm. 'I'm so glad you made the journey.' She led Evie through into the expansive gardens, where a quick scan revealed around a dozen adults and about as many children at play. 'Did you want to check on Jonas? We can together if you wish.'

'Might be good if I just see he's settled. Perhaps you can tell that I'm still learning how to be a mother to Jonas. You have a son, too, don't you?' It was common ground they could bond over.

Dodo gave her a beam that lit her face. 'Yes. He's sleeping through all the fun today. He's not yet a year. We're both mad for Butzi . . . we call him that as a pet name. He's yet another Ferdinand,' she said, drolly, 'born the year of our marriage.' She grinned. 'We wasted no time. You shouldn't either. Give Jonas a brother or sister?' Her warmth was irresistible.

'We're trying,' Evie said, giving a conspiratorial grin.

'Good. Come. I'm sure your little boy is fine. These are all lovely children, and they'll look after him.'

She wasn't exaggerating. Evie could see that Jonas was already comfortably embedded with a pack of blond youngsters, overseen by two older girls who seemed very good at making sure no one acted rough and everyone took their turn at skittles. The game seemed to have everyone's attention at present. There was lots of laughter and Jonas barely noticed her standing nearby. Evie couldn't help but think of his sister, who in Max's words had been black-haired and exquisite like her mother. The child who'd died before being given the name of Sarah would not have fit in here.

Shaking off the grim thought, Evie grinned at her new friend. 'He looks happy – it's wonderful to see him around other children.'

'Let's get you a cool drink and you can meet some of our other guests.'

The next half hour passed most pleasantly. Evie found herself, despite her reservations, among agreeable company, surprised by how easily she was accepted. Most of the women were of a similar age to her own and they all looked fashionably casual in capes or bathing gowns with wide skirts. Evie felt conspicuous and was looking for the right moment to excuse herself to change. German women, it seemed, fretted, laughed and gossiped about all the same things that British women did. Topics ranged from weddings to children, fashion to the new favourite eating spot, from the vagaries of husbands to the latest hairstyle.

The aroma of meat landing on a hot griddle wafted near to make her hungry and added to the carefree atmosphere she was in, as more French champagne was poured to top up glasses.

'Oh, I love this brand,' someone said to Dodo.

'I insist Ferry always has a supply for me of this one, Petra. Do you know it?'

Petra nodded. 'Delancré, yes. We visited it after the war as a family. My father took us all through the Champagne region, told my sister and myself: "Girls, this is part of your important education."' Everyone laughed as Petra continued. 'We were quite happy learning about champagne, I'll admit.' She grinned. 'From memory, it's a small winery but I was fascinated that the champagne-maker was a woman not much older than I am now. And her husband, who she'd thought was lost to the war, returned after nearly four years. We met them both – it all felt so romantic. The husband told us his wife is an alchemist when it comes to champagne.'

What a different life these women led, and yet they all presumed Evie's was like theirs and that she, too, likely subscribed to the Aryan philosophy. She glanced over at Max, where his head was tipped back laughing at something Ferry was muttering; other husbands were joining in the merriment. And while not all of them were as dashing as her husband in their shorts and casual shoes, he fitted the perfect mould. Tall, athletic-looking, square-jawed, blond-haired . . . and then there was Jonas, growing up in that same mould. He'd inherited none of his mother's looks, it seemed, and he sat squarely in the desirable Aryan box, golden-headed and fair-skinned with eyes a brighter, more summery version of his father's. Their dazzling Viking appearance was the very armour that had likely kept them safe until now . . . and might protect them from whatever was coming. Perhaps not Jonas, though. His mother's blood betrayed him. The thought of this sweet little boy that she'd come to love being sent into some sort of ghetto – or worse – was horrifying.

It hardened her resolve like cooling steel within. One way or another, she was going to access the secrets that this house protected.

One of the wives leaned closer. 'He's very hard to stop watching.' She winked. 'You drew the lucky straw.'

Evie hid her surprise at the woman's candour. 'Anna, am I right?' she asked as a deflection.

'What a memory you have. I lose someone's name within moments of being introduced.' She laughed. 'How are you finding us?'

'Very friendly, I'm grateful to say, although maybe it's being Max's wife. He's very popular.' It was a probe and Evie waited to see what it might discover.

'Good-looking men like Max are admired by men and women alike. That's your cross to bear, Evie. You'll never fully have him to yourself. While I, married to Rumpelstiltskin over there'—she pointed to a short man with a large nose and a couple of chins, his loosely buttoned shirt unable to hide his belly bulging over the top of his swimming trunks—'will never have to fret. I do love him, though – he's given me three beautiful children and a wonderful life. He treats me like a goddess.' She chuckled. 'Plus, he's rich and very well connected. What more could a wife want?'

'When it matters to have Max, I do,' she said playfully.

Anna laughed at the innuendo. 'Oh, I like you, Evie!' She squeezed her arm gently. Then her glance cut sideways. 'And how do you handle this one?'

Evie followed her gaze to see Giselle arriving into the room, making her salutations. She looked exceptionally tall and lean in a silvery blue pantsuit that did her icy glamour plenty of favours. Evie blinked back at Anna and sighed. 'One of the crosses I do bear,' she remarked.

Anna smiled without amusement. 'You'll work it out, Evie. Just steer clear of the SS, pay your party dues and stay on the right side of her, playing magnificent support to your glorious husband, and you'll sail along.'

'Why would the security forces be interested in me . . . or us, for that matter?'

Anna gave a look of slight surprise. 'Because they're interested in everyone; making sure we all toe the right line. And *she*'s like a snake in the bushes to remind us to walk the safe path.'

'You really don't like her.' Evie felt a thrill.

'I really don't. I find her provocative and dangerous. She preys on men . . . yours in particular, I'm afraid to say. She's had her eye on Max for years, as I understand it. No one took greater pleasure than her when his first wife passed away, and no one was more amazed and furious, I think, when she learned he'd not only married again but married a foreigner. We're all thrilled to meet you, of course!'

Evie smiled at the compliment but pursued Anna's remark. 'Do you know Max well?'

'Our families know each other. I remember him being around most of my life and he's always been lovely to me.' She smiled sadly. 'I was like a distant cousin.'

'Should I worry for Jonas?'

Anna gave her a thoughtful look, dropping her voice. 'If I were you, I'd be getting him abroad. Nothing I hear is good for anyone with Jewish blood in their veins, no matter how pale they look.' She dropped her gaze. 'I've said too much,' she said, as the glamorous 'snake' arrived in their midst.

23

'Evelyn,' drawled the familiar voice, 'you look very pretty today.' The compliment sounded hollow. Evie didn't care; pretty and vacant suited her. 'How are you enjoying Stuttgart?' Giselle continued.

'Hello, Giselle.' Evie brightened her voice to suggest innocence and watched her enemy blow out smoke from a cigarette she held in her long, narrow fingers. 'You look gorgeous,' she said, meaning it. 'I've barely glimpsed Stuttgart, actually. We came straight here from the railway station. I didn't know you were coming.'

'Ferry invited me.' Giselle leaned in to kiss the air near to Anna's cheek. 'Hello, Anna, dear. Family well? I see Franz has got himself a new middle-aged paunch,' she said, her tone light but her effect cutting. She waited for the injury to bleed a little. 'Suits him. You know the Chinese say a round belly means prosperity.'

'Do they?' Anna said. 'I guess you wouldn't know what roundness feels like, Giselle, as you haven't had a pregnant belly yet. Any gentlemen on the horizon?'

Giselle laughed off the insult. 'Well, Max is back!' she said, loading her voice with irony. Her cool hand suddenly gripped Evie's wrist. 'You know I'm only jesting when I say that. Max and I had a flirtation some years ago.'

'Giselle, you were teenagers!' Anna interjected. 'Hardly relevant. Don't upset our new guest.'

Giselle ignored the remark, still addressing Evie. 'People may talk behind my back that there's a flame still burning, but honestly, darling, don't feel at all anxious about that silly gossip.' Evie could see Giselle trying to make her smile appear sweet.

'I don't.'

'What, darling?'

'I don't feel in any way anxious. I know Max loves me with all of his heart,' Evie said, making her tone wistful, as though she couldn't hear the offensive note in Giselle's words.

'That's it, darling. Proud of you. Believe that and cling to it. I'll head out and say hello to the men.'

Anna cut Evie a look as Giselle departed and Evie shifted her gaze to the other women, who seemed to possess similar opinions about Giselle, based on the sour looks.

'I think I'll head out and protect my husband,' Evie said, winning a gust of soft amusement from the others.

She walked through the open doors, waving to Jonas, who spotted her, and followed the sound of boisterous laughter to where a lot of smoke was emanating from a large barbecue. Ferry was in the midst of it all, loading sausages and cuts of meat onto the sizzling hotplate, while holding court.

It was an idyllic scene . . . everyone happy while their country was secretly getting itself ready for war. She felt ill.

Giselle hadn't made it to Max yet but Evie was happy for her to sidle up to him; he would know to keep her busy. He spotted her approaching and reached out a hand to grasp hers.

'Ah, everyone, this is my new and very beautiful bride, Evie.'

A chorus of welcomes and approving looks ensued. Ferry put down his tongs, wiped his hands and stepped up.

'Beautiful Evie. Sorry, I'm chained to the barbecue right now. Welcome to our home.'

'Thank you. Your lovely Dodo has made me feel so welcome.'

'Yes, she's a sweetheart and been dying to meet you. Has Butzi woken yet?'

She shook her head with a grin. 'I'm looking forward to meeting him.'

Most of the fathers drifted away, leaving Evie with Max and Ferry.

'Ferry, do you want me to take over here?' Max offered, glancing at Evie. She caught on fast.

'Oh, would you, Max? Ferry promised me a guided tour of his designs.'

'Erm . . .' Ferry looked torn but also suddenly hesitant.

'You go on,' Max encouraged gently. 'Or she'll pester you. I've never known a woman to like engines as much as this one. She's already been up to my offices to ogle the models we have.'

'I saw a wonderful photo of a Porsche racing car and have made Max promise he'll take me to a race some time,' Evie chimed in.

'Well, well,' Ferry said, more than impressed. 'Who was driving?'

She thanked her lucky stars for Max's knowledge and insistence the previous evening on giving her as many pointers as he could. 'Even the smallest titbit might save your life, Evie,' he'd said. 'Be a good student and just listen – I know you have a sharp memory.'

She'd listened closely and now retrieved one of those tiny items he had mentioned, to impress her listener further. 'It was this marvellous shot of the racer, Hans Stuck, piloting the Type A to a hill climb victory.'

He nodded. 'Max, who have you married? A dream girl! She loves cars and racing.' He gave Max a friendly backhand to his arm.

Max shrugged. 'She has many talents.'

'Well, Evie, now you make me feel guilty. I have to tell you, my father's design couldn't entirely keep pace with Mercedes-Benz that year, despite a couple of victories.'

'But now?' she asked playfully.

'Now we'll whip them,' he promised. 'Especially if I'm driving!'

Evie clapped. 'Do we have time?'

'If you go now,' Max urged. 'Or risk Dodo's wrath.'

'All right, all right. A quick tour. Max, those sausages will need fifteen minutes at least from now. Follow me, Evie.'

She caught Giselle's slit-eyed gaze taking stock, but hearing Max call, 'Giselle!', she knew her enemy would be helplessly trapped as he welcomed her with a kiss.

'Where are we going?' she said to Ferry.

'Upstairs to my study.'

Her stomach clenched with anticipation. 'Oh, Ferry, I feel a bit guilty now pulling you away from your party.'

'No, no, you're not really. We shan't be long. It's a rare woman who is even vaguely interested in engineering designs. I can count the women I know on one hand, and you and my darling Dodo take two of the fingers – not that she's too intrigued in my work these days.'

'Oh yes, I heard you met at Daimler-Benz.'

'We did,' he said, spying his wife and catching her attention on their way past. 'Is our son still sleeping?'

'The apple fell far from the tree, my love. Our Butzi loves his rest – he doesn't possess your ability to sleep for mere snatches of time. Where are you two off to?'

'I want to show Evie some of the latest designs,' he said.

'Evie, you really do not need to be polite. Surely you're not interested in cars?'

'Actually, I am,' Evie lied. 'I come from a family of engineers,' she said, continuing the lie. 'Plus, I've married one. And now I discover that Jonas is engine mad! But the truth is, I'm quite in love with Porsche cars.' That was not a fib. When she'd seen one parked outside their apartment building she couldn't take her gaze from its sparkling, sleek lines. She decided to test Dodo. 'And Ferry says he's now designing aircraft engines, which is exciting.'

'Oh, Ferry, don't bore Evie, please. And, darling, should you be showing those?' she said, sounding hesitant for the first time since Evie had met her. 'I thought—'

'I've no intention of boring Evie with anything, least of all aircraft engines.' He pecked his wife's cheek. 'It's the new car I want to show Evie. We'll check on Butzi too.'

His wife gave a small shrug of acceptance, but there had obviously been talk of secrecy, enough to frighten the seemingly unflappable Dodo, who now changed topics. 'Evie, if you want to change, your bag is in one of the guest rooms. Show her, Ferry, will you?'

'Of course, come . . .'

'Thanks, Dodo,' Evie said. 'I might as well change now.' That might buy her some time.

They made for the house, Ferry talking as they walked. 'The design of 1934 was a radical change from what had gone before. You see, Benz employed a front engine, whereas our design used the unorthodox layout of putting the V16 behind the driver . . .'

Evie was listening, but taking in as much information about the house as possible. She counted the stairs as they ascended. She had no idea if this was going to help her but in her increasing fear she wanted to know everything she could in case she had to get back out in a hurry.

'. . . for optimal weight distribution, you see,' Ferry was saying.

She smiled, looking dazzled by the information. 'I do,' she agreed, not knowing what she was agreeing to.

'Now the chassis . . . Oh, wait, let's check on Butzi.'

She was shown into a child's bedroom, the daylight dimmed with drawn voile curtains; it was still and silent, save the sound of a softly breathing infant. The room was painted a parchment colour but all around its cornice trailed a hand-painted pattern of cars.

'Your idea?' she whispered, glancing at it with admiration. 'Starting him early?'

'No.' He laughed softly. 'All Dodo. I have no say in the décor of this house. I simply make the money.'

Evie stole a peek into the cot. Ferdinand III possessed the heart-shaped face of his mother, but dimples that were all his father were obvious in his red cheeks.

'Teething,' Ferry assured in a murmur at her frown. 'He gets a bit feverish with it. My wife just lets him sleep as long as he likes, but I don't think it's healthy.'

'I've very little experience, Ferry, but I think a sleeping child is a happy one.'

He grinned, his own dimples deepening. 'Spoken like a perfect mother.'

'He's beautiful. He manages to look like both of you at once.'

'He actually looks like my father, but with luck he'll grow into his mother's beauty.'

She grinned.

'Come on. He's fine. He'll let us know when he wants away from this cot.' He led her down the corridor. 'There's a bathroom at the end of the hallway if you need it?'

She shook her head but took note of its location.

'I have an upstairs study,' he explained as though she had queried it, and then answered the obvious question. 'I know that's unusual, but I deal with highly sensitive material and designs – whether it's cars or tanks, or aircraft engines. Dodo said it made sense to shift from downstairs to here, and then no one could have access.'

'She's right,' Evie said, feigning concern. 'I've been saying much the same thing to Max with his war railway. Not that I am a political creature,' she added, keeping her expression angelic. 'I take no interest in what governments decide – I just want Max safe. Me, I'm a nomad. My parents always said so,' she lied and continued to embellish. 'We've travelled all over England as my father was posted from station to station. And he was always impressed that I adapted so easily. Meanwhile, my sister raged at losing friends or changing schools.'

Ferry smiled. 'You're a chameleon.'

'I hope you're not calling me reptilian?' she said lightly.

'Would I dare!' He let out a laugh that depressed his dimples in genuine amusement. 'I meant you adapt to your environment.'

'I suppose it does describe me,' she admitted, wondering how shocked he would be if he only knew the truth of what a brilliant chameleon she was.

At the barbecue, Max was determined to keep Giselle by his side.

'Where's the little woman?' Giselle sneered.

He didn't want to set her straight. Let her believe that Evie was uncomplicated and transparent. 'Oh, around,' he said. 'Probably looking out for Jonas.'

'Well, you've certainly got the mothering all sorted for your son.'

Max nodded. 'I am very fortunate that they have taken to each other as well as they have. How about you, Giselle? No thoughts in that direction?'

She gave him a lazy smile. 'Are you offering, Max?'

He gave a gust of a laugh. 'No, I meant, do you think you'd like children?'

'Not really. My parents were dreadful with me and I suspect I would behave quite similarly. I might as well spare this generation and the next all the arguing.'

Against his better judgement, he cast her a look of sympathy. 'You may be a far better mother than you imagine,' he lied, believing her the last person on earth who should be encouraged to have a child. 'Look how you are with Jonas,' he said. He really didn't know what he meant by that – it just sounded right.

'When I look at Jonas, I see you, Max. I'm glad I don't see your former wife or . . . well, let's not think about what that would mean for him. But he is a replica of you. He is easy to love.'

Her final remark was loaded so he turned it on its head. 'Can that protect him?' he asked, hoping to appeal to whatever last remaining sense of fairness she might possess.

Her response was a cruel shrug. No words accompanied the gesture but the intent was clear. *How much less could I care?* it asked him and he could see she was enjoying this.

Whatever it takes, Giselle, he said silently. *I will open myself up to all the pain you wish to inflict, as long as it keeps you distracted and having fun at someone's expense.*

It was as though she could listen into those private thoughts. 'I can't imagine why Evelyn would leave us alone for so long.' She looked around.

'Because it doesn't occur to her to think badly of anyone, I think. She hasn't been exposed to the world that you and I have.'

'You mean she doesn't feel threatened by me.'

'Oh, I think she's careful. She doesn't wish to offend anyone.'

'Don't you find that boring, Max?'

Play into her hands. 'Well . . . I know what you mean, when you ask that,' he said, deliberately not answering her question but making her feel as though he had.

'The Max I remember needed stimulation, intelligence, wit, worldliness. What's happened to you?'

'Oh, I'll take sweet and affectionate for now, Giselle. I've been through enough. I want very little now,' he lied. 'I want a quiet life.'

She actually laughed. 'I don't know who you think you're fooling, Max Hall. Certainly not me. Life positively brims from you. It's like a vibrant aura. Your masculinity oozes from every pore and you know it. Every woman at this gathering wants you.'

'Yes, but I don't want every woman, Giselle. I don't know why you think I would.'

'Why not? Life would be interesting . . . and just a bit dangerous.'

If only you knew, he thought. 'You're dangerous,' he quipped with a grin, knowing it would please her.

She arched her back in a sort of feline show of pleasure. 'I'm glad you think so. Little Miss Perfect is going to smother you with love, Max, but I give it a year before all that affection leeches the vitality from you.'

'You think so?' He was flirting and loathed himself for it. *Come on, Evie, make it count.*

Ferry led Evie into a bedroom that was bourgeois with its silks and tassels, thick upholstery and drapery, showing few of the traits of Germany's minimalist skills in this decade. The eau de Nil colour was soothing, but she was glad she didn't have to make that bed each morning with its heavy silk eiderdown and ruffles. But then neither did Ferry or Dodo, she thought, with maids at their beck and call.

'Oh, this is so pretty, Ferry,' she cooed. 'I would live in here and never emerge.'

He laughed. 'Save the praise for Dodo. I have no hand in all of this.'

She walked over to the French doors, which looked out over a private side garden. Ferry opened the doors. 'My wife likes to take her breakfast out here sometimes.' There was a Juliet-style balcony and hidden iron steps at one side leading down to the small garden.

'It's charming,' she remarked, stepping briefly onto the balcony. It was the right thing to say.

'. . . through our bedroom suite,' he was saying, 'to my study.' He opened an adjoining door.

Evie turned to look to where Ferry was standing. 'Oh, that's clever.'

'All Dodo's doing. She's determined to keep my work away from prying eyes.'

'Are you sure I should—'

'I didn't mean you, Evie. Come in, don't feel awkward.'

She entered a large study with only one window. If the adjoining bedroom was utterly feminine and classic in its era, then this space was all masculine and very much in keeping with the times with far less clutter and dominated by a polished walnut desk. A lamp, which depicted a sinuous and athletic-looking woman holding up the bulb like a moon, would have made a stunning member of Streicher's Night of the Amazons festival troupe.

He took a set of keys from a box on his desk and she paid attention to the one he favoured; it was the third one on the ring, counting in a clockwise direction from the key ring, which looked like a blob of metal. He saw her looking at it and she realised she would have to be more careful, or risk being caught.

'That is curious.' She pointed. 'What is it?'

He held it out for her to examine more closely. 'It's painted metal, crushed into this rough cube shape from the first car design that I was fully involved in.'

'Brilliant!' She smiled, handing it back, and he shrugged but clearly enjoyed her praise.

She watched him as he turned his back and began pulling out wide, narrow drawers from a purpose-built chest against the wall.

'Here,' he said, proudly. 'These are the *very* hush-hush blue-prints for the new Porsche car that we will be releasing in 1937.'

Evie looked over the huge sheets he was smoothing out on the desk. The technical detail couldn't hide the sleekness of what she now understood to be a highly recognisable Porsche design.

Ferry lifted one. 'It's a new racing car I'm working on, but honestly, I can see it being adapted for a sporty street car.'

She gave the expected sound of awe. 'Ferry! How incredible. Look at these beautiful curves . . . but it's so low!'

'Yes, isn't it?' He chuckled. 'We get more daring with our aerodynamics.'

'When might you have this one ready?' She made sure she sounded enthused while her mind was reaching towards the other drawers.

He gave a slight shrug. 'It should be on the racetrack for trials by mid next year. You and Max should come along.'

'Really? I'd love to hear the roar of this engine and know I had a glimpse when it was newly out of your imagination.' She touched the ink of the drawings to make him smile. 'And I can say I felt its beauty even when it was still a drawing.'

'You're an old romantic, Evie.'

'Guilty,' she admitted, raising a hand and making him laugh. She looked further, needing to get to the bomber engines. 'Oh my, what's this?'

'Ah, they've somehow got into the wrong drawer. These are the early designs, although when I say early, it's probably our fifth incarnation of the Volkswagen.'

'This is the German People's Car that the Führer is promoting, isn't it?'

'Indeed. He's very excited by it. The problem is, he wants it available for a price so unrealistic that I just don't know how our firm can deliver it. We keep trying to trim, and we are getting closer, but he wants so much for so little . . . Anyway, I think right now this is too boxy.'

'How do you fix that?'

He drew a curve in the air with his hand in front of the drawings. 'I think if we round it out a lot more . . .' He grinned. 'I know it's daring but I can even see it beginning its curve from here' – he pointed at the back of the wheel on the drawing – 'cutting out all that squarish shape and turning it more like a pod. Here, like this.' He picked up a nearby pencil and quickly sketched on a notepad.

She tipped her head to show she was giving it thought. 'Like a little beetle.'

'Ha!' he exclaimed. 'A beetle? Yes, I suppose so. But I'd build it like a tank . . . heavy and capable of a long life.'

'Is that part of the brief – to be like a tank?'

He nodded. 'In a way. Hitler told my father he wanted something that could move a small team of soldiers quickly over terrain. But there are two projects being discussed right now. I'm afraid I shouldn't talk about them as they are highly secret.'

'Oh, Ferry, you can't do that to me now. I'm invested!' she teased, trying to quieten the klaxon in her mind. 'I'm also just a girl,' she said, in a derogatory way that made her gut twist, remembering how 'girls' like Deidre had taken over at the Levisham signals box to help keep Britain going through the Great War while all the men were absent. 'Who am I going to tell?' She frowned. 'Do you mean Max?'

He shook his head. 'Max is fine. While we each have different bosses, we share the same ministry in government . . . and it's the most powerful one – road, rail, air, sea.'

She could tell he was not keen to show her and that she shouldn't push too hard in case he mentioned it to someone like Giselle. 'Then don't show me. I completely understand.'

He shrugged. 'All these drawers are full of designs, from a new amphibian craft that the Porsche company is involved with to tanks. I'm not at liberty to—'

Those were the drawers she had to get into, then. 'No, no, please. Don't feel awkward, it's fine.'

'They're not nearly as exciting as a car. I am a racing-car driver as much as I am a designer, and there's nothing on earth like flying around a racetrack at the highest speed that I can push the car's engine to . . . and myself. Now real flying?' He gave a moue of distaste. 'But what the Führer wants, the Führer gets, and no one dares deny him.' He put the drawings away.

'Does he scare you?' Evie asked.

'Yes, actually.' She was surprised he admitted as much. 'But I have enormous admiration, too, for what he's doing for Germany. His singlemindedness and passion for the betterment of his people are helplessly inspiring.'

She desperately wanted to challenge Ferry but if she was honest, she couldn't care less how Ferry might justify Hitler's plans or even his actions to date. Ferry was a nice man, a good father and a loving husband, but he was – hapless or not – part of the machinery that was promoting war, promoting cruelty to certain sections of society. She was happy to be doing something that might just help bring down that machinery. And so, she kept her smile fixed and even, and her tone neutral as she nodded. 'I can appreciate that,' she agreed, knowing the remark would sound right to Ferry. She watched her words land on him lightly like a gentle squeeze to the shoulder, as though giving him approval to be inspired – and indeed financially improved – by supporting Hitler's projects. She sighed, her belly twisting with the knowledge that her worst fears were already being hatched. 'I'm glad I don't have a son of age; even so, I can't help but fret for people like Max and yourself.'

'Don't. Max and I, and others like us who are engineers, are considered essential and they will not risk us. Max is needed for that railway into Poland, and railways to come. Besides, we aren't going to war just yet, Evie.'

'No?' She didn't trust his sentiment. 'I feel unnerved.'

'I like to think that people like Max and I are future-proofing Germany. When war erupts, we will be more ready than any other nation. Our Führer, who fought in the previous war and felt the humiliation of Germany's loss so keenly, has vowed that the country will never be powerless again.'

Evie felt sure Ferry was lying to himself, finding a way to distance himself from the preparation for war, not to mention all the cruel strategies promoted by the Nazi Party hierarchy.

'We should probably get back.' She grinned. 'Max will definitely burn your sausages otherwise.' She watched him return the keys to the box on his desk and turn towards the door. She was going to need to get back in here quickly.

But how?

24

As they exited Ferry's study, Evie turned. 'Well, thank you, Ferry. I feel newly educated,' she remarked as he waved his hand demurely. 'I might get changed for the pool as Dodo suggested.'

'Head past Butzi's bedroom to the next room on the left.' He gestured down the hall.

She smiled. 'Thank you. What about Butzi? If he wakes, shall I . . .?'

'The maid will be up soon enough, I'm sure. You just get changed,' he said. 'See you downstairs,' he said and pointed again to the bedroom that held her change of clothes. 'Dodo's left bathrobes for everyone.'

She dutifully entered the room and then began to pace, nerves crowding in. It really was now or never. What was she going to do? What *could* she do? A diversion? Fire? No, that was a crazy idea – then everyone would definitely be looking for her. No, she needed to find a legitimate reason to be left alone upstairs for long enough to get back into the Porsche bedroom and Ferry's study.

She pulled off her clothes, having already taken the precaution of wearing her swimming costume beneath her dress, and belted on one of Dodo's bathrobes. She rummaged through the items in her bag. The tiny camera she placed into her robe pocket. What else could she use? The magnifier was useless, as were the tiny scissors that unfolded from a small notebook. She picked up the copper penny, to all intents and purposes a spare English coin. But it had been cunningly fashioned to hold a tiny blade. Was that any use? Hardly. Not unless she was found out, thrown in prison and decided to slash open the vein at her wrist before the executioner could deal with her. She discarded it, placing it back into the bag, and then frowned as an idea formed.

Could it work?

With no other inspiration or opportunities, and all too aware of the clock ticking away the minutes, she made the decision, smiling grimly at the old adage that leapt to mind: *in for a penny, in for a pound.*

Haste was now the key.

Evie hurried to the dressing table and before she could change her mind she pulled back the small, curved blade that sat flush against the edge of the penny, made out of similar copper that had been worn and aged so to a passing gaze it would go unnoticed. The blade's tip was small, pointed and razor-edged.

Do it! she commanded herself as butterflies flapped urgent wings in her stomach. *Don't think, just do!*

Evie pulled back her hair so she could see her forehead clearly and hesitated just for a heartbeat before she pressed the blade against one side of her hairline and jaggedly dragged it down. It was more the ghastly feeling of her skin being slit open than pain that made her expel a ragged breath that she'd been holding. Blood bloomed as she'd anticipated and then flowed. Head wounds always bled freely and she let it, making sure the blood ran down her cheek, through her hair and dripped off her jaw onto the towelling robe she was wearing. It looked ghastly as rivulets split and took new pathways down her face, one finding her lips, another tracing to her chin. Trembling slightly at her own daring and the sight of all that bright lifeblood being wasted, she closed the blade and flung the British penny back into her bag to be lost among the other belongings.

Now she had to play her role properly. What was coming was the harder part; *cutting yourself was easy*, she reminded herself with a mirthless gulp.

Evie hurried down the hallway, careful not to drip blood. It wasn't a long corridor, but might as well have been an aeroplane runway; she felt like it took forever to get to its end. Glancing down the stairs, it seemed no one was around; everyone must be getting their meals, sitting down, certainly all out in the sunny gardens. People would start looking for her any minute.

Be convincing, Evie, she said again and again in her mind.

She quickly tiptoed three-quarters of the way down the stairs and then girded herself. This had to look real. There were only four stairs to negotiate. She could do this. Evie heard footsteps on the tiles coming from the kitchen and so it really was now or never. Holding the bannister for safety, she let out a scream that convinced even her as she carefully toppled down the final stairs, making sure the camera stayed safely hidden in the pocket as she landed at the bottom in a tangled heap. Mercifully, she felt nothing crack, though her ribs felt as though they'd hit one of the stairs and would be bruised. A trifling injury in comparison to how bad she hoped it would appear.

As anticipated, two of the staff had come running at her shriek. They looked at her with shocked, disbelieving silence, which she filled with groans before hands were suddenly around her.

'Don't move her,' one of them said. 'We have to make sure she hasn't broken anything. Get Frau Porsche.' The other one fled. 'Frau Hall, it's Erika.' Evie had deliberately kept her face down but now she turned over with a sigh, groaning and flicking blood in all directions. 'Oh, my heavens. Frau Hall, you're bleeding,' Erika wailed, pulling off her apron and putting it behind Evie's head. 'Please don't move.'

Voices came riding over hurried footsteps and sounds of shock. It was Dodo, Anna, Max and Ferry, from what she could see. And through the blood that had dripped into Evie's eyes, she could see Giselle leaning against the doorway into the sitting room and smirking, taking it all in.

'Evie!' Dodo was on her knees in a blink. 'What happened?'

'Max?' she groaned tremulously.

'I'm here, Evie.' He sounded more shocked than Dodo. He gripped her hand. 'You've hurt yourself. You're bleeding profusely.'

'Don't let Jonas see.'

He nodded.

'Erika?' It was Dodo, taking charge. 'Make sure the children stay outside please, especially Jonas Hall.' The younger maid disappeared again. 'Evie?'

'I think I tripped,' she said, trying to sit up. Everyone collectively told her to remain lying down, Dodo gently pushing her back. The apron was removed and cushions that Ferry had fetched replaced behind her head.

'Is there pain anywhere, Evie?' Ferry looked pale. 'Should we call ahead to the hospital?'

'I think a few bruises. Please, no hospital,' Evie groaned. 'I was stupid. Hurrying to get outdoors with everyone and I must have tripped, I don't remember . . . Did you say I've bumped my head?'

'You're bleeding all over Dodo's nice carpet,' Giselle said in a sardonic tone, leaning in and blowing smoke Evie's way from a lit cigarette, helpful as always.

'Oh, Giselle, be quiet,' Dodo said. 'Right, we need to see to that head wound. Are you sure there's no pain anywhere, Evie?'

'Only the pain of embarrassment, Dodo.' Evie allowed her voice to lose its tremble as she began to feign regaining her wits. 'I'm so sorry, Max. In front of your friends.'

'Don't be silly,' he said.

'Bring her into the drawing room,' Dodo said.

'I'll carry her upstairs?' Max said to the Porsches, no doubt sensing this was where Evie wanted to go. 'Evie's modest. She really won't appreciate all the attention,' he murmured.

She'd like to kiss him right now for helping. 'I think I might just lie still upstairs, yes,' she said. 'I'll admit, my head does ache a little.'

'Pick her up, Max. We'll get her to one of the bedrooms, onto a bed, and properly assess any damage.' Dodo made a clucking sound of dismay.

As Max carried Evie upstairs, he shook his head as if frustrated but he gave her a wink. She wanted to smile or cry, or both; the first part of her spontaneous plan was underway, but the mountain was still ahead of her to scale. She just hoped she was up to it.

'Well, it's a horrible cut to your head, Evie,' Dodo impressed, but luckily you can hide the wound with your hair until it heals.' Ferry's wife had guided them to the spare bedroom where Evie had changed.

'At least that's convenient,' Evie replied with a tone that spoke of despair at her own clumsiness. 'I still don't know how I managed to fall.'

'Don't worry about it. I am wondering whether it needs stitches, though.' She looked at Max. 'This beautiful girl can't have a scar.'

'She'll be fine, Dodo. She'll tell you she's made of strong stuff from Yorkshire. I doubt Evie would think a scar is anything but some sort of badge of honour of life.'

'Evie . . .' Dodo began, dismissing Max's remark.

'I'm fine, Dodo. Feeling slightly better already. Thank you for cleaning me up.'

'Shall we get you out of that bloodstained robe?'

Evie startled, thinking of the camera. 'No, I do feel a bit shivery. I think I'll keep it on just for few more minutes.'

'That's shock. Sit with her, Max, and then help her change. I'll fetch a warm robe from the airing cupboard.'

Dodo left but they knew she'd be returning shortly.

'Dramatic,' Max commented but he looked impressed. 'One hell of a cut on your head.'

'Keep everyone away from me as best you can, especially Giselle.'

'I'll do my best.'

'I plan to be feeling quite ill from the fall shortly, and we'll need to leave, all right?'

He put his finger to his temple and saluted her. 'I'll be waiting for the signal.'

She gripped his wrist. 'Max, if this works, we have to be ready to flee.'

'I have ears, Evie, you just—'

'Not just Stuttgart. I mean Germany. We'll go tomorrow.'

His features became sombre and she squeezed his arm as he nodded.

Dodo was back, fussing with a fresh bathrobe. 'How are you feeling?'

'I'll take some aspirin and just lie here for a little while if that's okay?'

'As long as you need. Are you comfortable?'

Take your chance, Evie thought. She made a show of looking around at all the coats and bags she was sprawled among. 'I don't suppose . . .'

'Oh yes, how clumsy and thoughtless of us to lie you down here among everyone's belongings. I'm so sorry. Come on, Max,' Dodo said. 'Pick up your wife. Carry her to my bedroom. Follow me. She'll be far more comfortable in there than here. I'll bring her bag and clothes in case she decides to get dressed.'

'You don't have to take me to yours; any bedroom will do, Dodo,' Evie tried, hoping against hope that their host would insist.

'No, I insist,' Dodo said, as if Evie had her under a spell. 'I don't want you down another wing of the house. We want to keep you close.'

'Thank you, Dodo,' she replied, even though she was really thanking whichever lucky stars were guiding her way. At least now she would be in the right room.

'There, much better,' Dodo said, once they'd got her settled. 'It's warmer in here too, because the afternoon sun reaches in. Stay as long as you like.'

'You're very kind,' Evie said and then closed her eyes.

'Let her rest,' Dodo whispered. Evie heard her open her side drawer and uncap a bottle. 'Two of these, Max,' Dodo murmured. 'There's a glass and a flask of water in the bathroom.'

Max nodded. 'Go back to your guests, Dodo. I'll be down shortly.'

He stayed a few minutes more, keeping up the pretence for a little longer, not sure that everyone had left the first floor yet. He removed the aspirin and put them in his pocket. Then he fetched the glass with a small amount of water and placed it at the bedside as though she'd drunk from it. 'Perhaps you should take them in case your wound does start to ache?'

'No, I need to stay clear-headed. I'll be fine. Go,' she urged. 'It's up to me now.'

He nodded.

'And, Max . . . if anything goes wrong—'

'It won't,' he said. 'It won't,' he repeated, softly and more emphatically. He kissed her hand. 'Be careful.'

Once Max had left the bedroom, she swung her legs to the ground and stood. The wound throbbed slightly, but it was negligible compared to the feeling of adrenaline; she would have sworn she could feel her heart leaping around in her chest, as though it had untethered itself from whatever strings held it in place. Evie was worried that the nervousness she was experiencing would deepen but she took three slow, deep breaths; it passed as she reminded herself that this was why she was in Germany. Whatever she achieved next might be her ticket home to Yorkshire and the pardon for Max to bring his child home to Britain.

She tiptoed to the study, let herself in and took the keys she'd seen Ferry use from the box on the desk. She didn't hesitate in gently pulling open the wide drawers that held the schematics of the Porsche war machines.

Evie flipped through pages showing a small tank that was called the Schwimmwagen. She stared at it for longer than she knew she should. 'A car in the sea?' she queried aloud. To her it looked like a tub on wheels. 'Wehrmacht' was stamped at the top of the page and there were signatures at the bottom – 'Ferdinand Porsche'. The father, no doubt.

She hurriedly pulled out the camera and promptly forgot how to make it work. It took her a few moments to realise she had to pull it open before she pushed it closed to move on the film. Stepping back, she took a photo of the army stamp, the signatures and a rough long shot of the schematics; she would need to take dozens of photos to get any workable close ups but they hadn't said she needed anything more than proof . . . here it was.

And then the camera jammed. She heard a loud whistling of fear in her mind.

25

Around the barbecue, Giselle was pumping Max for information.

'How do you think she fell?'

'I have no idea. She's clumsy, I know that much.'

'She doesn't strike me that way.'

'Oh, she is, believe me. If it can be dropped, spilt, kicked over, tripped over or broken, Evie will be on the end of it.'

'Truly?'

He nodded.

'How odd,' Giselle said.

Max wasn't convinced his explanation had helped. She sounded even more intrigued. 'Come on, we should join everyone – they're already eating.'

'Should you not be with your wife?'

'I left her resting. Dodo gave her some painkillers, so I think she'll doze for an hour or so and then we'll probably head home.'

'She shouldn't sleep if she's hit her head.'

'I think she'll be fine,' he said.

'Shame to miss all the fun this afternoon.'

'It is. Jonas had been looking forward to today and being with the other children.'

'Max? Giselle? Come on, the sausages are getting cold,' Dodo called.

Upstairs, Evie was cursing Leadbetter in every colourful German way she could think of, ending for some reason on a sheep's bladder. So much for his precious prototype – the camera was properly stuck. That could mean the film was ruined, twisted or even that it had never worked in the first place. She didn't know about these things and wasn't briefed on this sort of technical problem solving. She found a flat manila folder in the drawer as she returned the drawings of the Schwimmwagen and upon opening it, her eyes widened to see the details of a memorandum of understanding. It was a carbon copy of the original on a thin tissue-like paper. The original letter must be filed at the Porsche factory, almost certainly under lock and key or in the company safe.

Nevertheless, this was surely a true copy. It carried the Wehrmacht stamp and she glanced over the short points describing the car. As she read, she realised that Porsche's overlords were planning for the company to develop a massive number of these amphibian vehicles for the Wehrmacht. Why would Germany need amphibious craft – and in such numbers – unless it was planning invasion . . . war?

She tried one more time with the camera, but to her ever-increasing fright and frustration, it refused to take another photo. *Make a decision!* She did. The camera, in her untrained opinion, was now useless to Leadbetter because the film could be damaged, thus compromising the photos she had taken. But this memo was surely a prize even more valuable.

She took two deep breaths in an attempt to stay calm but she was beginning to feel sweaty with nerves that this was all in vain.

Even if she memorised the letter she was looking at, who would believe her? There was nothing else for it; she was going to have to steal it. It would be damning evidence if she was caught, but there was no time to stand around trying to calculate the risk.

Evie took the single page, folded it in half and then rolled it like a cigar to put down the front of her bathing costume. She had to risk a few more moments in the study checking the other drawers, where she found similar drawings; they looked like crude designs at this stage – some for ground tanks, and then what looked like bomber engines. She'd seen enough; Leadbetter and his colleagues would have to take her word for it, along with the single sheet she was willing to steal to prove that she'd viewed the schematics of the Porsche war machines.

Time to retrace her steps. She took off an earring, remembering something that Rosie had told her once got her out of a scrape. And right now, she needed every trick she could muster because she had a cold feeling in the pit of her stomach that her luck wasn't going to hold much longer. She needed to move before she was discovered, get dressed, hide the letter and ditch the camera.

She closed and locked the drawers, returned the keys and tiptoed back out of the study. Hurriedly, she pulled on her dress over her swimming costume, glad that the tight fabric would hold that letter safe against her heart. She wanted to be rid of the camera – it wasn't worth the risk trying to get it back to London, but it would be incriminating if anyone found it. She could risk taking it back to Munich but what if everything went pear-shaped from this moment? She needed as few implicating items as possible on her person. Most items, such as the penny, were well disguised but the camera might as well be the executioner's axe.

Max couldn't hold Giselle's interest much longer. The other men had dispersed towards wives and children, while she had followed him back to lurk near the barbecue when he'd offered to sizzle up the last of the hamburgers. He'd deliberately taken her back in time, recalling memories of their youth; they had made her tip back her exquisite, oval-shaped face and reveal her perfect teeth in genuine laughter. But even her mirth was encased in a frigid cold that would never know true warmth.

'Max, don't char that meat. It is well cooked,' she warned.

'Yes, just thinking the same. Ah, Helga,' he said, touching the elbow of the passing maid. 'Could you help me?'

'Herr Porsche has just asked me to check on his son, sir.'

'Where is he?'

'Here I am, Max. Are you burning my hamburgers?' Ferry said, arriving to *tsk-tsk* near the barbecue.

'Shouldn't we check on dear Evelyn?' Giselle asked.

'Yes, we should,' Ferry answered.

Giselle's eyebrows, which she'd plucked and then drawn back on firmly in pencil, Max noted, now lifted in query. 'What was she doing upstairs in the first place, I have to wonder?'

'She was changing into swimming clothes,' Ferry said.

Dodo arrived. 'The children are swimming. I've got all the parents taking turns keeping watch. Everyone but you, Giselle, will take a turn. Oh, and Evie if she comes down. Maybe I'll check on her.' She threw a smile her husband's way. 'Did you manage not to bore her in your study, darling? I hope that's not why she became dizzy and fell.' She pinched his cheek affectionately.

'Not even a whiff of boredom at the Porsche design.' Max watched Ferry blink as though regretting his words.

Giselle's lazy gaze now slid with fresh interest to Ferry, who avoided it. 'What do you mean, Ferry?'

He shrugged. 'Nothing really . . . I just showed Evie some sketches.'

'Of what?'

'The new racing car. Don't worry, Evie isn't interested in war machines and I certainly didn't show her any.'

'But you told her about them?'

Max sensed Dodo's unease. Fear had suddenly crept between their quartet like a gleeful wraith. 'Oh, Giselle, please. Let's not talk about work now. This is a social gathering . . . a family get-together,' Dodo admonished her.

But Max could see Giselle was not to be dissuaded. 'Ferry, what did you tell her?' Her tone sounded official, although Max had never grasped how she had acquired the belief that she had any authority to be the eyes and ears of the Nazi Party.

'Her name is Evie,' Max reminded, 'not *her*. Exactly what are you getting at, Giselle?'

She didn't hesitate, turning on him. 'That no one, particularly a stranger in our midst, should be privy to whatever the Porsche company is working on for the government.' She sounded waspish and her attitude stung her three companions, who met her words with sighs and dismissive hand gestures.

Max deliberately raised his eyes to the sky. 'You're paranoid,' he told her, wishing Evie would arrive. 'My wife is *not* a stranger.'

'Not to you, perhaps, Max. But to us? What do we know about her? Even Herr Frick has put a question mark beside her name. You know he hasn't released her passport. She got herself taken in for questioning for flouting German law. Don't think Gestapo haven't got eyes on her, Max, or you'd be terribly naive.'

Ferry cursed under his breath.

'You see, darling,' Dodo said, vexed. 'This is why I told you not to.'

'Not to what?' Giselle said, shifting her attention, like a dog catching a scent.

Max breathed out slowly as he made a show of helping Ferry to load the last of the meat onto a platter while really watching

Dodo's discomfort, willing her to throw Giselle some sort of bone that she could run after.

As usual Dodo was reliably cautious about Giselle's insatiable inquisitiveness and her dubious, almost shadowy role within the Nazi hierarchy. She chose her words with care, Max saw. 'I don't know why I should explain myself, but I simply told Ferry not to bore Evie with designs for the People's Car and asked whether it was appropriate.'

'And I said,' Ferry continued, sounding wearied by their guest, 'it's just a car engine design. Nothing new about it, either. It's been shown in various prototypes to all and sundry, anyway.' Max knew Ferry was lying but no one could know just how close Giselle was to the truth. 'Even people like Max have seen them in his division . . . isn't that so?'

Max nodded and stretched, as if the conversation was beyond tedious. 'All the engineers who work for the Reich Ministry have. Which incarnation is this one, Ferry?' he asked, trying to push the conversation out of the swamp they'd found themselves in and onto firmer, safer ground.

Ferry knew what he was doing as he laughed, waving the question away. None of them liked the notion of a Nazi snooping at their social events. 'I've lost count, my friend. But my new racing car is going to be our best ever.'

'So she was shown the racing car and the new family car?' Giselle pressed.

'What are you doing, Giselle? What is this suspicion of our wonderful hosts?' Max asked, trying a new tack to get them off the topic of Evie and what she had been shown. 'You're going to get yourself left off the guestlist if you keep making even your old friends feel uncomfortable. What are you? A spy?'

It was a mistake to say the word. It had slipped out while he was trying to nonchalantly make her feel guilty. It backfired.

She slow-blinked, looking as satisfied as he imagined a spider might at having a fly suddenly trapped and squirming in her web. 'No, you were the spy, Max. And while you were spying away from Germany in enemy territory, you picked up a wife. Wouldn't you say that was convenient? Herr Frick thinks so.'

'Oh, for heaven's sake, Giselle,' Dodo said as both men let out groans of disbelief. Their hostess turned on her heel. 'Come on, Ferry. I'm not pursuing this conversation. Let's bring that food – some may want seconds.'

Ferry followed with his plate of cooling hamburgers like an obedient child, casting Max a wounded look of apology.

'Yes, but *I* am pursuing it,' Giselle snipped, ignoring their hosts and returning her full glacial stare to Max. 'You don't think it was a fast and opportunistic marriage?'

'I am sensing jealousy here.' It was a last-ditch attempt to deflect her but again she resisted.

'I won't deny I carry a torch for you, Max. That's no shock to you, surely? But I also know you to be a measured, deliberate decision-maker.'

He frowned. 'And?'

'You would not marry anyone in the blink of an eye.'

'Then I've proved you wrong.' He didn't have to fake this. 'I fell in love with Evie from the moment I met her.'

'I don't think I am wrong.'

'And that's your problem in life, Giselle.'

'What do you mean?'

'It's why a beautiful woman like you finds herself lonely . . . and risking becoming bitter. From what I see, you have no close friends and never will so long as you make everyone around you feel as though you're a puppet for Berlin, mistrusting all, snooping on anyone who allows you into their life.'

'How dare you.'

'How dare you call my marriage into doubt.'

She smiled, which caught him by surprise. 'I do, though, Max. Your good little wife runs far deeper than she presents.'

'I'm not sure what that means.' He had to keep Giselle talking until Evie reappeared. They would deal with whatever the fallout might be once he knew she was safe.

'I just get the feeling she's making a mockery of all of us.'

He frowned.

'Pretending to be one thing . . .' Giselle paused.

'While being what?'

She demurred. 'I'm not sure, darling Max. But I intend to find out.' Giselle made to leave.

Max was desperate to stop her. He caught her elbow. 'Giselle,' he said. 'Listen, let's not be like this. I've always . . .' He made a deliberate show of searching for the right words, as though trying not to incriminate himself. 'How shall I say . . . admired you.'

He suspected he had caught her unawares with the remark, just as she had caught him moments earlier with her sly smile. He hated himself for falling back onto his charm, but he had always been cognisant of the effect he had on her, even though he'd never fully understood her devotion to someone who did not return it. But right now, he had to use every weapon he had. It was obvious to all that he was her weakness, and he would have to lean hard on that if he was going to save Evie.

'Admired me?' She looked back at him quizzically. 'That is a vague word, particularly as you were just ready to spit at me.'

He shook his head. 'Never. You embarrassed me in front of our friends, suggesting there was something deceitful about Evie. But you are a beautiful woman. A very desirable one.'

She blinked twice . . . quickly. She was disarmed. *Good.*

'I . . . Look, Giselle,' he said, feigning self-consciousness and a struggle to select the right words. 'If we're honest, our timing has always been wrong, hasn't it?'

She grasped his intent immediately, like a starving dog that digs up an old bone. 'I loved you, Max, long before you married the Jew.'

He nodded, not displaying the revulsion he felt at her insult. 'I know.'

'But you've never—'

'You're wrong,' he lied. 'I've simply fought it.'

'What?' She looked visibly shaken. He hoped Evie was forgotten in her mind. 'What are you saying?' she demanded.

He shrugged. 'Our circumstances were never aligned. We were kids, and then I left for Berlin. But I do want you to know that it's hard to be around you because of those old feelings that sometimes simmer.'

Her voice sounded stretched when she spoke. 'You had every opp—'

He nodded to stop her. 'I know, I know. I was young and wanted to see the big city. I left home, I studied, I met Rachel and suddenly we had Jonas. I had to leave behind my youth and the people I loved.'

'Loved?' She managed to make it sound like an accusation.

Max felt ill, wondering where this might lead but he had to keep her trapped . . . just a few minutes more.

Evie was dressed to flee but with a subminiature camera in hand and looking around wildly now for ideas to rid herself of it. She thought about flinging it out of the French windows into the garden and she got as far as opening the doors and stepping onto the balcony but then wondered about where to throw it. She'd have to aim for the shrubbery. Was her aim good enough? Her arm strong enough?

And even if both were up to the task, would the lightweight camera simply lob and land on top for anyone to see, especially Ferry or Dodo from this vantage? No, as much as she tried to convince herself it would be a great hiding spot until she'd left Germany, she couldn't presume it would fall conveniently into the middle of the bushes – they looked too tight-knit to let it through.

Time was moving inexorably towards her capture if Evie didn't make a decision. People would start coming up to check on her and that was a scene she didn't want to contemplate. Fear was closing in like a fog, making her thoughts blur. She scoured the Porsche bedroom. Everywhere looked like it was dusted, cleaned and tidied regularly, meaning there was nowhere to hide it, short of flinging it under the bed. Even then, a member of staff, if not Dodo, would find the camera too soon. She needed to give herself some distance from it . . . just long enough for it not to be found until she left Germany.

Evie moved to the bathroom, casting about for inspiration; she began to feel clammy with her desperation. About to give up and resign herself to smuggling the contraption out with her – after all, she assured herself, she had got it in, so why not back out? – she happened to glance up at the toilet cistern. The decision closed like a trapdoor in her mind. No reason for anyone to check there in a hurry. She climbed up onto the toilet lid, tested the porcelain sink next to it and decided it was sturdy enough to hold her weight. She hauled herself into a precarious position to reach the lid of the cistern; if she fell now, she would definitely hurt herself and find it hard to explain why she had been found sprawled on the bathroom tiles with the camera in hand. The cistern lid was heavier than she'd imagined, as well as being awkward to lift with her arms at full extension, but fear was driving her now and helping her to find previously unimagined strength. With a cursing grunt she managed to squeeze the camera through the tiny gap and heard the satisfying metallic clunk of Walter Zapp's cunning invention falling to the bottom of the bowl; instantly harmless and invisible, its film decaying already. She had to now rely entirely on the single sheet of paper that was hidden next to her skin.

Getting back down was as dangerous as climbing up but now was the moment to go downstairs and claim how unwell she felt. Evie knew she would not have to fake this; at this point she was trembling and exhausted. Added to this was the uncertainty of whether anything she'd done was going to be of any practical help. All she had in her head right now, apart from that very loud alarm, was the cemented notion that she had proof. That and the surety that she wanted to go home now with every bit of will in her body. War was being spoken about as inevitable by those in the know – like Ferry – and although she had no idea if that might occur tomorrow, next year or much further into the foreseeable future, she needed to be in England when it did.

She needed to see the moors, smell their mist or run a hand through their drifts of heather. She wanted to hear the sounds of Levisham: iron and steel complaining against each other, the cough of smoke and the piercing shriek of her father's whistle. She wanted to feel Alf's hug and hear Rosie's whingeing. She was a station-master's daughter. Doubts that she'd kept at bay since she'd first left for London began to crowd in, joining the shrieking alarm of her mind as she pushed her belongings into the bag. There would be no going back if the thin sheet of paper she carried at her breast was discovered; there would be no arguing against her treachery. An axe and a chopping block awaited. She could all but picture the axeman, his short-handled, brutal tool raised in his hand, the sleeve of his dark coat-tailed suit slipping back to reveal a white cuff of his shirt with spatters of blood on it from a previous execution. Evie's fears crowded closer. Were her legs shaking too? She was sure her teeth might start chattering next.

As sardonic as he sounded, she couldn't imagine Hugh Leadbetter of Whitehall doing anything so tasteless as jesting about beheading a woman . . . or indeed anyone, especially her. She banished the image of the infamous German executioner; he would never get within yards of her.

Even so, Evie could feel perspiration on her hands that were rarely damp. Cutting through the fog of her thoughts, the ringing in her ears and the tightness that was now enveloping her chest, she heard a voice she recognised. And it was not friendly.

26

Max felt helpless. His awful lie to Giselle had stalled her for a few more minutes; the admission that he had secretly kept a flame burning for her had certainly captured her attention in a way that perhaps nothing else could. It was no rattling skeleton that they had once . . . very briefly . . . been lovers. But, as Max had explained to Rachel, and more recently to Evie, they had been seventeen, just beginning to explore sex and take their desire further than kissing and fumbling.

The truth was, there hadn't been a hot-blooded youth in their circle of friends who didn't fancy a tumble into bed with Giselle. She was a statuesque beauty even then with style and sophistication, and how she had made the most of that beauty as she moved into her fourth decade was obvious to all. Giselle, older than Max by a year, was a glorious-looking 32-year-old woman; to Max, that was the kindest thing he could say about her. Beyond that she was empty, in his opinion . . . as hollow and insincere a person he had ever known. Unfortunately, her obsession with him was one of her darkest parts.

He'd lied about his feelings. Back in their teens she was part of the tapestry of growing up, discovering sexuality, acting on desire.

She'd led him on, in fact, because there was no doubting how much she'd wanted Max. He had wanted her like any man might, but not because he held any grand affection for her. Giselle had been a dangerous character even then, wielding her attractiveness to lure people and then using them for her own needs. Blackmail was never out of the question for Giselle, who had known only wealth and privilege.

At seventeen, when he'd toppled into her bed one lazy Sunday . . . and several Sunday afternoons after that, when her parents went visiting, he was simply enjoying sex with a willing partner. In the meantime, Giselle was losing her heart. For someone as cold as her, it sometimes seemed impossible to him that she had a heart, or that her blood was warm. If she were cast as a creature, he was convinced she would be a cold-blooded serpent of myth. But love him she had; since their time together, Giselle had kept a flame flickering for him, waiting with reptilian patience for her moment. She'd had many lovers since, as he understood it, but they carried value for her in other ways: what could they give her, or what could they do for her. None lasted longer than a brief affair – until they were no longer of any use, or until someone more important and useful moved into view. Giselle seemed content to be a determined single, committed to the Nazis, whose ideals seemed to dazzle her and take the place of family and friendship . . . but when it came to Max Hall, she was weak. He was the chink in her armour . . . and he had always sensed this.

'Max, why have you never told me this?' she said, still looking at him with incredulity.

'What was the point?' he reasoned. 'When our paths crossed again after so many years, I was married to Rachel and I had a child. I was not the cheating sort.' He still wasn't – but he needed Giselle to believe it was possible.

'But you never wrote, never contacted me,' she said, her voice thin and angry.

'No, I didn't.' He shook his head. 'Maybe it's how we men are wired. I just presumed you would be snapped up in your twenties.'

'You were wrong.'

He shrugged. 'I was married.'

'And now you're married again.'

'I needed a mother for Jonas. You're right in your presumption of Evie. Motherhood, family life . . . that's all that's in her head. It doesn't make her shallow; she's just more one-dimensional than you,' he lied. 'Rachel wasn't any different.' He gave a helpless grin and ran his hand through his hair, knowing she was watching him with a fresh eruption of desire. 'I must be attracted to that sort of woman.'

'Needy?'

'I know you're not.'

'I do need you, Max. I have always needed you.'

He remained neutral but gave her a long stare, the type that would potentially make her insides twist with the incredible notion that there might be potential for them. 'I don't know why. Look at you. You could have anyone you want.'

'I know that. But it's only ever been you. And now you tell me you were mine all along? I think I want to kill you.'

He laughed. She didn't. 'As I said, our timing is out of kilter.' How many minutes had he bought? Another six or seven? Could he hold her any longer with this ridiculous conversation that would surely come back to pinch him?

'I must think on this.'

'What's to think on? There is no "us". I'm with Evie and I have to admit that I love her in my own way. You are . . .' He pretended to search again, shaking his head.

'I am what?'

'You're the one who got away. The one I should have always been with.'

'Max, stop it! You're breaking my heart.'

'I shouldn't have said anything,' he said in a rueful tone, watching her.

'I'm astonished but despicably happy that you did,' she admitted. 'I want to scream for all sorts of reasons but, Max, thank you. I do need to ponder this because, my darling, there is always a way. *Always*.'

That sounded ominous. 'Where are you going?'

'To find your wife.'

And there was nothing more he could do without giving away that Evie had something to hide.

Giselle met the maid in the corridor of the main family wing. She couldn't remember her name but watched the poor wretch try a sort of half curtsy with Dodo's and Ferry's son in her arms. She barely acknowledged her in response. *Ugh* . . . She hoped Dodo was not going to breastfeed now, retiring to the sitting room to lay a baby blanket across her top half as she'd seen other mothers do before suckling their babies. The child was practically walking, for heaven's sake. But some women just loved a child at the breast. Giselle couldn't understand it. While she had no intention of getting pregnant, she thought if she did have a baby, she would have it on the bottle immediately. Then someone else could feed it.

Mind you, if it was Max's baby . . . She glanced over her shoulder at the burdened maid and child. Maybe she'd feel differently about a son from Max. A bright, yellow-headed Aryan god in the mould of his father, growing up to make her proud, joining the Hitler Youth and the party as soon as he was old enough to buy his ticket. There were times when she wished she had been born a man. She would make such a fine addition to the Nazi hierarchy, and was quite certain she would have been one of the Führer's most trusted servants. Some women simply followed their husband's idealism, or perhaps just their husband's loyalty to the Reich. But she wholly believed in everything Adolf Hitler promoted. She held utter faith in Germany and its potential supremacy, and its dire need to re-assert itself in Europe as a major power. Mistakes had been made in the last war but would not be in the one coming. She might not have been a man or a party member, but they'd made concessions for her and she had the ear of most of the influential men in the Reich. Money always talked. And her devotion had been noted. If she could now somehow put Max at her side, they could become one of the nation's most powerful couples.

It was a dazzling daydream, so bright right now it felt overwhelming. And despite Max's reservations and conservative sense of duty to this new wife of his – clearly a burden to him . . . a child in a woman's body – she could find a way for them to be together. While Evelyn Hall suited Hitler's vision for women perfectly, she didn't suit Max. Max needed strength beside him. He needed sophistication and style alongside to match his family's pedigree.

'Did you see Frau Hall?' Giselle called back, grabbing the maid's attention before she descended the stairs.

'I haven't seen anyone except you in the last few minutes, Fräulein. I gather she is in Herr and Frau Porsche's suite.'

What was in Dodo's head, giving a stranger her room?

'Where is that?' Giselle demanded and the terrified maid pointed.

She marched straight up to the door and, without knocking, flung it open.

It had been Evie's plan from the moment she'd entered the house to find something incriminating, get proof of that material and then get out. They could then make a run for it out of Munich and into greater Europe. Leadbetter had said he could extract them from almost anywhere with relative ease, except from within Germany. It was a loose and dangerous plan because it lacked any structure; even Evie could surmise that much. Dithering in the Porsche bedroom, it had occurred to her to simply remain there and pretend to be resting, begging off as soon as she dared, citing her fall and desire to make the long journey back to Munich while she still could.

But Evie no longer believed she was capable of maintaining a neutral expression while keeping up the pretence of her injury, or being able to conceal her anxiety. The rolled sheet of paper poked at her breast, reminding her that it was her death sentence if discovered, and she was increasingly of the opinion that waiting around for it to be found on her or for anyone to check in Ferry's office for tampering was lunacy. Besides, if she was going to die, she'd rather do so on the run towards England rather than meekly accepting her fate with Giselle sneering on.

And it was the sound of Giselle's voice that had spurred her race to get away; it was the first time she'd felt herself lose control since this whole idiotic idea of hers to become a spy had taken control of her life. How had she ever thought she could do this? She had been so confident that morning, never really believing that a swimming party and barbecue could turn as dangerous as it now presented. Too many memories, fears and desires had rolled together at the moment she least needed them to. The yearning for Yorkshire and her previously safe life was undoing her; the fear of being discovered as a spy threatened three lives, and she had started to imagine Leadbetter having to tell her father and sister that she was in a German jail, awaiting her sentence to be carried out.

None of these thoughts made her feel brave or capable of saving herself; in fact, the opposite was happening. She found herself unable to think mechanically. Spies were tutored so their training kicked in over and above fear or circumstance; their preparation made sure that even a blurred mind could act decisively. But without training, all Evie had now was basic animal instinct, and an animal under threat only has two options – hide or flee. She momentarily considered hiding under the bed or in a closet, but that was not going to help – she'd have to emerge at some point. There was nowhere else to hide in the bedroom or the study, which is why she had left the Porsche bedroom and now found herself standing on a ledge to one side of its balcony, holding onto a drainpipe. She figured if hateful Giselle glanced out of the window, then she was hidden and safe for the moment. If the Nazi idealist stepped out onto the balcony, then Evie knew she was as good as dead because who clung to a drainpipe, clearly trying not to be seen, if they had nothing to hide? She would be hauled in, questioned, probably searched, as Giselle was probably already too suspicious of Evie to leave anything to chance.

She held her breath as she heard the door being flung open and her name being called. More distantly, she could hear other doors opening and closing . . . Giselle was presumably determined to find her and rallying others to her cause.

'Where is she?'

Another voice, muffled from behind the door, spoke. 'She was here, resting.' It was Dodo, she guessed.

'Then help me find her. Where's Ferry's study?' There was nothing muffled about Giselle's voice coming from directly behind the glass of the doors.

Whatever Evie was going to do, she needed to do it now. She couldn't risk climbing back onto the balcony and being seen through the doors, so she was going to have to make a leap of faith in every sense. Her only options that she could see were to make the drop of one whole floor and hope for a soft landing on the grass, rather than the concrete pathway, or to launch herself at the iron railing beneath the balcony and clamber around to the steps – hand over hand – hanging off the edge and hopefully remaining unseen.

She chose the latter, imagining that a landing from as high as she was almost guaranteed a broken limb – at best, injured ankles. She wouldn't be able to explain that away. This move, as precarious as it was, gave her a chance of getting to the ground in one piece.

Again she heard raised voices; they were back in the bedroom and would be at the doors in moments if they decided to look out again. *No time to contemplate, Evie*, said a small voice. *Go!*

She jumped.

'What are you doing here?' Giselle demanded, blinking with puzzlement as she arrived at the bottom of the main staircase in the house and found Evie on all fours.

'Oh!' Evie exclaimed, not having to fake shock; she was still trying to calm her breathing from her exertions. Her hand clasped her chest. 'You gave me a fright, Giselle.' After jumping towards the railing beneath the balcony and hanging on for her life with her clammy hands, she had taken a few short breaths and then swung slowly beneath and around the edge of the balcony towards its stairs. It felt like it had taken hours, though in reality it was less than a minute, and her hands hurt as she hauled herself in a desperate, far-from-ladylike way onto the stairs. No time to catch her breath or look back and congratulate herself on the feat achieved.

'I asked what you are doing,' Giselle said more loudly, the note in her voice suggesting she was addressing some sort of idiot.

Evie pasted on a look of dismay. 'Oh, sorry. I'm distracted. Er, I'm looking for an earring that I must have dropped when I fell,' she said, pointing to her naked left ear. 'It looks like this,' she said, pulling back the hair around her right ear. 'Can you help me find it, Giselle?'

Giselle appeared speechless; no doubt mute with rage. Here was Max's wife with her usual innocent persona in place – if only Giselle knew what it had taken for Evie to reach this spot without raising anyone's suspicions.

Once Evie had reached the iron stairs beside the balcony, she had padded down as quietly as she could, far slower than she wanted, fearing the metallic reverberations being heard. Wanting to kiss the ground when she finally stepped onto the concrete path, she moved around the corner of the house to relative safety, out of sight from anyone in the bedroom. All she had to do now was get back into the house and make up some sort of excuse for how she'd got from the first floor to the ground floor without being seen. She could hear the cheerful noise of the children's voices carrying from the swimming pool and the low drone of adult voices, still outside enjoying their day.

Go, Evie. She tiptoed around the perimeter of the house, not knowing what she was going to encounter. At one point she had to pause, holding her breath, while a maid was hanging out tea towels to air. Once she went back inside, Evie continued, ducking beneath the level of the kitchen window where she could see the staff were gathered, working. *Damn.* She'd hoped to enter through the kitchen but if she did that, she'd have a gang of surprised maids. She kept moving, her thoughts firmly on Giselle and Dodo, who were no doubt confused, having likely exhausted the potential for Evie to be in any of the upstairs rooms.

A side door came into view. She risked peeping in through the glass and worked out it was some sort of boot room; that would do. She turned the handle and entered, giving herself a few moments to catch and calm her breath. There was a mirror on one of the cupboards and she used it to check her appearance – flushed. She couldn't help that, but she used another few precious moments to tidy her hair and straighten her clothes. She tiptoed out into the hallway alongside the kitchen and, not giving herself a chance to hesitate, skipped across the hallway and was on her knees not a second too soon. Giselle had arrived at the top of the flight of stairs just a heartbeat or two later.

She could swear she could hear Giselle's furious breathing, as ragged as her own but for different reasons, as she continued to look around for the earring.

'There you are, Evie! How are you feeling?' It was Ferry, with a beer in hand, his wife arriving at Giselle's side down the sweep of stairs at the same moment.

Evie regarded them all, embarrassed. 'I was just explaining to Giselle that I think I dropped my earring . . . or rather it must have fallen off.'

He blinked. 'Oh, I see. Yes, I remember you were wearing them.'

'Can you help me, please? They're tiny diamonds that Max gave me, and they mean the world.' They were no such thing, of course, just a cheap pair of earrings she'd won at the local fair at Pickering in Yorkshire, but she was counting the fact that neither would get close enough to check.

'There!' Dodo said, pointing to where Evie had flung the cheap earring moments earlier.

'Gosh,' Evie exclaimed, sounding appalled that she hadn't seen it sooner but delighted that it was found. She made a show of pouncing on the earring. 'How could I not see it?' She carefully returned it to her ear. Who would have thought this silly prize won from throwing three hoops around a milk bottle might save her life? Thankfully it appeared that Ferry and Dodo accepted her story; it was only Giselle who still wore an expression of suspicion. Would she push the issue, or let Evie leave with Max?'

She turned, cold with fear but with the memory of Levisham burning in her mind and the notion that her father, and any helpers he might have roped in, could well be busy picking cherries this very moment from her precious trees. Evie dug deep into herself and found the courage to look them all in the eye. 'Can we find

Max, please? I don't feel terribly well, but I want to say thank you for everyone's kindness and I'm sorry for all the nuisance I've caused.' She gave an innocuous, self-effacing grin that none could know how much bravery it took to deliver.

Her enemy frowned. 'How did you get past us?'

'I'm not sure what that means,' Evie replied.

'Dodo and I were upstairs looking for you.'

Evie shrugged. 'I walked down these stairs,' she said, sounding baffled. 'Oh, I did use the spare bathroom at the top of the landing. Perhaps we missed each other?' She looked at Dodo's kind expression. 'I didn't wish to use yours, Dodo. You've already been far too generous.'

Giselle shook her head. 'Something's just not quite right here, and yet . . .'

'And yet? I rather like being mysterious.' Evie laughed.

'You aren't mysterious,' Giselle said flatly. 'But you are confusing . . . one moment the adoring mother, another the giggling nymph. At Streicher's party you were direct and in the Hofbräuhaus you were obtuse. You baffle me. But more importantly – and I don't know why I feel this – but I don't believe you dropped your earring.'

'Just stop, Giselle. Why must you believe everyone is alive to outwit you? I'm tired of this conversation.' It was Dodo, who pointed, looking vexed. 'Evie looks ready to faint. She needs her husband.'

Giselle's mouth twisted. Evie would have loved to tell her just how ugly that gesture made her appear, but then there was the ugly personality within, so there was no point. Her concern now was extracting herself from everyone's scrutiny and getting the precious letter back to Leadbetter.

'Evelyn, I have to admit I am not satisfied. In that study is highly classified information, if my information is correct?' Giselle threw Ferry a warning glance. He nodded. 'You have no business being in there, no matter your reason.'

Evie frowned as innocently as she dared. 'Study? But Ferry took me in there. All I did was admire the sketches of his new racing car.'

'And what else?'

Evie couldn't look at Ferry, but she knew he'd forgive her the lie because she could feel him squirming in the corridor of his own grand house, as small and frightened a person in this moment as she was. She wondered if he too was thinking of an executioner's axe, or perhaps the rope's noose. *Look at her squarely, Evie*, she heard in Leadbetter's tone. *Don't back down!* She eyed Giselle firmly. 'Giselle, I was shown a racing car and some sort of bug-like car that Ferry said is an old prototype of the People's Car. He didn't show me the latest drawings of anything, by the way. And actually, having seen those, I'm now convinced that railway engines are the ones for me. No offence, Ferry.'

'None taken,' he murmured from behind Giselle.

Before Giselle could speak, Evie continued. 'What danger is there in showing a housewife the drawings of a car? Now, I'm feeling quite uncomfortable at this constant badgering.'

'Giselle,' Ferry said in a commanding voice. 'Either join us for dessert, or don't. I'm not ruining my day over your unfounded suspicions. Evie was in my study at my invitation. Let's leave it at that. No harm done, except to this poor girl's head.'

There was a tense moment. Dodo broke it. 'Come on, everyone. Out into the garden and, Evie, let's find Max for you.' She linked arms with her husband and led him off.

Giselle finally turned away, unable to resist the final word as she began to follow. 'As I say, I'm not satisfied.'

Giselle reached Max before Evie could. Jonas was with them, dripping in his swimming trunks. Evie saw her say something to

Max that made his expression cloud but in that heartbeat she was too relieved at saving her skin to give it further thought.

Evie touched Ferry's elbow as he passed. 'I'm sorry, Ferry,' she said.

'Don't be. The mistake was mine. I should not be showing our designs to anyone – no matter how innocently – because Berlin's spies are everywhere,' he said in a droll tone.

So are Britain's, she thought, feeling a vague pang of guilt for what she'd just done to him.

Max approached with Jonas, who looked tired but happy, clutching an ice cream with two scoops. She could smell the cone; it had been recently cooked, if the scent of toasted sugar was anything to go by.

'We have to go, darling. I'm sorry, I'm not feeling too well.'

Max took her hand and kissed her cheek so he could whisper, 'Giselle is onto you. Be careful. I'll say our farewells if you can help get Jonas dressed.'

Dodo arrived. 'Helga is fetching your bags from upstairs. And, Max, you'd better get this girl home – she was flushed a few minutes ago and now she's pale. I'm so sorry this happened.'

'I'm too clumsy for my own good,' Evie said, not wishing to remember her recent athleticism. She was grateful for the years of trekking over the moors that had given her the stamina to do what she had.

Helga arrived with the bags, and Evie busied herself helping Jonas pull off his wet things, wrapping a towel around him and getting him into dry clothes. She looked up to see Max and Giselle talking. It appeared an intense conversation, with Giselle managing to pout while at the same time appearing triumphant, even cutting Evie a sneering glance. What had been exchanged?

Dodo had returned. 'By the way, I don't want you taking the train all the way back to Munich. All that waiting around on station platforms, especially as I suspect you're not feeling well.'

'I'll be fine,' Evie assured her, watching Max's expression, which looked grim against Giselle's victory smile.

Anna strolled up. 'Sorry you fell, Evie. What a pity and I hope you're not hurt. It's good to see you back on your feet, though. And I hear Giselle's been her usual hateful self,' she remarked, mostly to Dodo.

'She wasn't really invited, you know, but people like her seem to think they can stroll into anyone's gathering.'

'She acts like she's Gestapo.'

Dodo cut her a warning glance. 'Hush, Anna, dear. Don't jest like that.'

'I'm not sure I am,' Anna murmured. 'I've just overheard her mentioning to Max that his wife could be a spy.'

Evie could have sworn her belly was full of tangled snakes all moving at once.

'Ooh, that woman!' Dodo said, looking mortified, her hand at her throat.

Anna kissed both of Evie's cheeks. 'Get away from her, Evie dear. This is all jealousy, but unfortunately she has managed to ingratiate herself with the people who are suspicious of everyone and everything. As I say, Giselle's dangerous because a mere rumour from her can snowball.'

Dodo put up her hand. 'Enough, ladies. Evie, I was trying to explain that I've already organised a car and driver to take your family home.' As Evie began to protest, she squeezed her wrist. 'No, it's the least we can do.'

'Thank you, Dodo. It's been a lovely day.'

'I wish it had been entirely that for you, my dear. But come again and we shall not let Giselle know next time.'

There won't be a next time, Evie thought as she hugged both the women.

27

In the car Max and Evie avoided discussing their situation for fear the driver might overhear and potentially report back any conversation. So they kept it light with lots of pointless chatter about the house, its décor and how much she enjoyed the family and new friends. All the while, they had to keep their nervous energy at bay.

Once back in the apartment with Jonas tucked into bed, they went into the bedroom, turned on the wireless, and then stepped into the bathroom, switching on the cold taps so they could talk.

'That was uncomfortably close, Evie,' Max said, pulling her close.

She nodded, only now feeling her pulse begin to slow. 'I thought my heart was just going to explode from my chest.'

'Tell me everything. Leave nothing out.'

Evie explained, watching his expression dissolve into one filled with fear.

'You stole it?' He sounded understandably incredulous. She retrieved the tissue-like copy from beneath her clothes. He blinked, perplexed.

'I have to hope all my fear and clamminess hasn't dissolved the ink. I've got to get this to Britain.'

'Well, not by any traditional means, you won't. I don't trust Giselle for a moment. She is almost certainly going to report you as someone to watch, at the very minimum.'

'Then we send it via Hannah.'

'No, you'll throw a spotlight on her for the Gestapo.'

Evie looked distressed. 'I can't do that. She's important to Leadbetter and embedded in German life.'

'You have to protect her by not drawing any attention to her.'

'Then how, Max?'

He sighed. 'I have an idea. But you're not going to like it.'

She stared at him. 'Go on.'

'Let's go downstairs.' He flicked off the wireless and turned off the tap. 'Jonas is fine. We won't leave the apartment building – I feel like a cigarette.'

She followed him, clueless as to what he might have in mind. Once downstairs, he stepped outside, holding the door for her. It was mid-evening and the traffic was light; a few people from the neighbourhood carried groceries or were perhaps returning from their weekends away. The night would be balmy.

'Do you only smoke when we're whispering?' Evie teased, despite the tension she felt.

'No, I only smoke now and then if the situation calls for it. Sometimes I do at work as it can give me cover if I need it. You can learn plenty over a cigarette with a stranger.'

She looked at him, perplexed. 'Are we being watched?'

'Possibly, so lean on me now and then as though you're feeling ill from your tumble.'

Evie watched him strike a match from a matchbook, touching it to the cigarette end so the tobacco caught and its tendrils glowed. He inhaled shallowly, then blew out the smoke, going through the motions of flicking ash from the end of the cigarette . . . not that there was any yet.

'You're convincing me but you wouldn't convince a real smoker.'

'Impressions are everything.'

'What were you so deep in conversation with Giselle about?'

Max frowned. 'When?'

'Just before we left.'

'I was asking her to stop being so hostile towards you.' He sounded strained.

'And?'

'And nothing.' He shrugged. 'Giselle is Giselle. I don't think she cares who she hurts. When she wants something, she won't stop.'

'She wants *you*, Max.'

He gave her an admonishing look. 'Well, you've stopped her having that.'

Evie sensed he was protecting her; hiding something. 'So, she'll make a report, do you think?'

'Yes, I do. But I've asked her to consider how damaging that could be.'

'What does she get in return for—'

'She retains my friendship,' he said, cutting off any further protestation. He gave a sad smile. 'We do have to leave immediately, Evie. Not in a few days. Tomorrow. My plan is that we just get on a train and get out of Germany. Leave everything behind – no packing, no looking back. We don't tell anyone; we simply go to the station, get on a train for Paris and leave.'

'That's too dangerous with Jonas in tow – they could stop us. Imagine what could happen to him if we are both detained. There would be no sympathy, Max. None. The way they speak about Rachel should tell you how little they care about the welfare of Jonas. We are his only defence. We need a valid reason that takes the suspicion away.'

'Where's this valid reason going to come from?'

'Give me forty-eight hours.'

He shook his head. 'Impossible. Giselle could have you arrested, locked up and interrogated with pressure, in that time frame. Let's not forget they have Jean.'

'All right, twenty-four hours.'

'What are you hoping for? A miracle.'

'No, just some Leadbetter magic. And, Max.' Evie put a hand on his arm. He looked at her as he flicked his cigarette to the gutter. 'It's all of us, or none of us. Come on, I'm going upstairs to pack a few things. We need to be ready to go. And then I need to find my pack of cards and make a call to your cousin at Ditchling in Sussex.'

Leadbetter was at home in Surrey, sipping a whisky. He had been tempted to splash the Scotch over some ice, given it was such a warm evening, but that would have meant a lot of unnecessary palaver, digging around in the ice box, and he was too distracted to be bothered. And, to be fair to the Haig whisky in its familiar dimpled bottle, it needed no help to be delicious; besides, his father might turn in his grave to see him watering down the precious nectar.

His family was away in Hove visiting relatives for the weekend, and although he had planned to join them this evening, he'd returned home from the office at around midday with a low headache and couldn't face the journey south. Something he had never admitted to his wife, Nancy, was an old superstition he'd harboured since he joined the Secret Service. He felt silly thinking about it, but he was yet to be proved wrong that this headache often pre-empted bad news . . . usually relating to work. It had occurred three times previously and although he refused to fully commit his faith to curious clairvoyant abilities, Hugh Leadbetter – like any good spy master – had learned to trust his instincts . . . especially his intuition. The headache, he'd schooled himself to believe, was that sixth sense at work.

And as his head continued to protest after he arrived home and took aspirin, he waited for its source to show itself. It was Saturday evening, about to dip into night; he should be having a family knees-up on the coast instead of feeling vaguely ridiculous as he waited for something he wasn't sure would ever come.

Hugh inhaled the spicy toffee aroma whirling up in pleasant fumes from his glass and tasted the first sip, roughish on his tongue, before allowing its smoky warmth to penetrate. It always surprised him as to how that initial rawness oozed into a caramel-sweet finish in his throat. He sighed his pleasure. It smelled like fudge cooked a little too zealously over oak logs. He was just tipping the glass for a second joyous sip when the phone jangled on his desk and startled him.

He snatched at it. 'Hugh Leadbetter,' he answered, half expecting it to be Nancy, scolding him for not being with her, though his work antenna was still anticipating someone calling him about trouble . . .

'I have the Munich telephone exchange, Mr Leadbetter,' said a crisp voice from the London exchange.

There it was. He put the glass down, frowning with concern. 'Thank you,' he said, swallowing his anxiety. He listened for familiar clicks. 'Jean?'

'Gretchen.' That was code for a swap in spies. This woman was his only other Brit embedded at the exchange. Her real name was Josephine.

'Tell me.'

She continued in the matter-of-fact voice of a telephone exchange operator. 'The number requested is out of order, sir.' He closed his eyes. She'd just told him that Jean had been arrested.

'And what about the other line? Is that one still working?' This referred to Evie Hall.

'No, sir. I'm sorry. It is being tested now and that one might also need to be placed out of order. I will be requesting documents for this.'

'So we can't get through at all?'

'I'm afraid we cannot escape the fact that this one too may be relegated to out of order, hence the request for documentation.'

'Right. Thank you for your help, Munich.'

'Thank you, sir. And thank you, London,' the woman said to London Exchange.

He rang off, eyes downcast. So Jean had been captured. Her real name was Alice and he was glad she had no family that he needed to feel guilty about. But she was one of his best on the ground in Munich especially, but also across all of Bavaria. She was a professional, though; she knew the risks and he hoped she might escape prosecution with a warning of being observed for dissident behaviour, or something similarly inane. He didn't believe her arrest would have been in conjunction with Evie, but more likely a ghastly coincidence related to eavesdropping on government department telephone conversations. Alice would play dumb. If necessary, she would say she had been listening in out of boredom.

Even with Alice unable to help, his newest spy, who had no training and was about as far from professional as one might be, had at least got her message through to the hairdresser, Hannah, and warned everyone that Alice had been compromised. The message also made it clear that Evie was ready to come home – perhaps she was spooked or, he hoped, she had something tangible he could use to prove to Westminster categorically that war with Germany was imminent. The word 'escape' that Gretchen used meant immediate extraction, which could only signify that Evie believed the authorities were onto her. And, to boot, the mention of documentation meant Evie no longer had a passport, which complicated her situation inordinately.

To his surprise, the phone jangled again. It couldn't be another call from Munich – no one would risk that. 'Leadbetter?'

'Hello, Hugh. It's your cousin calling from Ditchling.'

'Oh, hello um . . . Clara,' he said, wondering where on earth he'd dug up that name from. He had no cousin in Ditchling; he didn't even know anyone called Clara. But he certainly knew this was the final protocol being triggered by Evie; she had contacted one of his people to ensure he knew she was in immediate danger. Now he knew there was no time to wait and see. He had to act.

'How are you, Hugh, dear?' she continued.

'Not too bad. How's the family?'

'Oh, desperate to get home, apparently. I mean, really desperate. They were planning to stay on for the Olympics, but Elspeth has been struck down with something and they just want to be back in Sussex . . . You know how it is when you get ill . . . far from home and frightened?'

'That's a shame to hear. Can I help?'

'Yes, well, that's why I'm calling, Hugh. I rather hoped you might pull some strings with the Home Office. My silly sister has lost her passport.'

'Oh, I see. Well, it will have to be generated out of Europe, but I can see what might be done to hurry things along.'

'Thank you, dear Hugh. Anyway, look, anything you can do is much appreciated. Perhaps we can talk tomorrow?'

'Yes, let me get something happening if I can. I'll call you, Clara. Night-night.'

He put the receiver down and rubbed his face. Tricky. The urgency was more pressing than he'd grasped. Evie had triggered the Queen of Hearts. Time to get her out.

Had she achieved something . . . or let him down, proving herself to be just that young Yorkshire lass who should never have been put in harm's way by his team? The guilt turned his second sip of whisky sour on his tongue and he knew he had a responsibility to get Evie out no matter what.

He picked up the phone again and began dialling, the flavours of his excellent whisky forgotten.

The telegram arrived while they were having a late breakfast. They'd agreed to stay in to play some games, despite the beautiful morning, and perhaps go for a stroll around the neighbourhood in the afternoon to pick up some groceries. As far as Evie was concerned, the extra day she'd asked for gave London time to achieve something – though she had no idea what. But she was now weighing that against the realisation that Jonas would be due back with Giselle the day after tomorrow. If they were going to make a move, it had to be tomorrow morning.

Max and Jonas were playing on the carpet with trains, building some new great rail track through the apartment, it seemed, while Evie was in Jonas's bedroom putting a few essentials into a duffel bag. She'd already packed one small suitcase for herself, and Max had impressed that he'd need nothing.

'Surely you need something?' she'd queried.

He'd shaken his head. 'If we have to move fast and I have to carry Jonas, then I want both arms free. There's nothing I'll miss that I can't buy at the other end.'

Evie didn't believe him, thinking about the model railway set alone that seemed to matter so much to both of them. But in comparison to their lives, of course it had no value. She had thrown a few spare items for Max into her case anyway. Now, closing the locks of Jonas's bag, there was a sharp rap at the door.

'I'll get it,' she called, moving down the hallway to open their apartment door. 'It's probably Frau Speigel.'

It was not their neighbour. 'Frau Hall?' said a man in uniform.

'Yes?'

'Telegram for you,' the young man said.

Evie signed and took the envelope, feeling momentarily anxious. Whatever this contained, she was sure it was about to make a major change to their situation. She returned to the sitting room. 'Telegram.' She held it up.

'You keep playing, Jonas,' Max said, then got to his feet and walked over to her. Maybe her expression betrayed her because he offered, 'Do you want me to open it?'

She shook her head and moved into the bedroom, Max following. She quickly undid the envelope, reading it, swallowing bile. 'Er . . .' She sounded shaken when she spoke, looking towards the wireless. He nodded. She paraphrased for him. 'It seems my darling father's had a heart attack. He's in hospital.'

'Oh, Evie,' he said. He reached for the notepad and pen by the bedside and began to scribble while he said, 'I'm so sorry, my love. What else does it say?' He held up the paper: *False?*

She shrugged, took the pen and wrote: *Prob Leadbetter*. He nodded with obvious relief.

'No, nothing more. It's from Rosie. All she says is hurry home.'

They both looked towards the wireless that was presumably filtering their conversation back to those listening in on them.

'I'll book train tickets for Paris,' he said.

She nodded, speaking equally clearly. 'Do it today, darling. The fastest route possible. We'll have to be gone in the morning.'

Sadly, for Evie, Max did no such thing. Kissing her goodbye on the pretext of walking straight to the railway station to book their tickets, Max made his way to his office first and rang Giselle.

28

Evie felt so tense even her teeth were aching. She wanted to run to Munich's railway station but, for the sake of Jonas, she was determined not to show nervousness.

That she was going to risk getting on a train out of Germany without a passport felt even more dangerous than leaping off a ledge towards a thin iron railing. But she was counting on her ability to play the flustered mother as she realised they'd left their documentation at home, creating a scene and hopefully being allowed to alight at the next terminus – but outside of Germany. From there she had to pray that Leadbetter's tentacles would reach out and offer help. She couldn't know. She simply had to trust.

The taxi ride felt as though it were taking an eternity, and Jonas was fidgety with extreme excitement that he was going on a long train ride. His eyes were glistening with wide-eyed joy.

'Do you think we're being followed?' Evie whispered to Max.

'I suspect we're being watched,' he said. 'But I called into the office yesterday and even though it was Sunday, I let all the right people know that I would only be away briefly.'

Evie couldn't pin it down, but she sensed that Max was behaving awkwardly. Something in his body language, perhaps, or his slightly taut tone. To her, Max was always reliably relaxed; she knew he felt anxiety and tension as naturally as anyone else, but he'd taught himself to control it, to not show it on his features. He'd been at this spy game longer than her, but she also believed he had an inherent skill to give off a casual, distant air. She could forgive doing neither today but even so, it caught her attention. 'Are you all right?'

He nodded, hugging Jonas, who was on his lap, even closer.

'It's going to be fine, Max,' she assured him, trying to make herself believe it.

After unloading themselves and two small bags at the railway station, alone on the concourse with the taxi paid and gone, Max turned to her. She noted that Jonas had wandered a couple of feet away to stare at the bank of turnstiles they had just come through. She watched him beginning to chat with one of the ticket inspectors, no doubt about trains, and gave her attention to Max.

He glanced around to check no one was close. 'I have to tell you something.'

It was not that she'd been expecting it, but she wasn't shocked to feel like an admission was coming. 'What is it?'

'I've booked tickets on the train to Paris.'

'Right . . .'

'Except we won't be going that way.'

Evie smiled, feeling relief. 'I knew you were up to something, but I figured that out last night when you talked about booking the tickets for their benefit.'

He didn't smile back, which confused her momentarily. 'You need to focus, Evie, in case . . .'

Evie frowned. 'In case?'

'We may get separated.' She began to protest. 'No, listen. We don't know what's waiting for us in there. I'm just hoping I've laid enough false clues. I actually have booked and paid for tickets to

Paris and made sure I was seen doing that. But then I went to the office and used a back entrance to return to the station and book tickets using a different route, and I need you to be sure you have that memorised.'

'Where are we going?'

'We're taking a shorter trip into Vienna, changing trains and travelling into Switzerland before heading into France and onwards into London. It's a lengthier journey, but if we get spooked or worried, we can get off the train in Innsbruck, Zurich or Paris, even Calais.'

'I think the precaution is wise but, Max, I have no documentation. You know Frick still has my passport. What are the authorities going to do with me in Vienna . . . if we make it that far without me being picked up?'

'You will,' he said with a confidence that baffled her. 'You've let Leadbetter know you have no paperwork?'

She nodded. 'But he's thinking Paris, right? He doesn't know about Vienna.'

'You let me do the worrying now, Evie. So long as you're outside German borders, we are going to keep you safe.'

She looked back at him, pained.

He squeezed her hand. 'Will you trust me?'

'I have to.'

'You must trust me,' he urged. 'No matter what happens today, trust me on every decision I make from here on.'

She frowned. Max sounded intense and as though he had a hidden meaning, but she couldn't fathom it and he didn't give her the opportunity to do so. 'So you've got that routing all in your mind, just in case of any unseen situation?'

She smiled, still baffled. 'Yes, Max. I actually have a very good memory for detail.'

'Where's the—'

'Safe,' she said, shutting him down. He stared at her and she refused to say more. He appealed with his silent expression. She shook her head. 'First lesson in spying,' she murmured, 'Don't share information when you don't have to.'

'Come on,' Jonas whined. 'Let's go!' He had wandered back from the turnstiles and was pulling at Max's sleeve.

She turned away.

'Evie?' Max said. Glancing back, she saw only pain. 'I love you and Jonas more than anything in the world.'

'I know that, Max. I've always known it.'

As she heard the familiar, delicious sound of a steam train sighing and wheezing at the platform of the *Orient Express*, Evie looked at Max with wonder. 'Really?'

He found his smile, much to her relief. 'Might as well flee in style,' he said, lifting up Jonas to carry him on his shoulders.

Jonas was struck dumb with awe, staring at the carriages of the distinctive, regal blue of the famous train that carried first-class passengers in true luxury. He leaned forward to touch the shiny gold emblem that was the badge of the Compagnie Internationale des Wagons-Lits. 'Are we going on this, Papa?'

'You are, my boy. What a treat, eh?'

Jonas clapped, laughing, and Evie was deflected from something that snagged in her mind, watching her stepson. Her amusement was combined with sheer relief as much as pleasure to be taking such a legendary train and travelling in such flamboyant fashion.

Max consulted the tickets. 'We're down a couple of carriages, I think. Ah, the steward's there,' he said, pointing, and they began making their way towards their car. Others awaited too, including two women with mink coats slung over their arms. They were expecting cooler weather in the east, obviously.

Max lifted Jonas down to the platform and the little boy took Evie's hand. 'Are you excited, Evie? We have a Märklin train set that looks exactly like this.' His eyes sparkled with pleasure and she was captured by his excitement.

'I am so looking forward to this journey, Jonas.'

'Evie, tell me again the route,' Max said.

She did so, sounding vaguely vexed. 'Max, please.'

'You have a number for Leadbetter?'

'Of course. Memorised.'

The steward bustled over. 'Now, I'm guessing you are the Hall family. Is that right, young man?' he asked.

Jonas laughed. 'Yes, sir, I'm Jonas Hall. This is my father, Max, and my mother, Evie.'

Max glanced at Evie and she could tell he was torn between heartbreak and total joy at the innocence of his child.

'Well, well. Thank you, young sir. My name is John. May I show you to your home for your journey?'

Jonas nodded and began clambering up the tall steps.

'Oh, let me help you, junger Herr – that's a big gap. We can't have you slipping to the tracks.'

Stepping on board, Evie and Max gave sighs of pleasure, nodding at other guests as they followed John to the compartment, noting their names on the door.

'Here we are, Herr and Frau . . . and junger Herr. I am looking forward to ensuring you have a wonderful journey with us.'

John took some time explaining the services, plus all the features of their carriage compartment. He showed them how the beds would fold down and how cunningly hidden their bathroom was, winning all the right noises from his new guests.

'Well, I shall leave you to get comfortable.' They heard a shrill whistle. 'Ah, good. We shall be departing in twenty minutes, so I will see to my final guests and I shall return shortly. The dining carriage is a short stroll from here and we shall be serving morning coffee as soon as we leave the station and luncheon service begins at midday. I hope you're hungry, Jonas,' John said, rubbing his belly.

Jonas laughed. 'I'm always hungry.'

'Excellent.' John departed and Evie sighed.

'Thank you, Max. What a treat.' She stood and flung her arms around him and he seemed to welcome her hug, holding her close and not letting her go as quickly as she imagined he might have in public. In fact, despite the open door and Jonas trying to push them apart, he took the time to kiss her. It wasn't just a kiss; Evie felt like he was making her really experience it, remember it. It was deep and tender.

'I'm pleased you're happy,' Max said, and again she noted that strange look in his gaze. 'I love you so much,' he said, making a second declaration. It felt fraught; maybe he was more nervous for them than she had anticipated. He looked down as if blinking away dampness. 'Now, Jonas. I need you to be on your very best behaviour because this is a very grown-up train.'

'I will be, I promise.'

Evie watched Max give a lingering kiss to the golden mop of Jonas's head. 'Good boy.'

'Max?' Evie said.

'Mmm?'

'What's going on?'

Max shook his head. 'What do you mean?'

'You know what I mean.'

He shrugged. 'I'm emotional, I suppose. I doubt I'll ever be back. Just feeling the pangs of not visiting Rachel's grave to say goodbye or taking Jonas to see his mother in farewell.'

'Oh, Max, I'm so sorry. How insensitive of me not to realise . . .' Evie's face fell as a figure arrived into their doorway.

'Hello, Max, Evelyn . . . and little Jonas. I heard about the crisis back home.' Evie swallowed hard to see Giselle looking her glamorous best. 'I thought I'd come and wish you a safe journey, although you should have checked about taking Jonas away first.'

Evie glanced at Max, who held her gaze, but there was a sheepishness to it. 'You knew about our trip?' she said, turning back to Giselle.

'Max told me, darling. Now, a quick search and you'll be on your way.'

'Search?'

'Just protocol, Evelyn. I'm sure you have nothing to worry about . . .' Giselle hesitated. 'Do you?'

Evie shook her head, thinking about the letter. Did Giselle know she had it? Had she somehow wrung out of Ferry what might have been found in his desk drawers if a person had snooped? Or had Max said something . . . was that why he was behaving so awkwardly? Her mouth had turned so dry, her tongue felt suddenly too large for it. She wasn't able to say anything except make the appropriate sound of disdain at Giselle's remark.

'I see you're wearing that divine Hermès scarf of cherries, Evie, and matched it perfectly with a darling little red summer dress. I could wish to wear that outfit myself. Now, turn out your pockets, please, for the police.'

Giselle had brought the police? Evie felt instantly sickened; bile churning deep but threatening to rise. She had no choice but to obey as a burly man in uniform stepped into the compartment. She glared at Max as he did the same, refusing to make eye contact. Evie ran back over what Giselle had just said. *Max* had told her? Why would he tell her anything?

Giselle had the gall to rifle through Jonas's pockets and his little holdall of model trains, making him giggle innocently. The man in police uniform now began systematically dismantling their luggage.

'What are you looking for, Giselle?' Evie asked pointedly.

'Anything incriminating, Evelyn.'

'I'm baffled,' Evie persisted. 'Incriminating in what way?' She could barely swallow.

'I don't trust you, Evelyn darling, and I've told you that previously, so you shouldn't be surprised. So I'm doing my duty and making sure you leave Germany with nothing that doesn't belong to you.'

Evie didn't like the way Giselle glanced at Max with those words. 'Go ahead. You'll find nothing,' Evie said calmly, though her heart felt like it was escalating towards its final beat. She dug out the telegram to stop her hands from shaking. 'Here, this is why we're leaving Munich briefly. My father is potentially dying.'

'And I'm sorry to hear that,' Giselle said, with the cutting insincerity she could muster so brilliantly. She took the telegram, glancing at it momentarily before returning it. 'Even so. I do have to search you, Evelyn.'

'I've already turned out my pockets,' she protested.

Giselle just smiled and mimicked lifting her arms. 'Rather me than him, Evelyn,' she said, nodding at the sombre-faced policeman. 'He's one of Frick's,' she added for extra weight.

Evie could feel perspiration trickling down the narrow cleft of her spine, beneath her brassiere and the silk of her slip. She was glad Leadbetter had insisted on the scarlet dress from Selfridge's that was made from a thicker fabric and now added some protection. If the angels would smile on her, Giselle would never know how panicked she felt right now.

Reluctantly, she raised her arms, glad they hadn't dampened beneath the sleeves. She turned her face to one side, closing her eyes against the offence as Giselle began pressing and feeling over her body. Her heart felt as though it were pounding somewhere in her throat; would she find the letter?

Evie forced herself to open her eyes and regard the pale puddles of Giselle's, wishing she could admit to her that, in her opinion,

Giselle shared the same stare of the dead that Frick did, and they should both go to hell. But Evie held her tongue. 'Nothing, as I told you,' she said, fighting to keep her voice even; amazed that she did and had managed to sound so affronted.

Giselle moved around to check in Evie's hair. *Her hair!* 'I'll be careful with your wound, fret not,' she said with her horrible grin. Evie suffered the intrusion, all the while staring at Max, who refused to look at her.

'Why, Max?' Evie finally asked, putting the pieces together in her mind and coming to the conclusion that Max had brought this about. It explained his strange behaviour of earlier, all the declarations of love and the lingering looks and kisses. His guilt had moved with them all of this morning, and his shame was crowding the small compartment right alongside them.

'Because he's a good German, Evelyn,' Giselle answered for him.

Now Max did look up, and Evie was surprised as much as she was convinced that his expression disagreed with Giselle's assessment.

'I'm a good German boy,' Jonas said gravely.

'No, Jonas, my love. You are a Jew, but out of kindness to your father, I won't tell,' Giselle said to the confused expression of the boy, but Evie knew she would just as soon commit Max's son to the fate of the Jews in Germany as hug him.

'Anything?' Giselle said to Frick's man, who had finished searching Max and the luggage. He shook his head. She turned back to Evelyn. 'Well, well. That's a surprise. I *will* get to the bottom of whatever you were up to at the Porsche house. But for now, you are free to continue your journey.'

Evie shouldn't have said another word, but she loathed Giselle more in that moment than she could have ever imagined. 'If you think I'm guilty of something, why let me go?'

Giselle gave her snake-like smile. 'I have some insurance,' she said cryptically but before Evie could ask, she tapped her nose. 'But something tells me you have been very lucky, Evelyn. I suggest you don't test my patience or largesse any further. Take your little trip. My regards to your family in its grief.'

It was wise to not push Giselle any more but still Evie spoke. 'He's not dead yet,' she said, unable to resist a jab.

Giselle ignored her. 'Max, a word, please.'

He left but not before turning and giving Evie a look that contradicted his apparent betrayal.

'Max, really? We're leaving in minutes,' Evie bleated.

'Come along, Max,' Giselle ordered over her shoulder, before stepping off the train.

'Relax,' he soothed her. 'There's still more than ten minutes. I'll only need a couple of them.' He pecked her cheek. 'I'll explain everything.'

Something wasn't right. She couldn't work it out, as she watched Max step off the train, trailing after Giselle. In that moment, Evie heard the tell-tale sound of the locomotive preparing to depart. She knew the sounds of steam engines intimately and this was no longer one idling in readiness. This was one that was about to take the brakes off. Another whistle sounded. Doors were being slammed up and down the train.

'Stay there, Jonas,' she said and hurried into the corridor where many of the passengers were already waving goodbyes. 'Max!' she shrieked in a low breath. She raced to the door and opened the window, leaning out. What was he thinking? How could he do this to her and risk not being on board?

They found each other's gaze. He was standing next to Giselle, who'd wrapped a protective arm around the man she loved. Evie saw only the smirk she wore, heightened by a slash of scarlet lipstick. Max's expression was filled with pain.

'Max!' Evie yelled, already knowing it was helpless.

'Safe travels.' Giselle waved before turning Max's face towards her and leaving the mark of her red lips on his like blood.

He wiped it away and with Giselle unable to hear him above the screech of wheels, Max began to talk to Evie silently. She read his lips.

It was the only way. Love Jonas for Rachel, for me, for all of us. Know that I did this for the safety of you both.

Tears erupted and ran down her cheeks to cause rivulets in her face, freshly made-up for the journey. She reached out of the window. 'Max . . .' was all that would come. Jonas, too, had realised that his father was being left behind and had come to stand behind Evie at the window. Feeling the emotion of the moment rather than understanding, he began to cry. Evie pulled Max's child to her hip and hugged him, sobbing with him and for him, but with her gaze firmly on her pretend husband.

And as the train jerked forward, Max mouthed three more words: *Wait for me.*

John the steward was at her side. 'I'm so sorry, Frau Hall.' His fallen expression told her he had been in on the ruse. 'Herr Hall and I had no choice but to lie to you about the timing. It was the KriPo; we cannot argue with any of their demands.'

But Evie wasn't listening; she was watching Max disappear into the distance through the blurring gaze of her helpless tears.

She couldn't cry any more. Now it was anger that she felt, ringed with despair; how had she missed the signals? She was like a train out of control, blundering along, so focused on one track that she'd missed others that had departed from her path. Max was one of them, choosing to sacrifice himself to Giselle in order to protect her and Jonas. What had he promised her?

There was a more pressing problem to solve, though, and she could no longer keep picking at the scab of the wound inflicted in Munich. Jonas's tears had finally ceased and he had fallen asleep, and she was alone in her painful thoughts. They were now well on their way towards Vienna, and Evie's burning question was what all the risk had been about if Max had always intended to stay behind . . . Why had she come in the first place? Why had he inflicted this on her, leaving her with the fresh risk of getting the letter out and with no passport? Had he always planned to be with Giselle? Was that the driving factor? Perhaps his going along with Evie's plan was only ever about getting Jonas out of Germany?

The thoughts collided and meshed and tore themselves apart as she analysed them, measuring them up against all that she knew . . . had listened to . . . felt in her heart.

No. Max had always intended to come back to Yorkshire with her and while, yes, she was Jonas's ticket out of Germany, she believed she would have sensed that she was being duped by Max if that had been his plan. She'd not just heard it but felt it through every chill in her body when he'd hidden his revolt whenever Giselle took the opportunity to sneer at Rachel or herself. Evie was sure she'd have known if he had kept a flame burning for Giselle or been unfaithful to her. Every look from him while the Nazi servant had humiliated Evie on the train was in direct opposition to what Giselle claimed.

And then those three words: *Wait for me.*

Did he have an escape plan too?

That was probably it. Max was going to get out of Germany and find his way to Yorkshire, but the only way to achieve safe passage for Jonas was through Evie. Plus, he could only ensure safety for both of them by using himself as a bargaining chip. Giselle was so obsessed with Max that she could look away from her sense of duty to the Reich and allow Evie to disappear. As far as Giselle knew, all she was taking with her was Jonas.

This realisation didn't make her sorrow any easier to bear, but it helped her to move past the knot of pain in her mind and focus on the passport officer, whom she had heard moving down the carriage as they presumably approached the border with Austria.

There was nothing for it. She would have to lay herself at the mercy of the authorities, praying they were Austrian rather than German. If so, when they alighted in Vienna, she and Jonas would become a Viennese problem and its people would presumably contact London. If the officer on board was German, he would likely put them straight back on the next train to Munich. It crossed her mind that she wouldn't put it past Giselle to taunt her in this way, to allow Evie to feel as though she'd escaped, only to have her returned to face formal questioning, prison and everything else that would follow. However, if Giselle had pulled a trick like that, she wouldn't have Max . . . and Max's affections were presumably all that mattered to Giselle with regard to this business. How far would he have to take this ruse?

Ugh! The thought of Max making love to Giselle sickened her, and though she was convinced it would sicken him too, she would never know.

'Passports, please, ladies and gentleman. Please have your passports ready for inspection,' the man called just a few suites down.

Jonas began to stir. Evie readied herself to plead, to beg on bended knee if necessary.

Doors opened and closed. The voice of the passport inspector got closer and finally it was their turn. There was a rap on the door. 'Passports, please.'

Evie smoothed her dress and took a deep breath. She opened the door.

'Good afternoon . . . er, Frau Hall, and son, Jonas Hall?'

'Yes,' she uttered, finding it hard to speak.

'Your passports please?'

'I . . . um. Oh yes, we should have them here,' she said, turning to rummage through bags. 'I saw my husband put them in here. Just a minute.' Her mind was racing. She had to come clean; no point in putting it off. Evie could see the glint of an axeman's blade in her mind, Jonas dirty and barefoot, and so thin she barely recognised him as she imagined what his life might become if he didn't have the protection he had now. He would beg for food, for warmth, for a roof over him.

'Thank you, Frau Hall,' she heard the man say. She turned, puzzled.

'And I see young Jonas is on your passport, thank you. All in order,' the man said genially. He gave her a wink and handed her a precious blue British passport. 'Oh, and Mr Leadbetter asked me to say hello,' he said. 'Welcome to Austria.'

Her mouth was still agape when he closed the doors and continued down the corridor. 'Passports, please, ladies and gentleman. Have your passports ready for inspection.'

They were met at London Victoria by none other than a guilt-ridden Hugh Leadbetter, together with Clive Elliott and Ed Cartwright. It was quite the welcoming party, but all three were sombre of face when the *Golden Arrow*, the elegant English train that linked with the *Orient Express* to carry the European passengers into London, sighed to its rest.

Evie alighted, grim in her expression too, with Jonas holding her hand; he was quiet as he leapt down the steps. She'd had to lie that his father had been held up with work and would join them when he could. Her mind had been too addled to say much more and, while she hated the lie, she would deal with the fallout later. And Jonas, it seemed, was used to the excuse of work taking preference where his father was concerned. For the time being he was showing his feelings only through the constant holding of her hand.

She knew Hugh Leadbetter was watching her as she paused; he was taking a measure of her mood. Evie looked directly at him and as Leadbetter took two strides forward, she seemed to fold into his arms, though she didn't let go of Jonas. She would never let go. She wept, but the emotional outpouring didn't last long. She gathered herself within moments and pulled away from him, straightening her bearing and smoothing her clothes with her free hand.

'Ed, perhaps you could take Jonas for a walk around the station,' Leadbetter said. 'Feel like stretching your legs, young chap?'

Jonas looked up at Evie. 'Ed's a friend, Jonas. You'll be fine,' she said.

They watched him leave with Ed's protective hand on his shoulder. She turned back to Leadbetter. 'Hello, Hugh, Clive.'

They sheepishly said, 'Hello, Evie,' together.

'Thank you for the passport. You might well have saved our lives and I'm grateful for your intervention, especially to have Jonas put onto mine.'

Clive said nothing, looking between them. Hugh simply nodded, watching her carefully. 'And are you all right?' he finally asked.

What a terribly British query, Evie thought, the response to which was always, 'Yes, I'm fine', even if they were dying. There was little point in explaining. She'd conveyed it all when she'd arrived and collapsed into him. Now she needed to stay composed.

'Your head is wounded,' he observed.

Evie shrugged. 'It's fine. Did you know what was going to happen?'

He nodded again, still watchful and cautious. 'Max got hold of me.'

'How did he have your contact details?'

'I gave them to him, Evie,' he admitted with a sigh. 'In case you did anything reckless and I needed to do something dramatic. What I didn't expect was his cunning. I don't know how much you know, or whether he explained what he was going to do . . .'

'He told me nothing. I hate you all, plotting behind my back.'

Clive shuffled uneasily but Hugh absorbed her insult, seeming to accept that he deserved it. 'I understand.'

'No, you don't. Max and I love each other and you put us both into untenable positions. We were your puppets. And now they'll kill him.'

'They won't. He's been smart. He brokered a deal with the security services.'

'Which is?'

'To allow you and Jonas to leave.'

'He has sacrificed himself!'

'Not quite. He feigned loyalty along with a lie. He told them that you were pretending to like Germany, but that you really wanted to return to Britain and he couldn't stand the tears any longer. He wanted to annul the marriage, and apparently there's some old flame involved?'

'A hideous woman called Giselle Kleist, who is close to the Nazi hierarchy and part of the reason I had to get out so fast.'

'He told me.' Leadbetter sighed. 'He's a better man than I credited. Apparently, he was going to pretend that he still carried the flame for her and had only married you as a convenient mother for Jonas. But he hadn't expected you to be such a burden . . . or such a lightweight.'

'Lightweight,' she repeated with a bitter smirk as though it was a filthy word.

'This Kleist woman clearly couldn't see past her own obsession with him and wanted you out of the picture – and the child, since he is half Jewish and problematic.'

'And what about when they all discover what I've stolen?'

Leadbetter's demeanour changed. He shifted his weight and his expression helplessly lit up. 'Max will have a story. He'll distance himself from you and it . . . whatever it is. He wouldn't have risked himself if—'

'Yes, he would, Hugh, because he's got the hero streak that none of you have. All of you sit behind your desks and move people like Max and me around like chess pieces on a board. And if we get swallowed up by the opposition, we're all dispensable. None of you risk anything other than embarrassment – least of all your lives. Can you get him out?'

Leadbetter looked like he was going to give a small mirthless laugh at the idea, but Elliott did it for him in the background. She ignored Elliott while Leadbetter rearranged his features to neutral. 'No, Evie. I cannot do that. Max has indeed made the sacrifice for you and Jonas. Now he has to live it until he can extricate himself.'

'He's staying permanently?' she asked, shocked.

Leadbetter shrugged. 'This was the only quick way he could see to get you safely out – he used himself as the bait. Why don't you tell me what his life is worth, Evie? Show me what you stole.'

Evie momentarily closed her eyes, then opened them as if tamping down the rising heat of her temper. She fiddled with the scarf around her neck, pulling it free and unravelling it so its cherries formed their full pattern, revealing a letter that had been rolled into a tiny cylindrical shape and hidden within the scarf's folds.

'I'm sorry about your camera. It's lying at the bottom of a toilet cistern, not only because it incriminated me but, you should know, Hugh, it jammed and let me down. I could have brought you fifty pictures of schematics for a small, amphibious craft, and potentially an aircraft bomber engine for the Luftwaffe that is being designed by the Porsche company.'

Both men stared at her, open-mouthed.

'Instead, this is all you have, unless you wish to pick my brain and I can tell you what I saw. You will note Hermann Göring's signature at the bottom of this page,' she said, offering the cylinder of paper. 'Check it. I'm confident you'll find it authentic – and chilling. They are gearing up for thousands of these amphibious craft alone.' She cleared her throat, glad to be rid of the burden that had felt like a lead weight around her neck since Stuttgart. 'War is coming, gentleman – and there's your firm proof. Now, I can't confirm when these are being built but I can probably tell you where. As to the aircraft, I know very little. There will likely be other companies working on similar projects, according to Max, but I viewed genuine diagrams from locked drawers in Ferdinand Porsche II's household study.'

Leadbetter blinked as he stared at the unrolled sheet. 'Evie, I don't know what to say.'

'Well, as it happens, I do. To hell with you all. Leave me alone . . . every last one of you.'

He cleared his throat. 'We may need a debrief.'

'You can do it in Yorkshire. I'm not staying in London long enough. Jonas and I will catch the afternoon train.'

'Please let us—'

'I don't want you to do anything, Hugh. You've done enough for me . . . and to me. I wish I'd never been such a patriot. I knew in my heart that Max was no agent for Germany and if only I'd trusted my heart and not said anything, we'd still be living and loving in England.'

Leadbetter obviously didn't want to burst that bubble for her and chose not to say more on the notion that they would have tracked him down eventually.

'He was never giving secrets to Germany and he's still working for Britain, but now he's alone and in a deeply dangerous environment. Now, tell me my father is fine,' Evie demanded.

'He is. I'm sorry about the telegram,' Leadbetter said, clearing his throat. 'It was all I could think of in the moment.'

She nodded, holding out a hand. 'Goodbye, Hugh. Clive,' she said over her shoulder. 'Hope to never see either of you again.'

They had to watch her walk away towards the approaching Ed and Jonas, where she stopped briefly and found a smile for them.

'Are you just going to let her leave, sir?' Elliott asked in astonishment.

'Yes, I am, Clive. She's right in everything she says. I find her rather amazing and she owes us nothing.'

Epilogue

North Yorkshire

April 1945

The woman with a smudge of oil on her face left the tiny hut next to the southbound track at Levisham Station and grinned widely at the tall youth who'd flung his cycle down and loped on long, gangly legs across the tracks towards the kiosk, probably expecting to find her there rather than polishing the brass in the signals box.

'You're back so soon,' she called. 'So?' she asked, hoping it was good news.

He swung around with a smile so reminiscent of Max that she caught her breath. 'I won!'

'You did not!' Evie exclaimed, letting out the air that had trapped itself in her chest, laughing and running towards him. She wrapped her arms around the son who, at fifteen, was now taller than her. 'You ace! Really?'

'No one even close, Mum. I thought I was going to explode on the train back from York because I had no one to tell.'

'Congratulations! Schools Chess Champion for 1945. Gosh, your father would be chuffed. You must let the family know down south – they'll be thrilled. And we should celebrate.'

'Can we go to the cinema?'

'Something like that.' She grinned.

'I'm starving.'

'I can never fill that endlessly empty belly of yours. Go to the house and wash up. I'll be home shortly to make a sandwich.'

'I just want to see Grandad . . . tell him the news. Where's Aunty Rosie?'

'She's taken Sarah into York for a girls' big day out.'

'So instead of coming to watch me up against one of the best under-18s in the country, they went shopping instead, I suppose?'

'Can't stop those two. They're addicts. Birds of a feather, who neither appreciate nor understand chess.' She looked down. 'I wish I could have been there. But you know I have to help Grandad.'

'I know. Anyway, I would have been nervous if you'd been in the audience.'

'Where's your trophy?'

'I got to hold it, that's all, and be photographed for the newspaper. They're giving me a medal next term. The school will want to make a fuss, probably.'

She was sure it would. St Peter's was one of the most eminent boys' schools in the country, and certainly the oldest. Max's people, who were wealthy, had been determined to give his son the top education that she couldn't afford. She didn't mind and had never felt offended; she only wanted what was best for Jonas, and it was his birthright after all. Evie gave him another hug. 'You make us all proud. Meanwhile, I think I'm turning into a man,' she said, gesturing at the men's boots she'd bought in a second-hand shop and secretly loved stomping around in.

'You are, but Grandad and I think you're the most beautiful woman in the world . . . well, apart from Jennifer Ferris.' He gave her a cheeky grin.

Evie knew Jonas was sweet on one of the girls from St Margaret's in York. And she also knew that Jonas, now preferring to go by the more anglicised Jon among his peers, had a horde of female admirers and she understood why. He was a tall lad, and although he was still a bit like a giraffe – all legs – he had developed a slightly remote air that girls found irresistible. Evie had never had to wonder from where that trait had been derived. His father had been aloof when he'd first begun visiting Levisham and his pauses during conversations gave additional distance. His frame was yet to fill out fully, but the rugby and soccer through winter, the tennis and rowing in summer, plus all the bike riding he did all over the moors when he was home from boarding school, meant that he had developed an athletic body. The Nazis would have considered him a poster boy for their cause if not for the blood that still ran strongly through him.

Jonas had told his family that he was aiming for a Rhodes Scholarship to Oxford; he had already demonstrated that he was as capable in maths and physics as he was in English literature, and he was equally talented in sport, from the most boisterous of rugby to the more strategic, such as chess. She would desperately miss him if he headed south to university, but she refused to stand in his way.

In looks and temperament, Jonas was Max Hall all over again, and while that had moments of joy for her, it could also make her feel melancholic. But sorrow right now was a mindset that had to be set aside, for the world was feeling the early tendrils of excitement. She was privately pinching herself that more than five hideous years of war seemed to be drawing to an end after a firm belief a year ago that it might never end. So many lives lost, so much hardship and heartache. Joe had passed away from a vague illness he had never discussed and, with no one to replace him, plus all their fine young blokes being scattered in the battlefields, she had shouldered all the responsibility for the running of the station with her ageing father. When Jonas was home from school, like now on half term, he threw himself into station work, never complaining, as happy to be around the steam and smell of metal as she had always been.

Rosie, happily married to a local policeman, and with children too, ran the summer kiosk and even gardened for the station, while Evie managed everything from parcels to signalling and stopped just short of wearing her father's uniform and blowing his whistle.

She wouldn't swap it. There was nowhere she'd rather be – that was the truth – but the war had pressed her shoulders so low that if not for the members of her enlarged family, she might have drowned in the suffocating misery. They'd taken in children from London and done their bit for the war effort, turning the once fine lawns around the station into vegetable gardens.

The cherry trees still stood proudly and they didn't seem to care about war; each year they blossomed into their resplendent pale mantle of beauty, reminding her of a time when war was a vague, albeit unbelievable threat, when she'd resigned herself to pretend marriage vows to a spy she had loved and who had, by now, presumably given his life for Germany.

She had noted with relief that Porsche's bomber aircraft had never come to fruition, but the air raids over Britain's cities attested to the fact that Hitler had spread his commissions far and wide for the war effort. The Schwimmwagen had been manufactured, though, so the danger she'd risked had not been entirely for naught. Whether her brief life as a spy had made any difference to Britain's preparedness, she couldn't know. It was doubtful but she'd acquitted herself as well as she could, and it had cost her so much.

Since that time, she had resisted all efforts by Whitehall to contact her, save the debrief soon after she'd arrived home to York. Leadbetter seemed to understand her overriding emotion, especially that she needed to blame someone for the fact that she was now raising another woman's child alone while the man she had adored was gone. Their love had burned brightly for a moment and been extinguished through circumstances out of their control.

Evie no longer went by the name of Hall – it had been fake, anyway – and although Jonas's family in the south had tried to make an early claim on him, his fierce resistance to leave Evie had proved far more ferocious than they'd imagined. So, from the summer of 1936 he had become an Armstrong-Hall. He now visited his relatives regularly at his own request, so he had a solid relationship with his father's folks, all of whom Evie liked, but he had been raised on the railways with the Armstrong family and she knew that Jonas couldn't be happier. Well, perhaps if his father was in his life – but Max Hall was now a fond memory and she had quickly become his son's most important person.

Peace was on the horizon. It felt like a new and shiny concept, but it was one to be treasured. Just as they had following the previous war, men would be demobbing and arriving home; they and their families would need support and patience while they re-integrated into life. She sighed at the notion that she would likely soon have to relinquish her role at Levisham to a man, but times were changing, and women had shown themselves once again to be fearless while the men were away. Evie could imagine a time – and maybe it wasn't far off – when a woman stationmaster would walk out on the platform and wave a flag or blow a whistle. That might be her, she thought, and it spread a warm feeling through her.

She knew Jonas daydreamed of being just that – a stationmaster – but his talent as a scholar was too obvious for him not to fulfil all the promise he was showing, and she felt she owed it to Max to give their son every opportunity. *Their son.* Yes, Jonas was hers, and she wouldn't let anyone naysay her.

She checked the time. Only one more train today, due shortly from London via York. Soon she imagined they would be getting back to regular services and life would become busy again.

She should shower and change, especially if they were going to celebrate Jonas's win. Perhaps they could go to the local pub and have something from its menu or, better still, she should make her son's favourite meal and then everyone could go out to see a film as he'd suggested. They all wanted to see *Son of Lassie*.

Yes, that sounded perfect. She made the decision, but then her gaze fell on the resplendent cherry trees, which were in their full regalia of white spring blossom. The fragile petals of the delicate blooms were being loosened with even the breath of wind. She didn't know why, particularly while looking as untidy as she did in her work clothes, with her messy hair pulled back, but Evie felt like walking among the falling blossom before the train came and released more petals or added sooty grime into this happy moment.

She tiptoed around Rosie's well-tended vegetable patch of beetroot, rhubarb, potatoes and spinach – all of them thriving and ready for picking before her summer harvest flourished. Rosie's domesticity had been a big and welcome surprise, but it had come about during Evie's absence when her father had only Rosie to lean on. Rosie had shouldered her duties and proved herself more than capable, and Evie was perceptive enough not to try to take back her more superior role. She had not been emotionally strong enough all those years ago anyway, and Rosie had been her rock through those first months while she re-embedded herself into her former life.

Nearly a decade without Max. She could still taste his kiss – still yearned for it every day.

Evie stood beneath the now tall trees, remembering when they had planted them and worried about winning the prize length. Now they just concerned themselves with keeping Levisham Station running smoothly. The cherry trees were their one bit of showing off, and many people deliberately stopped there or made a specific journey onto their line in spring to see the spectacle of their gorgeous station in full cherry blossom bloom.

Over the years of the war, Evie and Jonas had trained some of the smaller trees to climb against the fencing and now those branches trailed off to the surrounding meadows, giving the impression of the blossom disappearing into the countryside. They were going to have a bumper crop of fruit this year, and she'd need to get some help picking and then preserving it, baking with it for the kiosk – pies, tarts, her infamous cherry cakes, of course, perhaps selling it by the bucket . . . Every little bit would help her father.

Evie looked up into the branches of the trees and let the featherlight petals fall around her. Closing her eyes, the vision she conjured was of Max. She wanted to feel him once more. Just once, and then she would let him go to find his place in her memories, but no longer allow him to hold her back from life. She'd hidden away here in Levisham for the past nine years, happy to be a mother and a stationmaster's daughter again, but with no ambition for herself . . . not even in love.

She wasn't looking for it any longer but, as Rosie continued to counsel, she wasn't making herself available for it either, and there had been several soldiers – officers – who'd shown keen interest on their rare breaks. But Evie knew those dates had been more out of kindness to the men who were witnessing so much carnage and despair. They had each been lovely men, but she'd managed to disentangle herself adroitly, using widowhood, family and duty as her main weapons. Fate had stolen the two loves of her life and so she'd accepted married life was not to be hers. Family life was enough.

The last train of the day screeched in the distance; she'd already set up the signals for it, so Evie decided to stay among the blossom and watch from the vantage of the sidings. Her father arrived onto the platform as he always did, uniform pristine, hat on, checking his fob watch against the station clock. He was a bit stooped now – certainly shorter and greyer – but he wasn't ready to hang up his hat yet and she hoped that day was still a long way off. Satisfied with the time, he tested his whistle with a short peep as he awaited the train. She didn't imagine anyone would be alighting at this time; it was still too cold for anyone but locals to be getting off here.

Evie anticipated that Rosie and Sarah would be on this train from York, no doubt bursting with fashion news and all the exciting talk of peace plans from the big city. Evie smiled. After the screaming halt of the train, she coughed through its steam, sad for the thousands of petals that had been launched from their parent blossom, perhaps not quite ready for flight. Gosh, she was becoming romantic and fanciful at the grand old age of thirty-six.

There they were, the women in her life. She waved to them as they spotted her beneath the trees.

'What are you doing?' Rosie called.

'Hello, you two. I'll be up in a moment, just grabbing some of this blossom.'

'What will you do with it this year?'

'The usual, but I thought I might try to make some tea with it, too. Could be fun?'

'Oh, come on, you lunatic. We have lots to share.'

'Is Jonas back?' Sarah yelled.

'Yes, up at the house – all good news.'

Sarah squealed her pleasure and Evie grinned as they headed for the house. She turned back to start filling the basket she'd left for this purpose; she wanted to collect the newly fallen blossom before it bruised. She waved to passengers in the window as her father blew his whistle and the train eased out of Levisham.

Bending, she got busy, being selective about the petals she toppled into the basket. She was genuinely interested in the notion of cherry blossom tea. It might be a fun addition to their summer menu; plenty of tourists would try it, and it could be a new seller in small jars.

'This year's crop is going to be huge,' she murmured to herself.

'Evie?'

She turned. The voice was familiar, but it was out of context and she struggled to place it. The late afternoon sun had dipped just low enough to strobe in across her line of sight, meaning she couldn't make sense of the approaching silhouettes.

There were two of them. 'Yes, sorry. I'll just get myself out from the trees,' she said in an amused tone. Evie emerged onto the platform, making the slight ascent with her basket, shading her eyes. 'You'll have to forgive my appearance,' she began and then halted as the words caught in her throat. 'Hugh?'

'Hello again, Evie,' said Leadbetter with a smile that spoke volumes.

Her gaze now shifted to his companion and she had to blink; she might have even shaken her head. Words no longer caught . . . they simply were no longer there.

It was a ghost. It was *his* ghost.

'Evie,' Max Hall said, and it was his voice that confirmed that this tall, gaunt, barely recognisable person was indeed the man she'd always considered her husband, even if they'd never legally married.

She dropped her basket of blossom as she covered her mouth with her hands. Never one for histrionics, not even now would she permit the shock to escape in the shriek that was rising so sharply from her chest. Instead, it came through large, uncontrolled tears that welled and spilled and coursed down her cheeks to wet her hands.

Hugh looked on helplessly and Max seemed not to know if he was permitted to touch her.

'Mum?' Jonas was at her side in a blink, arms around her. 'Mum, are you all right? What's going on?'

'Jonas?' Max's voice was thick and croaky, swelling with emotion. 'Is that you?'

Evie clutched Jonas. She was half sobbing now but trying to pull herself together for her son's sake. 'Jonas,' she wept. 'It's your father.'

She watched the golden-headed youth turn and take in the hollow-looking man, whom even he couldn't deny he unmistakeably resembled. 'What . . . what are you doing here?'

Max tried to reach for him but Jonas took a step back, understandably shocked, perhaps reluctant to embrace the man he'd loved so much but who had disappeared from his life at a German railway station. He shook his head. 'No,' was all he said, as Max tried again. Jonas strode away, across the tracks, back towards the station cottages they called home.

Evie found her voice. 'Max, give him a moment. This is threatening to stop my heart. Imagine what it's doing to the child who feels you abandoned him.'

Leadbetter cleared his throat. 'I'll just be over here with your father, Evie.' She glanced at the doorway of the kiosk where Alf stood, and nodded at him.

Evie and Max were alone on the platform moments later and she turned to walk into the waiting room, where her frames still adorned and brightened the space.

'I look a fright,' she said, touching her hair and smoothing her overalls, knowing it was shock talking as she didn't know what else to say.

'I think you look marvellous,' Max said. 'Oil smudges, your hair woven with blossom, station overalls, scuffed boots . . . You're a treat.'

Evie laughed but again her throat caught and she stopped, gulping back more tears. 'I thought you were dead.'

He nodded. 'I got close . . . several times.'

'Where were you all of this time?'

'France, mostly. I managed to get transferred out of Germany's essential services in 1940 to work in France, first on repair and maintenance of railway tracks, and then I was based at a place called Wizernes, near Saint Omer.'

'Why?'

'I was part of the team working the V2 launch site. It was probably the last of Hitler's winning strategies. But as soon as I could make the right contacts, I deserted and joined the French Resistance.'

'Why did they trust you?'

'I got word through to London about the Bauvorhaben 21 – that was the code name for an enormous concrete dome and network of tunnels beneath, designed as storage for warheads and fuel. The British spy circuit in the north knew from the information I could give that the site was being prepared to fuel and launch dozens of missiles daily on southern England.'

'Oh,' Evie said, still trying to make sense of the fact that Max Hall was talking to her in real life, not in her daydreams or memories.

'I managed to desert in 1943, but the whole while I was feeding news from wherever I worked back into the Resistance networks.'

She blinked. 'You've been working with the Allies?' Her voice was thinned by shock.

Max nodded. 'I worked with several British circuits and was responsible for blowing up and disrupting German transport, as well as repairing when the Allies needed a way through.'

'Couldn't you get word to me?'

'I tried a few times, but then I gave up, deciding you might be better off not knowing. The life of a resister was mostly short. It wouldn't have helped you to lose me twice.'

'Oh, Max. I rang the apartment too but there was never an answer. You obviously left.'

He nodded and she didn't want to know any more about that time right now. She couldn't resist him, that was the truth of it. She reached up and he grabbed her, pulling her close and burying his head in her neck among wisps of hair and blossom.

Neither of them wanted to let go but finally Evie pulled away.

'I was frightened to come here today,' he said. 'More scared than running across a German line,' he jested.

'Why?'

'In case you were married, engaged.' He shrugged.

'You told me to wait for you,' she reminded.

He smiled. 'I meant it.'

'I don't want to ask what you had to do for Giselle in the deal you brokered.'

'Then don't. Just know my mind was always with you, and fortunately I could claim we were still married. Can you live with that? Accept that we've all had to do things we didn't want to?'

She stared at him. 'Not easily,' she answered, knowing she would. Giselle was not important any more but she had to ask. 'What happened to her?'

He sighed. 'I know that when I left, she also headed east to Berlin, ostensibly to stay close, but I know she was chasing after power and influence. I didn't care. I didn't want her anywhere near me.' He gave a soft shrug. 'Berlin is certainly not a place to be now, especially as a woman and a known Nazi collaborator. The Russians . . .' Max frowned, couldn't finish his thought. 'Evie, I don't even want to think about all of that now. I just want to look at you and never stop. May I kiss you?'

He was what she had wanted for too long. Why would she make this hard for him? *Let go*, her inner voice commanded. 'Kiss me and never stop, Max,' she said.

The familiar taste of him, the body she knew so well – albeit so much rangier now – the feel of his thick hair sent spangles of desire she hadn't felt in a decade through her body. Kissing Max felt so natural, so easy; there wasn't a moment's awkwardness as they rediscovered their love and made a silent promise never to be parted again.

When they pulled away, she smiled through fresh tears and he grinned at her. 'You look so wanton. I love you like this.'

'Smelling of Brasso?'

'Perfumed by cherry blossom,' he corrected.

She touched his face as though needing to reassure herself that he was real. She felt the graze of his beard beneath her fingertips; it was so familiar it threatened to make her start crying again. 'You'd better go and see Jonas. He's a wonderful boy – you will be so proud when you learn about him, but he's at a tender age. As far as he's concerned, you deserted him, but also me for another woman . . . so you may need to absorb that bitterness for a while.'

Max nodded. 'I expect nothing from him. If he'll let me slowly back in, that would mean everything.' He hugged her again. 'Thank you for raising my child,' he said in a gritty voice, full of emotion.

'He's mine now too,' she assured him. 'I love him with every ounce of myself. Jonas got me through the hardest times; his affection, his laughter, his need for parenting. He's a joy. And Max, he knows you didn't leave me for another woman. I assured him of that. Go and discover all that your beautiful son has become.'

'I don't want to let you go.'

'I'll be here. I'd better speak to Hugh – I was pretty horrible the last time we met.'

Max nodded and, as she watched him cross the tracks towards the cottages, she shivered with fresh disbelief.

Hugh Leadbetter sidled up. 'Sorry for the shock. I didn't believe you'd take my call. Max was so nervous about returning.'

'It's actually quite nice to see you, Hugh.' Evie pecked him on the cheek.

'Good grief. Wonders never cease.' He grinned. 'You look splendid.'

'Don't lie, you wretch.'

'No, I think you look quite the part. You're like an advertisement for the women who have kept the home fires burning.'

'Well, thank you for that but I feel a wreck. How is he?'

'Still in shock. He doesn't sleep much, I gather. Eats like a bird.'

'I can tell.'

'You're the tonic, Evie.'

'I thought you didn't care about him,' she teased.

'I didn't. That was until I began to hear reports about a German who was based in the French Resistance around northern France and sending extremely helpful reconnaissance information via our spy circuits. Real acts of daring and heroism; apparently he was quite reckless with his life. I started finding out more about this fellow, who was hard to pin down, to be honest. But I learned his particular skills were connected with railways. When I discovered he used a code name of Scarborough, I started to put a file together on him. I'd lose track for months at a time and then he'd bob up somewhere else, blowing up bridges or repairing tracks, depending on what was needed. He moved around the Resistance with ease because his French was impeccable but so was his German, and I even heard of daring occasions where he stole uniforms and walked into enemy territory, speaking his perfect German to find out information that he would then relay in flawless English.'

Evie smiled.

'I didn't want to get my hopes up but it had to be him, and my intuition that I trust so much told me to find him. Then I heard he was badly injured and I knew I owed it to him – and to you – to get him out. That was a couple of months ago. He's been convalescing on the Isle of Wight for six weeks. He didn't say much for four of those weeks, but he let me visit and . . .' Hugh shrugged. 'Here he is. The best place for him, if you'll have him.'

'I can't believe it. Nearly ten years I've grieved for him.'

Hugh dropped his head. 'And I've felt every tear land on me, Evie. I know you've thought me a monster, but truly, I did care about you and the guilt has been burdensome, to say the least. I feel terrible about all you went through, so this was one way I could repair the damage.'

'Thank you, Hugh. Thanks for breaking your own rules.' She paused. 'By the way, what happened to Jean?'

'Brave to the end. Let's leave it at that.'

She squeezed his arm and he covered her hand with his. It was a sharing of silent sorrow.

Evie could see Max returning across the tracks to their side of the platform with Jonas. They were not touching but looked more at ease walking alongside one another. Evie felt her heart settle. It would take time, but she was optimistic that they seemed at least friendly.

'Heavens, they're like carbon copies,' Leadbetter remarked.

She nodded. 'I've been living with the younger version of Max all these years,' she said, smiling. 'Now, I think we all need a calming pot of tea. Plus, there's one more hurdle for Max to jump.'

'Oh, yes?' But Evie had already reached the doorway and was smiling at her men. 'Come on, Hugh. No better time than now.'

He followed, intrigued, smiling at Jonas. 'Hello, Jonas. You won't remember me, but I met you on the day you arrived into England. I'm Hugh Leadbetter.'

Jonas shook his hand. 'I do remember, sir. You made my mother very angry, as I recall.'

Leadbetter tipped his head back and laughed. 'Indeed, I did. I have that capacity with her.'

The family had gathered outside the kiosk and there were no travellers still left in the station. Evie began introductions. 'Max, you remember my father, Alf.'

'Sir.'

'You're like a wraith, back to haunt us,' Alf said, but continued, obviously noting that his daughter was flushed with happiness. 'Welcome back. Leadbetter tells me you've been a bit of a hero. I'm sure we'll hear your adventures soon enough.'

Evie gave her father a smile of thanks. 'And I'm sure you can't have forgotten Rosie,' she said, moving on.

'Rosie,' Max said with a sigh of pleasure. 'You're even more beautiful than I recall.' He kissed her on both cheeks.

'Oh, you charmer. My beauty didn't work ten years ago,' she admonished. 'But I'm married now. Len's a policeman and they wouldn't let him sign up, so he does everything but pick up a gun!'

'Good for you, Rosie. I'm glad you didn't flee to London as Evie told me you likely would.'

'Len caught my eye just in time.' She winked. 'We have two children now, Max.'

He turned to the eight-year-old who was leaning against her grandfather, Alf. 'Is this your beautiful daughter?' he asked Rosie.

Everyone but Evie gusted laughs.

Max smiled, perplexed. 'What did I say?'

Evie moved forward to put her hands on Sarah's shoulders. 'Max, this one's mine. She's *your* daughter, Sarah.'

'My silly sister,' Jonas said, with only affection in his tone. Sarah gasped and gave him a shove.

Max was staring at Evie, open-mouthed. What only they knew was that the daughter who died with Rachel was going to be called Sarah.

'Sarah,' he said, his voice threatening to break. 'My daughter?'

Evie nodded, eyes glistening.

'You are beautiful, Sarah.'

She smiled shyly at the compliment. 'Mum's always saying that. Nice to meet you,' she said, glancing up at her mother.

'We'll take it slowly,' Evie said softly to Max.

A baby's cry from the kiosk broke the awkward moment and Rosie sighed. 'There goes our Beth. Come on, let's get the kettle on for tea.'

And as everyone began moving into the kiosk as one, Max watched Evie with damp eyes. *Will you marry me?* he mouthed.

Through her own tears she laughed and nodded, whispering, 'Yes,' knowing this time it would be for real, with cherry blossom for confetti and all those she loved around her.

ACKNOWLEDGEMENTS

After visiting my perfect branch railway line and picture-book station in a sleepy hamlet of North Yorkshire, I was blessed to discover that Simon Barraclough, the stationmaster, has a wife who has spent a lot of her life on the English railways with a long railway lineage. She became a brilliant resource of regular information from afar – when Covid-19 prevented me from travelling – for behind the scenes at Levisham. Thank you to Beth, her mum, Hilda, and her aunt, Elizabeth, for all their help too.

In Germany, big thanks to Dr Matthias Georgi, MD, from Neumann & Kamp, historical projects in Munich and Stuttgart, who also came to my rescue when travel was no longer permitted. He donated his time and help when I sent out an SOS that I couldn't revisit Germany to grab those extras I like to layer in. Matthias was so generous in educating me and stepped into my writing life at the perfect moment when I didn't know how else to find the information I needed.

Alex Hutchinson in Britain is always behind the pages of my historical books. Her expertise in sniffing out fabulous historical locations, such as Levisham Railway Station, and general history on just about anything I am hunting is second to none. She's like a bloodhound with a real nose for exactly what's needed to fill a gap, and no doubt her own historical novels (as Penny Thorpe) based around the famous Rowntree's Quality Street chocolates benefit enormously from her knowledge and research. Alex is now much in demand on podcasts and TV . . . particularly in relation to chocolate and its history. What a dream job! Thanks, Alex, for all the generous help and the great friendship we share.

Pip Klimentou and Sonya Caddy in South Australia – first readers, fine critics, great friends. Always supportive but capable of laser-like attention to what needs to be done to make the story better from its earliest drafts. Big thanks.

To all in the Penguin Random House team – thanks for all the camaraderie and support. To my publisher, Ali Watts, thank you for being such a reliable and wise partner . . . and to my new partner in the editing process, Amanda Martin – I love your work.

Arms around the family – my lovely men – who make it so easy for me to write my stories. Thank you, Ian, Will, Jack.

Most especially to Ian, who got me into and out of Britain and Germany during early 2020 on a whirlwind location hunt and information-gathering blitz, just fast enough to gather up what I needed to feel confident to start work on this story. Your help with reading the tower of material that we do for each book, for taking on so much work behind the scenes to give me more time at my craft and for the flowers on my desk, is rarely acknowledged.

Fx

Book Club Notes

1. Evie is a stationmaster's daughter but what attributes does she possess that can be leveraged to make her a spy?

2. Evie makes a number of very bold moves throughout the course of this story. Which act in particular did you think was the boldest of all?

3. Did you think Evie was a brave character or a foolhardy one?

4. Evie tells Max, 'Everything about you is a secret.' Were there any aspects of his life about which he was being true?

5. 'Now that I'm in love, I don't know how to be out of love with you.' Can you appreciate Evie's predicament, or should rational thought override emotion in such a scenario?

6. Evie describes her love for Max as intense and frightening. Is this ever a good thing?

7. Do you think Evie is convincing in her role as the good wife of the German engineer?

8. Evie learns the first lesson in spying: 'Don't share information when you don't have to.' What other important lessons does she learn about espionage in a time of war?

9. Evie and Max are told that 'no problem's too great when there is love'. Do you agree?

10. Did you sympathise with Max's motives in becoming a spy for the Germans? Is there anything you would not do for your own child?

11. Evie believed that Max withheld the truth from her for all the right reasons. Is there ever a good reason to do so?

12. The novel features some stunning picturesque locations. Which have been your favourite settings in this book and other novels by Fiona McIntosh?

FIONA McINTOSH
FIELDS of GOLD
FIONA McINTOSH
The LAVENDER KEEPER
FIONA McINTOSH
The FRENCH PROMISE
FIONA McINTOSH
The TAILOR'S GIRL
FIONA McINTOSH
NIGHTINGALE
FIONA McINTOSH
The LAST DANCE
FIONA McINTOSH
The PERFUMER'S SECRET
FIONA McINTOSH
The CHOCOLATE TIN
FIONA McINTOSH
The TEA GARDENS
FIONA McINTOSH
The PEARL THIEF
FIONA McINTOSH
The DIAMOND HUNTER
FIONA McINTOSH
CHAMPAGNE WAR